ZACHARY'S HORSES

ZACHARY'S
HORSES

STAN KRUMM

TouchWood
Editions

TouchWood Editions
touchwoodeditions.com

LIBRARY AND ARCHIVES CANADA CATALOGUING IN PUBLICATION
Krumm, Stan, 1954–, author
Zachary's horses / Stan Krumm.

Issued in print and electronic formats.
ISBN 978-1-77151-042-4

I. Title.

PS8571.R82Z23 2014   C813'.54   C2013-905987-3

Editor: Edna Sheedy
Proofreader: Sarah Weber, Lightning Editorial
Design: Pete Kohut
Cover images: Horse racing: rollover, istockphoto.com
Victoria image: Glenbow Archives NA-674-69
Author photo: Tim Reeve

| Canadian Heritage | Patrimoine canadien | | Canada Council for the Arts | Conseil des Arts du Canada | | BRITISH COLUMBIA ARTS COUNCIL |

We gratefully acknowledge the financial support for our publishing activities
from the Government of Canada through the Canada Book Fund, Canada
Council for the Arts, and the province of British Columbia through the
British Columbia Arts Council and the Book Publishing Tax Credit.

MIX
Paper from
responsible sources
FSC® C016245

The interior pages of this book have been printed on 30% post-consumer
recycled paper, processed chlorine free, and printed with vegetable-based inks.

1 2 3 4 5 18 17 16 15 14

PRINTED IN CANADA

To my children and grandchildren, who have inherited a world so much more complicated and confusing than the one I describe here.

Chapter One

WITH PARTICULAR CARE AND CONCENTRATION, I was able, during the first half-dozen years of my life in the little colonial capital city of Victoria, to live the life of an exemplary citizen. Any shortcomings of my social character were minimal and discreet, and with good reason, for I was still, and always would be, a fugitive from the hangman, never able to prove my innocence. So the altercation in which I was involved on that morning in the late spring of 1870 was brief and inconspicuous.

The day had begun at a horrifically early hour when we had come down to the docks to see Uncle Boon, with his family and servants, off on their trip to the mainland of British Columbia, where they would pass a week visiting friends (and possibly some of Boon's dubious business associates) before returning briefly to Victoria and thence back to San Francisco. Six of us had accompanied the Boon entourage from the Celestial Hotel—myself and my wife, Sue, our son, Ross, already a bundle of energy well before the sun was up, my wife's father, White

Lee, and then the boot boy and the front door girl. Once we were sure the luggage was aboard, the two servants returned home while the rest of us passed a tedious two hours until the steamer finally hissed and shuffled out toward the open sea.

White Lee, for some reason, hurried up the hill while Sue and I took the slope at a more leisurely pace. I was feeling that it would be a relief to be done with relatives living with us for a while, after ten days of their company. I spoke my thought to my wife, who answered in a critical, somewhat offended tone.

"Shame on you, my husband! They have been only pleasurable company all the time. Uncle Boon likes you very much. You told me yourself that you like him."

"And I do. Yes I do." (He was, in fact, my father-in-law's uncle, but he was only a few years older than me, and we got along well.) "It's just that I'm not used to having extended family about the place every day. I feel a little bit tied to home, a bit crowded. And it makes my brain tired trying to decipher Boon's English. They are all fine, wonderful people, but you know very well that there are limits to my social tendencies."

"I often wonder, husband, why you chose to become a hotel owner if you find the company of other people so distasteful."

It's a fairly steep hill that leads from dockyards to hotel, so the fact that I was a bit breathless as I answered might have given my voice a rather romantic tone as I answered. "I purchased the half-share in the Celestial Hotel solely because I had fallen deeply in love with you and wished to be by your side forever."

"Oh, really? You should shut your mouth, Lincoln Zachary. There is nonsense coming out of it."

"And the price was right, of course . . ."

"Half ownership of a wonderful hotel just for paying off our debts . . ."

"And to become your husband, and the father of this wonderful boy . . ." I was carrying Ross, fast asleep, over my shoulder. His moods shift rapidly.

"Ha! I know you very well, and I know nonsense when I hear it."

That was the end of our conversation, but I knew that in spite of her brusque manner she was inwardly pleased that I had actually spoken the word "love" out loud—so much so that she made no objection when I flopped Ross down on his bed, then slopped down to my room and stretched out on my own.

In perhaps five minutes, as I was dozing off, I realized that we had left the luggage cart down at the dock. I muttered a curse, first in English, then in Chinese, since it was one of the only phrases I knew in that language. When multilingual cursing failed to solve the problem, I sat up and laboriously pulled on my boots. I could have sent one of our staff to fetch it, but at that hour everyone was involved in greeting guests and making breakfasts, so I decided to go myself. I wasn't all that tired, really, even after rising ridiculously early.

I was about halfway down the street when I first heard the shouting. It did not have the industrious tone of sailors and longshoremen calling to each other, so my curiosity was aroused. I could hear rough laughter mixed into it, while one voice contained no hint of humour at all. When I rounded the corner, I was greeted by the sight of a man in clerical costume partway down the nearest wharf, standing at the edge and shouting down at some ruffians below him near the water's edge. Their heads were about level with his feet, so it was a little too high for him to jump down, although he was threatening to do so if they did not stop what they were doing.

"Leave that man alone! Stop that!"

The situation, as I saw it, was that two of the scoundrels, one holding a bottle of liquor by the neck, were exercising their boots against the backside and ribs of a third, who was prone and helpless. While the

3

first villain took a turn at kicking, the second laughed uproariously and showered abuse upon the clergyman. Like any port city, Victoria has its share of derelicts who have been washed ashore and are unable to find their way off the island and on to the next stage of their personal purgatory.

"Leave him alone! Don't make me come down there with my stick!" He carried a walking stick that would not have frightened a cat.

Be it understood that I am no churchman, nor was my father a churchman. If his father was a churchman, it was a family secret never revealed to me. Still, it seems somehow inherently wrong that a pair of useless drunkards should be allowed to disregard and insult a man of God who confronts them in the name of justice. I was only a dozen strides away at the foot of the wharf, so without pausing I jumped down and ran at them, grabbing an oily plank about four feet long on the way. The fellow preparing to land another kick had his back to me, and I brought the lumber down square on the top of his head. He dropped to his knees without a sound. I then turned to his companion and swung the plank like a broadsword at his midsection. He was surprisingly spry for a drunk, and I missed him completely.

"Watch it, guv'nor!" he shouted, backing quickly away. "Watch where you're at with that thing! You almost hit the bottle!"

His friend was now on all fours like a dog, attempting to crawl away, but I clubbed his buttocks so hard that his face hit the dirt.

"That's enough, friend! Good play, but that's enough! That's enough!" The minister was shouting at me now, as he ran down the wharf to where it was safe for him to jump. By the time he reached me, the pair of miscreants were hurrying along the path behind the warehouses, once again laughing. I was pleased to see that at least one of them was now moving with a limp. As the minister bent down to examine their fallen companion, or whatever he was, the battered fellow began to snore, and it seemed to me that the expression on his face was vaguely content, although there was a bit of blood in front of his ear. As for the rest of him, it was hard to tell what was blood and what was mud on the fellow, who probably made his home in one gutter or another. "I think he'll be all right," my new friend said, shaking his head. "His breathing is steady. Foul but steady. Well done, by the way. Thank you for your work with the big stick. Avery Elliston." He reached forward and we shook hands.

"Lincoln Zachary. And it was nothing, Reverend."

"Please, Mr. Zachary—not Reverend. Call me Avery. Please not Reverend." He fingered his dog-collar uncomfortably. "I wouldn't be wearing this thing except that I have to be at a morning meeting in half an hour. And now this! I can't believe how these sad people treat each other sometimes! What can we do with him?" He was gazing down at the sleeping drunkard with an expression that might have been sympathy and might have been disgust. I myself opted for the latter.

"Leave him here." I suggested. "The other two won't be back."

"But he's close to the water, and if the tide was to rise . . ."

"The tide is on its way out."

"Someone should be available to him if his injuries are worse than I've guessed. And there's rain coming, I think."

I was about to reply that in Victoria there was usually rain coming from one direction or the other, but instead told him that I was on my way to fetch the hotel luggage cart, and we could haul him somewhere in that.

So Avery Elliston waited with the injured man while I fetched the cart and brought it to the foot of the wharf. Then the two of us each grabbed a handful of his jacket collar and dragged him down to it. Avery held the cart steady while I lifted the man up and dumped him into it.

"Look, I think he's coming around," Avery said, and the fellow did struggle his way into consciousness—staying awake just long enough to lean sideways and vomit on my boots. He then returned to his stinking slumbers. My kind-hearted friend stared sadly at my feet and spoke soothingly. "It will all wash off."

"Yes," I admitted, then muttered, "but its memory will linger on forever."

Avery insisted on pulling the cart up the hill, with only occasional assistance from me. He wasn't much older than me—perhaps thirty-five years of age—but a clergyman's costume has a way of making the best of them look older and a bit frail. He was still fussing about what to do with the derelict we had rescued.

"There's a mission for these characters," I suggested. "Somewhere over on Wharf Street, I think."

"Of course. I put in a few hours each week there myself. It's run by a close friend of mine." He shook his head. "But there's a very strict rule to the place. The man has to be sober when he arrives, and coming on his own initiative."

"Well, then, my hotel is only another block away—look, you can see it there—and we can unload him in the wagon shed. I'll check on him in a few hours and make sure he's alive."

"You actually own this hotel?"

"Yes. Not much of a hotel, mind you. The Celestial Hotel. Chinese, you understand. I married into the business."

"A hotel and a Chinese wife!" Avery beamed. "How wonderfully intriguing!"

We dumped the drunkard onto a patch of loose straw and rolled him onto his back, after which Avery once again told me he must leave for his meeting. We chatted for ten or fifteen minutes. I smoked the last of a packet of little cigars that one of our guests had forgotten on a bedside table when he left. Avery seemed profoundly interested and pleased to hear of my unusual position in life—not the most common reaction I receive from strangers—and for my part, I thought he was about as amiable a fellow as I had met in quite some time.

"Forgive me for my presumption, Mr. Zachary, but I must ask you how you've been received by your new family. Is that an improper question?"

"Not at all. Everyone in my wife's family seems to accept me gladly. Not the whole community, mind you. When I married Sue, I was made well aware that there were about a hundred Chinese bachelors for every eligible female. But the family was happy to have me. Do you think that unusual?"

Avery nodded and laughed. "As much as there's anything usual in any such matters. It's something I've noted with the people my brother Jack and I have met on our travels. We've been travelling for a couple of years now, you see—Spain, America, South America, Mexico, California . . ."

"You must love the open road then, or the open sea."

At this he frowned thoughtfully. "Not completely, really. Not always. It wasn't our own choice, you see. Things happened in England, and our father—who must never be disobeyed—rather expelled us from our native soil until he deemed us to be worthy . . . But I shouldn't defame the man. He sends us more money than we deserve, and, well, I really shouldn't be boring you with my family history, should I?" He suddenly blushed and apologized. Then, "I'm late for my meeting . . ."

I was oddly—for me—reluctant to see him leave, so I interjected quickly. "I would invite you to meet my family, but we've just now seen off my uncle, who's returning to San Francisco, and we're all a bit worn out. Uncle Boon—a good fellow, mind you, and sort of the head of the clan. Runs some sort of mysterious business down there. I like him, and I think I managed to make him like me quite a lot."

"Ah! How good for you."

"There's a reason. You see, we were all of us spending a sunny Sunday by the water at the bay last week and his son—eight years old—slipped off a slimy rock into deep water. Over his depth, at any rate, and he doesn't swim. Nor could anybody else in the group, as it turned out, so it was up to me to be the hero and I did my duty."

"Bravo."

"It didn't feel heroic at all, mind you. We were in about seven feet of water and I got myself under him—fully clothed, of course—so I could push him back onto the rock. He had a hard time of it, though. Slimy rock. He couldn't get a grip. He would put his foot on my head and push up—with me going straight down into a muddy bottom—then lose his grip on the rock and flounder around until he could stand on my head again. This seemed to be repeated about a hundred times, until someone helped him out. A great deal of hugging and caressing the young heir to the family fortune, while I stood around on the sand, belching sea water like a drowned dog. I lost one of my best boots to the mud and the tide . . ." I looked down at my current, vomit-soiled footwear. "It's been a bad week for boots." Avery was laughing now, as I hoped he would be. I added, "But at least my uncle Boon now considers me his absolute favourite."

At last, he departed for his morning meeting. We agreed that we should get together again sometime, but of course that is a sentiment often expressed and rarely brought to fulfillment.

WHEN AT LAST I entered the hotel, I found that breakfast had come and gone, and the dishes in the dining room were already cleared away. I prefer to eat in the kitchen anyway. The staff had disappeared to other duties, but I found a great mound of eggs still hot on a pan at the edge of the cookstove, as well as slabs of ham on a platter on the counter. I think that perhaps Cook had temporarily lost his sense of proportion after daily feeding the extra eight people in my uncle's travelling household.

All this food was left over after serving my wife, son, and father-in-law, three long-term residents, and one Scottish traveller. Seized by a sense of duty not to waste it, I took the pan and the platter over to the table and consumed as much as I could. My normal breakfast meal consists of noodle soup and coffee, but eggs and ham were fine for a change.

After eating so heavily, I felt it was only civilized to lie on my bed and meditate for a while. I stood at the top of the stairs, outside my room, and paused to appreciate for a moment the silence and lack of activity. Ross was outside with his governess, my wife and the downstairs girl had taken the cart of linens down to the laundry at the end of the block, and White Lee would be scribbling accounts in his own room. It was wonderfully serene. Perhaps my love for privacy and quiet was one of the reasons that the Celestial Hotel lost a considerable amount of money every month, although it was certainly not the only reason.

Boon and his family would be gone for a week. A weight was taken off my shoulders, and another had been loaded into my belly. I lay down on my bed and closed my eyes. As was unfortunately my habit of late, my first idle thoughts concerned the state of my finances. I had arrived in Victoria a half-dozen years previous, dragging with me so much Barkerville gold that I thought I would never see the end of it. Now, lo and behold, there was the end of it—well within sight. The end of my storied fortune was not exactly close, but I could now measure my finite wealth—rather easily, in fact—and that disturbed me. It disturbed me for about ten minutes, then I fell asleep.

It was almost two o'clock when I awakened, and I felt a bit embarrassed as I lurched to my feet as if I was a man who had affairs to attend to and had wasted the better part of the day. As I strolled down the stairs on my way to see if the boot boy had removed the residue of vomit from my boot, I spied Sue in the kitchen, polishing mugs with Cook's helper. Sue saw me, as well, but did not acknowledge my presence until I spoke to her. She loves me, as I love her, but she does not always approve of my daily habits.

"I'm off for a walk," I told her brightly. "I thought I might take Ross. Is he about?"

"He is busy with his governess," she replied coolly. "Miss Green is teaching him reading and arithmetic, because someday he will be a man who maybe has to work for a living and an education is necessary for that."

"Good. I'm off then."

I THINK IT'S rather unfair of me to have begun my description of the city of Victoria with vagrants brawling in the mud. It is, in fact, a beautiful little city, ideally suited for a man who enjoys a stroll. The sea is always in evidence, of course, with a thousand varied views of the inlet and the salt smell following you inland. Rambling roads and farm fields, stands of pine on the high ground, arbutus and ground-cedar along the rocky shore. The city itself exploded almost overnight in 1855 from a few hundred Hudson's Bay Company workers and a few sod-breakers to five thousand miners and miners' followers, desperate to go north and get rich. Now that the gold rush had peaked and ebbed away, there were about three thousand souls in the city, which had become the capital of the new colony of British Columbia, and they were finding new ways to survive. It was a modern port with proper streets and laws and firemen—even gas lighting. There were plenty of saloons and a number of churches. There was music, a theatre group or two, an opera singer once or twice a year (if that sort of thing appeals to you), and horse racing. Horse racing. And of course there were taxes upon taxes and bylaws enough to swallow a man.

There had been a good squall while I was sleeping, from the look of it, and now the sun was turning back the clouds into a more than decent day. I was three miles from town, casting an eye toward the distant whitecaps on the water, when I remembered the vagrant that the

English preacher and I had picked up, and that I had promised to look in on him. I shrugged it off, presuming, as was later proved to be correct, that the fellow would by now have roused himself and strolled off in his own direction.

So it was about six o'clock when I arrived back at the hotel. My wife met me on the front porch, where she was sewing something, and told me to wash and change my shirt before dinner. Also she said that a pair of Englishmen had come to visit me, and that they might return later in the evening, she thought. Almost no one comes to visit me. I have continued to live the life of a near recluse ever since I arrived in Victoria, when I was actively sought by the law for a panoply of crimes—only a few of which I actually committed. And so I knew at once that the aforementioned Englishmen must be the Reverend Avery Elliston, and probably the brother Jack, of whom he spoke.

I remained at the hotel for a couple of hours after supper, in case they returned, then picked up my black book, along with pen and ink, and told Sue that I was off to a saloon—probably the Whale and Sail—to have a drink and write for a while. She said she would be going to bed soon, and kissed me when I left.

There was a spring in my step as I strolled into the gathering dusk. In addition to my writing apparatus, I was carrying almost a hundred dollars in cash—recently received in exchange for gold from one of White Lee's confidential money changers—and I had a good feeling about that night's card game. The card game was the only logical reason to make your way to the Whale and Sail. It was a tiny, low-ceilinged place on the docks that smelled of smoke and fish, but it was run by a dour barrel of a man named Abbingdon who knew the rules to every card game ever invented and would allow no violence on the premises.

I had developed my own theory as to how to win at gambling, a theory that I was pretty sure would prove true if given enough time. I wanted nothing to do with this business of betting on the odds or the averages, or whatever, reasoning that such a strategy would only get you average results. My belief was that luck blew back and forth and around a card table, very much like the weather, and just as a good seaman or a seasoned outdoorsman can intuitively foretell a great surge in the weather, I was developing a subtle but ever stronger sense for the unpredictable changes in direction that fortune so often took. As witnessed by the greatly diminished pile of gold hidden behind a false wall in my closet, I had invested a good deal in the development of this intuitive power. I had high hopes for that night.

By ten o'clock I considered that I was doing pretty well. I still had about eighty dollars, and the feeling was upon me as the cards were being dealt that I could sense a certain shift in luck's barometer. There were four of us playing—single-draw straight poker—and the men on both my left and right immediately tossed in their cards and forfeited their ante. The skinny American with the long moustache across from me was another story, though. He had already taken some of my money, and he wanted more. He wagered thirty dollars before the draw and I matched him. We each took three cards, and I found myself sitting with a pair of nines—not at all a bad hand at that game. The American sat impassively for only a moment before he pushed forty-five dollars forward and left me to decide if he was bluffing.

I ordered another tall whisky—my third, I believe. This is another point of strategy that I have decided upon. When a person allows himself to become too excited, I believe, he wagers badly. A certain amount of alcohol in my system dulls my emotions and keeps me steady.

As Abbingdon was bringing my drink, I looked past the American's shoulder at the two men sitting at the far table. One was a tall fellow I didn't recognize—well groomed, well dressed, and visibly out of place at the Whale and Sail. His companion I recognized vaguely because of his long cascade of snow-white hair, but I didn't know him either. They seemed to be observing the game with interest, though, and the first fellow surprised me by smiling in my direction and actually giving me a wink. I paid this no attention. I had a large wager to consider.

The American sat as expressionless as a cedar plank. I took a long drink and tried my best to hear the sound of fate and fortune swirling around us, the pair of nines looking better and better as I did so. Sitting with one hand on my glass and the other on my money, I prepared to commit myself, but first took the time to lecture my opponent on the philosophical comparison between a habitual liar and a gambler who bluffs once too often. In the midst of this, the tall gentleman from the other table stood up and stepped past us on his way to the bar with his empty glass. To the surprise of everyone, he looked down at the cards the American held cupped behind his hand, raised his eyebrows dramatically, and gave a low whistle of appreciation.

The two players who had already folded gazed up at him in amazement. I shut my mouth, shrugged, and threw my useless cards in, my money still under my left hand.

The American was furious. He positively shrieked a string of curses at the Englishman that took a full minute to pronounce—some of them, quite unfairly obliquely cast in my general direction. In another saloon, fisticuffs and probably bloodshed would have ensued, but our patron, Mr. Abbingdon, knew his role and practised it well, simply placing his considerable bulk directly behind the American's chair, so that the frustrated gambler could not push away from the table.

"Arr, that's enough then, lads!" he pronounced. "Gaming's over for the night I think, says I."

I needed no persuasion. I swept up the remains of my money, leaving one coin on the table. "For you, Mr. Abbingdon." Gathering up my journal and ink bottle from under the table, I slithered away toward the door, hearing as I left the English gent's ongoing apology thrown up against the American curses.

"Honestly, I am so, so sorry. I wasn't paying proper attention and thought the wagers had all been laid, and then I happened to see your cards—all that royalty in one hand—and I wanted to compliment you. Now I've ruined your game and made you hate me. What can I do? Please! Allow me at least to buy all of you a round of whatever you're drinking . . ."

The other two card players settled back into their chairs, but the American—still pinned against the table by the proprietor—bellowed after me.

"Zachary! You owe me! You owe me . . ."

"I owe you the chance to try again, my friend, and you shall have it. One week tonight. Count on it."

As I stepped outside onto the board sidewalk, I found the white-haired fellow standing at my shoulder. "If don't mind, Mr. Zachary, I think Mr. Elliston be along in about a two minute. Spreading bit of oil on the trouble-water, if you reckon a meaning."

It was closer to thirty seconds when my quixotic rescuer placed his hand in mine.

"Lincoln Zachary. So happy to meet you. My name is Jack Elliston, and this is the intrepid but sadly soon to be unemployed Lucas, who I intend to see leaving Victoria in the morning quite hung over or possibly still drunk. He's up to Nanaimo in the morning. But before we two begin our night of debauchery, I believe you owe us both a drink."

"I believe I do. And would you then be brother to the Reverend Avery Elliston?"

"I'm proud to hear that my clerical brother admitted to my existence."

"Do you know, I halfway recognized you when you stood up back there."

"Ah! Kindred souls, no doubt. Perhaps we knew each other in a former life. My professionally Methodist brother gets wonderfully irritated when I say nonsense like that. I too recognized you immediately, but that was because your lovely wife said you would be at that place, playing cards."

I was a bit taken aback. "I told her I was going there to do some writing."

Jack shook his head. "I am sorry to tell you that she did not appear to give that story much credence." He sighed. "Women are like that."

Lucas agreed. "I was married once. Wives know such kind of thing."

"Damn," I said. "I still have a lot to learn. I suppose I should . . ."

"You should buy us that drink and let me present an opportunity to you. Let Lucas and I get hold of our horses, and we'll find a more pleasant drinking establishment at the top of the hill."

Three men and two horses, we strode slowly through the darkness.

"You play cards at that place often, do you?" Elliston asked.

"More often than I should," I admitted.

He nodded. "Actually, having observed your facility at the game of poker, it's tempting to say that you shouldn't play such games at all. At least for money. You were about to give that American about fifty dollars without a fight, weren't you?"

"I had a pair of nines."

"I think a blind man could have spotted the glare from all the face cards that card sharp held in his hand. He had queens and jacks, you know."

I shrugged. "I had a feeling that I suppose I shouldn't have trusted. And there's always a risk."

"There's a risk to wrestling with alligators, Mr. Zachary. There's just no point to it. Still, I liked your speech at the end there, where you were talking about bluffers and liars and comparing them both to, well, what was it, exactly?"

"Politicians, maybe. Did I say toads? I don't really remember now. I'm satisfied with forgetting the matter completely. So tell me, am I right in assuming it was you and your brother who tried to find me at the hotel earlier on?"

"It was the two of us, in all our splendour."

"Sorry I missed you."

"Not at all. I had the chance to speak to your lovely wife, albeit briefly."

"You're lucky she stopped moving long enough to speak to you at all. Lovely woman indeed. But she works too hard."

"And we met your remarkable young son as we were leaving the yard. Do you know, he accused me of being an Arabian pirate?"

"Not surprised." I shook my head slowly. "You're lucky he didn't stab you with a pointed stick. He didn't try that, did he?"

"No," Jack responded thoughtfully, "but I wouldn't have second-guessed him if he did. We have far too few people looking out for Arabian pirates these days. But he was under supervision at the time."

"Ah. That would have been Sarah. Miss Green, his governess."

"We conversed for a few minutes. Another lovely young woman, making it two in one day, and rarely in my travels have I met two lovelier in such close proximity. Miss Green. She lives at the Celestial Hotel, I understand."

"She told you that?"

"No, but I have other sources."

"She hasn't been with us long. English, as you no doubt observed, but more recently come up from the south, from the territories."

"And the young men of Victoria haven't discovered her yet? Amazing."

That was as much about Miss Green as I felt comfortable saying. She was a very private person, like myself, and she said conspicuously little about her past. Sue had decided immediately, as women do, that there was a high quality to her character, so there seemed no reason to pry into her secrets. To change the conversation, I turned to the other man.

"So Mr. Lucas, you're leaving Victoria?"

"There be no *Mister* to my name—just Lucas, thanks, and yes, I'm gone up island of the morning."

"You've been here long?" I was merely making conversation, and figuring so far that I would have to drag the words out of him. I wasn't really expecting the animated speech that he addressed to me as we arrived outside the saloon on Government Street, where they tethered their horses to a rail.

"Been here on to six year. Surprise to me you don't recognize who I am."

I had bought whisky for the other two, but myself switched to beer. "Well, I'm not very good with . . ."

"Been right-hand man to Bingham family that whole time. Older or younger. And you know *that* name."

"I recognize the name, but . . ."

"Got about as much clout, maybe money, maybe both be as any single man in Victoria. Be as the older, of course, but the younger coming into it—that's Mac, not Lloyd—but he be Mr. Bingham always to me. Lloyd, not young Mac. Grand bastards, be a pair of them. I the right-hand man. You want it done, I done it. What I done all, you don't want to know. I don't ask neither. I just done it. Loyalty. Loyalty is me."

"But didn't Jack say . . . ?"

"And right-hand man to young Mac when he get back to the island and no question, because Mr. Lloyd said it, and that be that, and some rough work good and bad both I done for the younger. Loyalty to one is loyalty to both. And a year be more like fourteen month, and then the young bastard takes away the position." I raised my eyebrows, and both Jack and I grumbled our disapproval. "And unholy bastard won't neither even come tell me to my face, but stead he sends this man what going to take my job. Wiggly little weasel. Slimy as a codfish and him all smiles. 'Poor you. Poor you. But I got your job, Lucas,' as he says. I should have punch a good smile down his throat, but stead I was to see Mr. Mac, who claims to be busy at first, to put me off, but I wouldn't have it. 'What the hell?' as I say, and now he's all wiggles, and poor Lucas, and I'm saying, 'I'm loyalty for six on seven year, and he's here a two month and who's got my job? And it's him? Is it him?'"

"Not right at all, would you say, Zachary?"

"Certainly not."

"'And what's a reason?' says I, and it's 'Good man for you, Lucas, but Roselle has a knowledge for business in the new way of things.' Knowledge of business! I be the one knows how to get it done in Victoria! Knowledge of business? This slimy weasel bastard only got one job before in his life and that be some government job up in Barkerville!"

I shifted uneasily in my seat, as I always do when mention of Barkerville is brought up in conversation.

"What knowledge the bastard is going to get watching over mud ugly miners in Barkerville?"

I always hated to think what knowledge someone from Barkerville might suddenly recall, particularly if they had worked at a government post.

"I tell you, I figure maybe it's some other knowledge or some kind of power he's got over Mac Bingham is what, because the big man is still all wiggly when he tells me I'm to go up Nanaimo and look after the coal wagons as they have and oversee and such like. Coal wagons! After being right-hand man or close on full-time six year, maybe more, and I'm down to watching the coal wagons!"

I looked over to Jack Elliston and could quickly see that he had heard this diatribe all before, and I fancied he might just be enjoying having the harangue repeated in my face. I didn't mind. Sometimes a fellow just needs to vent his frustration, and poor Lucas, already throwing back his third whisky, had evidently been badly done by indeed.

"Well," I said, "It sounds like they're a bunch of thankless sons of bitches and they deserve each other."

To my surprise, Lucas was instantly on his feet with a finger in my face. "I won't have you bad-mouth Mr. Lloyd, there! Not Mr. Bingham proper."

Jack may have been ready for it and quickly interjected: "Zachary was referring to Roselle and young Mac." I hastily agreed. "The boy will never be the man his father is."

"Not the half!"

"Business will suffer."

"Can't help but!"

"And speaking of business and Binghams," Jack swung around to me, "before I forget it, there's one piece of business I offered to do for them, Zachary, and it involves you."

"You work for the Binghams as well?"

"No, no, not at all, and never. But we have partnered up on a limited and very temporary basis for one short enterprise. The horse race. I'm in charge of some of the preliminary arrangements."

"What horse race is that?" I asked. He gave me an incredulous stare. "I don't follow horse races," I added.

"Do you live in a hole in the ground and cover your ears, then? What do you mean, you don't follow the races? It's the only real sport, the only diversion, the only civilized entertainment in the colony!"

I bristled as a matter of principle. "There's more than just that. Why last month there was an opera singer . . ."

"You don't favour that sort of thing, do you?"

"Not myself, but I heard she was quite good . . ."

"I'm relieved. She couldn't have been much of an opera singer for that matter. Maybe she was shipwrecked here. Or just worn down to the stage that they would only listen to her in the colonies. In my opinion, they'd do better to shoot lame opera singers and let horses just limp around. I need to educate you on this matter of horse racing, Zachary. The sport of kings and gentlemen."

"I'm neither one."

"And the better man for it. Kings and gentlemen are largely a bunch of idiots, but they do have good taste in horses."

"You mentioned some business that might involve me."

"That I did. It was my brother Avery that thought of it, really, but Mac Bingham and his associates need to rent a room. These are the characters who are organizing the big challenge race about which you apparently know nothing. The only person in the city who is not deeply interested. My God! Bingham lives a distance out of town, and they need a place with a central location and a big room where they can get together between now and the race and argue about details. It might run to a half-dozen meetings, and when I mentioned it to Avery today, he thought about your hotel."

I shrugged. "We have the back dining room that isn't used much. Big table . . ."

"Wonderful!" Jack chimed as he poured more whisky for himself and Lucas and called for another beer for me. "And by race time, you'll be fully tutored in all forms of equestrian competition."

My thought was, though, that these races involved the kind of crowds and public appearances that I made a habit of avoiding. "I'm not sure if it's really my sort of thing," I began. But Jack cut me short.

"And yet you gamble on cards, which, having watched you play for a while tonight, is a dozen times the risk. Frankly, it looked like you were just throwing coins out to eager children. Why not do some *real* wagering? Get a knowledge of the competitors, weigh the odds, use sound, measured judgement—then bet on a sure thing and win yourself a bundle?"

At that exact moment, the train of my greedy, worried thoughts began to turn about toward a new direction. I hesitated. "But horses! Horses and I have a mutual disregard. I know about the same amount regarding horses as I do about kings and gentlemen and social propriety in general."

Jack assumed a deeply philosophical expression. "Well," he said, "I've been travelling too long to remember much about polite society, but I can bloody well tell you enough about horses to let you place a dead-sure wager on the challenge race."

I was warming to the idea at great speed.

"Well, I suppose we should certainly discuss it."

"Capital! I shall begin your education tomorrow afternoon. Or will you be available there, at the Celestial Hotel?"

"I will indeed."

He paused, still smiling, then added, "And your son?"

It was my turn to pause, not immediately sure what he was getting at. Then I understood. "Yes, Ross will be around the premises somewhere. With his governess, Miss Green, no doubt."

"A lovely girl. Did I already say that?"

Chapter Two

I HAD FIRST SET EYES on Sarah Green only a few weeks previous to this, and that by chance in passing. It was perhaps ten o'clock in the morning, and when I emerged from a general goods store on Government Street, where I was checking out pocket knives, I glanced across the street and down a bit to see her and her companion standing irresolutely near the corner. A pretty young woman, a bit dishevelled, her eyes pinched and anxious, she would probably have made little impression on me, but the man beside her was more than a little remarkable. He was a Negro, over six feet tall and well beyond two hundred pounds, dressed in a standard dull cotton shirt and black wool trousers held up by suspenders of a most uncommon lemon yellow. Suspenders of any colour would have been memorable, simply because they somehow managed to extend all the way around this huge fellow, top to bottom and front to back. They had but one fairly large travelling bag between them, but I assumed that they had just arrived on the day's steamship up from Port Townsend. The brightly coloured bag obviously belonged to the woman, and if the big black man had been around Victoria for any length of time, I would have noticed him. I assumed he was her servant.

They were standing together and talking in low voices, clearly unsure of where they were. I stopped briefly and watched them. Nothing draws the attention of passersby more quickly than two people trying to look inconspicuous. After a moment I headed on down the street after my own affairs.

It was probably two hours later that I arrived back at the Celestial, carrying whatever it was that I had accumulated on the way, and as I approached I noticed the same large Negro leaning casually against a railing outside the gate of the lumberyard just across the street and down. The young woman I found inside, sitting in the lobby, conversing with my wife. Her posture was perfect, her hair carefully combed back, and she had managed to remove the traces of mud from the train of her dress.

Both women looked up at me and ceased speaking. I was immediately uncomfortable. I smiled, nodded, and headed toward the door that led to the kitchen.

"Mr. Zachary." I am never made more comfortable than when my wife speaks to me formally. "May I introduce Miss Sarah Green, who has come to us to be Ross's new governess."

I dropped my package onto a sofa and stepped across to shake her hand.

"Ah!" I said. After smiling at them for a couple more seconds, I may have made some slight motion toward retrieving my package.

"You should ask her any questions you have," Sue suggested in that firm tone of voice that indicated it was not merely a suggestion.

I had no questions. Actually, I had a lot of questions, but none of the sort that my wife had in mind and, seeing this in my expression, she began to volunteer the answers to the questions that I *should* have been asking.

"Miss Sarah Green has just this day arrived from the Washington

Territory in search of employment. She has all number of skills and qualifications but unfortunately no reference papers, but that's not really a problem because we are in need of a governess, don't you think? And this is Miss Green's speciality. Ross is growing up. School soon enough, but right now I have no time to teach him things and you teach him nothing, just how to get into mischief."

"Ah!" I repeated. Then, turning to the young woman, "Pleased to meet you, Miss Green. Mind you, my dear wife makes most of the decisions in this house and does all the hiring for the hotel, so I'm not quite sure why she thinks I should be consulted on this one particular occasion. But nice to meet you."

We all three smiled at this amiable statement of the obvious, but it was Sarah who now spoke. "I suppose I actually asked that you meet me and give your approval to the arrangement. As head of the household, the boy's father . . ."

I was just about to tell her that as head of the household, I tried to avoid decisions and responsibility as much as possible, when one question did occur to me. "Well," I began, "I did happen to notice that you are in the company of a very large . . ." My vision strayed in the direction of the lumberyard down the street.

"Yes. The Negro gentleman. His name is Othello. He is a hired companion, as it is most unsafe for a woman to travel alone in this modern world. Othello is not what you might usually expect for this position, but he is reliable and quiet. I could not afford to hire anyone else purely for the sake of appearances."

Quiet and reliable, I thought, *and capable, from the look of him, of repelling the attack of three villains and a rabid dog.*

Another question came to me. I asked her, "Why Victoria, Miss Green? And why would you decide to look for employment in such an unorthodox establishment as our hotel? A Chinese hotel?"

I was not paying as much attention as I should have if I had known the role she would play in our lives in the near future, but as I recall, it was at about this point that I noted a sort of flickering of her attention, as if she were holding the moment very carefully, and—just for a second—almost dropped it. Her eyes fell to the carpet just to her left and lost their focus. Her shoulders slumped. She drew her elbows tight against her, took a deep breath, and then was suddenly once again in possession of herself.

"I am a British subject," she replied, "so a colonial city seems my best choice to begin with, but as to the position I am seeking, I have no letter of reference, Mr. Zachary, and very little money in hand. A more prestigious family would probably not have me and I need to begin work more or less immediately. Given the normal passage of time, I naturally hope to work my way up in the world, so to speak, but you needn't worry. I won't leave any job partly done. If I was to apply elsewhere any time in the future, I would give you whatever term of notice you require. Would you like me to sign some sort of contract? I don't know much about such things."

"Not to worry." I nodded, quite businesslike, adding, a bit grandly, "I happen to know that written contracts are not as important as many people think. I once intended to study law in Illinois."

"I once intended to do all sorts of things," she blurted out, then turned bright red at her own response. She quickly assumed an expression of innocent gravity. "I will certainly do my best to provide satisfaction."

At this point Sue rose to her feet, indicating that the interview was concluded. Sarah stood up as well and they walked together toward the door, my wife telling her that by the time she had fetched her belongings, her room would be prepared and they could go together to meet Ross.

"Miss Green," I called after her.

"Yes sir?"

"This may not be totally relevant, but I notice that you walk with a bit of a limp. My son tends to run more often than walk. Are you sure you'll be able to keep up with the rascal?"

Her expression this time was calm and self-possessed as she looked me in the eye. "My injury is just a slight sprain, aggravated by travel. It will not be a problem."

It was the only time that I can recall Sarah actually lying to me. Her broken leg had, at that point, not completely healed. As she turned away, though, I felt oddly as if I, not she, had just been examined and approved. Sarah went out the front door and Sue, after giving me a quick kiss of approval, hurried upstairs to make sure that the room she had in mind was properly arranged.

Walking to the parlour window, I watched as the big man, Othello, strode up the street with the travel bag, which he passed to Sarah in exchange for some coins. They spoke briefly, shook hands, then stood facing each other for a second. It looked as if they each took a deep breath and sighed, then Othello turned smartly and headed up the street, while Sarah turned back toward the hotel's front door.

I observed an expression of abject terror on her face as she approached, and I considered what I might say to calm her, but by the time she stepped through the front door it had magically disappeared and been replaced by a look of calm and calculated industry.

Curiosity seized me.

Stepping out the side of the building, I slipped purposefully around to the front, where I was just able to catch sight of the Negro turning at the corner, evidently headed back in the direction of Government Street. I jogged after him, out of sight, carefully waited for him to turn the next corner, then scurried along behind. I don't know why I was following him or what I wanted to find out. He had turned at the corner of a rooming house, and when I myself reached that vantage point, I peered around in a manner that I thought stealthy enough for the occasion.

He stood there facing me, not three feet away. His expression was unreadable, but there was no need to read it. He was looking me eye to eye and had one huge forefinger pointed back the way I had come. And that was the direction in which I returned. I had no argument with the man.

I did not see him again for quite some time.

Chapter Three

ON THE DAY AFTER I met Jack Elliston, mid-morning found me standing with my father-in-law at the top end of our driveway, in front of the old shed. It was a decrepit building, rotted away in patches from top to bottom and jammed full of castaway miscellany. We needed a proper stable and workroom, and I had procrastinated and made excuses far too long. Now Lee stood with his abacus in hand and, as we paced off a logical size and began to figure exactly how much lumber we would need, I was thinking my own thoughts.

I had to quit gambling or at least cut down on the frequency of my card games and the size of my wagers. I had probably, over the past half-dozen years, seen as much money float away at poker games as I had spent renovating the hotel and subsidizing it through its fallow seasons. At thirty-four, I was approaching the age when a man is simply incapable of learning how to make an honest living.

White Lee barked out the number of timbers we would need for the structure. I guessed at what each timber would cost and came up with a total figure that was regrettable but still reasonable. I said as much to Lee.

He shook his head. "Timbers not a bad part. Not big money. Planks is plenty money."

So we agreed on the height of the walls, and he returned to his clattering beads.

I needed to quit drinking. Or if not quit completely, I should establish some rules for the pastime. I did not believe I was an alcoholic—I felt no compulsion to drink, I rarely ever drank in the daytime or until I was actually drunk. Still, I didn't often go through a full evening without a couple of glasses of whisky. Maybe I should just quit drinking while I gambled.

Lee told me how many feet of planks we would need. I was a little shocked, started to figure out the dollars involved, then stopped myself. There was no need to specify the bad news prematurely. This was the day when the sawmill owner we preferred was in town, taking orders. He set up his office one day every two weeks in his brother's smithy across town, so I would go there when we were finished and get him to quote us a price. It frightened me to think how much of my remaining hoard of gold would need to be cashed in just for this project.

"Now," White Lee continued, looking skyward at the upper stage of our imaginary building. "We need roof."

"Damn it!"

"We got to decide for roof what, uh . . ."

He couldn't find the English word. "Shingles?" I guessed. "Shakes? No? Rafters? What then?"

Looking past him, I saw Jack Elliston coming down the street at a rapid stroll, head and shoulders back, hands in trouser pockets. He turned in at the gate.

"Go inside, Father Lee. Get someone to give you the right word, and when you come back, we'll figure it out."

29

He did so, and I went forward to greet Jack. We shook hands and chatted amiably as we wandered up toward the hotel steps. This may seem like nothing at all, but for me it was somewhat remarkable—not only that I could slip into conversation with ease, but that I would actually enjoy it. The hard habit of a criminal in hiding is to speak to strangers as rarely and as little as possible. Already, Jack Elliston did not feel like a stranger but a friend. If he did become my friend, he would be a rarity indeed—unique, in fact. Perhaps his easy manner and clever speech inspired this feeling in everyone.

"This is truly a fine-looking establishment, Zachary. I'm sorry Avery and I didn't see your hotel before we took the rooms we now have. I like the look of this place, the ambience, the atmosphere . . ."

I grimaced. "It could really use a coat of paint."

"Nonsense. That would make it ostentatious. It's a mature hotel, an experienced and learned hotel, bravely shrugging off the woes of the passage of time."

"Good. I'll try to remember that next time Sue brings up the painting idea."

"And the name—the Celestial Hotel. Is there a story to that?"

"Not really. Celestial more or less means Chinese."

"No story. Pity. When Avery and I were dodging about the Caribbean islands, we stayed one night in a hotel called the Marianna. When asked, the proprietor told me that it was named after his dear dead wife, which is all good enough, but as an afterthought, he mentioned that she was buried in the basement."

"Ah! Did that improve your night's sleep?"

"Not at all. And tell me, what's that racket I hear from around the back?"

Following the sound of bellowing and banging, we discovered my son shouting angrily and throwing rocks at three bales of hay stacked against a sheet of tin. Sarah Green was ignoring this and reading a book on the back porch.

"Hello," said Jack with a smile, receiving a half-smile in return.

"Ross!" I shouted. "Less noise. Less noise, please!"

When he saw us he jogged over, still holding a rock in each hand. Jack turned to him. "Well, Chum, how goes the battle with the Arabian pirates?"

The boy glowered. "My name is Ross."

In a low voice from behind, Miss Green informed Jack that pirates were yesterday. "Today, I believe he is repelling a large army of invaders."

"Really?" Jack asked Ross. "And what scoundrel would dare to attack Her Majesty's colonial jewel of Victoria?"

Ross's glower continued as he answered. "Mr. Napoleon."

"Napoleon?" Jack shouted in amazement. "You know, one of his horrible soldiers shot the toes off my grandfather's left foot."

"Really?"

"The man still walks with a cane! You'd best get back at him, my friend. Don't let him get a proper foothold."

The boy held up his two rocks. "I've almost finished bombing him with bombs. Then I'll charge." And he was off.

"This will be the extension of some history lesson, I presume?" I addressed Miss Green. She nodded ruefully.

"Well, then, Zachary," Jack chimed, "shouldn't you introduce me to the lady?"

Sarah laughed. "Have you forgotten me from yesterday?"

"Of course not! How could I? I just want to hear your name spoken again."

I obliged. "Mr. Jack Elliston, this is Miss Sarah Green."

"There! You see?" he demanded of her. "Your name sounds so completely different when he speaks it. It's like a lovely piece of music played by different musicians." Sarah sighed, rolled her eyes, and resumed her seat on the porch chair. "You rush the name out entirely too quickly, and it loses something. Zachary here puts a subtle emphasis on the sibilant juncture between the first two syllables and makes it sound rather like an orchestra putting extra emphasis on the string section."

"You do talk complete rubbish, Mr. Elliston."

"Not complete rubbish, Miss Green. In order for it to be complete rubbish, it would have to be untrue, which it is not. No, this is only *largely* rubbish, in that I am babbling nonsense in an attempt to impress you."

"Ah, I see."

"And are you impressed?"

"I haven't fully decided. Not a lot, I don't think, but you needn't stop."

Ross had begun his final assault on the hay bales and was now using a gardener's trowel to thrash Mr. Napoleon's troops to the left and to the right. I looked beyond him and saw White Lee standing patiently, waiting for my return, holding a sheet of paper now, as well as his abacus. I excused myself. Sarah and Jack continued exchanging mildly amusing drivel.

"Pitch," said Lee when we were face to face.

"What?"

"Pitch of roof is what you deciding. Steep, not so steep . . ."

"No idea. An average pitch, I suppose."

"But to figure order of how many beam, how many rafter . . ."

"Someone at the sawmill will be able to figure it out for us."

"What? No no. No no. These men send you all kind of wood you no need. Cheat you like . . ."

Lee was always worried that he would be swindled by white businessmen, and not unreasonably, for in local commercial circles swindling a Chinaman was considered not so much a crime as a challenging diversion, if you could get away with it.

"They won't cross me," I assured him. "I have ways with those people." And with that, I took the paper and pencil, scribbled down the various figures we had come up with, and left him.

Sue was standing on the front porch, looking in my direction. The gloom that had been hanging over me a half-hour previous had miraculously lifted, and as she stepped forward to greet me, I gave her a light kiss on her forehead. She looked rather merry herself, as she tipped her head sideways to direct my gaze to the window of the front parlour. I heard the discordant clang of the piano begin to sound from within. The instrument was really only ornamental and had never been tuned. I saw that Jack Elliston had seated himself before it, though, and was attempting to draw music from within. Sarah Green was seated on the sofa next to it, Ross beside her, slumped across her lap. She was holding a cloth against his ear or the side of his head. It would have been a sweet and tender tableau were it not for the grossly off-tune melody of the piano.

"Was Ross a casualty in today's battle?" I asked my wife.

"It would seem so," she sighed. Then, after a pause, "He ran with his trouble to Miss Green."

"The nearest female," I explained quickly. "You were busy somewhere else, no doubt."

"No doubt," she agreed. As Jack stopped, stared at his instrument in frustration for a moment, then began a new tune, Sue, still without looking at me mused, "And if you were to be injured, would you run to a woman like me, or to a woman like Miss Green?"

I replied without the least fraction of any hesitation. "To you, my dear. Only to you—even if it meant running all the way across town." She squeezed my hand by way of thanks. "And speaking of across town, I need to run this paper over to Becker from the mill. I won't be long. Tell Mr. Elliston, if he happens to look up and notice that I'm gone, that I'll be right back."

I had to walk about halfway across town, which was not really that far, because the Celestial Hotel was not as far to the north as the truly Chinese part of town. The real Chinatown, or Tangren Jee as it was also called, was—when White Lee arrived in 1858—only a scattering of shacks north of the ravine, along Cormorant Street—completely lacking sanitary facilities or board sidewalks. Only three narrow footbridges connected the area with the properly developed centre of the city. Lee was a forward-thinking man from a good family, with some money at his disposal. He therefore built his establishment (at considerable expense) on the south side of the Johnson Street Ravine, where the Jews and Americans were building. It was a bold venture and marginally successful while the rush was on and every room in town was occupied. Even later, in 1863, he was awarded the prestige of having the Victoria Gas Company install a gaslight on the street almost directly across from him. When the economy began to slow, however, patrons of any nationality became scarce. He had borrowed money from various Chinese moneylenders (the words "usurers" and "extortionists" are difficult to avoid), and the calling in of loans was being mentioned at the time when I arrived, needing an inconspicuous place to live out the winter under an assumed name while the authorities gradually forgot about Zachary Beddoes. (In retrospect, I should have chosen a name more common and less memorable than Lincoln Zachary. I could have called myself Bill Smith. The former user of that name had changed his to Amor de Cosmos and started up the newspaper that was now pushing British Columbia to become part of Canada, rather than its natural neighbours, Washington and Alaska.) Once I was safely installed at the Celestial, it seemed somehow natural to buy the majority share of the place and marry my new partner's daughter. She was one of a very few unmarried Chinese women among a host of Oriental bachelors, so I made no friends there. All the best for me.

A light rain was falling on Government Street as I walked briskly toward the miller and the blacksmith. The swirling clouds were competing with patches of blue sky, and it appeared inevitable that they would soon win out. I turned into a narrow lane at the top of the slope overlooking the buildings of the Legislature, pausing once again to shake my head in amazement at these bizarre buildings. "The Birdcages." The thought came to me that, since Victoria was becoming known as a centre for the importation of opium, perhaps the architect responsible was smoking the stuff when he designed the structures.

I hoped to drop off my paper and hurry home, but such was not an option. Becker was not at the smithy when I arrived, and when he returned, he brushed past me waving an excuse and went directly into the backyard, where I heard the door to the outhouse slam shut. He remained within for no less than fifteen minutes, while I strode silently back and forth across the smithy, staring at the forges and building up an unhealthy sweat.

"Becker," I told him, when he reappeared, "a proper man of business needs to get better control of his bowels! You could have missed half a week's orders while you were in there, filling the toilet-house."

He had no answer for that, but grumbled when I asked him to do the figuring himself for how many planks and shakes I'd need for the roof.

"I'm not a carpenter!"

"Well, someone in your crew should be able to figure it, or I'll have to find a different mill." Then White Lee's worry came to mind and I remonstrated further. "And nothing more than needed! I'm a hotelier, remember, and if you take me for a fool, I'll see you get no new business from any of the other hotels any time soon."

Truthfully, I knew none of the other hotel owners, save for one, whose business was not so much a hotel proper as a house of ill repute and gambling saloon. (I had never had anything to do with the women of the former function, but I had played cards in the side room more than once.)

By the time I made it home, Jack had made his apologies and departed, leaving me a note, which Sue gave me. It said simply, "Clear your appointments calendar for the next couple of days. You must come on a short trip with me."

Oddly enough, the idea delighted me. Wherever I was to travel with Jack, it would give me the opportunity to question him in depth on a topic that had been on my mind a great deal since last night. I wondered how much money a man could make wagering on a single horse race. If a person had the proper inside information, it seemed to me, and if there were no limits to the size of the wager, it would be like single-draw poker where you were holding a royal flush—or at least four kings—and you'd be a fool not to bet every liquid penny you had on the thing. I determined to go down and have a look at my own horse, Old Peter, before dinner.

Sarah came down the stairs and joined us.

"Ross is asleep?" Sue asked.

She nodded. "He's had a hard day repelling the French invasion. I thought he deserved a rest before dinner."

As they were laughing together—that chittery little laugh that women reserve for the discussion of small children—I thought that it was the happiest and most relaxed I had ever seen the woman, and I had little doubt as to the cause. It was as if Jack's silly talk and pathetic piano had filled her up like a fresh wind fills the sails of a ship. No more the downcast eyes and stuttered speech that we had witnessed on her arrival. Then we heard the sound of a heavy vehicle drawing up outside.

It was a brougham—a dusty, dirty brougham, with poorly matched horses at the fore, but an impressive coach nonetheless. We all three moved outside onto the porch, to observe a pair of well-dressed fellows descending. The first man was so big he had to squeeze himself through the little door. The other was small, thin, dapper, and I had the horrible feeling that I had seen him before.

The big man walked like a bulldog, striding up to me and taking my hand in his great paw. "You must be Mr. Zachary, sir. I'm Mac Bingham. Think you've heard of me and my business. Maybe expecting a call? Here's my assistant, Mr. Roselle." The second man reached around his employer to shake my hand lightly. Then Bingham turned to Sarah, beaming a florid grin. "And you must be Mrs. Zachary."

I might have tried to laugh away the misidentification, but as I glanced at Sarah Green, I saw that she was suddenly a different creature. Her eyes were focused on the floor to her left. Her hands were clasped in front of her, one squeezing the other. Her lips were pressed white together.

I stepped in front of her, took Sue by the elbow, and drew her toward me. "This is Mrs. Zachary, my wife. Sue—Mr. Bingham."

His surprise was only a flicker before he regained himself and grasped her little hand between his thumb and forefinger. "Of course. Excuse me. Pleased to meet you. Of course. I understand."

But Bingham had not forgotten Sarah. Looking past my left shoulder, he asked, "And this would be . . . ?"

"This is my son's governess. Miss Sarah Green." But before I had actually finished speaking her name, she had muttered something of which I only caught the word "duties" and turned around to shuffle hastily inside, still never lifting her eyes. Not relishing the awkward pause, I spoke quickly. "I've heard of you from the Elliston brothers, Mr. Bingham. Jack tells me you'd like to use one of our rooms for business conferences."

"Exactly that. I live the hell and gone out of town. My father's place, you see, and he's got no use for society. Reclusive. Fine man, my father, but reclusive, and so we're the hell and gone out that way, while the rest of the fellas, my partners and such, are all here in town. You have a suitable spot here? Nice building, by the way."

"The back parlour would suit the purpose, I think. Would you like to come inside and see?"

He bellowed a laugh. "That's what we're here for. Roselle? Where the hell are you, man?" His assistant stepped forward from the blind spot directly behind him. Roselle looked at me and wrinkled his brow—just a bit. I looked away and wrinkled mine.

"When were you going to need the room?" I asked.

"Well, tonight, for the first, if that works all right for you. I'm already in town. Probably six of us. Is that all right?"

"Certainly," I answered, and led them in to view the back parlour.

THAT NIGHT WAS the third and last night that Mr. Griffin of Portland stayed with us. He was a salesman representing three different factories in that city, all of which, according to him, were going great guns with exciting new products, although if that were truly the case, I would have expected him to be taking more prestigious lodgings than the Celestial Hotel. Still, he did bring in an expensive bottle of wine to celebrate the success of his visit, and since the rest of our guests—a Spanish-speaking couple and our pair of long-term Chinese residents—declined to share it with him, I lingered after my meal and took a glass. I was acting as host, at the head of the table, while the rest of my family ate in the kitchen, as was our habit. I don't care much for wine, preferring my libations to begin their life as grain, rather than fruit, so I was not too disappointed to be called away when Bingham, Roselle, and two other gentlemen arrived for their business meeting. We all stood in the front parlour making small talk, waiting for the rest of their company to arrive.

Through the doorway at the end of the short hall, I spotted Ross, sitting at the table with his mother. They had spent the afternoon together while Sue tended the row of flowers she kept along the front fenceline, and I hadn't seen Sarah Green, who commonly took some of this part of the day to herself. I had presumed, though, that she was there, in the kitchen with the others, and I was a little surprised when she appeared coming down the stairs from her own room. Her pace and posture were steady. She went directly to Mr. Bingham and spoke to him.

"We were introduced earlier today, sir . . ."

"Yes, we were," he drawled.

"And as I later reflected on the moment, it seemed to me that perhaps I was short with you. Perhaps I did not greet you with the warmth that is customary in this house, and I wanted to be sure to apologize when I next had the chance."

"What? No! Never even noticed."

"I'm afraid I haven't been quite myself lately, I had other matters on my mind, but I hope you will know that discourtesy is never the standard at the Celestial Hotel, and along with Mr. and Mrs. Zachary, I hope you will find the accommodations completely to your satisfaction." Bingham was about to reply, but Ross was by now standing at Sarah's side, and she continued. "Now if you will excuse me, my young charge must be prepared for bed."

I thought, perhaps unfairly, that Mac Bingham watched her with a trifle too much interest as she led Ross up the staircase.

I took nothing more to drink that night after my small glass of wine, but sat quietly on the kitchen porch, carefully putting a perfect edge back on Cook's selection of knives, until the meeting in the back parlour broke up an hour or two later. On the front porch, I bade them all goodnight and heard from Bingham that thenceforward the group would try to arrange their meetings during the day.

Roselle stared at me in a silence that seemed unduly flavoured with curiosity. I tried as much as I could to refrain from returning his gaze, but a cold and empty feeling was descending upon me heavily during those few moments.

From the porch, I went directly to my room and stretched out on my bed. I stared at the ceiling, but it was Roselle that I saw before me— pinched features on a grey-white face, spindly little arms and legs, long, fluttery fingers.

I remembered him now, but the question was, would he remember me?

At first I was confident that he would not. We had only stood face to face a couple of times. Then I doubted myself. At the end of things, I was the talk of the town, and probably everyone in Barkerville had spent a moment or two trying to remember if they had seen me and what I looked like. The curiosity I felt when he looked at me tonight was surely just a measure of my own suspicious nature. Even if he did have that common feeling that he recognized me from somewhere, he wouldn't pin it down.

Of course you recognize me, you miserable weasel! I thought. *But you won't remember it because there was hair all over my face and I was dressed in filthy woollen trousers and muddy overcoat, like the rest of them. You, on the other hand, always wore a clean shirt and collar in your little office, with elastic armbands and matching black visor over your forehead. You looked like a dealer in a gambling palace and you acted like the Prince of Persia. I looked like every other mud-grubbing gold digger in town.*

Chapter Four

JACK AND I HAD ARRANGED to start off on his overnight errand to Sooke next morning, and he had agreed to pick me up after breakfast at the hotel, since, by chance, both of our horses were being held at the same stable. He arrived at about nine o'clock to find me drinking coffee on the front steps. I offered him some.

"That's a New World habit that I haven't taken to yet," he replied. "It's still tea for me, and I've had enough of that for one day, thank you." He tossed his duffel bag onto the bench and sat down next to me. "Don't hurry. We've lots of time. You're packed? Stableboy going to have your mount duly prepared?"

I nodded. "Old Peter doesn't need a lot of preparation."

"Old Peter? Interesting. Tell me about him."

"He's brown and he can walk a long way without getting tired, it seems."

"Hmm. Local breeding?"

I shrugged. "I wouldn't know where he started out before he was eventually dropped off here. I obtained him in trade as payment from a guest who stayed for a while and then couldn't pay his bill."

Jack was beginning to show a look of concern. "Perhaps we'd better go and take a look at this animal . . ."

I finished my coffee and tossed the dregs onto the bush beside the steps. "Let's go get the horses. We can stop back here to pick up the bags and I can say goodbye to Sue and the boy."

As we walked down the hill toward the stable, I commented on Jack's horse. "He's a fine-looking big monster, isn't he?"

He laughed. "You may have a better instinct for the equine species than you take credit for. The Commissioner. He is both big and extremely fine to look at, and he is indeed capable of being a monster. He was much more monstrous when he came to me only five weeks ago, but he's exceedingly bright, usually reasonable, and we've negotiated a more civilized relationship in a very short time. In both horses and human beings, Zachary, the brain is always more important than beauty."

We arrived at the stable and, a few minutes later, Jack was examining Old Peter. The look on his face was hard to describe. "You say you got him in exchange for a hotel bill," he said after a minute. "How much did that amount to?"

"A week's room and board," I told him.

He grimaced. "I don't want to sound mean, Zachary, but from the look of him, he's not worth much more than a cup of tea and a nap on the veranda. Still, it's not a challenging journey, and who knows? I may warm to the old soul."

Back at the hotel, we tied our respective bundles to the backs of our saddles and prepared to depart, attended by a plethora of well-wishers, as if we were about to circumnavigate the globe. Sue and Ross stood on the bottom step to the porch, while Sarah waited at the far end of the top step.

On the porch itself, White Lee and half of the staff had gathered for some reason—Cook and the downstairs girl in the doorway, the maid peering out the window, and the boot boy loitering about at ground level beside the horses. I had to speak to Ross at some length, for he was worried about the chance of our meeting up with wild animals, robbers, and even dragons on the road to Sooke. Then my wife, knowing that we would spend the night at the home of strangers, felt it necessary to lecture me quietly on my manners, as if I were a child going off to boarding school. During this time, I witnessed Jack speaking softly to Sarah Green—something that made her laugh, then scowl histrionically, then laugh again. I'm not sure that she said anything much in return, but as we rode off it could be noted that she waved goodbye in his—not my—direction. That is, if one were keeping track of such things.

We rode without speaking for the first while, as streets gradually turned into rutted roads, and houses were soon separated by farmers' fields and patches of woodland. I think the two dissimilar horses were not much inclined to stride shoulder to shoulder, so there was a little distance between us, but it was still a bit out of character for Jack Elliston to remain in silence for that long. As if he were continuing a well-established conversation, he remarked out of the blue, "Yes. She's rather remarkable, isn't she?"

"I presume we are speaking of Sarah Green?" I replied.

"What? Well, of course we are. You've got to try harder at keeping up with the topic, Zachary."

"All right then. I agree. Sue and I are very pleased to have her in the household."

"As you should be. Not just a pretty face, that girl."

"You'll be pleased to hear that she doesn't seem to turn into a screeching hag as soon as people's backs are turned."

"What?"

"A joke, sir. Just a joke."

"Really?" He did not appear greatly pleased that I would jest about such a thing. With a serious demeanour, he pulled The Commissioner closer to Old Peter and asked, "But tell me more, would you? Damn it, the girl has caught my eye, you know. Enlighten me, my friend."

I scratched my head. "I haven't much to enlighten you with. She is in private as she is in public—level, pleasant, a good conversationalist when she chooses to converse, more than pleasant of appearance, although her employer should probably advance her the funds to buy at least one more dress to wear."

"Yes, I've seen all that, but where from and what family and for what reason . . ."

"Here is where I'm not of much use. English, yes. Up from the territories—I've told you that. Olympia, Washington, I think. A governess for a farm family there. Something came up. Did she say illness? I'm not sure. Children sent away to—hmm—I don't think she said. She came north because of her citizenship. No references, which sounds bad, I suppose, but that would account for her applying at a place like the Celestial instead of asking around at the wealthy families. I think she approached my wife just asking for some kind of position—any kind of work, even common domestic chores. I suppose she explained her situation to Sue in more detail and the idea of governess came up quite naturally. By the time I arrived on the scene, my wife was convinced that she was reliable, and all that was asked of me was to say 'Yes, darling, you've made a wonderful choice, as usual.'"

"That's it? That's all you know?"

"Everything I can recall," I told him, shaking my head. "Although you realize that if I did know more, and if I was a gentleman, it would be bad form for me to share it, wouldn't it?"

He pursed his lips and fiddled with his horse's mane.

"I believe you. She isn't saying much to anyone about anything, is she?" Then, after a thoughtful pause, "By the way, that business about gentlemen not betraying a lady's confidence is rarely ever followed by the gentlemen I've met . . ."

I laughed. "Well, then, if it's my turn for a question, I'd like to hear more about where we're going. Some farm out toward Sooke where you've apparently never been. And why do you need me along on this trip?"

The last part of my query seemed to take him aback. "Well, you're here so that I have someone to tell stories to! Avery was busy, and besides, he's already heard all of my stories."

"Oh. Good enough. I will try to listen carefully."

"Now, the reason we're going to the aforementioned farm—the residence and estate of the good Riordan family—is to pick up a racehorse and bring her back to Victoria."

"You've bought a racehorse?"

"No. This is Mac Bingham's horse."

"Then why doesn't he send one of his own men to get it?"

"Because they would be shot on sight, but really, Zachary, it would be better if you just listened to the story and caught these various details in proper context."

"I'm so sorry. I promised to listen, didn't I?"

"Yes, you did. And the story is a good one."

So I listened to the story as we rode. I render it as follows, although in actuality, it was broken up by sections of the road where we could not ride two abreast, a couple of strangers met and greeted on the way, and a stop or two for water or something to eat. I am forced to abridge it, for Jack's tales tend to wander a bit, with odd bits of lengthy description.

"Avery and I were stranded in Oregon while the boilers on our ship were fitted or adjusted or some such thing. He looked up various other fellows who were engaged in saving the world from the devil's clutches, while I rooted around the stables looking at horseflesh. Almost immediately I heard of a good auction sale that was being held only a few miles up the coast. I hired a horse and was there that same afternoon.

"The sale was good, but the town was small, so I was forced to bribe a porter to get a room in the town's one good hotel, whereupon I retreated to that establishment's dining room for dinner and perhaps a drink or two. I was the last person to arrive at the evening meal, and the food that I was given reflected the fact—mostly dry and cold. There was, mind you, plenty of liquor to be purchased, and one last person remaining at the table to drink it with—a big, sullen, brooding fellow named Mac Bingham."

"Aha!" I said, and Jack answered, "Well, you might say 'aha!'"

By this stage of the story, we must have been travelling the part of the road that rides high along the clifftops, giving remarkable views out over the open water of the inlet—laced with whitecaps under a clear blue sky. Momentarily, it was enough to take one's breath away, but when Jack Elliston is in the midst of telling a story, the mere extravagant beauty of nature is not enough to forestall it for long.

"It took no prompting to persuade Mac to recount the reasons for his downcast visage. He had come to this auction, he said, to redeem the honour of his family, and from all appearances, he was failing in his attempt. It sounded like a very English predicament—the lost honour of the family, and so on—so I kept a firm grip on my whisky glass and pressed for the details. Some years ago, it seems his father, Mr. Lloyd Bingham, was publicly embarrassed in the course of a horse race of some fanfare. You may be familiar with this part of the tale?"

"No. I've heard Lloyd Bingham's name, of course. Large amounts of money attached to it, but nothing about any horse race."

"It was a half-dozen years ago. Were you . . . ?"

"Just arrived in town about then, I suppose."

"At any rate, it was the biggest challenge race of the time, with money and prestige flowing toward the winner from all directions. Lloyd had a horse, a good horse, and he figured it was a sure thing for him. Mac didn't say specifically, but I get the impression that his father bragged it up pretty heavily. And I don't think he was much liked around town."

"That sounds like something still true . . ."

"Well, someone brought in a ringer from God knows where. No form, not even a proper name—just called it the yellow horse. They didn't even practice the thing properly, just waited for the day.

"Now this would have been bad enough—for Lloyd to have lost the race and his wagers and so on—but apparently—and this can't be proved—apparently everyone in town, or at least everyone close to the race, knew about the ringer except Lloyd Bingham. And they mocked him so badly when they collected their debts that Lloyd practically dropped out of sight and society."

"I've heard him mentioned as a bit of a recluse. So when you met Mac Bingham, he was trying to buy a horse that would win back his father's respect, I gather, going all the way down to Oregon."

"That's the gist of it, but there was an interesting wrinkle involved."

"Which was?"

"He had already discovered the horse, or his spies had found it, and he'd found it on a farm just across the way, near Sooke—bred and trained by some Irish horse people called Riordan."

"Aha!"

"Aha, again! Mac assumed that he would be able to buy that young filly, since he had money flowing in from sawmills and wagon factories like water flows down the great Tigris and Euphrates, so he set up this race—of which you are no doubt aware, Mr. Zachary—that would confound all his enemies and set the name Bingham back properly at the zenith of colonial horse racing."

"I recognize your tone of voice, Jack. This is where you tell me about the big problem."

"If you insist, I will tell you about the one big problem. The problem was that the family Riordan and the family Bingham were wildly at odds. Mac has been away in the east attending college until recently and was out of touch with such family matters, but when he attempted to approach the Riordans—who are breeders of some esteem, but very minor players in the local racing game—he discovered that there was a history of land disputes. Angry words, threats, lawyers—even shots fired at some point, I believe. The Riordans would not sell the horse to Mac for any price. They would not even discuss it. He tried everything, but they wouldn't budge."

"Stubborn."

"If stubbornness had a nationality, it would be Irish, and in addition to this, they showed themselves to be too clever to be played upon. Mac went all the way to Oregon with the idea that he could hire a broker to buy this filly for him, but the Riordans figured it out. They arranged a private auction, where only a handful of people that they knew very well would be invited. Mac was devastated."

"And was that when Jack Elliston arrived on the scene, booking the last hotel room in town?"

"It was. You are an astute listener, Mr. Zachary."

By now Old Peter and The Commissioner seemed to have taken a liking to each other and we rode side by side, close together although because of the height disparity between the two mounts, my head was about level with Jack's elbow.

"So did you arrange a peace between the two camps?"

"Oh, no! But I had two days to work with, and I found a good supply of better than average whisky on hand in the little town, so I oversaw negotiations about the purchase of the filly. It still stands that any Bingham ranch hand risks his life to trespass on Riordan's property. But let me mention one other thing, Zachary, by way of an observation on the rich and powerful in this world."

"I'd rather just hear the end of the story, but I'm open to a bit of philosophy if it's simple enough."

"One simple observation. Men of power like to surround themselves with this or that when they go out and abroad in the public eye. Some fellows travel about in the company of their private lawyers and bankers, some surround themselves with bodyguards—whether they need them or not—and others always have a troop of pretty women in tow."

"I've seen a bit of that."

"Rather repulsive to me in each case, but there is one exception, and that is the few men—like Mac Bingham—who travel with a retinue of horses. I don't care to gawk at other men's pet women or, God help me, their lawyers, but I will happily admire some rich man's horses. And Mac had already purchased four horses at the auction, perhaps just to soothe his frustrated soul. I admired one of these so much that I said I would take him in payment if I managed to negotiate a sale with the Riordan family. It would be a sort of commission for me on the sale."

I laughed. "And if it became your horse, you might even name it 'The Commission' or 'The Commissioner' to give it a rounder tone."

Jack beamed at me. "I have said it once, and I say it again. You are a careful and astute listener, Mr. Zachary."

"How did you do it? Did you get the whole Riordan clan drunk and offer them—what—all the rubies in India?"

"Well, the deal was struck while we were all very drunk, that's true. Do you know, some Irishmen simply loathe people from England, but the Riordans and I got on from the start like old school chums. Wonderful folks. You'll see. No, I had Mac pay them about double what they were likely to get at the private auction, but then I went at the issue of *pride*, and pride is what the thing is all about. I made Bingham promise that there would be a special box at the big race with a banner that will read 'Reserved for the Riordan family—breeders and trainers of Miss Deception.'"

"Miss Deception?"

"That's the filly's name. And one more thing: the horse will be ridden by Christy Riordan, the fair-haired boy himself."

"So the Irishmen get a fair bulk of the prestige out of this, it seems to me. And that was all right with Mac Bingham?"

"It had to be. He has this race half arranged, and he's running out of time."

SO WE FOUND the Riordan farm without incident, arriving near the supper hour. Introductions were made, and in due course we all stood around the filly called Miss Deception while each man looked for an adjective more flowery than the last to describe the little beast. For my part, my buttocks were so sore from riding the whole day that I was left speechless.

Dinner was a stew of either venison or that stringy range beef that tends to have a gamey flavour to it. Either way, it was very good and I was very hungry.

The Riordan clan was headed by the honest farmer James, a solid clump of a man, aged perhaps fifty years, who maintained an expression of serious intensity, while still seeming calm and friendly. I did not hear word spoken of his wife, but I presume she had died, for at the foot of the table sat Gran—straight backed and sharp eyed, with a high collar and much grey hair piled perfectly atop her head. The children were numerous, and—after a long Papist prayer—quite loud throughout the meal. I am not sure who was the elder of the two boys, Christy and John, but Christy appeared to be unmarried, while John's wife, Natty, was responsible for a baby on a blanket near the wall, along with another little fellow, who sat on his father's lap. The oldest Riordan daughter was perhaps seventeen or eighteen, and sported a gold band that I took to be a betrothal ring on her right hand. Three more younger sisters, although one of them spoke without the family accent, and I suspect she may have been taken into their number from without. Lastly came young Dominic—Dom—who was about the same age as Ross, and just as wide-eyed about the world, although more composed in his manner than my own son. It struck me that although the house itself—built half of logs, half of lumber—was only of a common size, the number of persons present exceeded the usual number of an evening in my hotel. They were also considerably more animated, apart from James and Gran. A typical sample of dinner conversation involved the two older sons declaiming to Jack and me the origin of their Christian names.

"I was baptized Christopher," the first informed us—loudly to be heard over the general ruckus—"named after the saint, of course."

I did not realize that there was a private joke being introduced here until the other brother leaned immediately past his son's head to gain our attention. Apart from being an inch or so taller, he was as like his relative as are two berries on a bush.

"And I was given the name John, also named after the saint, you understand, and a much grander saint he was," I was quickly informed. "Best friend of The Lord Hisself, and not just some wanderin' foreign bloke."

Christopher interjected immediately, "Of course, *St. Johns* are all sixpence a dozen—*St. John o' This* and *St. John o' That*. Me brother was, I believe, named after St. John of the Woodchucks, but there's only *one* good and proper St. Christopher."

Conversation was loud and scattered, and the food circulated continually until everyone was quickly fed. Then the men were on their feet, looking for boots, midstream in a discussion of horses. Natty Riordan called out orders to the female segment of the assembly, some to dishes, some to bathing babies. "Off you go, Father," she added to James, who seemed of two minds. "Go with the men and look at your pretty filly. She'll be gone tomorrow."

Young Dom shouted out at this, as if everyone had forgotten something very important. "But who'll play cards with Gran?" And the old woman, who hadn't spoken a word all night thus far, leaned forward in anticipation as if it were indeed a profound question. Jack Elliston it was who answered.

"Mr. Zachary might choose to join the good woman in a game. He's familiar with cards, and more interested than in horses." I was very tired, and grateful for the suggestion.

The boy brought us cards at the kitchen table—a very old deck, a bit larger than the type I was used to, worn to the fuzzy texture of fine suede leather, the designs all pastel pale. Once they were set before us, the old woman spoke. I understood not a word that she said. Perhaps she spoke Gaelic, or perhaps her accent was simply that thick. The boy was required to interpret.

"You're to shuffle the cards, but Gran will deal, as you're a guest in the house."

I nodded thanks, assuming that I had been done a favour.

Very methodically, she dealt out all the cards between the two of us, speaking incomprehensibly in a low, level voice—presumably explaining the game. The boy watched intently but did not interpret, which was just as well. All my attention was captivated by watching Gran's mouth. Her teeth were artificial—bone or white wood, I know not which—and they flopped in a hypnotic movement, oddly syncopated with her lips.

She laid down a card from the top of her pile, and I tentatively laid down one of my own. She scrutinized them, then laid down another. I followed suit. At that she smiled and gathered all four to herself. With the point of her chin, she gestured that I was to play next. Six cards later, she gave a little, cackling laugh and captured them all. I looked quizzically at the boy. He shrugged, his expression uncertain, possibly a little worried. We played on. I laid a card. She replied with a king of hearts, and I quickly took possession of both. She seemed a bit nonplussed, but when I pointed a finger at her hand, she played the next card. And so the round went, with me ad libbing my reactions and allowing the old girl to claim about two-thirds of the cards. Occasionally she would mumble some muffled clattering sentence, and I would respond with something like, "You're a cagey player, Madam," at which I think she seemed pleased.

A half-hour or so later, just as the women were finished cleaning up in the kitchen, the men returned, all loud and obviously satisfied. As they took off their boots, the old woman leaned forward across the table to me and spoke shortly. The boy told me what it was she said.

"She says you owe her two dollars," the lad whispered with some trepidation.

The experience had been too remarkable to protest, so I cheerfully pulled a couple of coins from my vest pocket, which she slipped quickly into a fold in her belt. Then she stood up and left the room—that was the last I saw of her. Everyone was simultaneously yawning and groaning. I was led to a bed that had been laid out on a pantry floor. I thought to myself that country folk went to their beds at a strangely early hour and immediately fell fast asleep.

I was, I think, the last person to rise in the morning—not for the first time in my life—feeling very refreshed, although my inner thighs were still tender from the unusual amount of time I had spent on Old Peter's back. On the little table just outside the pantry door, I found a basin of warm water set out for me, so I washed and shaved before I went into the kitchen. As I did so, I could hear the voices of two of the young girls, chatting while they washed up breakfast things. I began to pay attention when I realized they were discussing Jack Elliston. His height, his charming speech, and even the length of his moustache were approved. One of the girls said she honestly felt that he had smiled twice at her in particular the previous evening, eliciting a scornful guffaw from her workmate.

This is an odd thing. Not for the first or last time let me admit to a confusion regarding the mental workings of women in general. Their response to my friend was a good example of their quixotic machinations. Jack was certainly not an unsightly man, but neither could I spot anything particularly admirable in his physique. He was rather too tall for the weight he carried, bony about the knuckles and elbows, and endowed with uncommonly thick eyebrows and a bit of a knob in his nose. Women, however, consistently seemed to find such a combination of attributes enthralling—this well before they had opportunity to judge his wit and his wealth, which might have been more rational attractions. It was *the look of him* that whetted the feminine appetite. Trying to view the matter in all objectivity, I would say that I am at least as robust, clean featured, and well disposed. But standing next to Jack I was always of about as much interest to a female as a one-legged priest.

The girls did not realize that I had been eavesdropping and cheerfully offered me breakfast—which I refused—and coffee, the one item of civilized society that I absolutely demand of a morning. The pot was large and hot on the corner of the cooking stove, and they didn't seem to mind that I took two cups—one in each hand—with me as I went out into the yard. The Riordan men were all standing, along with Jack, by the rail fence that ran behind the barns.

There had been a sprinkle of rain in the night, and they had just now decided that the dirt track on the other side of the fence was dry enough to run. As Christy and John went into the near barn to fetch the necessary tack, James and Jack discussed something about the philosophy of running horses in a profound, Socratic manner. I was left out of the discussion, which was quite agreeable to me. At that time of day, I prefer coffee to conversation. I was, however, most intrigued to watch the young men, Christy in particular, prepare Miss Deception for her morning run. All the while that they were fitting her with the light racing saddle and bridle, Christy discoursed with the animal in the soft, low tones of a man addressing his sweetheart. When she was ready, he did not immediately mount her, but stood fondly facing her for a minute, the two actually leaning forward to press their foreheads together for a moment. She was indeed a beauty— slim and golden in the morning sun, but all muscle at the shoulders.

Then he leapt into the saddle, and she ran. After loping gracefully around the field for a while, swerving and striding at her master's command, she was brought to a stop perhaps a hundred yards down the track. James Riordan had two blocks of wood in his hand and when he simulated the sound of a starter's pistol by clapping these together, the filly took flight. She almost literally took flight. Her hooves just seemed to clip the dirt lightly enough to puff up the dust as she soared by. I was impressed. Jack was open mouthed with joyful amazement. He almost looked like he might start to weep.

An hour or two later, the sun was high in the sky when the two of us got back on our own horses and were ready to start for home, Miss Deception—a little skittish now—behind us on a long lead. Jack had been talking a lot with Christy, discussing details, making arrangements for his arrival in Victoria, when James Riordan came up to me as I sat atop Old Peter. He held out his hand—I thought at first just to shake mine—and surprised me by dropping into my palm the two coins I had last night paid out to his mother. I made to protest, but he would have none of it.

"Understand, Mr. Zachary, that she's just a bit daft and not whole-heartedly trying to cheat you. She uses a trifle too much of her intuition when she decides who has won at cards. You should take it as a compliment, really."

"Ah?"

"She wouldn't think to take your money if she thought of you as a stranger in the house. She must have decided you were a bit like family."

I told him, quite genuinely, that I looked forward to seeing them all in Victoria at the race, and we started out.

We rode pretty slowly at first, as if Miss Deception was too dainty to travel at a decent speed, but I imagine Jack was just giving her time to accustom herself to our formation. He was turned in his saddle, watching her almost continually for the first few miles.

"You'll get a miserable crick in your neck, Jack," I told him, at which he grunted and smiled. Then I continued. "Is she still everything you expected, as fast as you remember, or had you actually seen her go before?"

"Only a glimpse down in Oregon, and she's better than I remembered. You saw her! She's a wily little terror!"

"For whatever my view is worth, I agree with you." I had to wait for a minute before he turned around and I could see his face, then I began to question him in more depth. "How would you rate her among all the horses you've seen? Near the fastest?"

He laughed at that. "Among *all* the horses I've seen? Good Lord, Zachary, I've been watching horses since I was a tadpole, every good track in England, every premier race, and then here and there in France and Spain and all along the coast of the Americas! I doubt she's in the top one hundred, but that's no insult to our little filly. I've seen legions of horses bred by millionaires for a dozen generations and trained by the cleverest professionals in the world. It's just that when you find an animal this fast and spirited and beautiful grown up in a farm next door to nowhere, why, it's remarkable. Totally remarkable!"

I though for a while before I spoke again. "But she's as fast as any that you've seen around here—I mean currently?"

He leaned his head back, closed his eyes, scratched his chin, and answered. "The fastest, I think, or as close as I can see without putting a watch on her and comparing the times over a week or two."

I sighed and nodded. "So a person could safely place a wager on her?"

At this he really laughed—from the belly, deep and long. "You can bet your hat and backside, Lincoln Zachary!" Then, turning and pointing his bony finger at me, he said, "You're used to wagering on cards, you see, like a plain fool. Betting on a horse race is something akin to making your bet after you've had a chance to take a good long look at everybody else's hand."

"Oh, really? Then why do people lose their shirts at the racetrack so regularly?"

"Bah! It's because the vast majority of them don't know how to read the horses, or they don't take the time. Or they bet on a horse because it won a race last week and should therefore win every race forevermore. Or because it has the same name as their grandfather's terrier!"

I was beginning to feel rather excited about this, and now the two of us were riding along turned around in our saddles. "So," I said, "she's pretty much a hundred per cent?"

He raised his eyebrows at that. "Nothing," he affirmed, "is a hundred per cent. And remember the first and most weighty rule of any kind of gambling: Do not wager money you do not have to wager."

I shrugged that off, although another voice inside me was reinforcing and amending his advice. "Do not wager more money than you can comfortably afford to lose," it said. It was a harsh, shrill voice though, and one that I could easily learn to ignore.

We worked our way into the rhythm of travel after that, and I was watching the high sky and the leaves blowing down the ditches, thinking my own thoughts, when Jack suddenly asked, "Does she speak of me at all? Has she said anything about me?"

For one irrational instant, I thought he was still speaking about the horse, then I caught myself. "I presume you are referring to Miss Green?"

"Of course I am. It's a simple question, isn't it?"

"And the simple answer is that the woman is a closed book. She certainly doesn't recoil from your presence, as you've no doubt noticed, but her mouth does not reveal what her heart may feel or her thoughts conceal."

"That's meant to be poetry, is it?"

"I rather like it, although it may not appeal to your Philistine soul."

I broke the silence a moment later on a more serious note.

"Watch your heart, Jack Elliston. Fair women use men's hearts to wipe their feet more often than not, and I'm talking common sense, not poetry now. Watch out for your heart."

He nodded thoughtfully and looked across at me with a winsome grin. "It wouldn't be the first crack in the seams of my fragile heart. No, and really, I must admit to wounding one or two on my own—not intentionally, of course—but maybe it might be my turn to shed a tear or two." I joined him as he nodded again for a moment, then he added, "Or maybe not, damn it! Maybe it's my turn to discover the enchanted princess and, well, whatever and whatever!"

We both laughed for a bit before I felt compelled to add, "But it's only been a few days you've known her. You take your time and watch your heart, man."

Again we lapsed into silence for a while before a thought came to me. "But tell me the truth, Mr. Elliston—was this the true reason you invited me on this journey? To learn what you could learn about my son's governess?"

He took it in the right spirit and guffawed. "No, Mr. Zachary! I wanted you along so you could entertain me with your life's story. And you haven't done a bit of it! We've chattered on about nothing but me, and you still the enigmatic stranger. Begin, good fellow! Recount your history! Leave no detail undescribed, no anecdote unrecounted!"

And after a fashion, I did that, taking a couple of hours to do so and feeling warm and liberated for the telling of it. I told of my youth, my brief stint working at the Pinkerton detective agency, my journey to Barkerville, and my spring and summer in the goldfields. I told him about my stumbling through the wilderness and the creek where I finally staked my claim, about the miserable near neighbour that I still think of as "Greencoat," and the good men I knew who went down into mineshafts and were swallowed up by the earth because they had pierced their way into the wrong spot on her skin. I described the snow on my face in the morning, the blood on my frozen hands, and the mud and bugs that seasoned my supper. Then I said that I found quite a lot of gold and came back south a rich man.

Jack was a surprisingly good listener for a fellow who talked as readily as he did. He chuckled and groaned at the appropriate places, and when I came to the abridged end of my tale, he smiled and looked at me thoughtfully.

"You were a lucky man," he commented slowly.

"I was that," I agreed.

"A lot of gold it must have been for one man in one summer."

I shrugged. "I worked damned hard, you know."

"Ah! Hard work, good luck, and a safe, uneventful journey back to your peaceful destiny."

I frowned and looked away, trying to think what I had said that had made him suspicious. "I've told you my story, and I stand by it," I said.

We must have gone a further half-mile before another word was spoken. Then Jack spoke, rather abruptly. "You know, Zachary," he said very seriously, "there was a man and a woman who I met in Boston on my way here from England, and they were in a spot of trouble . . ." He paused—a lengthy pause.

"And?" I asked.

He turned to me and smiled. "And I'm not going to tell you anything more about what happened there. I only bring it up to illustrate that we can both keep a few little secrets to ourselves. And still be good friends."

With that he reached across the space between us and shook my hand. I can't recall what we talked about for the rest of the way home.

WE STOPPED SEVERAL times along the way, for no greater reason than that Jack felt like strolling along the verge of some farmer's field or staring for a while out over the rocks at the white-capped water. He was clearly in a pensive and an uncharacteristically quiet mood, and night had fallen in full several miles before we reached our destination. This was no great problem, for the road was broad and we rode under the steely light of a moon a good three-quarters full. Once we were within the defined boundaries of city streets, both The Commissioner and Old Peter seemed to step a little more brightly, recognizing, I suppose, that they were nearing home. Miss Deception, on the other hand, seemed skittish to me, blowing the night air loudly and creeping closer to us on the long lead, like an apprehensive child slipping closer to mother.

As we turned down the street that led to the Celestial Hotel, Jack pointed ahead of us. "That's Mac Bingham's saddle horse, there. I rather thought he might be waiting here to get a look at his new toy."

I could have done without the presence of strangers to meet us, but there was no choice in it. When we approached the front of the building, Jack suggested that I go inside and fetch Bingham and whoever was with him, while he took the filly across the street, where she could be better viewed under the gaslight. I tied Old Peter to the gate, and as I did so, saw that Miss Deception was now quite skittish indeed, although Jack was on his feet and calming her with quiet words and a stroking hand. I presumed that it might have been the gaslight itself that was worrying her. She might never have experienced such a phenomenon. She was an excitable beast, quite surely.

Three people stood to greet me when I entered the front parlour— Bingham, Roselle, and Sarah Green—all of whom seemed pleased to see me, and for three different reasons, it turned out. Bingham's pleasure was the simplest. "She's here?" he boomed out. "Ah! Good, good, good!" and he bustled past me and out the front door. Roselle did not immediately follow him, nor did Miss Green. The woman looked at Bingham's back with an expression of unmistakable pained relief, then turned on her heel and strode out through the kitchen, where I heard her open the back door.

"So, Zachary!" Roselle began, his one-sided grin giving him a conniving look.

"You must excuse me a minute," I said quickly and went after the girl.

She was standing with her shoulders sagged, leaning against one of the posts at the top of the steps and looking vacantly in the general direction of the moon. "Are you all right, Miss Green?" I asked without preamble.

"What? Yes, I'm fine, thank you, Mr. Zachary."

"You look tired."

"Oh, that. Yes, of course. A long day."

"And a bit distressed, if I may say so."

She tried to pass it off with half a laugh and a wave of her hand. "More tired than distressed. Your wife had to go out, and she asked me if I would act as hostess for the two gentlemen waiting for you and Mr. Elliston. I'm not good at that—playing hostess. I hope I haven't offended them with my lack of attention."

"You don't like him, do you?"

"What? Who?"

"Mac Bingham. I've sensed it a couple of times now. Has he said anything to you, done anything . . . ?"

"Of course not! No, no. His mannerisms are gruff and tedious, but his manners are perfectly fine. No, the fault is mine. I suppose he reminds of someone else, someone less pleasant. I don't know. My father, perhaps."

I took one step closer. "Your father?"

She sighed. "There! I shouldn't have said that, either. Not my place to judge my father, but he was stern, he was strong in his opinions, he was less than pleasant at times. Were you close to your father, Mr. Zachary?"

I shrugged. "I hardly knew him. To be honest, to this day, I don't know whether he's alive or dead." She seemed to shiver at this, and I tried to lighten it with a laugh, then turned and went back inside.

I heard Roselle's bootsteps in the parlour, so I headed for the front door via the dining room, but the man would not be so easily avoided. He halted me as I stepped through onto the porch. "So, Mr. Zachary, the mysterious Mr. Zachary. I've been looking forward to seeing you again." I nodded, not so hypocritical as to claim that the feeling was mutual. He continued. "You know, the thing is, I'm sure we must have met. I've thought about it for days, and there's just about half of a memory sitting there, and it won't come clear. It was Barkerville, though. I'm sure it was somewhere up there, and I know we were both there at the same time. I was the assistant gold commissioner. Did I talk to you there, in that capacity, do you think?"

I shook my head, keeping my face pointed toward the far side of the street, where Jack and Mac Bingham were making a big show of admiring the filly, who seemed to have calmed down now. "The gold commissioner I recall was a tall, skinny fellow with big side-whiskers. That was the only fellow I dealt with."

Roselle was staring at my profile against the distant gaslight. "What about the King George Saloon? That was my usual. Did you frequent the King George at all?"

"Never heard of the place," I lied.

"Or maybe you just can't remember it!" Roselle thought this an uproarious jest and emitted a long horse whinny of a laugh. Then, "Well, I've got one chance to clear the matter in my mind, and that's just next week. I've got an old Barkerville chum coming through next week—just for three days or so, Tuesday to Thursday, and then he takes ship on his way to Hong Kong. Hong Kong! Can you figure that? I can't. Hec Simmonds. You know the name by chance?"

I was frozen where I stood. I told Roselle I had never heard of Hec Simmonds, and silently I wished to God I had not.

"Hec Simmonds—part-time lawman and full-time drunk. He stayed on in Barkerville even after the big fire of '68, which is when I left. Old Hec will tell you a tale or two you haven't heard before, brother, and we'll have some fun—the three of us."

"I won't be in town those days," I answered coldly.

"What?"

"I'll be out of town on business."

"What? What kind of business?"

"The kind that is mine, and none of yours."

He suddenly took note of my coldness and quietly returned it. I regretted that. I hadn't meant to antagonize the fellow. He had the potential to ruin me, and my best defence was to make him unaware of me.

"So," I said in what I hoped was a placatory tone of voice, "I imagine you and Mac will want to be heading home before the moon disappears."

"No. We're staying the night in town."

Somewhat in dismay, I gestured toward the Celestial and began, "So are you . . . ?"

He barked a laugh. "Not bloody likely! A dozen hotels to choose from, and you think we'd stay here overnight? Maybe hold our meetings here, for the sake of privacy, but not overnight! We're not beggars, and we're not Chinamen."

WHEN AT LAST I went to bed, I was groggy with fatigue. Thoughts about Roselle, about my financial situation, about the long conversations with Jack Elliston—all competed forcefully for my attention, but evidently to no avail, for I had slipped into slumber for an unknown length of time when I was rudely roused by my son, Ross, shaking my shoulder. It was a difficult struggle to achieve full consciousness, but I rolled over and asked him what was the matter.

"Auntie is crying," he said in great distress.

"What? Auntie Sarah? She's crying?"

"I can hear her through the wall, in my room."

I took his little hand in mine. "Well, what am I supposed to do about it, my boy?"

"I don't know," he whimpered. "She's been crying a long time now—just quiet, but a long time."

I stroked his arm and tried to sound reassuring. "Don't you worry, lad. Women do that sort of thing. It doesn't really mean anything. Go back to bed and go to sleep."

"Maybe you should go and ask her what's the matter."

"No, it's just a woman crying, like a dog barking. Doesn't usually amount to much."

"Maybe I should go and ask her . . ."

"No, no, no. This you should learn now, as you're a big boy. When a woman is crying, or starts to cry, you say nothing—just leave the room. Maybe it will go away. Maybe some other woman will come and talk to her. You are a man. You get the hell out of there. Thank you for telling me, but now off you go to bed. Go to sleep."

"Come put me in bed?"

"I would, my boy, but my legs have stopped working for the day. Be a big boy and put yourself in bed. Sleep."

He consented, to my relief, and I had just closed my eyes when Sue came to bed. Lying next to me, she softly asked questions about my trip (I do not recall if I was able to answer) and spoke a bit about events at the hotel during my two-day absence. She is a good woman, a kind and understanding woman, so I trust she was not upset when I again fell into a deep asleep while she spoke. I sank into the deepest level of sleep and dreamed a Stygian dream.

In my dream, I was visited by a man, presumably named Ned, who I had shot and killed in the deep forest some distance from Barkerville. At the time, I hung the man from a tree to save his corpse from the attention of major scavengers while I was in the area, but now in my fretful sleep I found him hanging not from a tree, but from the beam above the porch in front of our hotel—upside-down, dangling by one leg. I stood a half-dozen paces in front of him, on the street, with my Colt .45 revolver in my hand. I remember that his hat was still pulled down over his eyes, and I worried that in his present position it might fall off and I would have to look at his face. Then he spoke to me in a rumbling, low voice that was tinged with a tone of sadness or regret.

"Well, Zachary," he said, "it looks like you'll have to shoot me again if you want to keep living in this place."

I was quite reluctant to do this. I looked at my gun, then at Ned, then back at the gun. The dead man growled at me again.

"Hurry up! Someone could come along and see us any minute!"

So I raised my pistol and fired, then fired again and again. Each time, the bullet would float agonizingly slowly across the space between us, then, just as it reached his body, it would burst into a soft puff of white smoke.

"Come on now, Zachary Beddoes! That's not going to get the job done, is it?"

Dead Ned seemed very disappointed in me.

I DON'T KNOW whether I awakened directly from the dream or whether it was later. Perhaps my wife somehow roused me when she softly arose to begin her daily duties, for it was just the pale beginning of dawn, the time when she normally does so. There was no question of my returning to sleep, even as fatigued as I was. My mind was spinning. Great, bleak emotionally charged ideas thrust themselves into my face.

I needed to kill Roselle, and the sooner the better. I would probably be caught, though. I was never very good at subterfuge. I was living on an island, and the law could just seal it off, trap me, and hang me. Crowds of angry white men would burn the hotel and stone my family.

Maybe if I ran away immediately and forever, it would spare my family and friends. Perhaps I should say friend.

Poor Jack! They might even think he was complicit in my crimes, since he was my only friend. And even if he escaped being tarred and feathered beside me, he was doomed by a tragic love for this Sarah Green, to whom I introduced him.

Who was this girl, bright and beautiful but frightened of strangers, weeping like a child in the night? No doubt she was mentally unstable. Perhaps she was dismissed from her position in Washington for exhibiting fits of insanity. If Jack took her to himself, he'd probably wake up one night to find her wide-eyed and strangling him.

All these irrational thoughts can feel like absolute epiphanies in the first moments after a fitful awakening. On and on they spun themselves.

I lurched to a sitting position, leaned sideways, and cracked my head soundly against the near bedpost. It is a form of treatment that occasionally works to confound undesirable thoughts, and that morning it worked wonderfully. In the space of one minute, my head cleared, my heart calmed, and the beginnings of a perfectly practical plan formed in my mind. Another minute of thought and I was ready to begin preparations.

I needed to go on a short journey to the Washington Territory.

I would avoid the repellent Mr. Hec Simmonds, map out an escape route for my family and myself, should my identity still be exposed (something I should have done long ago), and, while I was thereabouts, see what I could discover regarding the past circumstances of Miss Sarah Green. For better or for worse, my friend Jack deserved to know the truth.

I ATE MY breakfast alone. We had no short-term guests in the hotel just then, so I was served my soup and bread in the kitchen. As I ate, I watched Old Lee through the back window, smoking his long clay pipe. He smoked one pipe of tobacco each morning after his breakfast, after which he would retire to his room to attend to the hotel accounts, which he noted in a voluminous Western style journal, spilling Chinese characters all down the margins. He bowed slightly and greeted me as he passed through on his way upstairs, spilling one final sparking coal from his pipe-bowl in the process, which the cook deftly stepped on without comment. I lingered over my empty dish for a while.

Going upstairs myself, I stopped first at my own room, where I closed the door, then reached behind the little false wall at the back of the closet to obtain a sealed jar—one of only three now—half-full of gold flakes and small nuggets. From this, I filled a small cloth bag before replacing everything as it was. Then I wandered down the hall to visit my father-in-law.

When I tapped on his door and entered, I found him not at his work table, but at his telescope. It was a big brass device—or so it seemed to me—mounted on a swivel at his window, and with it he had an oversized view between buildings of two different street corners, as well as the length of an alley leading toward Johnson Street. He had a star map, bordered with Chinese characters, pinned to the wall next to his bed, but I don't suspect he got as much pleasure from the night sky. I asked him once if he didn't wish to move the thing from time to time, so as to see a different section of the stars, but he merely framed the angle of the bedroom window with his hands and said, "This is enough sky." Likewise, the view of two intersections and an alley was sufficient for him to study mankind. For my part, I was simply glad that he kept it pulled well inside, out of the weather, where it was barely visible from the street. We did not need to be known as "the hotel with the strange man at his telescope."

I sat in the chair facing his work table, and as he came and assumed his position across from me, we began a conversation that had become a sort of friendly ritual, having been repeated over the years many times.

"A favour again . . . ," I began.

"Yes, a favour."

"I have some raw gold that I would like to have exchanged for . . ."

"The coin of the realm?"

"Yes, the coin of the realm." The stilted phrase was part of the ceremony. I placed the cloth bag on the table, next to his scales and weights.

As he poured the sparkling stuff onto a tin tray and began to weigh it, he asked me thoughtfully, "This is not the last of your savings, I hope?"

It was a joke, really, and again it was part of our ritual discourse, but I think he was always a bit curious, a bit relieved when I answered, "No. Not yet."

I still did not feel comfortable being seen with raw gold in my hands, so from time to time I would bring my father-in-law small portions (this time it was a little more than usual), and he would take them to the Chinese money changer. I never went with him, but once I had the temerity to check that everything was being kept quite confidential and that he was not using any Western bank for his transactions. He seemed somewhat offended. The Chinese money handlers were the only ones a sensible man could trust, he assured me—best rates, right now, and no questions asked. "Very quiet people. Very hush-hush. Just the same as me. Am I not always hush-hush?" His English had definitely improved during the time of our acquaintance, but it was still privately amusing to me to hear him pronounce "hush-hush."

"So coin of the realm as always, for the most part," I said, "but this time I need some of it in American money."

"United States?"

"Maybe two or three hundred dollars?"

"Not a problem, I think. Lots of United States money around . . ."

"Only US Treasury notes."

"Greenbacks!" Lee liked the word.

"Yes. Don't let them give you any old California money, no Confederate bills, or anything."

"Just greenbacks."

The federal treasury had replaced all the old demand notes with these bills, printed in green on the back side, a couple of years before I went north to the gold rush, then a year or two later started printing them on special linen paper with little strands of colour and numerous sections of fine engraved lines, all serving to make them virtually impossible to counterfeit. When I was employed for a short time as a Pinkerton man, a lot of the agency's business had involved counterfeit versions of the money printed by various states. Banks sometimes collapsed because of this type of crime, but it was bread and butter to Pinkerton's. Now I wanted to see, during the trip I was planning to the Territory of Washington, how readily accepted the treasury bills would be. In the event that I had to flee my present home—an event that I now realized I had not adequately prepared for—paper money would be much preferable to raw gold, if it was reliable as legal tender.

As always with Old Lee, part of the formalities consisted of his having me take note and approve of the gold weight he had calculated. As he slid a piece of paper across the table with this figure written on it, he happened to flip over a small photograph that had been propped against a small stack of correspondence. It was a family photograph of his uncle Boon with wife and child. After glancing at the gold weight, I picked up the picture.

"Very nice."

"Yes. Very nice," Lee agreed, rather proud of his wealthy relative from San Francisco.

"A good likeness. Young Jon looks like a small but distinguished gentleman."

"They back soon, in plenty time for big race."

"Ah. So Boon knows about the horse race?"

"Yes! Yes, the horse race! My uncle loves a horse race. Loves all the horses. Is there much money, bets, wagers in this horse race?"

I laughed. "Money? Buckets of it changing hands, so I'm told. Buckets of money."

"And lots of people. Visitors. Hotel will be full. Maybe people sleep on the porch."

I laughed. "Not without paying a dollar a head. But we reserve all the rooms on the front of the second floor for Uncle Boon." White Lee knew this, but he was still pleased, I think, to hear me affirm the importance of favouring his uncle. "But perhaps, Lee, you should go to the money changer now, before the weasels start changing their rates with race day in mind. And don't forget my greenbacks. I'm planning a trip, day after tomorrow."

Chapter Five

THE STEAMER *ELIZA ANDERSON*, POPULARLY known as the *Anderson*, left Victoria weekly on Thursday mornings at an absolutely ungodly hour—if three o'clock can be called morning and not the middle of the night. It was black as a crow's belly when we weighed anchor and started out. I moved my way forward, placed my bag against a bulkhead, my back against my bag, then pulled my coat around my knees and my hat down to my eyebrows. In this position I gradually gained a bit better humour. I had brought along tea, and I drank it from my canteen, one of my oldest possessions. It was the first time I had used it in five or six years, and it made the tea taste slightly dusty and rusty, but not at all bad. In fact, it was a pleasing taste—a taste that brought back memories of wilder days, and it was a pleasing sensation to feel the wild air blowing into my face. For the moment, I had no schedule to follow save that of the steamship. The hiss of the boilers and the rumble and slap of the ship's paddles were so oddly relaxing that I soon dozed off, awakening to find that true morning was upon us, and we were well into open water.

I was without coffee or breakfast, though, and my mood instantly returned to the irritable anxiety with which I had left the hotel some hours before. I wished that I had brought along some biscuits and something stronger than tea to drink. There was nothing much else to do, so I slouched there in the chilly sea breeze and stewed about fate and fortune.

Life seemed to be treating me rather ironically—bringing me into the company of a man who seemed well suited to becoming my very good friend and almost simultaneously introducing a fellow who might ruin me completely. And then there was the enigmatic Miss Sarah Green, who seemed to be so attractive to my new friend, but about whom I was beginning to have reservations.

And so this was a voyage with a trio of objectives. It was a voyage of evasion, one of investigation, and one of preparation. I would evade Roselle's equally repugnant friend, Hec Simmonds—lately of the Barkerville police. I would investigate the unknown recent past of Sarah Green, if that was possible. And I would prepare for flight back to the United States, if the worst came to the worst.

Having reached this much resolve, I stood up, left my bag where it was, and strolled the decks. Gradually, I became used to the rise and roll of the ship—a sensation I have never enjoyed, particularly when land was only a dark line framing a distressingly vast panorama of grey. After finishing a slow tour of the main deck, I climbed the steel stairs to the upper deck, where, as chance would have it, I met up with the ship's master, a man named Lacerte, who was leaned against a railing outside the wheelhouse, sullenly smoking a short, black pipe and occasionally spitting dark phlegm down onto the deck below. He coughed with a disturbing regularity, bordering on the continuous, starting deep in his chest and coursing up through his throat.

"A bad cough you've got there," I ventured—a significant under-statement.

"Ah! Blast and goddammit. Bastard of a thing for a man of my occu-pation, and carrying on for the best piece of a year, goddammit. Lungs and bronchials and throat and all giving out at once." He hacked away into his shoulder for a minute, took a few puffs on his pipe and coughed the pungent smoke into the wind.

"That's a long spell of discomfort."

"I smoke the pipe when I can, and that helps, warms up the air passage and calms the throat."

I decided to find a more positive topic of conversation.

"Well, this seems to be a good, solid vessel."

He looked at me with a touch of amusement. "Then I'd venture you know nothing at all about ships and the sea."

"Nothing at all," I agreed willingly. "But these old sternwheelers are as dependable as the coming of spring, aren't they?"

"Well, for starters, the old *Anderson* is a sidewheeler, if you cast your eye in that direction. She's underpowered and overweight as an ancient whore. Rides in the water like a dead whale. She's been recommissioned and decommissioned again and again, but she refuses to sink. Truth is, though, she's made the bastards that own her more money than you and I would dare to dream. They brought her north just in time to ferry the gold miners toward the gold rush, and then floated them back south to die in poverty."

"Come now. Not all of them," I felt obliged to reply.

"Ah! You don't know what it was like, lad. A handful rich and thou-sands dead-bust or dead outright." He shrugged. "But the *Anderson* carted them along, one and the same, all alike. Then she ran the Port Townsend to Victoria to Langley run until they found a prettier ship. When *that* poor thing couldn't take the beating, they brought *us* back. So maybe you're right. Maybe she's a solid cork in the ocean, after all."

"And you're the captain."

He shrugged his shoulders, ran his gaze briefly the length of the vessel. "Aye. Not that it's anything to get all puffed up about, but captain I am. Born to the sea about the same time as brother Noah set forth with all the animals, and I'm better'n I started out. Better placed than I once was."

I was still looking for an opportunity to advance my investigations. Flattery never hurts, so I offered some.

"I would imagine that you run an efficient vessel. Clean, dependable . . ."

"Aye. All of that, damn it. You can't figure for the weather, of course, but no man will put me off course or behind schedule. I'll have no goddamn sailor aboard who won't keep his station under watch and under good order. No passenger, and no cargo from anyone who can't read the timetable or needs to stay in bed the extra half-hour. Of course the weather is a harsher master than me. You can't figure for the weather."

"And I've no doubt that you keep a close eye on all aboard, as well. I imagine you keep a clear account and record of all and everything that comes aboard the *Anderson*?"

Somewhat to my surprise, he shrugged his shoulders to this. "Well," he said, "I don't allow any frippery or misbehaviour, and I won't have fools shooting guns at whales and the like, but who they are before they come aboard and what they do once they're ashore is not my business and too much trouble to take much notice."

And just like that, the captain had given me a good piece of information.

On the positive side, there was hope that a person like myself could leave Vancouver Island on the *Anderson* without being too closely watched. Less helpfully, on the matter of Sarah Green's arrival at Victoria with the big Negro, he wouldn't be able to enlighten me.

The trip aboard the *Anderson* was pleasant, although it took two full days because of the stops it made at isolated outposts along the way. Past Port Townsend, we wound through what seemed like an endless warren of long inlets. We had good weather, though, and fine scenery across the water all down Puget Sound. I met with pleasant company—mostly men of commerce and government—but the closer I got to my destination, the more anxious I became. As these rocky shores and magnificent forests slipped by, I was haunted by visions of Roselle, and visions of myself and my family running from angry crowds, creeping fearfully across the wilderness. I had too much time on my hands and I used it to worry. It was with great relief that I arrived at my destination.

Late Friday night, I booked into the Tacoma Hotel in the centre of Olympia. It wasn't such a bad place, although I cast upon it the critical eye of a man who is—technically, at least—a hotelier himself. The Tacoma was smaller than the Celestial, but well kept, uncluttered, painted and papered fresh and bright. There didn't seem to be much lobby space—no comfortable place for a guest to sit, and the glimpse I got of the dining area did not greatly recommend it.

Suddenly there was a man at my shoulder, behind the main counter, who had arrived as silently as a ghost—a bland, fat little ghost.

"Good evening, sir?" It was a question.

"Do you have a room for a couple of nights?"

"Certainly, sir. Second floor, if that's all right. Front or back?"

"Front," I said firmly, although I really could have no preference without any knowledge of the place. I just wanted to sound like a seasoned traveller, a decisive fellow. It's a common incongruity—the strange need to impress all these milk-faced strangers who hold positions of authority, be it ever so minimal.

"Name on line one, occupation line two, permanent residence line three." He said this so quickly, all in one breath, that I barely caught his words, and while he spoke he used a practised flick of the wrist to spin the big book on the counter around to face me. The register. On this detail, the Tacoma definitely outdid the Celestial. We used a commonplace bookkeeper's ledger to register our guests, while here I was faced with a massive leather-bound volume that momentarily intimidated me. I held the proffered pen hesitantly over the page until it was ready to drip as I suddenly considered that I should be paying more attention to the danger of inscribing my name in such public records.

"Sir?"

I scowled at him, decided just to sign and be done with it, actually began to write the Z of my last (or was it my first?) name, then changed my mind again, made the Z into a T, and then finished scribbling the signature of Mr. T. Ackery from Chicago. My knowledge from working at Pinkerton's had kicked in at the last. Never pretend to be from a place you don't actually know, and use as your alias something quite similar to your real name. I don't exactly know the reasoning behind this last practice, but I knew from experience that confidence men and fugitives all across the country use false names reminiscent of the true, so they must know something. And I was thus Mr. T. Ackery, as far as the hotel was concerned.

From my window I had a good view of that little city, but there was nothing useful to see. I sat on my bed and tried to formulate some strategy for my investigations. The one thing that I had already decided was that I should focus my attention on learning what I could about Sarah Green, during which time I would be able to see about stagecoach schedules, small boats that might take on passengers discreetly, and where a man in a hurry might buy a horse.

I slept surprisingly well for a person with so much on his mind, and in the morning, after washing up, I strolled down to the dining room with a genial smile on my face. The room was just as small as I had guessed the previous evening, but I was the only patron. Either the hotel was relatively vacant, or I was the only late riser. I squeezed behind one of the three little tables as a stout, flushed woman with a smile as genial as my own approached through a door that presumably led to the kitchen.

"Coffee," I said with firm conviction.

"Coffee. Yes sir." She turned back through the kitchen door. After only three words, I could tell that her origin was in the deep south. In the years following the Civil War, a large number of southerners, both black skinned and white, had come north with next to nothing, fleeing that devastated, once proud region. Some went even farther, into British territories. We spoke more while she poured from a huge enamel pot. An unusual aroma was exuded.

"This is coffee?" I was genuinely confused.

"Better than that—it's sweet potato coffee, and my own mother's process. The secret is in the way you chop and roast the peelings. Very exact and . . ."

Without taking time to apologize, I slouched out into the street. The desperate fear came upon me that this might be one of those sad outposts where genuine coffee was not always available. In all my years in Victoria, such a thing had never occurred. A time or two, there had been shortages, but someone had always had a sufficient supply of the true beverage.

My fears proved unfounded. I was soon seated on the boardwalk in front of a bakery, drinking a pretty decent cup, while worrying a bit that if the southern woman actually owned the hotel, I might return to find the blankets removed from my bedroom and offered to a more respectful client. For a while, I sat and soaked in the rays of the morning sun, which did little to energize me. I watched the citizens pass me by on their morning errands, and in particular I watched a tall Negro woman with a huge upright brush of black and white hair as she swept the boardwalk across the street. I should say that such was her intent, but social demands made it difficult for her to do much sweeping. She greeted, to my recollection, every passerby—most of these by name—and exchanged one or two sentences of information, as often as not. White folks were content with nodding to her and speaking her name (Delia), while her black-skinned brothers and sisters generally stopped to chat and laugh. There are many more Negroes in Washington than in Victoria, so this conversation put stringent limits on the cleaning of the city's walkways. No one seemed to despise her position, though, and she smiled so continuously that it could be presumed that she would smile at the devil himself, should the devil pass by the dentist's office that morning. I was not sure that she was totally in possession of her mental faculties. She was intriguing to watch.

But now it was time for me to stroll the streets of Olympia.

It was an odd sort of town, in some ways, perched between a large lake and an ocean inlet, with what seemed like two quite separate ports. I walked a great distance to spy them both out, and learned very little, save that if I was on the run when I next passed through, any further flight would need to be taken overland after reaching Olympia.

I learned nothing new about Sarah Green.

I tried to recall what course of action we had taken when I was a Pinkerton man. If I had stuck with the firm a little longer, I might have developed skills suited to the task ahead of me, but now I felt aimless and frustrated. My impulse at that moment was to interrogate the nearest stranger until he'd told me the unknown truth—that, or simply thrash some character until he told me a few good lies. This was the preferred stratagem of one of my former partners, a Texan named Gilbert. It was a chancy strategy. If one happened to knock about an honest citizen, it was a total waste of time, and if the target you settled upon was *too* nasty, you put yourself in harm's way, still without learning anything. Once I was nearly killed—and I hadn't even taken part in the original thrashing.

At some hour approaching midday, I made my way south to the battered shack that passed for a stagecoach station. Standing a short distance from a trio of storage sheds and the most southerly residences of Olympia, it seemed to be just a larger version of the multitude of broken wooden crates stacked outside its west wall. The station building appeared to be already half consumed by layers of moss and mildew, and if the rest of the road that the coach travelled on was as deeply rutted as the yard in front of the station, it would be a bone-crushing journey should I and my family ever be forced to take it. Obviously this would not be my first choice of transport, but it deserved a look and I'd walked a long way to get there. A portly little man stepped forward from the back room when I entered.

"Good day, sir. And what can I do for you?"

"Schedules. Just checking to see what time the stagecoach leaves here if I decide to go farther along."

"And where would you be headed? Portland? Walla Walla?"

"I'm not sure. I just wanted to know the general schedule."

"Well, you must be going *somewhere*. And when are we talking about? Tomorrow? We don't run tomorrow. Next day?"

"All right, consider the next day. I'm not sure. I'm just, sort of taking the tour."

"Touring? We don't get many folks coming through here on the tour. Nothing to see."

"I think it's very nice. I like the coast district."

"Coast is way the hell west. At any rate, you'd be heading to Portland then, and we'd be up and out of here as soon as the mail arrives. And Bobby. He's late sometimes."

"But noon at the latest, then?"

"You want I should save a spot for you?"

"No. Don't do that. I really haven't decided quite yet."

"On tour?" he repeated somewhat incredulously.

I decided it wouldn't hurt to expand on my story a bit. "I thought I'd stop over here in Olympia and see if I could find a friend of mine who was living here, last that I heard. Sarah Green. You wouldn't know her, by any chance? Englishwoman. Pretty girl. Twenty, twenty-five, thirty. I'm not certain."

His look adjusted from incredulity to curiosity, or even suspicion. "But she's a good friend?"

"Of my wife. And of myself. Of course."

"Sorry. We keep to ourselves, pretty much, and I'm generally too busy to keep track of names and strangers. Actually, I'm pretty busy right now."

The clink of spoons on bowls and the smell of soup coming from the back room told me the nature of his business, so I thanked him and headed back into the centre of town.

At the bakery, I ordered a slab of bread with molasses and more coffee. The coffee was evidently still from that morning's brew, and by now, because of the principle of continuous brewing, it was about as strong as I could endure. If I came back again that day, the stuff would be strong enough to fight for its own survival. I asked the serving girl if she had ever met a young woman roughly her own age named Sarah Green. An English girl, single, quite pretty. I received a thoughtful look—a worried look, as I envision it now—and a negative response. At the Olympia Market, where I purchased a couple of apples and some beef jerky, the proprietor, Mr. M.R. Tilley replied likewise to a like question, with the addendum that he was not inclined to trade in old gossip.

I wondered what that meant.

So I sat and ate one of the apples on the broad boardwalk outside the Olympic Hall on Main Street, while I reconsidered. I then made my way to the offices of *The Washington Standard*. The sign painted on the door informed me that one John Miller Murphy was the editor, but the boy who met me at the front counter—Rodney by name—informed me that Mr. Miller was out for the day. I asked this Rodney if he recalled the name Sarah Green. He did not. When asked if back issues of the newspaper were available for my perusal, he replied that I would have to discuss such an arrangement with Mr. Murphy. From the obsequious attitude of the lad when he spoke his employer's name, I concluded that John Miller Murphy slept with smoke curling out of his nostrils and demanded to be fed a young maiden or a copyboy if he was inappropriately awakened. I left the building feeling dispirited and frustrated. Detective work often turns out to be time-consuming and fruitless of course, which was my main reason for leaving my post with Pinkerton's.

The sensible source of information on what Sarah experienced in this city would be the local police, but contrary to general counsel, the policeman was not and never would be my friend.

As I trudged down the main street of Olympia, aimed in the general direction of my hotel, I noticed the tall Negro woman, Delia, leaning against a signpost between the hardware store and the bakery. She was talking to a small black-skinned workman of some ten years of age who was toiling at chopping wood in the space between the buildings. As I stepped up onto the boardwalk and strolled toward her, her voice softened and she greeted me as she did all passersby.

"Good afternoon, sir. Good afternoon."

I stopped and addressed her. "A good day to you as well. Delia, isn't it?"

She was surprised and, I think, pleased that I knew her name. "Not often people recognize a humble soul like myself, such as I am, and me not even having a clue as to you. You're new to the city, I'm thinking?"

"I'm just travelling through. Taking a tour."

"Well, my goodness. You sure do be having the time of your life. We get no end of folk passing through Olympia, just taking the tour. Taking the tour! Nothing more beautiful on God's earth than this green land where the mountains roll peaceful into the sea and the rushing rivers ease themselves into the mighty, mighty ocean."

I could tell that my new friend Delia was unafraid of wasting time in conversation, and that if I didn't go directly to the meat of my inquiry, I would not have time to ask more than one direct question before the sunset. "I'm wondering, Delia, since you seem to know everyone and everything about this place, if you could help me. I was hoping, while I am here in Olympia, to hear some news about a friend of mine—a young Englishwoman named Sarah Green. I believe she lived somewhere hereabouts until quite recently, and I think she might have travelled farther along for some reason. Would you recognize the name? A lovely girl. I'd dearly like to know what happened to her."

The Negro woman shook her head and looked up to the sky with a light laugh. She had a shrill, silly sounding laugh, and one was tempted to assume that there was nothing but fluff and dust inside her head, but I had an inkling that there was a little more to her than met the eye. "Don't recall the name. Don't see no whole lot of English young girls about this town, but what am I to be saying for sure? My goodness, there's people coming through this town now every day—new, like yourself, and long time like me, and the numbers is growing day by day by day. Railroad, too! Soon! Don't you believe the word some folks are talking that it will end up Tacoma way, don't consider no place but this natural railroad town. And soon, sure as sunshine, we also gonna be a full, true state of the United States of America, based as it is in the city of Washington, with the president and all, and why wouldn't they want a state with the same name as that city and the very first president, and we would be like the little baby sister to them all?"

Listening to her was like trying to keep track of four different conversations at the same time. I did not hesitate, but pressed on. "Or perhaps you might know a fellow she is said to be travelling with—a sort of guardian. Othello. Large Negro man. No hair. Bald, but a good reliable man, I understand. Othello?"

Her glance in my direction was fleeting to say the least, but as her eyes met mine for the briefest instant, it was as if I had glimpsed a face looking out through a window and gone so fast that all I could say for sure was that the curtains had stirred. Then she lied to me.

"No, sir. I can't say I recall such a fellow, and unfortunately I can't say there be a lot of reliable men of my own race here in this territory. And no, I don't know anything about no Englishwoman named whatever you just called her. Now I should be busy about my work, 'cause this walkway don't get swept by itself."

She took to her sweeping, head down, and since I had no way to press the issue, that might have been the end of it, but at that moment the young wood-chopper was struggling his way up onto the boardwalk, arms loaded with kindling sticks, headed to the front door of the bakery.

"Jeesh, Delee!" he muttered. "He's talking about Naomi Phipps. And 'Thello . . ."

"On your way, you woodmouse!" she cut him off, "and don't talk around things you don't know nothing about . . ."

"Jeesh!"

"And pull those damn trousers up, boy. Your daddy working all day so as to buy you 'spenders and your pants hung down like that. 'Spenders like that cost money and you could've got nothing but a rope belt and my goodness, if you don't mind your business and get that wood inside, then who's gonna bake the bread and we all go hungry in this town? Hurry up! Hurry!"

When she turned back, I stood directly in her way, my own expression as blank as I could make it. Rather than querying her further, I waited for her to speak, and with the good lady Delia, that was never a long wait.

"Listen, sir, who I don't even know your name. You just go off and look for your English friend wherever English people be. Good luck, and off you go. And if you absolutely got to see big bald Negroes, you just as well be looking down to The Rascals bar as anywhere. Plenty of big, lazy unreliable Negro men down there. Off you go! Take something with you to fight with, mind. Off you go."

But I would not leave until she had given me directions to the bar, which she did efficiently, albeit grudgingly.

Checking the time, I saw that I could still make supper at my hotel and considered this preferable to visiting The Rascals for the first time just as it was getting dark. I was a stranger in this town, tired, not at my best. Then, just around the corner, I spotted another signboard, this one advertising the services of Mr. James G. Swan—Notary Public. I stood there in the twilit street considering it for a moment. Here was a man who was, to some extent, paid to keep track of public information. If he showed signs of recognizing my description of Sarah Green—by whatever name she went in Olympia—I might be within the bounds of propriety to offer him money for information.

His door was locked, his windows dark, but it was another possibility for the morrow.

The Tacoma Hotel served a better supper than their cup of so-called coffee, so I ate well. After this, being apprised of the fact that drinks were served until ten on the back veranda, the charges added to one's hotel bill, I sat in a warm spring breeze and drank whisky. Being alone and away from my home for the first time in recent memory, I felt almost obliged to do something that resembled carousing, but I was too tired to do any more walking, so this was it. I drink rather quickly when I am alone and bored, so I don't recall exactly what time I lost my lust for liquor, but I must presume it was close to ten, based on the way I felt in the morning.

I felt horrible.

It was a beautiful sunny morning. I began it by slipping past the front desk and the breakfast room with my hat pulled down low, hoping that no one would try to engage me in an exchange of civil words. My head was full of something hot and mushy, like bread that had mopped up wash water. It was still chilly as I headed down the street, but I seemed to be sweating bile. With some difficulty I made it to the wooden bench in front of the bakery, and leaned against the wall, a large tin cup of harsh, black coffee by my side. When I had finished the coffee, I closed my eyes and absorbed the healing effects of the sunshine until the bakery girl awakened me by pouring more dark brew into my cup. I must have smiled.

"The right idea?" she inquired.

"A grand idea," I replied.

The second cup became empty about the same time as a cloud passed over the sun, so I got to my feet and, after returning the tin vessel to its proper owner, I started out. I thought at first that I was beginning to feel better, but the sensation only lasted a few steps. Bypassing the more intimidating signage of *The Washington Standard*, I made my way directly to the office of James G. Swan, notary public, and jingled my way through his doorway.

His was a very small office—barely room for a single desk, a few chairs, a coatrack, and a filing cabinet. He kept the window shades pulled down, presumably to avoid having the room polluted by sunlight. The man was wearing a very wide black hat and sitting at his desk as I entered. He was young, small, and thin. While it wasn't yet noon, he grasped a full tumbler of beer in one fist as he glared blearily down at the papers strewn before him. This might have done little to inspire confidence in another client, but to me, it assured me that we were a pair of souls destined to do business. I would perhaps be reluctant to bring complex legal matters to such a man, but he struck me as an ally I could use in my present search, so I greeted him cheerfully.

"Good morning," I said. "Mr. Swan? My name is Tim Ackery. And how is breakfast?"

He raised his glass in salute. "Cheap and rough," he answered, "like myself. There's about a cup or so left in the bucket if you're in the mood."

I would like to say that I accepted the offer strictly as a courtesy, but in fact my hangover had returned in force and I needed to numb it a bit. I drank from a sealer jar that smelled vaguely of soup.

"What can I do for you?" His voice sounded as if his throat was falling apart.

My mind was blank, but the circumstances being what they were, I sensed there was no need to hurry, so I just replied, "Thanks for the drink," and stared at the beer for a minute. It was as flat as an abandoned snakeskin with just a little bit of poison left in it. I threw the last of it back, shuddered, and reached across to shake his hand.

"Wait a minute," he growled. He was rolling a cigarette, which ended up taking a bit of time.

I leaned back in my chair, closed my eyes, and rested my boots on the corner of his desk. I supposed that he would have assumed the same posture, but his side of the desk was covered with important papers and scattered tobacco. Remarkably, I think the beer had focused my mind a little. I explained that I was a businessman down from the Island Colony, and I had been given some rather sketchy references second-hand regarding a young lady who I might be interested in employing. She had apparently lived in this area some short time past and, since he dwelt in the centre of the community's active life, I hoped he might have heard her name spoken and be able to point me in the direction of someone who could authoritatively speak good or ill of the woman. Sarah Green.

He looked at me thoughtfully, then asked if I had some sort of business card. I did not, but gave him the name of my hotel. He scowled and asked me what position I might be hiring her to. "Governess," I responded with a transparency that I hoped would counteract his reluctance. He grunted and took another sip from his glass.

"What sort of information do you require?" he asked then. I replied that any background on her time spent in the Olympia region, either positive or negative, would be useful. As an afterthought, I added that since his was a profession that traded in information, I would certainly be prepared to pay for reliable advice. He snorted at that, and then there was such a long pause that I almost decided that he was refusing to reply. Or that he had fallen asleep.

"Sarah Green," he said finally.

I hesitated. "Or possibly Naomi Phipps," I countered.

There was another long pause. At the risk of seeming less nonchalant, I sat forward and watched as he emptied his glass of beer and thought for a moment. Then he spoke carefully.

"Phillips."

"What's that?"

"The name is Phillips. You have been discussing her with someone who has limited control of syllables. They missed one. Her name is Phillips."

"Naomi Phillips, then."

He opened the top drawer of his desk, inspected the inner regions, then closed it and sat back. "Who told you about me?" he asked.

"No one. I just saw your sign."

Then we sat in silence for a long moment, staring eye to eye. His eyes didn't look good, and I suspect mine were about as bad. After a pause, he asked, "Why would you come to me?"

"I told you that."

"Why not the sheriff? Why not the newspaper?"

"The newspaper would be my next stop, I guess. I already tried once, but there was just a boy. And I don't deal with people like the sheriff of my own volition."

He digested that for a minute. Then he cleared his throat of some great liquid mass, walked across to the open window, and spat it outside, along with the butt of his cigarette. After this, he shuffled over to a little alcove behind the filing cabinet, where he had a basin of water and a towel. He doused his head thoroughly, dried it off, and returned to me with the towel around his neck.

"Shit," he proclaimed.

I shrugged innocently.

"Total shit. Nobody comes all the way down to Olympia just to check the references of some governess. What's the truth, Mr. Ackery?"

Again I shrugged. "I needed a change of scenery as well. I'm on the tour, so to speak. And while I was here, why not check the background of my son's teacher? Miss Green. Miss Phipps. Miss Phillips."

I was almost telling him the truth, so I was rather startled when he became instantly furious, shouting, "You lying bastard!" and banging his fist down on the desk in front of me. Things then went from bad to worse as he shrieked like a woman, spun backwards, and fell to his knees. He had banged his fist down onto the little scissors he used to trim cigarettes, and he was now bleeding profusely from his right wrist. I got him to his feet and held the towel against it. There we stood, behind the desk, weaving together like wrestlers.

"Goddamn! Goddamn!"

"Hold still! Stop that!"

"Goddamn!"

"It's not that bad. Don't act like a girl."

It did bleed a lot, but it had missed the big veins, and he was in no danger. I used his tobacco scissors to cut a section off his towel and wrapped it in place with shoelaces that were sitting in the middle of his desk for some reason. While I worked on this, we talked about my reason for being there.

"If you've done wrong to Naomi Phillips, or if you're trying something smart on her, I'll bite your head off at the neck."

"Calm down. I'm a friend. She works for me. In Victoria. She really does."

"Like I said before—that's total shit."

"No, it's not. She's become, well, friends with my friend Jack. I've got a feeling about it, so I have to check things out."

"A feeling? What kind of feeling?"

We were done with the bandaging now.

"She avoids questions, Mr. Swan."

"And so?"

"I think something went wrong down here. Questions need to be asked, and no one is asking. My wife is Chinese and she doesn't care that much about questions that aren't answered. Jack is a gentleman, so he doesn't ask. I'm neither Chinese nor gentleman, but I get a little cowardly around women, so rather than ask her directly, I thought I'd just look around for myself."

"While you're touring?" he added, still cynical.

"I have other reasons for this trip. My business. Not your business."

"Who told you I might be able to help you?"

"No one. That's the truth. I don't know what you're getting at."

"Do you have a knife?"

"What? Why?"

He turned and reached into the top drawer of his desk as he said this. I didn't know whether to grab his arm or run. Neither one was necessary, though, for what he took from the drawer was a sausage—a large sausage wrapped in waxed paper.

"I'm not going to cut this with my little scissors, am I? Bring your hat. We can get some bread at the bakery on the way to the Pony Sample."

"The Pony Sample?"

"Saloon."

"At this time of day?"

"It's nearly noon. We can go around the back door if they're not open yet."

It was an oddly appealing idea. Then suddenly, just as he reached for the door, he halted, turned and thrust his face at mine. His eyes were about level with my chin, but his gaze was belligerent and dark.

"I might tell you some things, and I might not."

"All right."

"Why should I tell you anything at all? Give me a reason, one reason, why that's a good idea. She's a friend of mine, as you may have figured."

I thought for a minute. He glared. Then I continued:

"She gets along very well with my son, and he with her. She laughed the other day, and it struck me that maybe she hadn't laughed much in quite some time."

Swan nodded solemnly as he absorbed this, then turned back and swung the door open. "I hope you have some money. Lately they insist on getting money for their beer at the Pony, and I seem to be a little short at the moment."

When we arrived—he was carrying sausage and I had a loaf of bread in my hand—the saloon was indeed closed, but the good Mr. J.G. Swan seemed to have a way with locked doors, and we were soon inside.

It was a pleasant-looking place at that time of the day—tidy and as big as a schoolroom, although offering a different sort of education. There were six small tables for drinkers, another large one close to one wall for card players, and, against the other wall, an eight-foot-square platform raised on blocks about a foot off the floor. In the centre of the platform was a tall stool, against which was leaned a battered banjo.

Swan strolled around behind the bar, pulled two glass mugs down from the shelf, and began filling them from the beer barrel at the end of the counter. The first mug he ran half-full and drained it off in one gulp. Then he filled both to the brim and slid one across the bar to me. Before he joined me, he found a pencil and a scrap of paper beside the barrel and scribbled both our names at the top.

He hesitated. "How much money do you have, actually?"

"More than enough," I said.

"That's the spirit." He put a small *x* under each name.

We had just nicely seated ourselves at a table near the windows and begun to carve up sandwiches to go with our beer, when a large man with a reddish beard and a florid complexion came bustling in through a side door.

"Swanny!" There was a distinct tone of warning in his voice.

"Lucas!"

"Why should I have to throw you out before the day's even started, Swan?"

"No reason. My friend has money. We're keeping a tab on the counter there."

"We're closed. We don't open for another two hours."

"Well, we won't pay you anything until after, say, three o'clock, and you won't be doing business out of hours." Swan thought this very funny and laughed loudly.

"Contrary-wise," Lucas the barman replied, "we'll maybe be having money up front from you for a change."

This was my cue to reach into my pocket and pull out a couple of greenbacks, which he accepted readily, with not even a cursory examination—much to my interest. He may have noted that I had pushed quite a number of other treasury notes back into my pocket, for he turned and grudgingly went back to the bar, grumbling over his shoulder that we had best keep a proper tab, because he could tell how much beer was gone from the barrel.

Over our first mug of beer, Swan told me the short story of his life, beginning with his upbringing in St. Louis and relating the basics as far as his education.

"I had planned to be a lawyer," he told me, "and to do something useful for the common man faced with a country full of thieving bankers and political confidence men, and I actually got started. I tried it. Law school. A couple of months. Thrown out on a technicality. Misunderstanding. I got back into law school, lasted another few months, until I nosed around lawyers enough to realize they were all a bunch of the worst kind of thieving confidence men themselves. So I became a notary, which is sort of the same, only better and quicker."

"Remarkable!" I intoned. "We escaped from the same den of thieves. My father planned a career as a lawyer for me and enrolled me in a college in Chicago, but I couldn't stomach the idea, and I became a Pinkerton man instead."

"You're with Pinkerton's?"

"No longer. It was a fairly brief stint."

"Good." He nodded solemnly. "I don't know what I think of Pinkerton's. I might not be able to drink with you."

It was probably not until we'd had a third glass of beer that Swan broached the topic of Sarah Green, also known as Naomi Phillips.

"You really know nothing about her story down here?"

"Nothing," I replied.

"And you didn't know she and I had a close professional relationship?"

"I don't know a thing, and it doesn't seem as if the people of Olympia want to discuss things with strangers." I wondered to myself what constituted a "close professional relationship" in Swan's estimation.

He shook his head gravely and gave me a short lecture on how to deal with people, and strangers in particular—how to ingratiate oneself and earn their trust by means of politeness and words of kindness and, above all, by possessing proper identification. Proper identification stilled the unease of a suspicious stranger and could be readily obtained through a notary public. The long form of this lecture lasted well into the fourth glass of beer.

"And how did you develop a friendship and a business relationship with Miss Green—Miss Phillips?"

"She was a sad case by the time I met her, Ackery. She was a poor, storm-blown vessel on a cold, angry sea, and I was the lonely port she spied. Desperate, sir. She was desperate." In spite of the overdone metaphors, his tone was suddenly both sincere and gentle. He finished his drink in silence while he considered where to begin. Then he went behind the bar and got us more, just as the redoubtable Mr. Lucas arrived to take over that duty. When he was seated, Swan went on.

"All right then. Listen up and I'll tell you the gist of it. First of all, let's be clear—there's nothing but good to be said about that girl, and if you hear otherwise from someone else, send them my way, and I swear I'll set them straight by one means or another."

The first new customers of the day were arriving at that point—a big, jovial pair of lads who nodded at Swan as they passed our table—so I was momentarily distracted and didn't understand when he continued.

"Hans Chapman Canon?"

"What?"

"You haven't heard of him either. Bah. No, I guess not. You live up there in the goddamn English wilderness." Apparently the story had been a matter of much discussion and controversy locally some months past, although now it had been replaced in the public eye by the scandal involving the postmaster in Portland who had been convicted of robbery and then pardoned by the president.

"Hans Chapman Canon brought her out here to look after his kids after his wife died." Here Swan peered at me from under the brim of his big hat. "How did his wife die, you ask? Well, pretty damned suspiciously is the truth, but what's to be done when there's no witnesses? Two years ago. Ancient history. None of my business, and I'm a busy man." He took three more gulps to drain his glass at this point and waved to Lucas for more. "So Miss Naomi Phillips came for honest work, and on the day she arrived and met the man, Hans Canon looked like an honest fellow. Just fine. Respectable. Respectable as hell. Clean clothes, trimmed whiskers. Bright red suspenders over his big belly. And they had a written contract. I notarized that contract without a word, because that's what I am—a damned notary. The girl wasn't stupid and she'd been figuring things out on the way up from Oregon, so she knew exactly what she wanted written down on paper. She just didn't know that documents don't mean much out here. I'd had a few drinks when they marched into my office and I could barely keep up with what she was dictating. I had opinions. I had suspicions, but I am a schooled public servant and I just kept my mouth shut while I was scribbling. Damn it. I should've warned her about the bastard anyway, right then.

"Hans Chapman Canon. The sheriff called him a murderer to his face not more than a year ago, but they had to let the wife's death stand as an accident. So I didn't say anything to the English girl. They showed up together and I wrote out the bloody details as fast as ink would come out of the pen.

"You knew she came from England? Of course you did. Why would she come to America alone? Some family problems maybe. None of my business. If your friend is planning to marry the woman, he might want to look into that, but it's none of my business. I talked to her a little bit, later on . . ." He paused thoughtfully, as if to assure himself that what he spoke was true, then shrugged. "From England, she arrived at Philadelphia. Goddamn Philadelphia. Then she carried on west in response to a newspaper advertisement. 'Nanny and lady's companion for a wealthy family in Portland.'" Swan informed me that when she arrived at the end of her long overland journey, the aforementioned wealthy family, in spite of the fine references they had offered, were now neither wealthy nor living in Portland. She was stranded and running out of funds. She thought it was her good fortune to spot an advertisement in the Portland newspaper offering a position in the Territory of Washington to a woman willing to serve as governess to three young children. She applied, was accepted, sight unseen. So north, farther into the wilderness, to Olympia. Her philosophy at that point was doubtless "in for a penny, in for a pound."

"She must have travelled that last leg with trepidation, though," Swan continued, "and she revealed some cynical good sense when she led Mr. Hans Chapman Canon directly to the nearest notary, Mr. James G. Swan. I liked that young lady from the very start, and not just because of the pretty face. I liked the businesslike way she carried herself. And I thought it was sort of touching how she kept glancing toward the window—toward the wagon, where Canon had left the little boy and the two little girls.

"Then I didn't see her for some time. Half a month it would be, because that was part of the contract. Twice a month she was to be given a day off and transportation to town, to spend the day by herself, as she chose. And the two weeks' pay in her hand. So that was that and Canon kept true, and two weeks or so later, Miss Phillips walks into my office with her pay, or most of it, I suppose. I think she took out a bit to spend. She asked me where she would go to buy material to make herself a new dress, but most of the money—most of it she plopped on my desk. He didn't pay her too badly, as far as I could see, and this was one of the things she said in his defence when—just in passing—I referred to him as an untrustworthy and dangerous old bastard. She pointed out that he couldn't be all bad if he was willing to spend such a large portion of his income to have his children educated properly."

Swan leaned forward now and banged his fist on the table so hard it spilled beer from my glass. "At the same time, though," he shouted, "at the same time she pointed out that he was regrettably hard on the three little ones. I ask what she means by hard, and she admits he beats them every day, at some point or other. She could see I didn't like that idea, so she jumps right in that he doesn't do it to be cruel—he just believes it's the proper way to discipline children. 'It takes a hard hand to keep them on the right path,' he says. I know this is bothering the woman. I think it scared her already, back then, and I started getting a bit riled up, but just like that, all of a moment, she becomes very calm and she returns to the issue of her pay. 'Will you look after that for me, Mr. Swan?' she says. I tried to get back to the issue of how dangerous the old man was, but she'd have none of it. 'Will you look after my savings, Mr. Swan?'"

He paused to glower across at the other two men who were drinking in the saloon. They were becoming a bit boisterous, laughing, singing their favourite colourful ditties. Swan told them to shut up, and they answered back the same thing. Swan returned to his story.

"My first suggestion was that she leave it with the bank just around the corner, but she said that was unsuitable because they only kept regular business hours. Ten o'clock 'til three o'clock. And she didn't trust bankers, which is further evidence of her intelligence. So I offered to hold the envelope myself. I have a small safe in my office for documents and where I keep a half-bottle of spirits for emergency mornings. If I'm properly knockdown poison drunk at night, then I can't undo the combination and get at that bottle, so it's still going to be there next morning when I positively, absolutely *have* to have a drink. She was very grateful. She promised not to 'presume upon my good graces' beyond that one service." After another long drink, he added, "I would have done anything she asked, mind you. It was the one thing I looked forward to was twice a month I had a pretty young woman come into my office and treat me like I was a good human being. Talk to me with respect. She knew I was reliable."

"Reliable?" I said, raising my eyebrows. "Ah!"

"I *am* reliable," he growled back. "But only as regards what's important and worthy. And what the hell else is important and worthy in this godless, useless town? This hindmost pimple on the buttocks of the world?"

"I rather like this town," I said, "but we'll accept your opinion as spoken. So Sarah—Naomi, I mean—she visited you every couple of weeks and brought you her money? What did she do with the rest of her day to herself? Did she say?"

He shrugged. "Walked around town, I suppose. Looked at things in the shops, I imagine, her being a woman."

"But she had no friends?"

"Actually, she always went to the hotel, the Harbor House, and sat in the back for a while with the niggers that work there. Drank tea with them. She liked them."

"How many were there? Did you know them?"

"The niggers? There's a bunch of them work at the Harbor House. Don't know them. Don't mind them." He cocked his head to one side, pondering. "Actually, I think I like niggers."

"And Canon—did she ever complain about Hans Chapman Canon? Beyond beating his children, of course."

"Complain? Complain? No. Not complain, as such. But the second time she showed up, when she reached out to shake my hand, I saw she had a bruise on her arm—a big, blue bruise. I would have commented on it, but I wanted her to sit and chat with me for a minute, and I didn't want to scare her off, so I didn't presume to ask about it. And we had a pleasant little chat. I have no recollection of what we talked about." He drank. "I didn't forget that bruise, though."

He was drinking faster now. As he became absorbed with telling his story, he used the beer as a form of punctuation between thoughts. I felt obliged to match his stride, particularly since I was paying for all the beer. In spite of this, I think my description of the afternoon and evening events is fairly accurate.

"Third time she come to my office," Swan drawled, "she got a cut on her eyebrow. Just like about this long. Not terrible conspicuous, but a bit of a swollen eye and a spot of red in the corner of the eyeball. I wait 'til she sits down. Hello. Hello. Smile. Smile. Then I can't just let it pass. I say 'What the hell?' and back and forth, she tells me that she tried to step in between father and son when Canon was caning the boy. Accidentally, she was struck on the forehead. Accidentally. I get riled. Maybe I said I was going to do something. She says, 'No, no, no. He doesn't like to be corrected. He would take it out on the poor children. He might even . . .' And she didn't finish the sentence. She didn't say what else he might do. Instead, she said she was expected down at the Harbor House, and please don't do this or that and so on."

"And you did what?"

Swan smiled at the question. "You already know my style, don't you Tim? 'Course I had to do *something*. So Hans Chapman Canon was going to be bringing the buggy back to town to pick up Naomi at the end of the day. I knew that. And I knew his farm is out the north road, out the edge of the inlet, so middle afternoon, I strolled out the edge of town on the north road and I waited. He comes along, I stand in the road and stop him. He steps down. Three kids are in the wagon, but I figure what the hell. I drill him one in the nose with my left hand—that's my good hand—and he staggers back against the wagon. Before he sets himself, I swing a full-force roundhouse right into his knackers."

"Ow!"

"That's fair. He was a full head taller than me, so it's allowed I even things up with a questionable punch or two. Besides, when you're the shorter man, it's easier to reach the knackers. I used to try to use my knee against the other fellow's knackers, but that's harder than it looks."

"The angle is wrong."

"Exactly."

"Well, good for you, Swan. Someone has to stand up to a bully. You stand up to them once, and they run away scared."

"Oh, no." He grinned. "He beat the daylights out of me, there on the side of the road. Big man. Tough as leather. I couldn't hardly move, but I don't think it made his knackers stop hurting."

We both laughed quite inappropriately. I have noticed over time that rarely does anything seem more hilarious to a couple of men—particularly when they have been drinking—than the thought of some other fellow enduring a hard blow to his private parts.

"So what happened when you next saw Naomi Philips?" I asked at last.

"I didn't."

"What? Did she leave Olympia, then? Did she run?"

"No. At least not immediately. Two weeks later, she left an envelope at the post office for me, with her wages enclosed and a short note thanking me for my continued indulgence and my confidentiality."

"So you . . . ?"

"I did nothing. I thought about it. I resolved to go out to the farm and confront Canon again, but I honestly didn't know whether it would help the situation, or just make it worse. I vacillated. I considered appealing to the sheriff, but he and I are on shaky ground. I drank quite a lot, and time passed. Then, about a week later, there's a big uproar. Neighbour down the road came around to buy eggs and they found Hans Chapman Canon dead, lying in his own front doorway."

"Dead?"

"Completely dead. Now me, as soon as I heard his name whispered on the street, I ran for my horse. The sheriff had gone to fetch the doctor before he headed out, and they were in a buggy, so the three of us arrived at the Canon farm about the same time. Sheriff chased off the neighbour kids, but he didn't bother about me observing the scene. Being a notary, I suppose—it's much the same privilege as a lawyer, but less likely to cause trouble. You should consider the possibility of becoming a notary, Tim."

"So what did you see?"

"He was dead. That was the first thing. Stiff and cold and just a little bit fly-blown. On his face, in the doorway. Dressed in his shirt and his underwear. Dry blood all over the back of his head."

"Murdered?"

Swan shrugged and paused to drink more beer. Mr. Lucas had delivered a fresh supply, after I advanced him a bit more money. "Some would have considered that likely, but not our sheriff, nor the doctor. Their theory was that he had been getting dressed—or undressed, I suppose—and slipped somehow, banged his head."

"What?"

"Yup."

"What?"

"I was not about to disagree. It was their duty, between the two, to come to a decision, and it was none of my business."

"But surely that's pretty unlikely . . ."

He leaned across the table at me. "Actually, considerable less likely when you consider we found a half-brick on the kitchen floor with a bit of stuff on it looked like blood and hair. That's between you and me, because it was never considered worth mentioning officially."

"And the sheriff? The doctor . . . ?"

"You see, a year or more previous, this sheriff was forced to accept the story that Canon's wife had died from falling out of a hayloft and breaking her neck. This same doctor examined her body and found any number of bruises and old, badly mended broken bones never been set properly—he found that suspicious. But what can you do?"

"Canon dead, and where was Miss Phillips?"

"For the record, it was presumed that she had resigned her position and gone. A notice was put in the papers—Portland, Walla Walla, Port Townsend—that she should please contact the authorities, but . . ."

"The children?"

"Took the sheriff another week to find them, but they were unharmed—at the home of their aunt in Walla Walla. Their governess had seen them off at the stagecoach."

"So Sarah? Miss Phillips?"

"Disappeared."

Swan stood up at that point, leaving me to puzzle over this odd story, and strolled unevenly toward the back door, saying he needed to relieve himself of some liquid. Being deep in thought, I barely noticed when one of the other two patrons slapped him on the back as he passed. I believed it was just a type of barroom salutation, but it was hard enough to knock Swan off track a bit, and I saw him stumble against an empty table. I paid no attention. A bit of growling and a bit of laughter accompanied the exchange. The notary presumably found his way to the outhouse.

I had a number of questions to ask him when he returned, but as soon as he came through the back door, I noticed that he was walking a bit oddly. The reason for this was that he was carrying something in his left hand, holding it behind his leg. This turned out to be a short, thick piece of kindling wood, which came into view as he brought it down onto the head of the fellow who had shoved him on the way out. Swan only hit him once, and there was a moment of odd, motionless silence as we all watched him grasp his hands around his hat and keel over sideways, chair and all.

The partner jumped on Swan, of course, and the two of them crashed to the floor in a whirlwind of elbows and fists. I was likewise on my feet immediately, which sudden movement caused the full effects of all the beer I had consumed to land on me at once, like a bucket of hot water. I just stood there, weaving, for a second or two. Then the first fellow jumped on the other pair, so I had to scramble over to help Swan.

He was smaller than either of the other two, and I had invested a fair sum of money getting him this drunk, so I had no choice. Lucas, the bartender, came running and shouting from the next room. I threw myself at the man on top, knocking him away from the scramble, and the two of us rolled and skidded some distance. When we came to rest, we were at close quarters, face to face, each holding the other by the shirt collar, both of us half under the raised platform with the chair and the banjo—our heads and torsos squeezed between the two levels of floorboards. I can picture him quite clearly banging my head down—or perhaps up—against the boards, while I tried to get my thumbs at his eyeballs.

After that there are mostly blank spaces in my memory of events.

I recall awakening from a deep sleep in the city jail, realizing immediately that I was doomed. I was imprisoned—under a false name that I was prone to forget—and subject to summary prosecution. Doubtless, my true identity would soon be discovered.

But when we were once again awakened some hours later, I found to my great relief that being arrested for public drunkenness in the city of Olympia was not a cause for paperwork or investigation. We were released into the night after the sheriff had scolded us, insulted us, damned us to hell, and fined us a total of six dollars. I paid for both of us, of course. We were barely outside and on the street when my new friend Swan asked me what time it was—a tone of great urgency in his voice. Checking my watch, I informed him that it was just after ten o'clock.

"Good," he sighed. "The Pony is still open. My head is horrible painful. We'd better drink whisky this time around. It's getting late in the day."

To my current amazement and discredit, I followed him back to the Pony Sample Saloon, where we must have been willingly received. Perhaps I paid them some money for reparations. I remember nothing more of the night.

Somehow I made it back to the Tacoma Hotel and to my own bed, for the morning found me there, and in hell as well. A morning in hell. That describes it quite fully. As I say, I could remember nothing accurately after our return to the Pony Sample, but there was evidence on my bedside table of what had occurred. We must eventually have gone to Swan's office, for three things from there now lay before me.

The first was an envelope containing a small sum of money in a plain envelope with the inscription on it—"Miss Naomi Phillips. Money held in trust." One of us had evidently convinced the other that I should return this to the woman I knew as Sarah Green.

Beside this was a single page from a newspaper, torn from *The Washington Standard*. I did not read the pertinent article at that point, merely examined the blurred photograph of Mr. Hans Chapman Canon. Immediately I recognized a resemblance. It was not exact, by any means, but the body bulk and the hairline and the eyes were all remarkably similar to Mac Bingham.

The third thing that Swan had evidently given me was a duly filled out birth certificate on proper Territory of Washington stationery bearing the name of Thaddeus Hackney. I hope I did not pay too much for this forged identification, for Hackney's birthday had unfortunately been printed in at the wrong spot, written as yesterday's date, making me approximately twenty-four hours old.

I groaned and dozed on my bed all day, while I considered.

TOWARD THE MIDDLE of the afternoon, still feeling horrible, I stumbled outside onto the street. It was after three o'clock. I decided I had better keep going and try to accomplish some small thing before the day was gone. I had a ticket for the ferry heading home next morning.

The first thing I did, of course, was walk straight to the bakery and get coffee. I'm sure it was still the same pot that had been brewed at dawn and simmered all day, but the acidic black sludge was exactly the punishment I deserved. The girl behind the counter, who by now was pretty familiar with me although we spoke hardly at all, gave me a bread roll smeared with butter in a gesture of Christian charity.

I rested for a few minutes on the bench outside.

ALL THINGS CONSIDERED, my journey of exploration had already been pretty successful. If my information was correct, Roselle's friend from Barkerville, Hec Simmonds, would by now have come and gone from Victoria without spying Mr. Lincoln Zachary. In the event of being exposed at some point in the future, however, I felt that I now knew some of the pros and cons of attempting a flight southward. Lastly, I had learned quite a bit of the story behind Sarah Green's arrival in my city and at my hotel. There was still a large gap in that story, though, and I resolved to spend the rest of that day in trying to fill it. Once again, this decision was made in a spirit of self-punishment, as my next destination sounded far from desirable.

There was no point in going out to Canon's farm. I felt I knew well enough what had occurred there. There was also no question of checking Swan's story by visiting the newspaper, or the sheriff, who would by now remember me as a former drunken guest at his jail. I had drawn more than enough attention to myself among the respectable citizenry of Olympia. There remained to me only the option of asking around at The Rascals bar to see if I could find the man named Othello.

DELIA'S DIRECTIONS TO the place were easily followed. I recognized the bar, located one street away from the docks, by its sign, which was an elaborately painted *R*. One letter of the alphabet drawn out in six colours—something of an accomplishment.

It was getting on in the day, and when I pushed my way through the heavy door into the small, smoky room, the man behind the bar was just lighting lanterns. He was a tall, middle-aged Negro with a calm gaze and a certain air of grace. His curly grey hair was rather long and it stood out behind him as if he were facing into a heavy wind. When I stepped up to the rough cedar plank bar, he paused for a long moment, looking away, surveying the place, perhaps to give me time to recognize that I did not really fit into this particular establishment. Then, looking at me more directly, he probably saw in my eyes that I would fit into any place that served liquor.

"Good afternoon, sir. Would you care for something to drink, sir?"

It was unavoidable. "A beer for me, I guess," was what I answered.

He nodded, but made no move to draw me a glass. "Our beer is brewed on the premises, sir, and is not to everyone's liking. Maybe you would like to smell it before you commit yourself to buying a whole mug of the stuff."

The implication made me grimace. "I'm afraid I'm a little bit under the weather," I admitted, "and I gather that smelling your beer would not do good things to a sour stomach."

"Perhaps not, sir."

I sighed. "Then whisky, I suppose."

He pointed at the two bottles on the shelf behind him with raised eyebrows to ask me which brand I preferred, to which I grimaced and pointed at one or the other, which he brought down, pouring an inch or so into a remarkably clean glass tumbler.

"Thank you."

He nodded. Although he did not immediately speak again, he remained standing in front of me while I lifted the drink in the direction of my face, then abruptly set it back down, for as the first scent reached my nostrils, my stomach heaved dangerously.

He nodded again.

His name, I was to learn in the course of events, was Flood, and he had a mannerism of straightening his perfect white, collarless shirt, and placing his thumbs behind his suspenders while he talked.

"It's not always easy, is it, sir? Picking up where you left off last night."

"No," I agreed. "It might take me a while."

He seemed serious and sympathetic, as if he were seeing me off as I embarked on a difficult mission. Then, "If I could make a suggestion, sir?"

I was still staring grimly at the whisky as he retrieved it from me and deftly poured it back into the bottle. "Among the particulars we offer, here at The Rascals, is a variety of cures for what ails you. And some of these do not smell so dramatically like yesterday's mistakes. Let me get you something."

First he rinsed my glass in a bowl of clean water and wiped it dry. Next, he walked around from behind the bar and across to the little barrel heater in the corner, where a kettle was simmering. I saw that his trousers were far too short and that he wore no shoes, only heavy wool stockings, but somehow his dignity did not suffer from the revelation. He poured my glass three-quarters full from the kettle—a pale yellow liquid that smelled sweet. I think it involved rosehips among other things. Returning to his position behind the bar, he finished filling the glass from a mason jar that he kept under the counter. Then he watched as I took a drink.

It smelled and tasted of nothing but sweet herbs and honey, but my throat quivered a bit as it went down. I gave him money.

The clear liquid took its effect, and quite quickly I began to feel marginally better. I raised my glass to Mr. Flood. "My compliments."

His smile was faint, but sincere. "I believe you came to the right place, sir."

At that, I cocked my hat back a little on my head and assumed a friendly, slightly confidential tone. "You know," I said, "the truth is I came here on the advice of someone who said I might be able to find a certain person here."

"A certain person."

"A friend. Or not so much a friend as a fellow I met once and never got the chance to talk to. He did a great favour for me. Large fellow. Bald as a rock. Calls himself Othello."

Flood betrayed no emotion or sign of recognition.

"And you did not find him here, sir."

"Well, I haven't really started looking yet."

"Not much places to look here."

As if the idea hadn't occurred to me yet, I turned and surveyed the room. It was small, hot, and smoky. There were three small tables, at one of which sat two middle-aged Negroes with an open pouch of chewing tobacco between them. One was thin and the other heavy-set, but their attitudes were identical. They both sat with their heads back, their knees together, and their hands in their lap. A philosophical duo who, I noticed, had no drinks in front of them.

"I hoped a man in your position might know this Othello. Maybe you could help me get in touch with him."

Flood shook his head. "A man in my position, sir, does not speak about his customers. For better or for worse, you understand. I hear a lot, I see a lot, and nothing gets repeated. I am like a drain hole in the floor that takes in whatever there is, but shame on me if any of it comes back out."

I nodded. "Fair enough." I don't think he was really suspicious of me, but I understood his principles. Downing my drink except for dregs of weedy brown sediment, I asked for another of the same. "But perhaps a weak one. I think I'll sit down and wait here for a bit, if that's all right."

When he had finished the procedure of making my drink, he took one step back and watched me for a moment. Then he spoke casually, guiding my attention to the two other patrons. "The stout man is named Downey, and his friend is called Fikus."

"They don't have anything to drink," I commented. "Perhaps they would allow me to buy them a whisky."

"A beer, more likely, sir. I'm sure they would."

I sat myself down at the next table, upwind from the yeasty fumes. When they had finished thanking me and drinking my good health, I went straight to the question.

"I'm looking for a friend of a friend and I thought someone here might know him. Othello, his name is."

"Othello. We know him," answered Fikus.

"Yes, we know him," agreed Downey.

"I understand him to be a fine man," I suggested.

"A fine man," agreed Downey.

"One of the best," added Fikus.

I stared amiably at them and they stared amiably back at me. A pair of young Negro men came in the door, noticed me sitting at my table, turned and left without a word. I looked toward the bartender, who betrayed no expression, although we both realized I was costing him custom as long as I remained. For this cause, I walked over and gave him three one-dollar greenbacks. "I should buy a drink for those two if they come back, and another couple of beers for my friends when they're finished these."

As I sat down, Fikus spoke up. "Yes, Othello, he might be down here soon."

"Soon enough," the other concurred.

"After work."

"He works, Othello. Got a job."

"Good job."

At this point, I made a connection that I should have made much earlier. "Does he work at the Harbor House, by any chance?" I asked.

"Why, yes he does," Fikus told me.

His partner confirmed it. "Yes, he does. At a good job."

"He usual come by The Rascals after work."

"Usual. Right 'bout this time, usual."

And true to their expectations, Othello did indeed stride into The Rascals ten or fifteen minutes later. He recognized me immediately, and he did not seem unduly surprised to see me. Without wasted time or dissemblance, we found ourselves seated at two chairs in an alcove behind the bar that Flood called his office. We spoke in low tones, although I suspect everyone in the little room could still hear our every word. He knew me as Sarah's new employer, so it didn't take much time to gain his confidence.

"Miss Nomi, she's still all right?" He didn't pronounce the *a* in her name.

"I've always known her as Sarah, and I shall continue to call her that, but yes, she's doing well. She's adjusting nicely. The woman has been through a lot, but I see more comfort, more good humour in her as time passes."

"Good." His sigh was a sigh of satisfaction, and I realized that he too would be grateful for the information we could exchange. Still, he was a bit wary as he asked, "You know about . . . ?"

"I know all I need to know about that. I know about Hans Chapman Canon currently rotting in hell. I suppose I should be satisfied with the story as it stands, but I have one more day here in Olympia, and I was curious about the part that you played in events. I think I owe you thanks."

"No one owes me nothing. Nomi's a kind and a sweet thing. You'd never guess she was tough as hell. Smart? Oh, sure, you see that right off, but a skinny little thing, all pretty like that and speaking every word just perfect all the time . . ." He looked at me, suddenly stern. "A good friend. She's a good friend to me and to my missus and to my child. And we should've stepped in earlier on."

"Hindsight is cheap."

"That bastard Canon—we knew about him, everybody knew about him, and truth is somebody should've stood up right at the start, 'cause it was not gonna be good come out of that. No good at all. Could have been worse. But who would've thought that girl was tough like that?"

I shook my head. "I still find it hard to picture. I don't really want to try."

"Canon, he was always proper as a preacher, here in town, of course, and Nomi, she said he was mostly straight enough toward her, back at the farm. Toward her—not them poor children of his. He figured the only good way to train a child was with a stick and once a day was sometime not enough. Didn't have much faith in talking, but he did believe in that stick."

"So I presume that he eventually tried teaching Sarah something with that stick that she wasn't willing to learn."

"Something like that. The girl didn't specify."

"He was a big man. You're right. She must be a lot stronger than she looks."

Othello made a low whistling sound as he shook his head. "Hit him on the head, heavy and hard, but that's not the strong thing about her. No, the strong thing is gathering up those kids and putting them on a stage to their relations somewhere, and then, all quiet and unsuspicious, she makes her way to the hotel and hides for three days with my missus and me while she cries and cries and cries it all through." Again he shook his head sadly. "And then we get her the hell out of town to where it's safe."

"But that's something I don't understand yet," I said. "Why didn't she tell her story to the law?"

"Well," Othello leaned forward, "there's the question of getting hanged on a rope."

"Come on, man! The sheriff hated Canon. Everyone knew what he was like. The doctor and the sheriff cooked up the story that he just fell down and banged his own head!"

Othello dismissed that quickly. "You don't know," he growled. "You don't know. She's a woman. She's a servant. He's the boss. She's a foreigner. He's from right 'round here. You just can't be sure. If she's gone off, then that's strange, but convenient. But if she was still here, then maybe a trial has got to be. And some people get justice and the law and what's right and what's wrong all mixed up. So best she gets out of the country."

"If they had decided to charge her with murder, it wouldn't matter if she was out of the country, though. If they caught her. Did she believe she would be safe from prosecution if she made it to Victoria? Did she choose Victoria thinking that . . . ?"

He smiled. "It weren't her that chose Victoria. That was my idea. My plan."

"Really?"

He leaned back in his chair. His smile grew even broader and his big chest seemed to expand. "Mr. Ackery, I was the best friend and possibly the cousin of Charles Mitchell himself."

There was a long pause while I tried to place the name. Finally, I was forced to admit that I was unacquainted with Charles Mitchell. Othello was visibly disappointed.

"How long you lived in Victoria?" he asked me.

"A half-dozen years."

"Huh. I guess it was before your time, though you still ought to know."

"Tell me, then."

It was an interesting story, and it took place in September of 1860. Charles Mitchell was then a fourteen-year-old slave belonging to some sort of government surveyor from Baltimore, working at Olympia. It was an odd situation then, for although Washington was itself free soil, the territorial Legislature had ruled that ownership of slaves there could not be barred. Charles Mitchell decided to flee to British Columbia for his freedom. At that point, his friend, Othello, was working as a "temporary steward" on the *Eliza Anderson*, and he helped Mitchell stow away when the ship headed north. Unfortunately, the boy was discovered halfway there, somewhere around Tacoma, and he was put to work scrubbing decks to pay for his passage. As an additional misfortune, the acting territorial governor—a man named McGill—was also on board, and the foolish young stowaway confided to McGill's son that he intended to jump ship at Victoria. Mitchell was soon locked away in whatever served as the brig.

"At Victoria, though, events took a strange turn, for while the *Anderson* was docked there, word got out onshore that a man was being held on board against his will. A group of protesters—both black people and white—gathered at the docks. A lawyer went to Chief Justice Cameron and obtained a writ of habeas corpus. Mitchell was freed and never returned south, although the international repercussions of the incident carried on for some time."

"That surveyor fellow must have been annoyed," I ventured.

"Annoyed?" Othello laughed. "He's angry. Angry! The word don't tell the tale. Maybe angrrrry!" He growled out the centre of the word and laughed again. "Him and the governor, too. Governor says in the paper that if Washington was a proper state, not just a territory, then the president would have declared war. War!"

"I'm surprised at that—at how much he made of it. I mean, he himself hadn't lost his slave or anything."

"Maybe no, but a governor is a man with a stick in his hand that the law give him to beat people. Just like a slaver. People that believe in the stick believe that the stick is the only way, and if somebody take away the stick, then the world falls apart!"

I myself was laughing. "It seems that this particular stick got broken, and the world did not fall apart. But good for you, Othello, for your part in it." And I toasted him.

"So that," said the man proudly, "was why I knew that Victoria was the place for Miss Nomi. People there are kind, upstanding, and true."

"Sometimes," I admitted.

"They believe, yes, they insist on justice!"

"When it suits their purpose." Before he could interject again, I continued, "But it is you, my good man, who stood beside my friend in her dark hour. I salute you again!"

I should mention that by now I was finishing my third, or possibly my fourth glass of Flood's potent medicinal beverage. I had suffered enough over the last couple of days, though, that I recognized when enough was enough, and Othello and I soon exchanged our final compliments. As I stood to leave, I drew from my pocket a fifty-dollar US Treasury note and slipped it under the big Negro's beer mug. He instantly began to protest.

"I don't take money for godly kindness on behalf of . . ."

"No, no! This has nothing to do with the past, Mr. Othello, but rather the possible future. I need to employ someone here in Washington to look after my needs in the case of a certain eventuality. It's possible that I might pass through this town again in an unholy hurry. When that might be, I do not know. Maybe never. God willing, never, and you can spend the money as you wish. But what I want you to do is keep a constant eye out for horses. At any given time, you should know what is available and where. If I arrive back some time in the dead of night, you must be able to purchase a horse on my behalf—discreetly and immediately. One horse, or maybe more. I'm not too good with horses, so it should not be too fast, but on the other hand it must not be too slow in the case of an emergency. It should be a medium horse, of medium speed."

Steaming northward next day on the *Eliza Anderson*, I had time to reflect on all the things that I had learned, including the story of young Charles Mitchell. I tried to visualize a crowd of citizens from Victoria clamouring for his release. After some reflection, I found the image a bit disturbing, for I knew that the high emotions of the crowd that one day shouts for a slave to be freed can the next day demand that an accused robber and murderer be hanged without a trial.

For much of the trip, I played cards with the old seaman whose job it was to stand guard in the room where the mail was kept. It was about the warmest, quietest spot on the ship, so I did not mind losing seven or eight dollars to him, even though we were obviously playing with cards that he had marked.

Chapter Six

SMUG. THAT IS THE PROPER word to describe my attitude as I arrived back in Victoria. Smug. It is a short word, a little word that denotes a small state of mind—an attitude that life is simple and well understood, with the problems around me being under control and small enough to wrap up in a handkerchief and pop into my pocket.

To further complement my self-satisfaction, my wife was at the dock, waiting for me, accompanied by the boot boy Jing, who held the reins to Old Peter. I was not normally accorded such attendance, but then I rarely left town for any length of time. I was in no mood to ride, particularly with my wife walking beside me. I had a single bag, weighing a few pounds in total, so this was duly placed on Old Peter's back, and we started up the hill toward home. Sue took my arm and I drew her close to me, suddenly realizing how much I missed her after only a short time away. What would occur if she was to discover the truth of my past? Would she ever look upon me kindly again? We walked in close contact, which, due to the great difference in our height, made for an awkward, wobbling gait, but it felt wonderful. Our progress up the dusty hill to the hotel was slow, and the odd image came to my mind that we were like Mary and Joseph of old, returning to his hometown of Bethlehem, although instead of being followed by a donkey, we had Old Peter and Jing.

Our walk was subdued, sedate, serene. Sue asked me quietly if I had eaten proper meals while I was away, and I said that for the most part I had done so, but I might have had more to drink than was necessary on one occasion. I asked her if the hotel had run smoothly without me, and she replied that no real problems had arisen, but things had been a bit dull. She asked me if I had met any interesting strangers, and I answered that strangers on boats were rarely very interesting. I asked if she had by any chance seen Mr. Roselle and his visitor from Barkerville. She said that Mr. Roselle and Mr. Simmonds had come to the hotel asking after me more than once, but the visiting gentleman had by now taken passage on a ship. She asked me if I had seen any opportunity to do business in the Territory of Washington, and I replied that it would probably remain an uncivilized wilderness, unfit for commerce, for another hundred years.

ONCE HOME, MY wife left me to my own devices while she unpacked my clothes and bundled them up for laundry.

It was only a week that I had been absent from my minimal duties as chief shareholder at the Celestial Hotel, but I wandered about the establishment, room by room, with the vague expectation that things had probably changed a great deal over that stretch of time. Not surprisingly, all was virtually as it had been and functioning quite nicely. The only item of note to my eye was that one of the sofas from the front sitting room had been replaced and relegated to the back porch. I liked that sofa, as did my father-in-law—canvas seat and back somewhat stained, leather arm-rests revealing their stuffing—but evidently we had been outvoted by Sue while I was away.

Testing out the friendly furniture in its new location, I found that it was still soft beneath my back and the leather arms were warm from the sun. I began to dream.

In my dream, I was dancing (and only in my dreams do I dance). I danced a rather solemn circle with not only Swan and the two young men we had fought at the Pony Sample, but the girl from the bakery, the Negro sweeper woman, and the sheriff, among others. I turned to my right as we slowly pranced about, and I found myself asking Othello why we were dancing.

"This is the horse dance," he replied. "The dance to see what kind of horse you need."

At this point, I found I was dancing alone, under the watchful eyes of only Othello and his compatriots Messrs. Fikus and Downey.

"Big man is what you are, Mr. Zachary," opined Downey as he judged my steps.

"Yes, a big man indeed," agreed Fikus. "Long legs."

"Got long legs."

"Need a big horse."

"Need a big horse—a high horse."

"Not easy to find such a high horse."

"Not easy."

But Othello stepped forward and stood between us, smiling. "I can find you that horse if you need it, Mr. Zachary," he assured me.

"Zachary?" Downey asked. "Ackery!"

"Mr. Ackery Zachary . . . ," Fikus mused.

"Ackery Zachary . . . ," Downey said speculatively. They spoke the name not in jest, but in a contemplative tone.

And at that point, I was awakened by my friend Jack Elliston. I stood up and shook his hand, mumbling my responses to his questions and squinting into the sunshine.

"Come along, Zachary, Avery and I are taking you out to dinner."

"What?"

"We have to hear your impressions of the American barbarians living to the south."

"Jack. What? Avery's here?"

"Inside. And speaking of barbarians, we'll need to do something about your hair, man. Shall we cut it all off immediately, or just wash it out for now?"

I raked it back with my fingers. "Nonsense. This is all the style in London, I think. You've been away from the country too long." The sun seemed to have travelled over a good deal of its arc while I was testing the sofa.

In the kitchen, Avery greeted me with more traditional pleasantries than had his brother. "Welcome home, Mr. Zachary. We've all missed you." He was seated at the big table, with Sarah Green standing beside him. I looked at her with new eyes, and it seemed to me that she returned my glance with a silent expression that bespoke both curiosity and apprehension.

In response to Avery, I said, "My wife informs me that she prayed for me every day and asked you to do the same."

"As we did, my friend."

"But Sue a little more fervently, I think. She knows my ability to get myself into trouble."

"Get yourself ready now, Zachary," Jack interjected. "There's a table for three waiting up in the town."

"Ah. Really? It's that time?"

"It's past that time. Look. Here comes Cook to throw us out of the kitchen."

Again I ran my hands through my hair. "Look, I can't, Jack. I'm foul. I'm fatigued. Bad company all the way around." As both brothers began to protest, I hit on what I thought was a grand idea and silenced them both. "Miss Green." I addressed myself to her just as she was turning to leave the room.

"Yes, Mr. Zachary?"

"Would you be willing to favour these two with your company, since they are so intent on buying someone a meal? Take my place."

"But I'm sure your friends . . ." Both the Elliston brothers were already on their feet, smiling. "And there's Master Ross, who . . ."

"I'll see that my son gets fed with the rest of us. I should be telling him a few wild lies about my journey before he goes to bed, anyway."

"Come along, my dear," Avery added.

And with that, both brothers offered her an elbow. She graciously put one hand on each and they turned like dancers, although they had to break up the pose in order to walk down the hallway.

It must have been an enjoyable couple of hours for them, judging from the fact that by the time they returned, I caught only a glimpse of Sarah Green while she peered briefly in on Ross and me sitting by lamplight on his bed. I believe that in some households there is a tradition of telling children a story before they sleep, but in mine, we usually allow Ross to tell us a tale of his own at that time. It's an interesting experience, although I fear that the boy has inherited a wild imagination.

For my part, I tried to imagine, while I listened, what segments of my discoveries in Olympia I would recount to Miss Green and how I should phrase them.

AS IT HAPPENED, I had no opportunity next day to speak to her at all. There was pressing work for me next morning in the area of hotel management—duties quite specific to my portfolio. The order of lumber had arrived from Becker's mill, lumber designated to be the walls of our new stable, and it was now stacked beside the chicken barn—two full wagonloads. Meng, our Chinese carpenter, had declared the entire shipment to be twisted and knotted beyond usability, but Becker insisted that it was all of good quality. A quick inspection proved Meng to be completely correct, but such arguments must always be carried out white man to white man, so I went off into town to find the fellow and inform him that there would be no payment forthcoming until he removed the offensive sticks and gave us proper lumber. I discovered him lunching at a place on Wharf Street, looking about, no doubt, for some fresh innocent to swindle. Our discussion was surprisingly quick and amiable. The man probably tried to rid himself of his substandard goods at the beginning of every job, and easily fell back to the option of removal and replacement if the customer objected. I don't blame him too much for this, but it did waste my entire morning.

When I returned to the hotel, a fresh crisis was upon us. Christy Riordan had arrived—something that would normally have been both pleasant and exciting, but events had transpired of which I was unaware, and I now found the taciturn young farmer pacing back and forth on our front porch, railing at Jack Elliston in a loud voice, his Irish accent thickened by his agitation so that I missed much of what he said.

"Don't worry yourself, Christy," Jack pressed in when he could. "We'll sort this out, Zachary and I will." I winced to hear my name spoken thus.

"I might as well be off home," Christy shouted, throwing both arms out and nearly knocking a bowl of nuts off the shelf. "Off to my own proper home where a man is treated proper by his own people!"

"No, no. Patience, my friend! You Irishmen must have heard of that somewhere along the line. Sit your body down and listen to me. Zachary has a room set aside for you here where you'll be comfortable as home and looked after like foreign royalty."

"Yes I do," I agreed, although I was mystified by what seemed at this point to be the most violent attack of homesickness I had ever witnessed. "You'll like this place, Christy. You really will. Jack and I will show you the town."

"Thank you, but it would sure be saving the lot of us some grief if I was off on the road this hour and sleeping in my own bed by nightfall."

"Your bed is here at the Celestial tonight, man. Second floor front. We tell strangers it has a view of the ocean, although that's a bit exaggerated."

"Second floor?"

"It is."

"I won't sleep on top of other people's heads. Never have. Don't intend to, until my pa dies and my ma, and my kids have grown some and I've got to change to the upstairs room . . ."

"Zachary has other rooms, I'm sure. It's fine, my friend—just fine, and all to be sorted out soon enough. Calm yourself. You need a drink. Come on. We'll take you for a drink."

The suggestion did have a calming effect on the younger man. He stood still, glared at the floor, and muttered to himself. I cannot put the words of his monologue to paper, unfortunately, for that type of profane language may not legally be reproduced. It seems to be a standard aspect of the Irish dialect, however, and does not sound particularly objectionable when uttered with the proper brogue in the open air. Also, as Christy noted for me at a different time, there was no cursing involved, only vulgarity. "I do not never take the good Lord's name in vain. Not ever. And that's the bloody truth of it."

"A drink," he pronounced finally. "That's never a bad idea at such a time. But before that, where does a body relieve the pressure of liquids while he's in the city?"

Jack pointed him the right direction out the back door and suggested that he might want to wash up at the basin on the kitchen table as well before we set out. "Zachary and I will wait for you on the front porch."

Once we were outside, he told me the part of the story I had thus far missed. It was not the matter of lodgings that had upset Christy.

"Bingham pulled a fast one on us. The bastard didn't tell me ahead of time, because he knew I'd stand by the Riordans. A major part of the agreement was that Christy would ride Miss Deception in the race—family pride and all that; he that trains the horse rides the horse—but Mac played as if he didn't understand that and now he's brought in his own jockey."

"Well, he can just send that new jockey back where he came from."

"It's not as simple as all that. It's Billy Horne that he's brought all the way out from the east coast."

"I don't care who he is. I've seen Christy ride the filly, and I doubt very much you could improve on that."

Jack paused, staring at me. "You have no idea who Billy Horne is, do you?"

"Should I?"

"Only if you've ever been to an organized horse race."

I took this as some form of rebuke. "I try to keep track of things, although I admit I don't favour public events with my presence too frequently, and there are so many . . ."

"So many what, old sport? Ballets and operas? Grand expositions? This is Victoria, colony of the far-distant Queen, and the greatest form of organized public entertainment is the riding of horses in competition. Have you heard of it?"

Since he was my friend, I endured his irony with grace. "They race around Beacon Hill. There are grandstands. They wager money that they can't afford. I don't gamble, and the lure of horses has never really lured me. What else?"

"Billy Horne?"

"I don't try to keep track of every farm boy who . . ."

"Billy Horne is not a farm boy. He is—or was at one point—one of the best known and most successful riders in the business. He hasn't been very successful for the last year or two, but Mac Bingham and the straw-sucking farm boys out here in the west still seem to think he's a hero on horseflesh. He's a big name!"

"So he'll help draw people to the race . . ."

"Agreed. But he's not the winner that Bingham thinks he is. I've followed racing all the way during my travels, of course, and the truth is that he's now a pompous little fat man who still believes that the harder you whip a horse, the better it will perform."

"I don't like the sound of that," I said with a grimace. "But the public seems to like the man?"

"He's a public sort of fellow! While he's in the saddle, his nickname is 'The Albany Assassin,' but back on the ground he changes completely. He dresses like a ponce, but he's wont to justify himself with scripture quotes, having come from a New York preacher's family. He gained his notoriety initially by sharing his winnings with all and any sort of lost soul—as often as not in front of a newspaper man. I don't think he does that so much any more. He hasn't won a race lately."

"Bingham doesn't realize that?"

Jack snorted. "He's been told, but he chooses to believe otherwise. The man is an echo of Bingham's own belief: If you want to win, you just need to bully your way to the end of things."

"But they don't need some rascal from New York! Christy can win the race on Miss Deception. I plan on putting a fair sum of money to back that presumption."

Jack sighed. "Don't preach to me, Mr. Zachary. I've already put that argument in front of Mac Bingham myself—rather loud and rather long. But the Binghams—father and son, Lloyd and Mac—they take this race as life and death. Family honour at stake. Lloyd lost his place of local esteem, he thinks, in that race some years back—as well as a bundle of money—and now he's confident he can get it all back in one day. He believes that Billy Horne erases the last bit of doubt."

An angle came to mind that I thought showed remarkable insight. "Well, then, why would anybody bet against us? You can't make money unless people bet against you."

It was a valid question, and Jack knew the answer. "Well, a rumour is already going around town," he said, "that the horse is not all that it appears. There is a rumour that Miss Deception—note the choice of name, Zachary—is merely a local fallback after Mac's real choice came up lame down in California. There is a rumour that Bingham is not even wagering on his own horse. There is a rumour that Lloyd tried to have the challenge cancelled and get the money back that he set up for the prize, but the local stewards would not allow it."

"They could just ask the stewards about that part."

"There is a rumour that the stewards are being paid to keep silent."

I was beginning to catch on to some of the ramifications of horse racing. "And where would all these rumours begin . . . ," I mused.

"Are you suggesting, old man, that fine gentlemen such as the Binghams would spread false rumours to their own advantage?!" He winked. "Now here comes Christy. I think we should take him to that horrible place just down there, where he can shout a bit without bringing too much attention to himself. Do you think they'll have some kind of Irish whisky down there?"

They did.

THE PLACE TO which Jack referred had no proper name and probably no licence to do business, for that matter. It ceased to exist not long after this, the operators likely fleeing the law. It cannot be legal to serve the kind of liquor they thrust upon the public under an Irish appellation, although the three of us drank it readily enough, distracted as we were by our common distress. We would drink in thoughtful silence for a moment, then Christy would bellow out something descriptive, after which I would advance a proposal for how we would convince Bingham to return to the original plan. Jack would then reply that he had already tried that particular tactic, and Christy would howl another chorus of insulting vulgarity at the ceiling. His vocabulary here was particularly amazing to me, because I had only known him as a gentle and polite young fellow in his own home. I'm sure that the seasoned sailors in the room tried to memorize those admirably turned expletives for future use in the hellholes of Santiago and Valparaíso.

It didn't take me long to realize that Jack's only strategy was to drown Christy's anger in an alcoholic sea, and while my trip to Washington had sated any desire I had for drunkenness, it had renewed, to some extent, my innate belief that I could blunder my way through any problem if I started out with both fists clenched and a full head of steam. Wagering on this race was my big chance to regain financial fluidity, and I couldn't sit back and watch some fancy, Bible-spouting idiot from New York ride my fortune into the ground!

"I can't just sit here and do nothing, Jack," I murmured while Christy's attention was diverted. "I want to do something."

"Then go home, Zachary. I'll ride this out and bring the lad up later to sleep it off in your shed out back. Say hello to Sue for us and apologize for our behaviour in advance."

"No," I insisted. "We can't let Mac Bingham bully us around. You have to stand up to a bully, make him back down."

"Nonsense. We have several days. Something will turn up. You go home."

And so I did go back to the Celestial, but not with any peaceful intent. I had just enough bad whisky in me to imagine wicked things, too much to realize how stupid the ideas were, and not enough to make me fall down flat without putting them into practice. My big .45 revolver was resting on the top shelf of my bedroom closet, and I stomped off to fetch it. I figured I would discuss this matter with our erstwhile partner, and he would reconsider things with the scent of gunpowder in his nose.

The gun was where I expected it to be, but I could find no bullets at first. On the verge of confronting my wife with the accusation that she had hidden them, I found them in my top drawer, where they were supposed to be, concealed behind my socks. I loaded the weapon and placed it in the deep pocket of my long black coat, which I rarely wore and now carried over my arm.

As I came down the stairs, I saw Sarah Green beside the doorway in the front foyer, speaking to a wrinkled old man, some five feet two in height with a white moustache that drooped down well below his chin. She was clearly discomfited, as he stood very close, thrusting a paper envelope toward her.

"Look. Here is Mr. Zachary," I heard her say. "You had best give it to him."

Turning to me like a weathervane on a stake, the old man tried to hand over the envelope, but I chose to ignore him for the moment, speaking to Sarah instead.

"Good afternoon, Miss Green. Is Ross not about?"

"He's upstairs with his mother, getting a bath. This gentleman has come with a delivery of some sort."

"Well, I'll take care of it, then. You might as well get yourself some tea or something." And I turned to face the old fellow, who once again thrust the envelope in my direction.

"For the boy. For the horse-rider boy."

"What?"

"From Mr. Bingham. Mr. Lloyd Bingham. Something for the Irish boy for his trouble, and that's all I know 'bout it."

The envelope had the feel of money.

"He doesn't have the nerve to face us himself."

The man touched his moustaches, one finger on each side, as if to ensure they were still safely attached. "It's just me you get, as Mr. Bingham—that's Mr. Lloyd, not Mr. Mac—is having himself a bad day with stomach and breathin' and all, and young Mr. Mac sticking close by."

I laughed. "That's the story, is it? Well, old man, I don't think it's good enough. I don't believe for a minute that . . ."

Sarah was still standing just behind me, and she intervened at this point. "I would suggest that he's probably telling the truth, Mr. Zachary. Mr. Bingham junior told me only yesterday that his father's health was worse than usual, and he likes to have his son close by at such times."

"Mac Bingham was here yesterday?"

"Why, yes. He was here several times while you were absent. We all understood that you had given him leave to use the back parlour for meetings involving the horse race."

"Well, true enough." Behind me, I heard the door open and close as the elderly messenger made his exit. I had meant to send a message of my own back to his master, but it was too late, and probably the better for it. "And that was it? Just horse racers?"

Sarah laughed a quick, fluttery laugh—just a trifle self-conscious. "And once he invited me to tea at a restaurant on Government Street. It was my afternoon off, and Mr. Bingham wished to speak to me."

"I thought you didn't like Mac."

(This may be the point in the conversation where I began to bury myself. On the other hand, one might decide that the whole discussion was doomed from the beginning to ruin me. Truth be told, the moment I decided to investigate Sarah's background, I was setting myself on a route that would inevitably be disastrous.)

Sarah's eyes fluttered as she paused briefly, then protested, "I don't believe I said I didn't like Mr. Bingham."

"But you were afraid of him. You could barely look him in the face.

When Jack and I came back from Sooke, you were like Daniel down in the lions' den."

"I may have been nervous when I first met him. Sometimes I don't do well with strangers . . ."

"I don't think that's it at all, Miss Green. I think he reminded you a lot of Hans Chapman Canon, and you were scared."

She staggered—physically took an unsteady step backwards—and I suddenly felt like someone who has dropped a huge burden onto a frail child, forgetting how heavy it was.

"Don't worry, Miss Green," I added quickly. "Your every secret is safe with me, and everything I learned about you in Olympia made me respect you all the more. You have my admiration. You were terribly misused and you reacted in your own defence. Self-defence. Everyone agrees. No one thinks badly of you, least of all me. You have my greatest sympathy and respect for everything you did. Everything."

While I rushed out this torrent of platitudes, I watched her in dismay. She stood there at the opening of the short hall next to the base of the stairs with one hand against the wall to steady herself. Her eyes seemed a bit out of focus as she stared at the floor just by her left foot, shaking her head slightly, slowly. It was distressingly similar to the attitude she had held while she was first frightened by Mac Bingham.

"I meant to tell you all this at a more convenient time . . . ," I stammered.

"A more convenient time?" Her voice almost too light to be heard.

"I mean this is very difficult to bring forward, and I normally would have hoped to . . ."

Without looking at me, she turned and started up the stairs quickly. She was about halfway up when she turned in my direction and spoke, looking at a spot somewhere above my head. "Would you please inform Mrs. Zachary that I am unwell and will not be taking supper tonight? Perhaps Ross can be put to bed by his father."

I could find nothing trustworthy to say. She continued up to the landing, very upright, still a little unsteady. How strange it can be—that an idea or an enterprise that for many days seemed perfectly logical and sound can, at a single tick of the clock, be revealed as blatantly, obviously asinine. It's like a magician waving his wand and turning a happy puppy into a rattlesnake.

What had I been thinking?

There was a chair in front of the window at the end of the hall next to the staircase. I trudged toward it, dropping my coat onto the floor. It thumped heavily with the weight of the revolver in the pocket. I sat.

Then, before she had entered her room, I heard her steps reverse and slowly descend the stairs. I seriously considered jumping out of the window. At the foot of the staircase, she turned the corner, spotted me slouched in my seat, and stared. If I had thought there had been time for her to procure a weapon, I would have expected to be shot. She spoke, though, in a calm and restrained voice.

"How could you—why would you do this, Mr. Zachary? To spy upon the most unfortunate tribulation of a vulnerable woman? I now admit that I thought it a strange coincidence that you should leave Victoria to consider business possibilities in such a place as Olympia, but I never believed you would be capable of this. Were you merely possessed of an unwholesome curiosity, or did you have more unwholesome motives?"

"Sarah! Miss Green! There was nothing unwholesome about anything in the whole stupid affair. I had other reasons for the trip that I cannot right now reveal. I just wound up in Washington, and while I was in Olympia, it seemed convenient to learn something about your story, your background. Not for myself. For Jack."

"Mr. Elliston?"

"Surely, Miss Green, you must realize that he has developed a fondness for you, and I thought it my duty as a friend—since your past was a bit of a mystery—to make sure that you were, well, a proper companion for him. It was not idle curiosity. I was doing it for Jack."

"Mr. Elliston put you up to this?"

And by this point, I had successfully buried Jack.

My protests that this was entirely incorrect were addressed to her back, as she had turned elegantly on her heel, but as she once again began to ascend the staircase, I saw her face, and it was chiselled in ice.

I may have called to her once more. I may not have bothered.

I returned to my chair before the window and sat. I scratched the top of my head with my fingernails but was unable to draw blood. I hauled at the tips of my moustache until hairs pulled loose.

Her footsteps climbed half the first flight, then there was a short pause, after which they began to descend again. I remained seated.

Once again, she faced me, speaking now with the forceful calm of a Medusa. "I must at this point, Mr. Zachary, give you one week's notice of the termination of my employment. I will inform your wife and Master Ross as soon as possible."

"Sarah! You can't! We want you here more than ever. You can't leave. What would you do?"

In the most businesslike manner possible, she replied, "There is always some other place to go, Mr. Zachary. Perhaps some other place where my person and my privacy will be better respected." This time when she walked up to her room on the second floor, she closed the door behind her and did not return.

THE NEXT DAY was a day of revelations and the repercussions of revelations.

When I awoke, a flurry of questions immediately thrust themselves upon me as if they had been sitting at the foot of my bed, just waiting for my eyes to open. I did my best to ignore them, since there were no answers to match them, and pulled the blankets over my head. I didn't want to face morning at the breakfast table. By the time I was up, quietly dressed, and inconspicuously down the stairs, the morning meal was finished. The hotel was ominously quiet apart from the distant wail of Ross singing something in the backyard. I entered the kitchen by the parlour door and found my wife and Sarah Green standing shoulder to shoulder, their backs to me, looking outside. They must have heard me approaching over the creaky wooden floorboards, but they did not turn, and I considered that although I would inevitably face this confrontation, I would refuse to announce my presence to begin it. I walked in measured steps across the kitchen and out of it via the dining room. Neither woman acknowledged my presence.

More than once over the years, some man or other has advanced the theory that all women are linked together in a vast conspiracy against the members of our gender, and more than a few times it has seemed to me quite plausible.

At the boot room, I gathered up boots, hat, and jacket in one swift operation and was down the street in search of coffee in a minute. I obtained that morning beverage along with a square of cornbread and a dollop of molasses at Stemple's, just around the corner, swallowing them down much more quickly than necessary. Sometimes even the worst of life's problems can be solved—or at least, functionally delayed—by walking and pondering. I think I was, at that moment, as anxious to get at my walkabout as a poisoned man reaching for an antidote.

I marched south, then a block or so west toward the water. At that point, I happened to hear a pair of acquaintances passing on opposite sides of the street, calling out to each other.

"Hey there!" one man shouted. "I thought we were meeting with the boys this morning."

"No," the other fellow called. "It's tomorrow morning."

This exchange had nothing to do with me, but it reminded me that

Jack and Bingham and all the rest were supposed to meet at the Celestial around eleven o'clock. My watch informed me that it was now past ten. I turned north at the next corner and started homeward, my step quickening as I visualized poor Jack arriving early to drop in, all unsuspecting, on his lady friend Sarah.

To my relief, no horses or buggies were yet on the street outside the hotel, and, when I stuck my head inside the front door, I did not see any evidence that Jack was there. I did, however, catch a glimpse of another figure standing at the end of the hall, next to the back parlour door. It was Roselle, and although I drew myself outside as swiftly as possible, I knew that he had seen me. I heard his footsteps coming, considered my options, and had just stepped off the porch into the street when he emerged, calling my name.

"Zachary!" He had to shout it again before I stopped. "Zachary!" Then, when I turned and gave him a restrained smile, he began to talk. "I had to think there for a minute—is that a Christian name or a surname? A first name or a last? People are so over-familiar these days out here on the far edge of polite society. You tend to forget."

I took another step—backwards, away from him—as I growled, "I have no time for this, Roselle. I have to meet someone."

"We have to meet, you know. We have to talk."

"I don't need to talk to you, Roselle."

"Oh, yes, you do. Yes, indeed you do."

At that, I turned and walked away, hearing him laugh behind me, going back inside. As nonchalant as I had tried to appear, I was on the verge of panic. My ears were ringing and the hair stood up on my forearms. When I reached the corner, I stopped and hunched down with my back against a stable wall, trying to breathe deep and slow. I looked at my hands and watched them shake. The butcher and his boy passed by, giving me an odd, cautious look, as did a trio of sailors, who laughed among themselves after they were past.

I presumed that if Jack had not already arrived for his meeting, he would come this way, and I could catch him before he got to the hotel. When I did, in fact, see him approaching only a few minutes later, my thoughts were all in a tangle and I felt the absurd inclination to call out, "He knows! Roselle knows!" But Jack was Jack, all beaming back at the new morning and telling me what a fine day it was before I even had a chance to speak.

"But what's the bother with you, Lincoln Zachary? You're all red in the face as if you'd just run a mile, and I happen to know that you never run anywhere at all."

"We have to talk, Jack. I need to tell you some things."

"All right. Good enough then, but I should go to this damned conference with the horse race people first. One more chance to fight for Christy's cause, for what the fight is worth."

"No, Jack. Right now. I need to tell you something before another minute passes."

By this time he had recognized the severity of my discomfort, and we stopped, facing each other, only a few paces from the corner.

"What is it then, old man?"

"It's Sarah Green, Jack. I need to tell you about her."

"Nothing bad, Zachary. Please, nothing bad. What has happened?" His face immediately clouded in fear. Looking past me toward the Celestial, he started to stride onward, thinking she was in trouble, I supposed.

"No, no." I grabbed his arm and stopped him. "Nothing has happened to her. She's fine. Wonderfully fine, in fact."

"Don't scare me like that, then! You know damned well that she's taken hold of me, heart and mind. Everybody probably knows. I can't put her out of my thoughts for more than a few minutes before . . ."

"But there is something, Jack."

"What? What do you mean?"

"She killed a man."

He stared at me, his mouth gawping open.

"What? Just now? Who?"

"No, not now. Some time ago. Not here. Down in the Washington Territory."

"What?" He blinked repeatedly and shook his head. "What? What are you saying? Who is this man she supposedly killed? In the Washington Territory? How do you know this? Did she tell you this herself?"

Having been given a string of questions all at once, I began to answer them in reverse order. "No," I said. "She did not tell me herself . . ."

"Then I don't believe it!" Jack interrupted.

"But I felt I had to, sort of, well, introduce the story and discuss it with her, and she did not deny it. She more or less admitted it to be true."

"She killed a man?"

"To defend herself. And to defend the children she was attending. Self-defence."

"But she killed him!"

"Brick on the head. Served him right."

"She never said a word about this to me," Jack mumbled, then, looking up, "How did you find this out?"

"When I was down there myself. I asked around and about and eventually . . ."

"That's why you took your trip? You travelled all the way down there to try to find out . . . ?"

"I went to Olympia for other reasons. Things I might tell you about later if you absolutely need to know. Other strong reasons! But since I was there, and since I was curious about that part of her past that she didn't ever mention, and since you were starting to develop, well, a certain closeness to her . . ."

"You were worried about me falling in love with a . . ."

"Here's the bad part, Jack. Here's the really bad part." I was having difficulty forming the words with my mouth. "You're my friend, man. You will forgive me, won't you?"

"Forgive you for what?"

"Just try to remember that my heart was in the right place."

"I can't forgive you if I don't know what you've done, Zachary."

"I muddled it all up and somehow I made it seem as if you had asked me to look into her secret past, and now she won't believe me when I try to explain."

"She thinks I told you to snoop around?"

I could feel my face hot as a steam boiler. "Eventually we'll bring her around. We'll set it right, I promise you. But right now you have to bide your time."

"Bide my time!"

"Please, Jack . . ."

And then we were interrupted by the rumble of iron wheels pulling up beside us and the sound of Mac Bingham's booming jovial voice.

"Hey there, Elliston! We'll give you a ride the last fifty feet. Look who's here, Jack. Look who we've got! Billy Horne!" Bingham was being driven in his father's carriage today—a rather ostentatious brougham, in spite of its one broken window—and sitting beside him was a smallish man with a face like a dried apple and a grin like a groundhog. He was, however, impeccably dressed—black suit and waistcoat, black shoes with white gaiters, white as snow shirt and collar, and a bright red bowtie. For once at a loss for words, Jack Elliston glared in confusion from Billy Horne to me, to Bingham, and then he was suddenly up, standing on the step-up, riding away down the street.

"Jack!" I shouted after him. "It's a secret! Remember it's a secret!"

I was aware as I said it that there is a sad irony in having to shout about secrets in the middle of the street. I plodded my way once around the block, muttering, trying to clear my thoughts, and ended up standing directly across from the Celestial Hotel, feet apart, arms crossed behind my back like a sentry, watching. Bingham and his boy Billy must have been the last to arrive—no one else came or went after them, and I certainly had no desire to join the meeting—so I had nothing to do but stand there. At various points over the next half-hour or so, I decided to go up to Government Street and drink, to go into the hotel and find Sarah, or to find my wife and get her advice, but my legs refused to be complicit in any of these actions, so I just stood. The same butcher and his boy walked past me again, pushing a barrow, and gave me the same suspicious look. I ignored them, staring off into the distance like a young Homer surveying the Aegean. Moments later a small boy and his dog passed by, and the little terrier decided I was too suspicious to go unmarked. He ran at me, barking, and refused to be called off by the agitated child until I kicked at him. The boy burst into tears and they both ran down the hill.

I thought, thereafter, that I should continue my vigil from a more inconspicuous vantage point. There was a box, half-full of rotten greens, at the edge of our yard, so I dumped this into the ditch, took it across the street to a position partly obscured by lilac branches, and used it for a seat. Happily, I discovered tobacco in my jacket pocket, so I was able to smoke while I sat in my cloud of gloom and indecision.

I don't know how long it was that I waited—at least an hour, I think—before the first members of the race committee began to emerge, chuckling compliments to each other and straightening their hats. The banker and the newspaper man came out together, then, a minute behind them, two others I didn't recognize. Bingham's driver brought the brougham around, and the big man and Billy Horne strode out, slapping at shoulders with a tall, grey fellow whom I recognized as some sort of political figure. The tall man walked off behind the carriage, having refused an offer to be driven.

Jack stepped out through the front door, his head down. He walked like a somnambulist, gazing at his hat. I ran across directly.

"Jack, Jack. Over here."

He gave me a blank look. "She won't even talk to me."

"Sarah? Ah, yes."

"She refuses to speak to me."

"I'm not actually surprised. So you and I need to . . ."

"No."

"What?"

"No, Zachary. Not now. I can't talk to you right now. I definitely should not talk to you right now." The expression on his face, to his credit, was not one of hatred or disgust, but rather amazement, incredulity. There was nothing for me but to watch him depart. When he disappeared around the corner, I couldn't decide whether to go inside or just go down to the water and drown myself.

Then Roselle came through the door and down the stairs, greeting me like his oldest friend. "Zachary. Dear fellow."

"The devil himself," I replied, not sure to which of us I was referring.

"We must talk. Yes, let us discuss!"

"Why the hell should I . . . ?"

"Come, come now. You know very well that we need to have this conversation sooner or later. You know that, don't you?"

I wished I was carrying my Colt .45. "Well, talk then."

He smiled with exaggerated tolerance. "Right here on your own doorstep, Mr. Beddoes? Or perhaps across there."

We walked across the street and he leaned against the hitching rail, the picture of nonchalance, smiling, saying nothing. He was enjoying himself. I was not.

"Say what you have to say, Roselle."

"Yes, yes," he drawled. "Where should I begin . . . ?"

"Tell me what you think you know."

"Oh, I'm very certain of what I know! The amazing thing is that I took so long to place what it was that bothered me about you. Or for somebody else to spot it. Why didn't anybody else in this little town connect you with your past? Of course, after a year or two, you would no longer expect to be discovered. This Lincoln Zachary person had established himself in Victoria, and who would suspect him of anything?"

I refused to respond to this, merely faced him, impassive. He continued.

"It was actually Hec Simmonds that struck the light for me. He came and went while you were out of town—I think you know that. I honestly only wanted him to meet you for old times' sake. I figured maybe we had all got drunk together in a saloon up there, or something, and you and I had forgotten it but he would remember. We came around to the hotel here. You were gone, and he laughed and mentioned that he had chased after a man named Zachary once before—Zachary Beddoes, the most despicable robber and the most heartless, murdering killer of the whole gold rush."

"I never robbed anyone," I blurted out at last, "and I never killed anyone. At least, never murdered anyone. Shot a couple of fellows, maybe, but self-defence. Pure self-defence."

Roselle laughed out loud and slapped his thighs. "You know, strange as it may be, I actually believe you! Partly, at least. I mean, I can't feature how a man could change from being a wild and desperate fiend, over the course of a half-dozen years or so, into a pissy little hotelkeeper, living among the Chinamen. Let's face it, man—you haven't got the gumption of a freshly hatched kitten! Maybe you really are innocent, but you're still a wanted man. Wanted by the hangman!"

"I am innocent."

"Then why did you run?"

"I couldn't prove it. Bad luck that it all pointed in my direction."

He let the silence hang for a moment before he continued. "There are stories about you." He nodded reflectively. "Some bad stories. I heard on good authority that when a bunch of men chased you up onto a rooftop in Barkerville and you were forced to jump, you shot a preacher in the street and used his body to break your fall."

"That's mostly a lie." For some reason, I felt like I shouldn't reveal what small part of the story was true.

"But the best story," Roselle intoned carefully, "is about how much gold and how much blood money you escaped with."

So the key point to the discussion had arrived. The negotiations had begun.

"It wasn't that much. I have none of it left."

"Now you're lying, Zachary Beddoes. I don't want you to lie to me anymore. That's enough, you see? I didn't tell Hec Simmonds what I knew, but we did talk over your history, and Hec worked for Judge Begbie back then. The reward money offered was considerable, and stories did come in, looking for a piece of it. An old Indian in Quesnelle Mouth. A ranch hand near the 70 Mile House. More. They all agree that there was a horse and a mule walking themselves to death with the weight of gold they were carrying."

"Nonsense. Most of what I had, I gave away, and the rest went to buy my share in that hotel. I have nothing left, Roselle."

He shook his head. "Well, that would be bad news for both of us, if that was true, because then there would be no reason for me to stay quiet. I would turn you in, maybe get a bit of a reward, if it was still being offered, and everyone in town would buy me a drink to listen to the story. And you'd be dead."

"Or I might decide to kill you right here, right now, if I'm such a bad sort."

"No, you won't even touch me, because you're still in hiding. You can't afford to have the law checking up on your background. And for the next while, I don't plan on setting foot outside at night, or anywhere that isn't in plain view of the public. Not until our arrangement is complete. Besides, I've made arrangements to protect myself. I've written a letter exposing you for who you really are, and I've left it in a safe place where it can only be picked up by my zealous friend, Hec Simmonds, who will pick it up when he returns from Hong Kong if I'm not peacefully waiting here to meet him.

"Don't look so distressed, Zachary! This doesn't need to wreck everything for you! You must have expected that something like this—or something a lot worse—would eventually turn up. Now all you have to do is pay up. Pay up! You end up a bit poorer, and I'm a bit richer, and we're both happy to be alive!"

"You think you'll be happy, do you, you blackmailing bastard?" I growled.

"Well," he paused in histrionic contemplation. "I'm pretty sure I'll be a bit happier than I am at present. Every whore and bartender in town will smile when they see me coming. Right now I can't even put a friendly hand on the backside of a serving girl without getting my face slapped. And you—you can relax again, right here—you and your Chinamen. You've become quite the yellow fellow yourself!" He was uproariously entertained by this witticism, but he may have sensed that he was treading on dangerous ground, for he calmed himself and carried on in a placatory tone. "No offence, man, no offence. Those Chinamen are not so bad for now. Good workers. Head down, dig a ditch. They're building the railroad for the most part, so I hear. I just hope they've figured a way to get rid of them when the ditches are dug and the railroad is finished. Don't worry, though. I'm sure they'll let you keep your little woman, if she's found a white man for herself."

"If you mention my wife again, I'll kill you right now and figure out the consequences later."

"Hey, now! No offence. I was trying to pay a compliment here. I've seen the good Mrs. Zachary in the hotel, what with all of Bingham's meetings, and I see she's a pretty little thing, and hard working and probably smarter than any white woman in the neighbourhood! Not that such is saying much . . ."

"She's a thousand times your superior, Roselle, and I *will* kill you if . . ."

"No, you won't. You certainly won't! Because whatever your excuse, once the law took a bit of a look at the circumstances, they would discover that she was *Mrs. Zachary Beddoes*! And that wouldn't do, would it? No, you'll just keep calm and quiet until I tell you exactly what I want and how I want it. And I won't make you wait very long. I'll be in touch directly, right after this stupid horse race."

"If you whisper one word about this, Roselle . . ."

"Relax, partner! It wouldn't be to my advantage just to *waste* you now, would it? And safer for me just to disappear quietly from this backwater town and leave you be, once I've tied up my last responsibilities."

And that was about as much as was said before the bastard strolled away. I was left standing there like an impotent idiot, sick to my stomach, with nothing but a frenzy of noise inside my head. I needed to think, and for that purpose, I made my way down to one of the private docks, where I sat on a stack of folded canvas, leaned my back against the boathouse wall, and stared out onto the bay.

I felt like an old man. I was exhausted, unable to defend myself against even such a mean and cheap rascal as Roselle.

After an hour, or perhaps more, I stood up, returned to my room, and wrote a short letter, which I then took to the wharfinger, who held things for the mail. He promised to see it sent off the next day.

Then I walked along the rocky shore for a while.

WHEN MY AIMLESS wandering eventually led me back inside the hotel, the place seemed very quiet. I found myself in the kitchen, where a large basin of clean, warm wash water rested on the stove. I thrust my head into this and held it there, in an underwater silence. It was not a matter of cleansing, more a ritual drowning if anything, and after coming up for a breath of air, I repeated the procedure. Then once again. After the third such submersion, I arose to find my wife holding a towel for me. As I took it, I said in a gasping voice, "Sue! My dear Sue, I need to talk to you."

"No," she replied softly. "It is not me who you should talk to." And with that, she walked away.

I learned several things from that very short communication. Firstly, I could tell that Sarah Green had spoken to my wife about my ill-advised investigation. Secondly, it seemed to be Sue's opinion that I should still attempt to reason with the young woman—to apologize and placate. Thirdly, it was confirmed to me that all persons of the female gender had joined their ranks to humiliate me.

I have come to realize that a wise man regards humility as a strength. Espousing this belief, I think that I have been humiliated so many times that I should be a venerable sage by now. One way or the other, I try not to shrink from abasing myself, since it so often becomes unavoidable. With my hair still dripping and the towel around my shoulders, I headed for the back door, through which I could hear the theatrical shouts of my son, Ross.

The boy had a short stick that evidently served him as a sword while he thrashed the distant willow saplings, which were probably attempting to attack our castle. As I expected, Sarah Green was watching from a distance, seated on a stool, her hands in her lap. I walked resolutely to a position beside her (I didn't think either of us felt a great desire to converse eye to eye) and spoke.

"Miss Green, I have come once again to apologize for my actions."

She said nothing, continuing to stare vaguely at my crusading child.

"Please, Miss Green. Will you not speak to me? I am admitting myself guilty of all charges and begging your forgiveness. Have you no answer for me?"

She sighed, drew a deep breath, and spoke with the flat tone of great fatigue. "If there is anything to forgive, Mr. Zachary, I certainly forgive you, but you've really done nothing so wrong, have you? A woman's privacy is a small thing, particularly before the man who honours her with employment. This is not a matter of offence and forgiveness, but a simple case of action and consequences. Something is done, something else follows. Unavoidably."

"Well, if you forgive me for my indiscretion, then there's no need for any other consequence, is there? We've done with it. Forgotten."

"I'm sorry, Mr. Zachary. It is not that simple."

"We've got to make it that simple. Carry on. Back where it was before curiosity made me a fool."

"Time doesn't move backwards. I can't look you in the eye when I know what you must see in mine. Besides, I've made new decisions. I repeat that at the end of the week I shall sadly be gone from your house."

"Decide a new decision, then. Decide to stay. As a measure of the esteem in which I hold you, I want to increase your salary."

There was a long pause. I leaned forward a bit and stole a glance at her face, but there was no expression there to read.

"You'll stay then, won't you Miss Green?"

She shook her head, still staring at the battle between the boy and the fence posts.

"No? Why not?"

She paused and then answered, in that uneven, liquid tone that presages a woman's tears.

"I have nothing more to say to you, Mr. Zachary."

After shuffling my feet a bit and looking up at the sky, I also discovered nothing more to say, to I turned and began a slow departure. She stopped me with a word.

"Mr. Zachary."

"Yes. I'm here."

She spoke hesitantly but clearly. "Tell me truly. Did Jack Elliston really know nothing about your, your . . . ?"

"He had nothing to do with it. He knew nothing about anything until this morning. I figured I had no choice by then but to tell him all."

She nodded to herself, and I walked away.

I THINK I was afraid at that point to go back inside and inform my wife that my discussion had been a failure, and we were about to lose a fine employee as well as someone who, I knew, had become Sue's friend. Or again, maybe I was simply in the mood to be punished by everyone in general. I threw the towel onto the back porch as I passed and headed for the Elliston brothers' apartments. It was a walk of some fifteen minutes at the pace I took, but during that time I made no mental preparations at all, save to resolve that if Jack decided to hit me, I would not strike back.

The front door to the building—a fine building of two stories with four gabled dormers—was propped open with a rolled carpet waiting to be taken outside and beaten. I mused, as I headed up the stairs, that I myself might soon be taken outside and beaten.

I walked down the second floor hallway and tapped at the first door on the right, which swung open to me. The first person I saw was neither Jack nor Avery, but Christy Riordan. He was sprawled face up on the sofa, one arm reaching the floor, eyes shut, mouth open, droning a raspy snore. Jack sat on a chair to his right, watching his somnolent guest in deep concentration.

"Amazing, isn't it?" he commented philosophically.

I pulled out my watch. "Well after noon."

"Irishmen work on a totally different timetable when they're drinking.

It has its own laws and limitations. Impossible for a lowly Englishman—or an American—to keep up with that."

"Have you been trying?"

"My Lord, no! Last night—yesterday afternoon and last night, I suppose—that was Christy's dash at drinking it all away, and he made a valiant attempt, I must say. Perhaps I'll take a shot at it myself tonight."

"Jack, I'm sorry. I'm so bloody sorry. I'm an idiot of the worst water, and if I've caused a rift between you and that fine young lady . . ."

"Forget it, Zachary. I think this particular crisis was bound to come up sooner or later, and I probably was just putting it off because I was enjoying her company so much. I half suspected there was something there—something hidden. Damn it. I could fix this thing if I was given a chance. I know I could!"

"You should know . . ."

"Yes, I'm sure that I should know a lot of things. At some point, I'll need to get the whole story from you, but right now I'm too miserable to listen. She won't see me, won't talk to me, and all I can do is sit here feeling sorry for myself and watching young Christy blowing like a beached whale."

"Don't give up on her, Jack."

"Give up on her? What? That's not on the program at all. I love that woman, Zachary. I love her! She's my first true love, if you'd believe that! An old fellow like me—thirty something, if the birth certificate's to be trusted—and I've never felt anything like it. I mean, I've had the occasional uncomfortable dalliance. I've courted and been courted, but this is something very strange. There's certainly no damned giving up to be done!"

"I think she might love you, too, Jack."

"Well!" He stood and began to pace back and forth the short distance across the room. "Well, we shall certainly proceed with that hope in mind!"

"But carefully, man. She's been ill-treated. She's been badly frightened. I don't think she can quite believe that it's all behind her."

"But it isn't!" he shouted, while Christy snored on. "These things don't just cease to exist when you start over in a different place! Whatever she's done, she's had to carry the secret around inside for too long, and it changes you. Secrets, dark secrets—they burn away little bits of your soul for as long as they're inside."

"I know." And I repeated, "I know, believe me."

"Ah, I'm not talking about your size of secrets—minor misdeeds, bad habits—everyone has those, but sometimes a person has to carry around a thing that is always there and never spoken, and it changes the whole way you live."

Once again I almost told him, right there. The pronouncement of my own culpability was on my tongue, slipping forward. But years of habit and fear prevailed, and I bit it back, saying instead, "Surely, the gentleman Elliston brothers haven't ventured into anything all that black."

He groaned and faced me square on. "There have been things, Zachary. There have been things done and things sadly repeated. No excuses. Fair is fair, and every deed has a consequence. We did not exactly leave England by our own choice, but I can't talk of all that right now. Maybe there'll be a time. Suffice to say that we are respectable gentlemen living on our father's considerable wealth as long as we remain abroad where we cannot besmirch the family name too publicly." He sat down again. "I write home for permission sometimes, you know. Like a schoolboy begging to be allowed to have his pudding after supper . . ."

"And there's nothing more to be done about that?"

"Nothing about that either. Not about father and not about Sarah Green. Nothing to do but wait. So we shall have to wait, and in the meantime, maybe we can do something about Christy Riordan."

I cleared my throat, taking a seat in the chair next to him and resting my feet on the arm of the sofa, next to those of our sleeping friend. "As far as that end of things goes," I said, "we'll just have to do something about Mr. Billy Horne."

Jack nodded. "You have a devious mind, Zachary. I like that."

So we talked for a while, but came to no real conclusions.

NEXT MORNING I was expecting Jack, but it was actually Avery who arrived at the Celestial to get me. I had agreed to accompany Jack and Bingham and their group while they took Miss Deception down to Beacon Hill for a run and a sort of reception. Bingham said he wanted to make a show of it for publicity's sake, and although I normally eschew any sort of public display, I figured all the attention would be on the horse, so I would hardly be noticed.

Avery was his usual ebullient self, singing out a rambling monologue about the wonderful weather—the breeze from the sea whistling a tune to the glory of God, and so on—as he approached, but when I stepped down to the street, he took my shoulder in hand and guided me back up the three stairs and toward the door of the hotel.

"Not meaning to speak offence, my friend, and not to give overdue emphasis to external appearance, but I've been sent on ahead to remind you that it's a public presentation, and we must all be dressed accordingly."

"Come on now, Avery."

"Very sorry, Mr. Zachary, but we just need to spruce you up a bit. Let's get a collar on that shirt. It looks clean enough. Of course it is. Your good wife wouldn't allow any less, but let's brush your hair, shall we? And your jacket. You'll need your jacket."

"I won't need my jacket. It's already too warm to need . . ."

"Public occasion, my good man! One does not dress for comfort. One dresses for propriety."

He was practically pushing me up the stairs.

"But I'll roast. I'll sweat like a pig!" I protested.

He said I would not and I said that I would.

"I always think," he added as he spotted a clean collar on my dressing table, "that at such times, all one needs to do is smile even more broadly and no one suspects a thing about your discomfort."

"I don't care whether anyone knows I'm uncomfortable or not. I just want to . . ."

"Your coat would be here in this closet, would it not? Ah, here it is. Is that your only hat, or do you have another that's weathered fewer storms?"

In a few minutes I was a marginally more presentable man, and we walked down the street, stopping at the corner. "My brother's instructions were to wait here for their arrival. He's very precise, is Jack. It can be a bit annoying at times the way he guides me so carefully along my way." Avery did not, I think, see any irony in this comment at all. For my part, I found it difficult to remain annoyed at Avery—the only member of the clergy who had ever amused me—so we stood there for a few minutes in the sunshine while he told me some story of their travels that I now forget.

Then the procession arrived, and a procession it was indeed. I had expected the horse to make the short journey in the company of Jack, me, Bingham, and probably the jockey, but I had underestimated Mac Bingham's sense of what constituted good publicity. In addition to the aforementioned, there were at least four of Mac's subordinates, all dressed up in their finest, two Negroes, one with a shovel and one with a burlap sack, as if Miss Deception's droppings were too valuable to be left in the street. The banker I had seen at previous meetings walked at one flank while a newspaper fellow followed on the other. Close behind, a man walked playing a banjo. By the horse's front shoulders walked Christy Riordan and Billy Horne on opposite sides, while Jack himself led the filly at the fore.

"There was a bit of a problem down at the stable," Avery told me in a conspiratorial tone. "Both riders wanted to lead the horse, so they compromised on Jack."

"*Both* riders?" I asked him. "I thought it was decided that Horne was in and Christy was out."

"Jack has badgered him into saying that the matter is still up for discussion, but I don't think either Jack or Christy have any illusions. And I suspect that Mr. Bingham wants them both hanging about insulting each other, to create the perception of dissension in the ranks, or some such thing."

"Well, that won't help Miss Deception's image, will it?"

"Oh, no! That's what he wants. The betting has been pretty slow so far, I believe, and it won't gather any momentum unless there is more doubt about the outcome. The odds, you understand, Mr. Zachary."

I laughed out loud at that. "The pompous ass has a bit of a problem, doesn't he? He wants to parade his perfect, pretty racehorse to an adoring public, but he hopes they'll think she might still be beaten. He wants a race where Miss Deception can't possibly lose, but he hopes the bloody gamblers will still bet both ways!"

Avery just nodded philosophically. "I suppose we should join the procession, then." So we matched the funereal pace of the others, trailing along behind the banjo player.

It was an odd sensation, an odd conflict of emotions to march in that company. On the one hand, I felt quite foolish, dressed up in my finest, humble as it was, ostentatiously following along up to the corner, then southward down Government Street, the horse's retinue all smiles and music. There was hand-clapping, shouts of greeting, and every once in a while the whole company waving their fists in the air and calling out, "Hurrah! Hurrah!" Included in this were not only Bingham's hired hooligans, but a middle-aged banker and a chronicler of events from *The British Colonist* itself. The snail's pace was maintained, although obviously

Miss Deception was anxious to move faster. No one was allowed to pass us in the street or look out from a shop window without being regaled by cries of "Just look at this horse!" or "Come on along!" or "We're running at the track!" Personally, I kept my dignity aided by the example of Avery Elliston, who, I'm sure, was used to all sorts of such odd promenades and processions, being a church figure.

"Don't you feel a bit ridiculous?" I asked him as we strolled.

He answered me, "Not at all. I rather like these silly festivities. Mr. Bingham actually offered me a small ceremonial capacity at the race itself, and I was pleased to accept. Be at the centre of things, so to speak."

"What are you doing? He hasn't got you blessing the horses or anything, has he?"

"I couldn't do that. I think I'm supposed to keep a righteous and holy eye on the wagers or something. What about you? Do you have a part in the play, Mr. Zachary?"

"No, no!" I assured him. "I'll keep my distance, thank you."

But there was another side to my conflicting emotions. In spite of myself, I was becoming caught up in the fun of it. Maybe the banjo player was to blame. For some reason, I felt a small, guilty pride in being part of the association, having small children run up to us enthralled and delighted, shouting, "Hello!" I found myself smiling and tipping my hat to strangers.

It began as a procession and worked its way quickly up to a parade. At the corner of Government and Yates, we were joined by another horse and another—albeit smaller—racing company. The horse was a grey who became a bit agitated by the commotion as we approached, and he was accompanied by three big working lads, a slim, sombre fellow, who was later found to be the jockey, and an old gentleman with a white beard growing all the way to his waist. He had two canes with which he manoeuvred himself on his wobbly way. I thought this might hinder our passage at first, but once we had spent some time shaking hands with one another and commending ourselves for what a fine spectacle we made, we continued on at a pace that the old man could easily match. The grey and his handler took the lead, while our more rambunctious group followed behind, still hailing all strangers and admonishing them to make their way immediately to Beacon Hill.

We had only travelled about halfway down the block when I spotted a third horse held in the middle of the intersection at View Street, surrounded by a half-dozen handlers and a small group of bystanders, all watching our progress. Avery had stopped to speak to some acquaintance, so I made my way forward and walked alongside Jack for a while.

"Wonderful, isn't it?" he laughed. His mood was jubilant, in spite of the distressing problems that had recently entered his life. "This is good fun. Good for the whole city."

"I had no idea what was happening this morning. You told me we were just taking the horse down for a training run."

"I didn't know myself," Jack told me. "I knew Mac would try to make a splash of it, but this is quite a surprise. Look up ahead. That's the big chestnut down from Nanaimo. They look like a serious bunch, don't they?"

They did indeed. Eight men, all dressed in severe black suits that nearly matched—as did the men, for that matter. If the grey's owners had the look of farm folk, these were definitely businessmen. Every one of them kept a manner of sincerity and dignity, and, when we met up in the street and halted to exchange greetings, every one of them stared me straight and level, eye to eye, as we shook hands.

"Nanaimo, you say?" I asked Jack once we were moving again. "Are they all such stern characters up there, I wonder?"

"Coal people," he told me. "There's money in those hands. Coal money tends to last longer than gold money, and the Binghams, father and son, intend to have a good share of it when this lovely horse outraces theirs."

I looked around the throng.

"Lloyd isn't here today?"

Jack shook his head. "Too sick. He's had a bad week, so they say. It's kind of sad, really, although I don't feel any great affection for the bitter old blighter. He's the one that's set up the whole party and now he's got to stay home in bed. They say he won't last out the year, although from what I've seen of him, when the devil comes to claim his soul, the belligerent old bastard might just kick him back downstairs."

"Where does the grey horse come from?"

"He's locally bred and trained. A nice-looking horse. They say he tends to lack the steam it takes to finish, but he's won one race at Beacon Hill and come close in others. Just the right kind of competition for us. He fills out the field but doesn't truly pose any major threat."

"Is that it, then? Just these three?"

"There's one more. A three-year-old mare from the mainland that's raced this track before. She's already out there waiting. Once again, she's good-looking company on the field, but Miss Deception will leave her well behind."

"It all sounds pretty cut and dried, according to you. Why would you expect anybody to bet against us? That's the point of a challenge race, isn't it?"

Jack glanced around before he answered me, but there was no one paying attention to our conversation. "Well, we won't be showing off our filly's true speed ahead of time, will we? We'll just use the training runs to keep her loose and to let her get used to the atmosphere. Besides, Lloyd Bingham is the kind of character that people love to bet against. When he lost badly in that big race a few years back, the town true and fairly smirked in his face while they cashed in their slips. Now the old man—and his boy—just wants to be sure to get the last laugh. And make a bit of money on the side, of course."

It's no great distance from downtown Victoria to Beacon Hill—we should have covered it in a half-hour or so, but as it was, we took well over an hour, even though we picked up our pace a bit once we got closer to James Bay. By then the parade had swollen to sixty or seventy people—racing people, idlers, and children—all in a festive mood. Bottles had appeared and were being passed around. Somewhere along the line a fiddler—a bad fiddler—had joined up with the banjo man.

As we neared the fields that surrounded the track that ran around that odd lump of earth known as Beacon Hill, an urgency common to all men struck me, and I was forced to climb up an embankment to relieve myself behind the high grass and bushes. While I was pursuing this endeavour, I gazed leisurely in all directions and was surprised to see another small group of men, a high-stepping horse at their centre, coming up the road from behind and about to catch us up. I buttoned my trousers and hurried back down the slope to rejoin Avery, who still walked with a jovial solemnity bringing up the rear.

"What's this then?" I asked him, pointing behind.

He shrugged. "I have no idea. It looks like another horse, doesn't it? Jack will know what's what."

Very quickly word of the new arrivals rippled up the line, and soon we were stopped—at least the majority of us. The chestnut and his attendants, along with many of the spectators, carried on over the low rise and across the field. In the distance, a band of discordant horns began to attempt a sprightly march tune. Then Mac Bingham arrived, bustling his way back to address our new companions, his face sweaty and red, clearly displeased.

"What's this? Why are you just getting here now?" he shouted at the company's leader.

He was a strange-looking leader of a strange-looking company. His skin was as white as good parchment, as was his hair, his jacket and trousers, and his hat. I have heard men such as him referred to as albino, although a doctor friend later informed me that if that was truly the case, his eyes should probably have been a pinkish hue, while I remember them as being blue or grey. He smiled broadly at Mac Bingham and, instead of speaking, struck a rather grand pose and looked back at his companions, like a general surveying the troops. There were seven of them, every one dark enough that I couldn't be sure whether they were Negro or some kind of American Indian from the deserts of the south. Very calmly, he answered in a rumbling bass voice.

"We were invited. By yourself, if you remember."

"Yes," Bingham spluttered, "but your time is all wrong. You were supposed to be either waiting at the track or joining us at a side road from town." He threw up his arms. "This is all wrong. You can't come in behind my party!"

It quickly became clear that Bingham had expected these fellows all along, but he was upset that they were changing the carefully orchestrated order of events. He had intended Miss Deception and her retinue to be the finale of today's parade. He spluttered a few more deprecations at the white man, but my attention now was on the horse itself.

It was a stallion, very large and muscular, black, with spatters of grey in its mane, which was carefully cropped short. If ever a horse could be described as fierce, this would be the one. It fidgeted constantly like a boxer in the ring. Its eyes seemed unusually large. They had given it a bridle of dark red, so its handlers were obviously well pleased to accentuate its intimidating countenance.

Another blustering man had arrived from the front of the pack. He wore a straw hat and a bad suit, and Bingham introduced him as one of the race stewards. He spoke in the same impatient, perturbed manner as Bingham.

"This horse—he's meant to run, is he?"

"He's meant to win," replied the white man. "His entry fee has already been paid to this gentleman," and he nodded his head toward Bingham, who acknowledged this to be true.

"I have not been informed of a fifth entrant," the steward grumbled, staring at Mac, who countered.

"I wasn't even sure they'd make it."

"I said we would be here with the horse to try the track today. It was agreed to be today, was it not?" the white man said in his low, even tone.

"Yes, yes," Bingham agreed, then recapturing his composure, added, "Very good to see you. Welcome to Victoria."

"Yes, of course," the steward added. "But there are papers that should have been filled out already. Posters will be going up this afternoon. Wagers may already have been made, although," he said, catching himself, "that's not the stewards' concern."

"They only arrived from California yesterday," Bingham informed him, "and they contacted me directly. I said it would be all right. They heard about the race through some friend of Buckley's down there, and Lord knows they've travelled a long way. There's always room for another runner-up, isn't there, Mr. . . . I've forgotten your name if I ever even . . ."

"Danny," the newcomer replied. "I don't like the sound of the word *Mister*. Just Danny."

"Well, then," the steward interjected, pulling out a stub of pencil and a scrap of paper, "we'd better get the name of this horse as well, shouldn't we?"

When the man called Danny gave his broad smile, he revealed the one part of his aspect that was not the purest white. His teeth were all stained dark and all crooked, with one or possibly two missing at the front. "Ojai." He spoke proudly. "His name is Ojai."

The steward spelled it out: "O-H-I-G-H."

Danny corrected him and added, "It's the name of a little town and a little valley in the hills above the ocean. The place where he was foaled."

"So the owner then is . . ."

"Smith. Mr. Smith from Chicago."

"Do we know . . . ?"

"Probably not."

The steward was by this time a little flustered and having problems with his pencil. "And a history of breeding?"

"None." Again the broad and crooked smile. "He's not raced before, but he's a natural runner and I wouldn't bet against him, if I was you."

In the end, there was no option but for the California horse to follow Bingham and Miss Deception over the rise and into the field, announced by the less than tuneful trumpets and tubas. It disturbed the perfect symmetry that the organizers had hoped for, but within a few minutes the groups were all separated anyway, each to their own enclosure, complete with coloured tents. The mare from the mainland was already there, as Jack had told me, but by now she looked like a very ordinary horse, attended to by very ordinary people.

All in all, the organizers should have been more than satisfied with the day thus far. The earth-shaking importance of this race had been duly impressed on the citizens of Victoria, as had the fact that the rest of the week leading up to race day was a waste of time if it was not spent on speculation, observation, and the levelling of wagers.

I ambled about. The band continued to drone and hoot, but I managed to ignore it. The sun was now playing with solitary clouds blown by a light sea breeze. I carried my jacket over my shoulder and strolled from enclosure to enclosure, watching the handlers conspiring together and brushing and saddling, while the various jockeys inspected their mounts gravely, each like Charlemagne judging his army. There was the condition of the dirt to be considered, from what I overheard, as well as the angle of the sun. In fact, I think none of them wanted to be the first to run his animal around the course. Finally, the local grey trotted its way around the track that encircled the hill itself. Light applause and shouts of encouragement rose from spectators who sat on blankets on the grass or leaned on the railing absorbing the summery warmth. There were two tea carts set up, one of which was selling sausages and pickled vegetables, a more than sufficient breakfast for me. I was feeding myself from a patch of butcher's paper that served as a plate when I spotted Jack Elliston, no longer quite so jovial, striding away from the enclosure where the horse from California was stationed. I called to him and he stopped for me.

"So what do you think of them?" I asked, nodding toward the Californians.

He only grunted, head down, massaging one ear lobe thoughtfully.

"Did you hear them talking to each other?" I asked again.

"Yes," he sighed. "Spanish. They're all Mexicans. Indios they call them, I think."

"I sense displeasure. You don't like them."

"It hardly matters whether I like them or not, but I think we'd best start keeping a couple of guards at the stable all round the clock, just in case. They play by a different set of rules when you get that far south of civilization."

I believe I raised my eyebrows at that. "And the horse. What do you think of the horse, Jack?"

"Now the horse—*he* is a problem. A very big problem. What the hell was Mac thinking, allowing a horse like that into our cozy little race?"

"I heard the pale fellow say that the beast has never raced before."

Jack laughed. "Of course not! And that woman in the back alley has never been kissed."

With that, he stomped off, probably to find the aforementioned Mac

Bingham, while I felt something like panic creeping up my back. I had to force myself not to run after him. I wanted to grasp him by the lapels and demand to know that it was still safe to invest all my earthly wealth in one grand but perfectly safe wager. I had visualized it all too many times to change my mind now. By now it seemed like my one and only heaven-sent chance to avoid a dreadful future as a common working man. I needed Jack to reassure me that I could still safely gamble my way back to glory.

But his pace was too determined, his strides too long. I stood for a moment with one hand half raised and my mouth half open.

Then I wandered sullenly away at a slouching pace to where they were arranging the grandstands. Two workers were sweeping them over with stiff brooms while two more—men who looked like carpenters—seemed to be taking measurements of the structure. Too late I realized that their work was being overseen by someone I knew all too well.

"Bunting!" Roselle chimed out as he came up behind me. "I've been put in charge of measuring for red, white, and blue *bunting*!" I stared at him without responding, trying to appear nonchalant. He continued, bowing to me in self-mockery, "Yes, Mr. Zachary, and not only has the great man put me in charge of tacking up the colours, but he has delegated to me the responsibility for erecting a wooden platform. Any minute now, I will tell those two builders, 'Build me a platform! Right over there!' and they will build it, and I will be a success!"

I could resist it no longer. "Are you really surprised that people hold you in such disdain, Roselle?" I sneered. "Pompous. Disloyal. If I was Mr. Bingham, I too would be looking around for someone to take your place!"

At that, Roselle narrowed his eyes and growled, "He's finished looking around, hasn't he? He's got your governess to take my place. One more reason I need your money in my pocket."

And that was when I first discovered that Sarah Green was leaving us to work for the Binghams.

TRYING MY BEST to hide my stunned amazement, I sneered disdainfully at Roselle, wandered away across the track, sat down on the grass, and watched the horses taking their turns cantering back and forth, leisurely running the round of the course, and generally accepting the adulation of the idle spectators. Surprisingly, I was soon quite caught up in all the intricacies of the spectacle. The other horses each took their bit of exercise until eventually the horse called Ojai was ridden by pale Danny in a wide circle in front of the tents. She walked the full length of the course, but she was never allowed to pick up the pace. Danny himself hardly paid attention to the exercise, merely smiling and waving to the ladies.

At last, both Christy and then Billy Horne were permitted a turn at riding Miss Deception. She seemed quite comfortable with both of them, and when it looked like her workout was about finished, I got to my feet, preparing to leave. My mind was half on the situation with Sarah Green and half on my newly diluted betting prospects.

Then, just at the last, Billy Horne rode the filly slowly down to the end of the stretch, turned her, and dug his heels into her ribs with a shout. She kicked the clay dirt in all directions and accelerated like a bullet. Within seconds, she was up to a speed that drew audible gasps from the young men hunkered down to my left, but that wasn't enough for Billy Horne. This was a planned manoeuvre. Sixty yards from the blue enclosure he raised his whip hand high and thrashed it down hard onto the animal's flank. She slewed a bit at the first blow—it might have been the first time she had tasted such a bite, and for an instant I hoped she might stop short and buck him off—but he held her head straight and bellowed into her ear, and she leaned into the wind even faster than before. He had a bit of trouble reining her in when she was past his chosen finish point, but when he did, it was to hoots of approval from the general public and loud applause from Mac Bingham, who strode out onto the track to meet them. He was ecstatic. He held his hands above his head as if he had already won the challenge race, turned in a short circle, and called out triumphantly to his partners. From my vantage point, I saw him shout something over his shoulder to Christy Riordan, whose disapproval was very evident.

"That," he called to Christy, "is why Billy Horne is riding for me and you are not!" Then, turning to the crowd in general as if they had all gathered specifically to be his audience—"I know exactly how to get exactly what I want out of a horse!"

Chapter Seven

JACK ARRIVED AT THE HOTEL next morning in a state of great distress. Between muttered curses, he informed me that Christy was off in the town buying some things to take back to the farm, and then he planned on riding back to Sooke in the afternoon.

I was surprised. "He's given up? He's not even staying to watch the race?"

Jack shook his head. "There will be no Riordan at the race. Not with Billy Horne riding. Christy says that if he's forced to witness that man whipping his horse like a donkey again—he still thinks of Miss Deception as *his* horse—he says he'll drag the bastard down and give him a whipping of his own."

We were by this point drinking coffee in the kitchen. I had other questions I wanted to ask, but Cook was banging about with his pots and pans and I didn't want him listening, so instead I asked, "Isn't it common practice to use the whip in a race, now and then?"

"Of course it's common practice, but not with the Riordan family. Matter of principle. They're more farmers than racers, really, and they don't hold with what they consider brutality—particularly on a filly they consider part of the family. I had hoped Miss Deception would absolutely refuse to respond to Horne's tactics, but he put the bully on her rather successfully, from the look of it."

"Does this mean that we're still safe to put all our money on her?"

Jack kicked the end of the wood pile. "Not in the slightest. He just surprised her. Next time she might just as easily bite back and go sideways. Horses are *so* much like women, Zachary! Nothing is ever predictable, but disaster is always close at hand."

I shrugged, took a long drink of my cool coffee. "Well," I whispered, "I'd say the next step for us is obvious . . ."

Jack raised one eyebrow.

There was a pause then, until Cook carried a basin of water out the back door to throw it out on the ground. I leaned forward. "How much money will it take to convince Billy Horne to withdraw his services?"

Jack gave a wan smile. "I don't know, but I agree with your train of thought," he replied calmly. "As a matter of fact, I've arranged dinner with the young man tonight."

"I'm not above an investment in practical bribery."

"Thank you, Zachary, and it really would be an investment, you know. If the famous jockey disappeared, the gamblers would take notice. It would change the odds on the race. Miss Deception would be far less favoured, and we'd win some of that money back with Christy in the saddle." He scowled. "Although for me, it's honestly more a matter of principle."

I nodded as if I were in total agreement, but in truth for me it was about money.

Another thought came to me. "But you say Christy's already gone, so what does it matter what we do?"

"Well," replied Jack, leaning back in his chair, "the boy's not gone yet. I told him I'd buy him lunch at the Goblet and Gander."

"It's actually the Gander and Goblet . . ."

"I've done due research and checked that the place carries liquor distilled in Ireland, so we will make more use of the goblet than the gander and ensure that our friend remains in town until it's too late to start off for Sooke today."

"Ah!"

"He should be nestled on my couch by mid-afternoon, in plenty of time for me to rest up for our dinner with Billy Horne. We'll need money and liquor—plenty of both—and we'll have one shot at convincing him. You will come along, won't you?"

"I should be able to come to dinner with Horne, but you're on your own with Christy. My esteemed uncle Boon is arriving back from the mainland sometime today, and I should be here to greet him."

"That's just fine. Dinner it is. I'll be drinking with Christy most of the day if things go according to plan, and although I have no intention of matching the lad stride for stride, I might be a bit unsteady during dinner. If I collapse forward and my face lands in the soup, I want you there to pull me out before I drown."

THE VENERABLE BOON Ten Jing did indeed arrive just after noon, with his entourage, walking single file up the hill. I happened to be out in the side yard, so I spotted him and was the first to greet him. He smiled broadly and made the slight bow that is traditional. I bobbed a bit myself as I tipped my hat, and we shook hands. He was the sort of man who shook your hand for about ten full seconds before he released it.

As to our relationship, I was never sure exactly what was either accurate or proper. I always referred to him as Uncle Boon, although he was actually my father in-law's uncle, making him a cousin of some sort to me,

I would think. When I addressed him directly, I spoke to him simply as Boon, which I suspect was improper according to the mysterious laws of Chinese etiquette, but I was never corrected, and I suppose the man was gracious enough to let it pass unremarked. I never understood him fully, but I admired him, in a way, and from a distance, and after the incident where I dragged his son out of the ocean, I think I was a bit of a hero in his eyes.

"Greetings, Uncle. Welcome, Boon," I spoke slowly and clearly.

"Greetings. Thank you, Mr. Zachary. I am so glad to be back here in Victoria colony and off the ship always rocking and now dry on the land!"

He was closely followed by one of his servants, looking rather odd by carrying a very nice embroidered chair with polished wooden arms in front of him. I thought at first that it might be a gift to us, but it was in fact a new chair, purchased on the mainland, that let him feel comfortable with his chronically sore back. The rest of their luggage was being towed up the hill on a cart well behind them. The man carrying the chair was one of his two valets—the shorter one, whose duties covered general assignments and manual labour. Behind him came the second personal assistant, a tall fellow with an even taller polished bald head that gave him, to my eyes, the appearance of an Egyptian pharaoh. He was responsible for Boon's clothing, grooming, and more personal matters.

Two steps behind came the matched set of bodyguards.

Bringing up the rear, distanced by another six paces, was the chef. He cooked always and only for Boon, which seemed a bit unnecessary, since the man never ate anything but rice and steamed white fish. Occasionally this was supplemented by some sort of clear broth. In addition to this, the cook was in charge of the whisky bottle, which was never far away, although I rarely saw my uncle actually drink very much. Another thing that I noted but never understood was the fact that this cook always preferred to stand or sit at least a few steps away from anyone else. I never knew why. Because I lived among the Chinese, my curiosity frequently went unsatisfied.

Once we were inside the hotel and greetings had been duly exchanged, Boon sat on his fine embroidered chair in the centre of the front parlour, facing White Lee and myself, side by side on the better of the sofas. His servants, our servants, and my wife all involved themselves elsewhere. I don't know where young Ross and Sarah Green were at that point. I think Boon was rather proud of his fluency in English, and the initial conversation was held with me, rather than my elder, his uncle.

"I own two hotels in San Francisco, but this one is better. You are always working all the time hard around this, I think."

"Yes, sir. We do our best. My wife is the hardest worker and the smartest at business."

"Good. But I think you and nephew Lee are maybe good at business too. Don't you think? Business all the time, working hard?"

"I don't know," I said, as I honestly didn't. Boon wasn't sure how to take the comment, so for a moment we just sat and smiled.

He projected an unusual strength, although he was physically unremarkable, and I felt that I should be careful and respectful around him—which is far from a natural inclination for me—but on the other hand, he made me feel that he was my friend. He was certainly no older than me, wearing a few wisps of hair on his upper lip that were intended to serve as a moustache, but everyone naturally deferred to him in matters of experience and wisdom. He dressed impeccably, with heavy gold cufflinks and bracelet, and he was invariably surrounded by servants, but his demeanour was that of a common fellow, and he often showed his impatience at being attended upon.

"And yourself, Boon? You are well? Your business is good?"

"Business is always good," he replied. "My family is always good, and my wife is good, and my son. I don't forget my son and you saved him when he is in danger. I don't forget." Then he turned off his smile. "My health is good except for my painful back, which is always bad."

"I'm very sorry to hear that. Back pain is a terrible thing, I understand. It's quite constant?"

"Quite constant. Yes. Quite. All the time quite constant. And nothing to help, although I try and try. What do I have in San Francisco? These American doctors? Very nice, thank you, but your doctors are all very new at arts of medicine. Not like my country, where knowledge is very old. And what do I have from China? Doctors who are cast away! Not good enough, too stupid, so send them off to America to look after poor Boon!"

"Are you comfortable now? Can I get you something?"

He placed his hands on the arms of his chair and the broad smile returned. "I am very well now. Thank you."

At this point, White Lee, whose English after many years was still not as good as his nephew's, interjected a question in Chinese—evidently a query about business. Boon replied politely in English, as if to remind him which language was currently in use. "Business? Yes, business is good, because silk and rice are always desired in these Western countries of America. A bit of opium sometimes. Then good rifles, machines, needles and pins—always desired in Canton." I knew he was a trader, an importer and exporter, but little else. "And now I have ships of my own! Two ships. The small one is coming to Victoria to carry myself back home after the horse race! You will see it. Also I have some goods for Hudson Bay Company and so on. Ships. That is a good thing. I did not have ships before. I worry to buy them, because what do I know? About ships? Nothing!" The three of us laughed, as if at a tremendous, self-explanatory joke. "But ships is simple. Just keep the water out. Silk and rice? Keep the water out. Ploughs and knives and needles and pins? Just keep the water out. And all of life, as well, I have learned. Build a good house? Keep the water out. Good hat? Good coat? They are going to keep that water out. And what about a good glass of whisky? Keep the water out!"

We all laughed loudly, although I suspect that Lee was mainly laughing because of Boon's story-telling ability and missed much of the content of the joke.

There was another suspicion, one possibly invented by me, that opium was a more major commodity contributing to Boon's success, but that might have been unfounded, based only on the fact that a number of wealthy Chinese men owed their fortunes to the growing appetite for opium and laudanum among Westerners as well as Orientals. It was a legal venture, but sometimes it allied itself to less savoury endeavours. Opium and prostitutes. Opium and crime. So polite white society considered it a very distasteful vice. As if to fortify this suspicion of mine, Boon continued with news that there was a certain amount of violence at the moment in San Francisco's Chinese business circles. "A tong war. Maybe all finished by the time I go home."

"A war? I know we have tongs here in Victoria, but I've not heard of violence . . ." I understood these organizations to be something between benevolent societies and private security firms.

"Maybe you got good tongs, no bother, no fights. In my city, some of these people got all heavy fighting over prostitutes and gambling and such bad things."

"And you . . . ?"

"I don't need some tong to protect me. I got trusted men, I got guards and servants. I got Canton Company and Six Companies, and I am a Sam Yup, most important thing of all. You cannot sell in San Francisco if you are not a Sam Yup. You cannot buy in Canton if you are not a Sam Yup. No tong for me. I trust my own men."

He turned in his chair as he said this and beamed a smile in the general direction of the two bodyguards who were now taking their ease on the front porch, although one of them was keeping half an eye on us through the window. He was at the ready as soon as Boon turned toward him, but he saw at a glance that he was not required. My uncle liked to keep his staff at just this distance. I wondered what people passing on the street would make of this pair of strong and stately fellows, who seemed not to speak or understand a single word of English—who rarely seemed to speak at all, in fact. Their demeanour was strictly Oriental, but they dressed almost identically in an odd amalgam of clothing—loose Chinese blouses, tucked into their trousers in the Western fashion, with neck scarves and boots of the sort that American cowboys wear. If the intention of this uniform was to draw attention to their vigilant presence, it certainly succeeded.

My wife returned to the parlour at this point, ushering in the downstairs girl with a tea tray. I decided it was time for the meeting to be allowed to carry on in a different language, so I excused myself and made my way up the stairs. I paused on the first landing, looking down on a scene that was both pleasing and at the same time vaguely unsettling to me. The three of them conversed calmly and amiably, while the downstairs girl lingered in the doorway, eavesdropping inconspicuously. The two big men stood on the porch outside the window. It was regrettable that my part in this tableau would always be peripheral. I spoke only a few words of Cantonese and had no hope of learning the language properly, but it was more than this. I was always aware, in the presence of my Chinese friends and relatives, that I might very well be sitting incorrectly or speaking at the wrong time or disgracefully ignoring something.

I did not belabour the point in my mind, though. I had an appointment with Jack Elliston and Billy Horne to prepare for.

THE CELESTIAL HOTEL was just the right size for my purposes—big enough to carry its own weight and small enough to allow me to remain inconspicuous—but if I was ambitious, I would probably have endeavoured to build my hotel into something resembling The Westminster on Yates Street. It was a solid brick and timber place, large, well built and well furnished, and in addition to its rooms, it maintained a public dining room that was open for supper from six o'clock until nine. There was also a saloon bar (foul language, fighting, and women not permitted) that did not close its doors until midnight. If one chose to linger over the remains of supper, drinks could be ordered and brought from the bar.

It was here that Billy Horne had been given lodgings, which, as Jack and I took places at a table around six-thirty, prompted me to comment that Mac Bingham was being pretty free with his money these days.

"Not just for Billy Horne, either," he informed me. "You and I will be eating on Mac's tab, as well, since our alleged reason for being here is to assure that the famous man is at ease and wanting nothing here in Victoria."

"All my best to the benevolent Bingham then," I toasted with an empty glass. "As an idle thought," I asked Jack, "what do we do if Billy says he wants a woman?"

At that point a waiter bustled over to our table and asked if we wanted something to drink while we waited for our friend. (Another servant had already been sent upstairs to inform Horne of our arrival.) Jack called for whisky—a full bottle. "We have a lot to discuss," he explained.

When the bottle had arrived and we had sampled it, I asked after Christy. "Did it go as you'd planned?"

"Pretty much. Not altogether pleasant. Over the course of the afternoon, he progressed from anger to self-pity without getting into a fight and without starting to weep. He drank enthusiastically though, and he'll sleep long and soundly before he's up to travel, whether it be homeward bound or bound for the finish line."

"And yourself, Jack? Are you still up to some serious swallowing? We should probably lead Mr. Billy Horne well into the middle of this whisky before we broach the subject of him taking our money and getting out of town. Do you have the stamina to drink with a new partner this late in the day?"

"Of course. It's one of my gifts. I'm practically stone sober." I accepted this without contradiction, although I thought I detected that his eyes no longer travelled at precisely the same speed as the rest of his head. "I am a noted expert on the art of drinking. That's the way you can tell me and my brother apart. He preaches. I drink."

I gazed up at the impressively expansive chandelier. "I wonder why Mac doesn't hold all his little meetings here, rather than the Celestial?" I mused.

"Oh, no! He knows that there's a time to be ostentatious and a time when you'd best just whisper behind the bushes." Then, "Sorry, Zachary. I didn't mean to imply that your hotel was anything but . . ."

"I understand completely, Jack. Look. Here's Billy Horne."

He had the smooth stride of an equestrian, as opposed to a jockey, and he was dressed impeccably in a very pale grey suit with a red rose boutonniere. He also affected two silver watch chains across his vest and black soft leather riding boots with heels significant enough to bring him almost up to an average height. Without them, the man was no more than five feet six inches. I also noted that, true to Jack's description, he was carrying a lot more weight than you would desire in a jockey.

"Good evening, gents." His smile was as carefully tailored as the rest of his attire. We answered him with robust greetings, and Jack immediately leaned forward with the whisky bottle. To our horror, he covered the glass with his hand. "None for me, thank you." He saw our surprise and laughed. "Don't worry. All the more for you two. Hey now!" The waiter had arrived with a tall bottle of mineral water. "They already know what

I want here! That's great, isn't it? This is a great place, yes it is. To your health, gents."

We returned his watery toast, each of us taking a pretty stiff jolt, as we considered what to say. Much of our strategy depended upon the abuse of alcohol. Most men can be tempted into a bit of good, honest fraud, given enough liquor to assist in the self-justification, but mineral water does nothing to build up a fellow's venal leanings.

"I have nothing against whisky," he continued. "I just don't take it myself. Do you want to hear a secret?" He leaned forward. "I've never actually tasted the stuff! Can you believe it?" He laughed—a little too much, I thought, for a sober man. Face to face at a short distance, I saw that he was older than I had originally thought—forty years or close to it.

The waiter was standing a step away, ready to receive instructions. They offered both roast beef and roast chicken along with vegetables. I chose chicken. Jack took the beef. Our guest ordered five scrambled eggs with fried potatoes. There was a wait of about twenty minutes, during which Jack and I gulped whisky and Billy Horne sipped at his water. We chatted. The other two discussed racetracks and racers, horses, and breeds of horses, while I became more and more uncomfortable and impatient. I stared at the portly Mr. Horne and tried my best to visualize him riding Miss Deception to victory and thus ensuring my financial stability for the near future. I couldn't see it. I felt flushed from too much quick whisky in an overheated room and, no longer able to hold my tongue, I stammered a bit as I burst into the conversation.

"Mr. Horne. Billy. That is, Billy, listen. Let's get this over with. We have something to ask you." I saw Jack hold up a hand to try to stop me, but I carried on. "We don't know how much Mac Bingham is paying you to ride Miss Deception, but we'll double the amount if you'll just claim to be sick and let us return to the rider we originally intended." His face was expressionless. Jack looked casually away. Billy Horne stared at me for about twenty seconds as if I were a complete stranger. Past his shoulder, I saw two waiters arriving with our meals. As they placed them on the table, Horne got to his feet.

"Gentlemen," he said softly, sweeping imaginary creases from his vest. "Good evening." Without another word or any look behind him, he strode away.

JACK AND I finished our drinks, staring at each other in silence. I started to apologize, but he brushed it away. "At least now we know," he said. He ate his beef and I my chicken, hardly noticing whether it tasted good or bad. Then a bit more whisky.

The last guest, apart from ourselves, was just leaving. He was a burly gentleman, a bit bent over and looking the worse for wear, but the waiter held the door open for him and bowed as he left, before coming across to our table.

"Bit of a celebrity there," he informed us, looking back toward the door. "Mr. Billy Barker himself—founder of the great gold rush city up north."

I was surprised. "I thought he'd gone bust."

The waiter nodded sadly. "Pretty close. The mines he bought all went bust. His marriage went bust. I suppose his wife still has some money and a lot of people he once called his friends, but such is life. Still, he was a good and a generous customer when he was rich, so I think he deserves a bit of respect now that he's . . ." He shrugged. "Can I get you gentlemen anything else?"

He left us the bill, Jack counted out some money, and we departed, shaking hands sadly in the street before we went our separate directions.

I walked home thinking about Billy Barker, whose hole in the ground beside Williams Creek reputedly dished out more than thirty thousand ounces of gold, most of which he brought to Victoria. I wondered where it all went—or for that matter, where was all the gold that *I* had brought back from the goldfields? I knew the answer to that, though. The question that remained was whether *I* would end up as a bent-backed pauper, or if not a pauper, a pathetic impoverished hotelier eating the leftover food from the plates of his guests. Once again there was a sick twist in my stomach.

I had thought this through several times already. If I didn't wager virtually all my money on this race and thereby double it, I would be reduced to some sort of manual labour within a very short time.

And now it appeared that my once seemingly secure wager was to be placed on an aging runt who ate too much, drank too little, and didn't see the good value of a dishonest dollar.

THAT NIGHT, WHEN it was time to retire, I sat on the bed and watched Sue while she perched in front of her mirror, applying complex layers of scented creams and lotions on her face, her hands, her feet. It took several minutes for her to complete this ritual and inspect the results, then I called her to sit beside me on the bed. I had something to say. She was puzzled as she came to my side, recognizing the unusual and emotional tone of my request.

I opened my mouth several times, but I did not speak. I could not speak. I could find no words. I could not even decide whether I wished to profess my love to her or to confess my dreadful guilt. After years of withholding the truth from her, I would of course have to admit my guilt as a liar in order to protest my innocence as a murderer. I think, though, that more than this, I merely wanted to describe to her how perfect and serenely beautiful she was to me. But I could not find the words. As wordy a fool as I am, I could find no place to start. So I said nothing, and for a while we sat in silence, her head against my shoulder.

AFTER BREAKFAST IN the morning, I went out to observe the builders who were going to be erecting the new shed. The crew was composed of only three men—the foreman, one labourer, and the stonemason who would set the cornerstones. There were string lines and levels run out like a spider's web, and I didn't understand much of what I saw, but I felt obligated to argue with them for a while since I was paying the bill, and I did so at length.

Re-entering the house after my discussion with the builders, I found that Mac Bingham and his party had arrived for another of their organizers' meetings. I was presented with an unexpected and intriguing scene. In the front parlour, Bingham himself was standing with my uncle Boon, formal and face to face. The aspect that immediately struck me was that Mac was showing respect to an Oriental man. I would not have considered that possible. He was listening intently, with furrowed brow, as Boon expounded softly, sedately about the best arrangements for placing wagers on the race. The words I heard as I opened the door were cool and even, but related that he hoped he had not wasted his time in making the trip north from San Francisco.

"Part of my thinking, you see, was that this be a game where men with very good strong mind play the game with weight of money. Heavy money. Is that proper English words?"

"I know what you mean, Mr. Boon. And I don't believe you've wasted a trip. There are a number of us who plan to put some serious money on the line. Heavy money, if you wish."

"But Mr. Bingham, I am happy and brave to bet, but where is my wisdom if I give such money to bookmakers I do not know? Who knows who? They have capital maybe. Maybe they just disappear . . ."

I did not want to be part of this conversation, but I enjoyed what I heard. My uncle had put Mac Bingham on the defensive.

"I assure you, Mr. Boon, that we have plans for carefully managed betting that would be every bit as, uh, carefully managed as anything you are used to seeing back down in, hmm . . ."

I slipped off my shoes and crept down the hallway past the entrance to the back parlour. Looking in as I passed, I saw that the rest of Mac's company were already assembled and waiting. I think a couple of them were looking out and eavesdropping on the same conversation as was I. Jack was not among them; these were the more well-heeled of the rogues. Someone was pouring whisky into glasses. Drinking one's whisky out of a glass is about as much decorum as can be expected from the horse race mob.

"Very, very much delighted that such man as you, Mr. Bingham, is taking hands in this. Forgive me this presuming and speaking and suggesting detail to you, but in San Francisco I learn some things because of all the heavy money, they are very careful."

"Please, please, go ahead! We heed the voice of more experienced gentlemen and we do indeed know the importance of every detail."

I wondered idly if Bingham realized he had just referred to Boon as a gentleman.

"Well, since it is my opportunity, so much my pleasure! Perhaps I must describe such fine system used in south California only September past. Desert Fall Competition."

As he proceeded to relate details of the system, I made my way into the kitchen, where I drank remnants of warm coffee, leaning against the small table. I noticed, looking back, that a number of heads were now turned to the conversation from the back parlour. They would never dream of having a Chinaman actually sit in on their meeting, but they recognized superior knowledge when they heard it.

A few minutes later, the parlour door closed behind Bingham, and Boon ambled casually to the kitchen, where he stood facing me in the doorway. For a long moment, he smiled benevolently in my direction, and I smiled broadly in return.

"This Victoria is very pleasant place," he offered.

"Yes, it is," I agreed, "and for once the weather is nice. Would you care to take tea outside in the sunshine?"

"Most certainly, Mr. Zachary."

"Jade May," I called, "would you make tea, please, and bring it out to the back porch." Jade May was Cook's niece, and she was now sitting at the dining room table, looking out the window. She was an unstable little thread of a girl, but she was still helpful from time to time. Boon and I repaired to the back porch, where we drew two chairs into the full sun with a crate between us that would serve as a table. I slouched out into a full stretch. He closed his eyes and turned his face skyward. After a minute, he spoke softly.

"Those men inside are already drinking whisky, and not even eleven o'clock. Is this common for Victoria people?"

I took my time in answering. "Not really common. But it's coming up to the race. And the weather is fine. There's actually heat in that sunshine." I undid my top buttons and removed my stockings. Jade May arrived with a teapot and cups on a tray.

"Here. I'll take these cups, girl, but I made a mistake. I gave you the wrong instructions. We don't want tea. We want whisky. Can you find the bottle in the high cupboard in the dining room and bring it to us, please?"

When we were once again indolently exposed to the sun, and the first little porcelain cups filled with liquor, I turned to Boon. "You amaze me, sir," I told him.

He did not look down from the sky or open his eyes. "I amuse you?"

"You amuse me only when you choose to. But you amaze me continually."

Perhaps an hour later we heard the bustle of people preparing lunches inside the kitchen behind us, but we were perched at a spot that was not visible from within. We heard someone being sent upstairs to find us, and the sound of that person returning unsuccessfully. We could not be found, apparently. We did not stir, did not move, apart from the motion of bringing cup to lip. Another segment of time passed, as did several little cups of liquor. It was turning into an exceptionally long week, as far as drinking went. I thought I might go up to my room to rest from the exertions of the morning, so I stood, took my leave, and re-entered the hotel with my stockings in one hand.

The racing committee was gone. My wife was assisting the front desk boy in greeting new arrivals—a trio of Canadian men who would share the last room we had available until after the race. My son, Ross, was kneeling beside the low table under the far window, laboriously putting pencil to paper under the guidance of Sarah Green. She looked up as I made my way toward the stairs and raised a tentative hand in my direction.

Her expression betrayed a mixture of emotions, none of them desirable. She showed anxiety, confusion, regret, and fear, all at once, without speaking a word. When I approached, she seemed of two minds—whether to speak out a world of worries or to say nothing at all. Then her eyes fell away to the floor at her feet, her breath caught an odd rhythm, and she rubbed one hand against the other. I recognized this posture.

"Miss Green?" I asked. I spoke softly, as I was aware of the registering guests only a few steps behind me.

"Mr. Zachary." She stuttered. "Mr. Zachary. I believe I've made a bad mistake."

Standing there before her like a barefoot beggar, I felt inadequate and confused. I would have liked to refer the obviously distraught woman to Sue's attention, but my wife was otherwise engaged. Sarah looked like a stiff wind would blow her apart, but she was holding herself calm behind a façade of dignity.

"Would you, that is, do you have an idea where Mr. Elliston might be? I've made a bad mistake. I don't know why. Honestly . . ."

Her speech ended in the middle of a quavering word. I told Ross to continue with what he was doing and led Miss Green to the relative privacy of the two tall chairs in front of the bookshelves. We sat and I waited. After a moment or two, she was able to regain enough composure to tell me about her contract with Mac Bingham. When she was finished, I agreed that Jack might be the one to advise her properly. I knew nothing about legal contracts, except that they became more and more abundant in the world now that trust and honour were disappearing from society. After instructing Ross to bring a book and read to Sarah for a while, I snatched up my hat and went looking for Jack Elliston.

At the boarding house, I found Avery, who told me that his brother had gone out with Christy Riordan, but if I wished to wait, they should be returning soon.

"They're calling on that Billy Horne fellow," he told me, "ostensibly to wish him well and claim no hard feelings, but I wouldn't be surprised if our friend Christy intends to advise him on strategy."

"I don't think Mr. Horne will take advice on that count. He seems to believe that you need to whip a horse from starting line to finish line."

"Well, Jack is there to referee, should fisticuffs break out."

Avery lit his pipe and smoked it in the sunshine next to the window of their little sitting room. "Did you have something urgent to discuss with him, Mr. Zachary? You seem a bit agitated, if I might say so."

"Urgent? Maybe. Maybe. And confidential as well. What we really need is wisdom, my learned friend. Would you mind hearing the matter out?"

He raised his eyebrows. "Confidential? I haven't had many people confide in me lately. Still, if you're going to tell one Elliston brother, you might as well tell them all. As for wisdom—don't count on much of that. I try to be kind and gentle in lieu of being wise."

"Come now, Avery."

"I could tell you stories that would prove my point, but sometimes a man should observe a certain confidentiality regarding his own history."

"This is about Sarah Green."

"Miss Green?" Suddenly I had his attention.

"I won't go into the background of it—I don't think that's necessary—but the nub of it is that she decided to leave my employ. Leave us at the Celestial."

"Really? I thought she seemed quite happy. She seemed admirably suited . . ."

"I made her angry, and rightly enough. I pried into her background. No business of mine, and if I'd just kept my mouth shut about what I learned instead of crowing about it to her face, well, maybe it would have been all right. I didn't realize it was so important to her, this secret. It didn't seem so bad to me. I told her that right away."

"A secret," Avery murmured through the pipe smoke. "Terrible diseases, these secrets . . ."

"I suppose I had the idea that this secret was something like a boil under your skin. You lance it. A little jab of pain, very quick. Then you clean it up and everything is fine."

"But it wasn't your secret to lance, Zachary, nor yours to choose the time and place. You don't understand this, because you don't have any great secrets to hide."

I let this pass and continued with my explanation. "As it happened, she had an opportunity waiting in the wings, so to speak, and on the spur of the moment—partly to sting back at me, I think—she rashly accepted it."

"An opportunity?"

"Mac Bingham. He wants a new personal assistant. Fed up with that man Roselle, I guess. He offered her the position while I was out of town, and he left it open. I return, I blunder, and she immediately sends word to him that she will accept his offer. Damn it, Avery! I have an ugly feeling, and I hope I'm wrong, but I have an ugly feeling about the man's intentions. I can't help but think that Bingham expects more to come out of this arrangement than just someone to write his letters and purchase his shirt collars."

"Does Miss Green suspect this as well? Did she suggest that Mr. Bingham . . . ? Did he say anything that would . . . ?"

"She said nothing concrete, but she's not a schoolgirl. Nor am I. These contracts can be like spiderwebs . . ."

Avery leaned forward, concerned now. "There's a written contract?"

"That's the problem, you see. They put it all down on paper, supposedly for her protection, but now time has passed, she's calmed down a bit, and she went back to him. She tried to cancel everything. He laughed in her face."

Avery was appalled. "He laughed in her face?"

"Well," I admitted, "at least he told her in no uncertain terms that he would be holding her to it. He claims he would take legal action if it was necessary. Now Sarah can't risk that. There are certain things that have taken place in the past . . ."

"Her secret."

"Yes, well, she couldn't countenance any litigation. Enough said about that. So now she's trapped, as far as she can see. And she's terrified."

"I understand."

"She blames herself, but it's my foolishness that precipitated the whole mess. And I have no idea how to help her. Contracts! That's the sort of thing that caused my quick exit from law school."

"And did Miss Green voice the idea that my brother might have some advice?"

"Yes, she did. Jack knows the background to this, so . . ."

"Jack knows her secret?"

I slapped myself on the forehead. "Yes, he does. I wasn't happy just making a fool of myself—I had to drag Jack into it! I meant well, Avery. Honestly. I thought I could see a certain, well, a certain affection growing between the two of them . . ."

"As have I. Jack has very strong feelings for her. I know that."

As if on cue, Jack Elliston's boots sounded down the hall. I braced myself.

IT TOOK ONLY a minute to bring Jack up to date on things. He took a deep breath and assumed a stolid expression.

"Well," he sighed, "what's been done can always be undone. Or nearly always undone. Usually, at least. Sometimes." A short bark of a laugh. "This time, at any rate! We shall see that things are set right. Bingham owes me a favour or two, I warrant, and if necessary, I'll just demand that he cancel the contract. Then we'll see how things stand with Miss Green." He grinned like a schoolboy. "She turned to me in time of trouble! Think of that!"

He continued. "Avery, my brother! I have to ask you to step into the gap for me. Seeing Christy off on his way back home took me longer than expected. He and Billy Horne had to debate the merits of the whip—I should have expected that—and now I'm bloody late. I have to be at the track an hour ago for these training runs. I've been made a steward—did I tell you that, Zachary? Go see Sarah, would you please, Avery? On with your boots and off you go! Like that fellow who took the good news from Ghent to Aix. Only faster. Tell Miss Green that all will be well, and I'll see her in an hour, or maybe two. As soon as I can get away. Tell her not to fret. Zachary—come with me. I have a boy holding our horses downstairs."

"Old Peter? You've got Old Peter down in the street?"

"Of course not," he replied as we stomped down the boarding house stairs. "If we took Old Peter out to the track, the other horses would probably refuse to run until the old beast was removed. I thought I would be collecting Avery, so I have the horse he normally rides. Don't worry—she's a sedate old mare with a very clerical spirit. She won't run out from beneath you."

We started at a brisk pace down Government Street, and I soon discovered that I rather liked Avery's horse. She was a patchy grey colour and she had quite enough spirit for me.

"Training runs . . . ?"

"Practice runs, sort of," Jack informed me.

"Do they always have training runs? Do the horses really need to practice?"

"Not always. Not normally. This isn't for the benefit of the horses. This is to show them off to the bettors and to lubricate those fools' purses. Advertising, Zachary!"

The streets of Victoria were lively, and I had no doubt that the upcoming race was to be credited for the festive air that I noted. A few more people bustling about, with slightly broader smiles, speaking slightly louder, dressed just a bit more brightly. It all adds up to a tangible sensation, particularly on a bright spring day. I found myself riding with a particularly straight posture, tipping my hat to strangers. As we passed Dennison's, I noticed a one-horse carriage in front of us moving in the same direction. It was the kind they call a whiskey, with a red canvas top that obscured the driver until we were actually passing him, whereupon we saw that it was the bleached-white man who called himself Danny, the rider of the big stallion. He hailed us with a wave of his white top hat.

"Hello. I know you two. You're on the team with Bingham, aren't you?"

We pulled in close, Jack on one side, I on the other. It was somewhat difficult to hear him over the noise of the wheels on the hard roadway. "Well, a bit yes and a bit no," Jack called back. "We helped a bit with the organizing, and we know the horse that's bound to beat you. Zachary's just a spectator, and I've been appointed a steward for this particular race."

Danny barked out an ironic laugh. "Really? A steward? If I didn't know better, I'd suspect you weren't all that impartial, brother!"

Jack answered with a laugh of his own. "Isn't it fair that the organizer of the challenge should have a representative on the Stewards Committee? And not to worry—I'm a fair man. Accused of all sorts of shortcomings and misdeeds, but everyone agrees that I'm fair-minded." He pointed at the shuffling nag that drew the carriage. "You'd get to Beacon Hill faster if you hitched your shay up to that stallion of yours."

Danny smiled and shook his head. "No, I don't think so. If you ever managed to hook Ojai up to this thing, he'd either bust the axle when he took off or bounce me out of this seat into the road."

I interjected a question. "Your men—the dark fellows—they're already at the track, I suppose?"

"Yes, they are. And they'd better have that horse brushed and saddled properly when I get there, or I'll skin the lot of them. Bunch of idiots."

"I would have thought your mysterious owner would have a better crew of minders for such a proud animal," Jack suggested.

"No," Danny answered with a gleaming glance. "These are not horse boys. That's not their main job. They're here for after the race, just in case your Mr. Bingham tries to cheat me out of my winnings. Then I send them over to burn his house down." He smiled broadly. "Or in case some steward tries to cross me." He winked at Jack. "You must give me your address, brother."

There was a bit of stilted laughter before he added, "All in jest, of course. All in jest!"

After that, we resumed speed and left the whiskey behind us. In spite of his rude manner, there was something about this Danny that rather appealed to me. When we arrived at Beacon Hill some minutes later, Jack drew up to the edge of the clearing at Miss Deception's enclosure and called for one of Bingham's farmhands to take our mounts. "Get these two some water," he instructed, "but no need to unsaddle them. We won't be long." Then turning to me abruptly, he slapped the side of his head and exclaimed, "Damn it, Zachary. I haven't told you about dinner. You're engaged for dinner tonight. Seven o'clock at Lloyd Bingham's. I'll come fetch you and we can ride out together. Wear something decent, won't you?"

"What? I don't do that sort of thing—dinners at people's fancy houses!"

He grimaced. "I was afraid you'd say something like that, but I won't have it. I promised the old man I'd get you there. Dinner for the whole team, night before the race."

"The whole team? I'm not part of any team."

"You and I are a team, man! I need someone to count my whiskies and hold me in check."

"Take Avery then."

"He has prior commitments. Saving souls, as likely as not. Come on— the food will be good, the liquor will be free, and the company will be bad, except for me. Two hours at the most, then I'll claim you have a case of the vapours and whisk you off before the dancing girls get there. Do this for me, won't you?"

"Why would the Binghams want me there? I just gave them space at the hotel for a few meetings. Made them bring their own whisky!"

He put his hand on my arm and walked me slowly toward the rest of the group. "They give you credit for bringing in all these new Chinese bettors, and for setting up this whole new betting arrangement. Actually they give your uncle Boon credit, but they can't very well invite a Chinaman to dinner—not the bloody Binghams—so you have to represent your uncle."

"I don't know anything about Boon's wonderful system."

"Oh, it's not exactly new, but the committee here had just assumed things would run like the little local races, and everybody would have private wagers, or lay a bet with one of these gents who act out of a little black book. They just weren't thinking, really. Now Boon has them centralizing the wagers at a neutral post, with winnings divided up and paid out properly after the race. He has bank tellers conscripted from that little fat fellow's bank registering everything very carefully, and all the money held at that structure they built to be the governor's podium."

"The governor's podium?"

"The old blighter wasn't going to come anyway."

"And all that money will be safe there?"

"They've hired the Victoria Fire Department to protect it. Stout fellows all, you can imagine."

"Really?"

"They paid the firemen with two kegs of beer, and they get to watch the race from a wonderful vantage point."

"They'll entrust the money to a bunch of drunken firemen? You know they'll all be drunk."

"Of course they need one sober person to oversee the firemen."

As Jack started toward the serious-looking gents in top hats, I asked one more question. "But why does this new gambling arrangement please the Binghams so much? What's in it for them?"

"Boon informed them that down south the administrators of the event take ten per cent of the wagers to pay out prizes and cover the costs—of the bank tellers and the firemen, I presume. Bingham will be spared the need to shell out any money at all." Then, just as he started to turn away, he remembered something. "And there's some other reason the old man made me promise you'd be there. I don't know what it is exactly, but there's something the old man needs to tell you in private. Not Mac, it's Lloyd you have to see at some point before we take our leave after dinner."

"But I've never even met Lloyd Bingham."

A quick wave, and Jack was gone. I strolled away looking for a spot to sit, but first I wandered across the trampled grass to the roped off area where most of the spectators' horses were being kept. I spotted Jack's Commissioner at a glance, tethered with a number of others to a line strung between a pair of pine trees. He looked marvellous when you stood him up in a row with a bunch of more pedestrian steeds, and when I approached him, he seemed to recognize me, nickering softly and lowering his head when I ran my hand down his neck. I couldn't help but speak aloud to him, chatting lightly about what idiots humans are when they get together in groups. I often don't respect horses as I should. I tend to avoid them, when possible. When I was a lad of ten, I happened to see one of my young friends have his finger bitten completely off in one snap by a temperamental mule, and I'm afraid that the experience left me with a permanent suspicion of all creatures with the same basic shape. This caused me no end of trouble and embarrassment during my brief tenure as a Pinkerton man, during which I was constantly being forced to introduce myself to new equine partners, all of whom seemed like potential assassins. It may well have contributed to my decision to leave that career. The Commissioner—graceful, strong, and well-behaved—was the exception to this generality.

Then, as I considered leaving, I decided I should at least say hello to Avery's mare, the one who had carried me thus far, and I turned to the big grey tethered behind me. Perhaps I reached out to the animal too abruptly, but it immediately took offence, rolling its big eyes wide, raising its head high, and tilting its weight back as if it wanted to rear. I am not the only person to have noted that horses holding that particular attitude look very much as if they might be able to breathe fire. As I backed away, I happened to glance between the beast's rear legs, to discover equipment that I knew Avery's mare did not possess. I had greeted the wrong grey.

From there, I went back to the track. There must have been a hundred or more spectators come to watch the practice running, and that number again of people who were involved or appeared to be involved with one or another of the racers. There were flower vendors, musicians strumming away, and boys rolling tea carts across the bumpy ground. Standing at the rail, I was approached by an anxious bookmaker, made more aggressive now by the competition with the new wagering system in place for the challenge. He assured me that he would be paying at better odds than the "official blokes," but I told him I wasn't a gambling man. The breeze brought me, among other things, the smell of meat boiling at one of the vendor's stands. I find that odour repulsive, which is strange, because the aroma of baking meat is quite wonderful. For some reason, boiling flesh smells like something to be served to starving prisoners in a jail—an image that I do not like to entertain.

I ducked under the rail, crossed the track, and found a grassy spot on the hill, now spotted with groups of racegoers, where I could sit. The first pair of runners was just lining up at the far end of the front stretch. At that distance, I couldn't tell at first which horses they were, but I recognized a familiar face sitting close by and asked him what was going on.

"They're running two at a time, just to let the horses get a feel for the track. It doesn't matter much."

His name was Alain Dubois, and I knew him as a cook at one of the other hotels similar to my own. In spite of his name, he was not French, but rather from a New York Dutch family originally named Baice. They changed their surname solely because it sounded nicer, which admittedly it does.

"It's that big black matched up with the Nanaimo horse," he continued. "There they go!"

Once pointed out, the horse called Ojai was easily recognized, and she looked formidable, even at a distance.

"Are they actually racing against each other?" I asked Dubois.

"Well, I think they want to try to get a bit of the measure of each other," he answered, "but it doesn't count for anything. Look at the way the black is running, though!"

Danny had taken a lead of about one length on the other horse and now ran along about six feet off the inside rail. Twice the Nanaimo horse tried to advance through this six-foot gap, but each time, Danny would pull his horse back in to cut them off. If they wanted to try to overtake them, they would have to go far wide, and Ojai looked as if she had plenty in reserve if they tried to go by that longer route. He kept the lead almost casually all down the stretch, slowing down to general applause from the spectators.

"Bloody hell!" Dubois shouted. "That's a horse!"

It was definitely impressive. Even I could tell that Ojai had expended only a small part of its energy to run away with it. "But the practice runs mean nothing, do they, Alain?"

"No, of course not," he admitted. "They arrange them at courses like this to encourage the local breeders and ranchers and farmers. In some of the regular races, there's horses might never have been on a real track before—never felt what it was like to be side to side with an angry stranger." He shook his head. "But that black looks like he'll be tough to beat—that's the word by me!"

The next pair ran a few minutes later—the local horse and the one from the mainland. As soon as they started, you could tell they had agreed not to make a race of it. They ran hard and smooth, but side by side in perfect rhythm. At the end of the stretch they slowed together, and you could see the jockeys talking calmly together as they cantered off toward their separate enclosures. The betting public learned little by watching that subdued display.

Almost at once the next two horses were cantering and dancing into position where they would start. Again it was Ojai, and this time he would be running against Miss Deception. Everyone on the grassy slope, including me, stood to watch. There had been plenty of gossip and a great deal of prognostication going around Victoria, and most of it had reached a consensus that these two were the horses to beat. As they prepared to run, I turned to Dubois.

"Is this the last run for the day?" I asked.

"No. They'll pair off differently next, and try to let everybody run twice. There's an odd number of runners—that's why the black is going again."

The thought came to my mind of what Jack had said the first time he saw Ojai and his company—that it might be a big mistake on Bingham's part. This was not the horse to invite to a cozy little race like ours, where they wanted to win with a maximum of fanfare and a minimum of competition. My stomach tightened and I felt a little sick.

They took off together (although from our vantage point we could hear no starter's call), and from the first stride it was apparent that this was no friendly practice run. Envisioning both Danny and Billy Horne, I could not imagine either man coming across any line—real or imaginary—in second place just because it "didn't mean anything."

Billy Horne didn't make the same mistake as the rider from Nanaimo. Miss Deception burst out like a bullet, neck and neck with the big black horse, and kept control of the inside. The people around me were all cheering and shouting, but it seemed to me as if the horses themselves were pounding their way down the course in absolute silence. The jockeys were bent forward into tightly coiled packages, neither one wavering an inch. Danny and Ojai were at their top speed now, straining to gain enough ground to edge around the smaller filly, but Miss Deception was flying like a hawk, like an arrow. To my own surprise, I felt my throat tighten with a crazy anxious pride as I watched her. She had passed the test already, I thought. She was as fast as Jack had said. If anything, as she passed us, she was nosing a little bit ahead with each stride.

Then, just as they passed our position, there came the situation that, as my friend said later, is every steward's nightmare. There is a fine line sometimes between competitive pressure and obstruction, between the ideal of close-quarters action and illegal contact. From my viewpoint—which was pretty good—nothing blatantly improper occurred.

Both jockeys had their whips out and both were swinging hard. I cringed, half expecting the filly to bolt or blunder, but she did not. Perhaps she even gained speed a little, I would reluctantly admit. I did not see either whip make contact with the wrong horse, although they were running so tight together against the rail that it would not have been impossible. I saw no appreciable physical contact between jockeys, nor did either man ever claim that there had been any. It appears to have been simply a very nasty, unpredictable accident, occurring at such a speed that it could not ever be accurately analyzed.

Billy Horne's foot caught something on the railing. What it was could not later be determined, but it caught hard, ripping him out of the saddle like the hand of the devil, and throwing him to the turf with a sound like a great sea wave dashing on the shore.

For a moment he did not move at all. Then with a bellow of pain, he tried to stand. Impossible. His leg did not have the proper appearance of a human limb—it was all limp and at wrong angles.

Miss Deception went into an obvious panic—running and spinning wildly. Men rushed toward the track from both sides. Ladies screamed, and someone collapsed not far from where I stood. At first I misinterpreted what I saw happening farther down the track, and I began to curse this fellow called Danny, as he seemed to be unwilling to stop and see what had happened. But he was keeping position with Miss Deception until both horses gradually slowed down, gradually sliding closer to the far rail about a hundred yards off—gently closing in and stopping the filly where she could be gathered up by her minders.

I spotted Jack at the edge of things, talking to three people at once, and I jogged over to his side. When he saw me, he asked me to wait where I was, then ran off to confer with another group. Ten minutes later he returned, very agitated, quite breathless.

"Zachary, I've got to go. I've got to catch Christy Riordan. I'll be back with him in a couple of hours. It could be longer."

"What? What do you mean? Isn't the whole thing over and done with?"

"That can't happen, old man. Too much already in place. Too much at stake. Christy can still ride the filly."

"But look over there! Billy Horne is half-dead!" (I believed this to be no exaggeration.) "Can we really just pick up our tools and go back to work on this thing?"

Jack grimaced. "I'm afraid so. I'm afraid so. But look—you have to talk to Sarah Green. You have to explain what happened and tell her why I couldn't come to her. Christy is already halfway home, damn it! Tell Sarah that I'll talk to her before you and I head out to Lloyd Bingham's tonight. Tell her not to worry. I'll fix things with Mac. Tell her how sorry I am and promise her . . . Damn it! Promise her anything—on my behalf. Anything!"

With that he was running hard toward the clearing where the horses were kept.

FOR A WHILE, I wasn't sure what to do. I watched while a small group of medical attendants arrived with a litter, then stood over poor Billy Horne for some time, discussing things at leisure, as if he were perfectly comfortable and they didn't want to disturb him too soon. After that, if I had not been in possession of a horse, I would have started walking home, but with the disposition of Avery's grey to be considered, I merely loitered about. There was a stream of people leaving the track, and I knew there would be an awkward muddle at the tethering area, then more congestion as the various carts and wagons were turned about and manipulated down the road away from Beacon Hill. I would wait until the worst of it was past. As I ambled my way upstream, I passed the enclosure assigned to the black horse.

Ojai himself was being blanketed and brushed by a couple of the dark Indians, while the rest stood in a scowling half-circle. At the centre of this, Danny sat on a stool with a towel wrapped around his shoulders. I decided to speak to him.

"Are you all right then, sir?" I spoke out, keeping my distance from his swarthy companions.

Hearing my voice, he looked up and stared at me with a severe look, and nodded once.

"A bit of a rough ride," I tried lightly.

"I did nothing wrong, damn it!" he barked back.

"I never said you did, Danny boy!" I don't know why I called him that, save that I was a little irritated to meet with such a defensive tone when I had come to pay him my respects. "I saw the whole affair from pretty close, and it looked to me like nothing but an accident. Wasn't it?"

He held my eyes, trying to gauge my intent, I think. "It was," he answered at last.

"I merely wanted say that I saw how you helped—looking to the filly after the crash. You did it very smoothly. I appreciate your efforts."

In reply, he merely nodded again. I tipped my hat and started to walk away, but he called after me.

"Tell your big man that if he finds another rider, I won't be holding back tomorrow! It doesn't bother me a bit if another rider or two hit the dirt when there's money on the line." I raised my eyebrows, and he returned a sardonic grin. "I'm glad the horse wasn't hurt."

Once again I surveyed the flow of the departing company, and once again decided to delay, particularly when I recognized a figure approaching from the area of the grandstands—a more friendly figure. Uncle Boon was coming toward me, one oddly costumed bodyguard on each side. When we came together, we shook hands and I asked him if he had seen the accident.

"Oh, yes!" he exclaimed. "Very exciting! Much drama! So sorry, you must tell your friend Mr. Bingham how it is so sorry about his rider. His rider doing excellent riding also!" I assured him I would communicate those sentiments, and he added, with a boyish twinkle in his eye, "So fortunate I already did not place a wager on Miss Deception! Now that black horse looking good, very good, don't you think?"

"You haven't made your bets yet?"

"Not for me! Surely not. Not so hasty. I am foolish sometimes, and who is not, but not foolish hastiness."

"Then, Uncle, do not be too hasty to bet your fortune on Ojai, as good as he does look. If Jack manages to catch Christy and bring him back, then we'll have an equally good rider in the saddle tomorrow."

"Ah!" I could see the thoughts spinning around in his head. "So fortunate! Do all people know this? Maybe more money to make."

"I wouldn't know, Uncle. Your invention is far too complex for me."

"Complex? No, no! Very simple. Deduction made for owners of race. Then all divided up in equal shares on the winning horse. Very simple. Take your ticket over there after race. Money goes out. Ticket goes in." He pointed at the big wooden platform behind him, erected specifically for this race, and now being decorated with red, white, and blue streamers.

I laughed. "I just hope those firemen don't just scoop up all the money and carry it off to buy more beer."

Boon also laughed (although his bodyguards, who evidently spoke no English, remained stolid and stern). "No problem with firemen, Mr. Zachary. They are to be watched by your friend, the man of God."

"The man of God?"

"The Reverend Avery. Is his brother Jack your good friend?"

"Avery is doing that?"

"Suggestion of my own nephew's child, your good wife."

"Sue suggested Avery?"

"Something wrong with that?"

"No, not at all. A good idea."

But I was looking beyond him. Over Boon's shoulder, I spotted the approach of another acquaintance. "You must excuse me, Uncle," I said. Roselle was walking toward us. Boon followed my gaze, assessed my expression.

"Something is wrong with this man?" he asked softly.

"No. No, nothing. I just have to discuss some business, I think."

Boon and his men continued off in the direction of the wagon enclosure, and I leaned against the railing while Roselle came to me. He exhibited a foolish grin, greeting me quite loudly while he was still a dozen paces off.

"Mr. Beddoes! Good to see you, old chump."

I looked around us in great irritation. Granted, there wasn't anybody very close by, but still, "Don't call me by that name. Ever!"

"Did I call you Beddoes? Slip of the tongue, sport. Won't happen again." He laughed and slapped me lightly on the sleeve, making us out to be the best of friends. He was dressed smartly enough, but he smelled as if he had been drinking something made of fermented beans. "Seriously, man, I had hoped to find you out here. I need some money. Time to gamble, and I'm fresh out of currency. A hundred should tide me over until we formalize our arrangement on Monday."

I stepped forward and stood with my nose about an inch from his forehead.

"I'll save you some grief, Roselle. I don't think gambling is likely to be your strong point. I'm not giving you any money."

I think he was actually expecting that response. He immediately threw up his arms and gazed wide-eyed around him, as if he wanted to share his amazement with a broad public. "But Mr. Beddoes," he said loudly, "I don't think you . . ."

I figured that was as good a time as any to sucker punch him. I hit him with as strong a right hook as I could manage at such short distance, while his head was turned about forty-five degrees to his right. The blow was solid, but it achieved mixed results. Roselle went down like he was a sack of flour dropped out of the back of a wagon. That was good. On the negative side of things, he had a sharp and solid jawbone that I caught on all four fingers between the top knuckles, and for a second, I thought I had broken all of them. I kept my composure, though, and stood over his prone figure as I snarled at him.

"You are a worm, Roselle, and I have a good mind just to squash you and take my chances with the law. Do not threaten me again. Remember that you could only expose my identity once, and if you aren't very careful with your timing and your demands, you won't get a penny for doing it. I am prepared to listen to your proposition on Monday, but between now and then, if I see your face within striking distance, I will knock it off your head."

Hitched up on one elbow, stroking his jaw, he attempted to sound defiant. "You'll be sorry for this. I think by Monday my price will have gone up considerably, *Mr. Zachary*."

As I turned to walk away, I added, "Make it Tuesday. Tuesday night. At the Empire Saloon. Eight o'clock."

I had already decided that I had to meet him after dark, but I guess I changed the day just to be objectionable. As of that point, I still had no real plan of how to deal with Roselle. Every option was repugnant.

Walking toward the clearing where Avery's grey was tethered, I reflected that it would be unfortunate if both Roselle and I were at Lloyd Bingham's dinner—one of us with a swollen face and one with an injured hand. Then I happened to see a curious thing. One of Boon's bodyguards was just now striding through the trees, leaving the Beacon Hill track. He had stayed to watch.

Chapter Eight

HALFWAY HOME FROM BEACON HILL, riding the grey with my aching right hand tucked under my left arm, one of those less than charming vagaries of Victoria weather came upon me. A solitary black bank of clouds floated in from the ocean, and out of the nearly perfect azure sky it began to pour rain. By the time I reached the stable and handed Avery's horse over to the boy, I was soaked. I walked the two blocks from the stable to my hotel, and when I arrived, the sun was once again shining in a near cloudless sky.

Sue met me at the front door and directed me, with as much kindness as was possible, to the back entrance and the boot room. Feeling dejected and uncomfortable, I went upstairs and shed my wet clothing. She arrived with a robe and a towel, and the news that a warm bath was almost ready and another basin of water was heating downstairs on the furnace.

"One of the great things about owning your own hotel," she reminded me, "is that you can have a soothing hot bath whenever you want." She often repeated this homily to me. I think part of her still remembered me as the filthy, bug-ridden miner who had arrived on her doorstep a half-dozen years previous.

"I need to talk to Sarah Green," I told her.

She pointed a finger at me sternly. "Not while you are dirty and naked. She is a proper young lady."

"Afterwards, I mean. After my bath. I might even take time to dress myself."

"She is feeling very poor. Very upset. The situation is complicated. Father made some of his tea for her, and she went to bed."

Sue's father's tea had the sedative quality of three large shots of brandy. I realized that I might not be able to pass along Jack's message before we left for the dinner.

As I lingered in the hot water, rubbing my chest with Chinese soap that smelled like some sort of flower, I came to the conclusion that Sue was right—a person of privilege might well enjoy a hot bath once a week, or even more. I also decided that if Jack did not make it back with Christy in time to lead the way, I was definitely not going to Bingham's house party alone.

JACK DID ARRIVE, more or less on schedule, with our friend Mr. Riordan in tow. There wasn't a room to be had in Victoria, so one of the maids and the boot boy were sent off to find a mattress and bedding, then prepare a makeshift accommodation in the cellar.

"Will that be all right, Mr. Riordan?" Sue asked. "It might be a bit warm when the furnace is first built up for the night."

"It will be fine, ma'am. Wonderful, it'll be."

"Are there rats down there, Zachary?" Jack interjected.

"Nothing half the size of Christy," I assured him.

While Jack washed up, Sue went upstairs and checked on Sarah Green.

The word she brought down was that Sarah was still sleeping, so Jack reminded her once again to pass along the message that he was confident that Bingham could be convinced to revoke the contract. He would address the issue after the dinner tonight. Then it was past time to leave. I borrowed Christy's horse, since it was already used to walking alongside The Commissioner.

"We'll have to get someone at Bingham's to water and feed them both when we get there," Jack muttered reluctantly. "They've already put in a long day."

"As have you, old man," I pointed out.

He was putting on his boots, still muddy from the day's riding. "True enough, Zachary." He stood and beat the dust off his coat. "This may be the one time in your life when you arrive at dinner looking better than me."

As we left, the aroma of Cook's dinner at the Celestial was becoming quite tantalizing, and my guess—later to be proven true—was that we would probably get a better meal if we stayed home.

There were still a few miles to go in Jack's journey, and when we started off toward Saanich, my companion slouched a little in the saddle. "I should be staying here, you know—waiting for Sarah to wake up, talking to her." I would have agreed to that in a minute, but it was a measure of his commitment to the horse race that he led us onward, looking back over his shoulder as we headed out of town.

The road was good, the sky clear, and the moon almost full, so it didn't take long to reach Lloyd Bingham's house. It was a huge place, but not particularly appealing—half log and half frame-built, under a single-peaked roof without even a gable or dormer to relieve the lines of utilitarian expanse. The yard was equally spacious, muddy now from the rain earlier, littered with little sheds and a pair of small rundown houses— all telling the tale of his rise from pioneer rancher to the builder of half the wagons going north and inland to search for gold. His nickname was "The Wagonmaster." His carts and buggies were now built by a crew of a dozen or more on the mainland at Fort Langley. On the island, he owned a brewery and a sawmill, but he had chosen for the last few years to live back here, on his original ranch.

We were the last guests to arrive, and three men had been detailed to wait for us on the verandah. Two of them took charge of our mounts, while the third charged back inside with the good news that Christy Riordan had been returned and secured to ride Miss Deception on the morrow. The cheering was still at a crest when we entered the great room, and we two felt very much the conquering heroes—myself only by reflection, having been mistaken by many for Christy, but it was an appealing sensation nonetheless. I was slapped on the back, congratulated, thanked, properly identified, handed a drink in a glass tumbler, and ignored. On the far side of the room, Jack was at the centre of a circle of intimates that had formed beside the seated figure of Lloyd Bingham himself. All smiles. They must have been receiving details of Christy's fitness, and his eagerness.

The drink I had been given was some sort of punch involving gin, lemon juice, and excessive amounts of honey. If mustard had been added, it might have served as a poultice, but as a libation, it was a horrible thing—evidently some sort of punishment for having ladies present. There was a long table at the shadowy centre of the big room where I could see whisky bottles alongside the punch bowl and crackers, so my first order of business was to find a place to dump the liquid I had been given and proceed on to better things. My search was not interrupted by conversation. There were twenty or thirty guests shuffling about, but none that I knew well enough to address with more than a word or two. I found a jar in one corner, a vase, I suppose, ornamental but too big for flowers, and after a quick glance around me, disposed of the gin concoction, after which I strolled over to the drinks table and poured the tumbler full of a more potable liquor.

I surveyed the assembly. There was no gas service that far out of town, of course, and in spite of the great number of oil lamps all along the walls and the candelabra on the serving table, the room was too big to light properly, causing most of the guests to settle in along the periphery, where I could examine them at my leisure. As long as I remained in the middle of the hall, I was not forced to approach any of these strangers. I recognized a few faces—the banker, the lawyer, and the newsman who had met with Mac at the Celestial. Most of the others had a similar look to them—money men and civil servants—nearly all with their wives. (I presumed them to be wives. They were not the sort of women a man would be seen with unless compelled to do so by the bonds of matrimony.) Most of these persons were themselves posing and pondering uncomfortably, and this made me feel more at ease. For a while, I was comforted by their discomfort. A fellow in a dark suit sat down at the piano and began to play, which was a welcome distraction, although once the fellow played about four songs by Stephen Foster, he was apparently forced to begin repeating them. Then—somewhat belatedly—the thought occurred to me that no one had extended an invitation to me that would include my wife. This would certainly not have been the fault of Jack Elliston, so I concluded that the Binghams preferred not to have her in the mix. It was disagreeable and illogical. James Douglas had, up until very recently, been governor of this colony, while married to a woman who was half Cree Indian, but a man with a Chinese wife was still expected to leave her at home. Good enough. Sue would not have wanted to be here, where her beauty and grace would have embarrassed these colonial crones.

At long last, a servant (clearly a cowboy in ill-fitting livery) entered the hall and shouted out that dinner was ready to be served in the dining room.

The capacious oak dining table was the one truly impressive piece of furniture in that vast, poorly finished home. It was all of twenty feet long and polished to a fine shine. I was pleased to see that I would be seated next to Jack, although this placed me quite near to the head of the table, just across from Mac Bingham and only three chairs down from his father. I had not realized that the old man was so ill, but he was evidently not even capable of walking. Two big men picked up his chair in the great room and, with considerable effort, carried him in to dinner. They were strong men—Lloyd Bingham must have weighed at least two hundred pounds.

No grace was said, no formal welcome voiced. People were simply directed to their chairs by two servants, and the food began to arrive. I noticed that our host's meal consisted only of a mound of uncertain vegetable mush and a never-diminishing flow of whisky. The rest of us were given great slabs of roast beef with potatoes, carrots, and turnips, all covered in thick, charcoal-accented gravy—a rather cold and waxy gravy. I'm quite sure that in a proper dinner party, there is soup served first, as a course unto itself. Not so here, and probably all for the best, as undoubtedly the chef would simply have watered down some gravy and brought it to us in bowls. Under the dour glare of Lloyd Bingham, it seemed inadvisable to return to the great room and refill my whisky glass, so I was forced to wash the food down with heavy red wine.

"That wine's from Spain! All the way from Spain!" bellowed the old man, with his version of a proud smile. "Ten cents for the wine, and two dollars to ship it here."

Even though he was an invalid, his presence had a certain power. He was almost bald, but his grey side-whiskers and moustache must have bushed up four inches high, and his eyebrows were so long they flopped forward, framing his eyes, whose fire was always bright, but whose motivation was indecipherable. He sat with his head thrust forward, which is sometimes a sign of defiance and sometimes of deafness.

I believe it was likely a bit of both in this case, although defiance was his specialty.

"I see you down there, William!" He was addressing the banker, near the end of the table with his timid little wife. "You're doing a good job of putting the widows and orphans out into the streets, are you?"

There were polite titters of amusement, although the group had not yet consumed nearly enough strong drink for the comment to be funny. Even Lloyd Bingham didn't laugh much, his breathy chuckles sounding a bit like a panting dog. I glanced across and saw that his son, Mac, exhibited no expression at all, making serious and methodical work of his beef and gravy. A minute or two later, a bit more jollity could be heard from the nether section of the long table—some sort of humorous remarks being thrown out by a tall, skinny man I didn't recognize, a big-eared, long-nosed character of twenty-five years at the most. Lloyd barked down at him in a tone that was neither angry nor light. Lloyd could not quite form words that were light.

"What are you bunch giggling about down there?"

"Canada," the young man replied. "About joining Canada."

"What?"

The other repeated himself, but again Bingham could not make out his soft speech, which was for the best. Lloyd was not at all the sort of person you would want to invite into controversial conversation. Rather than ask for a second repetition, though, he turned and bellowed at someone at mid-table opposite.

"Matthew! You're not drinking my wine! Is it not good enough for you?"

This fellow seemed to have experience in conversing with our host. "I'm sure it's the best a man can buy, Mr. Bingham." He spoke loudly. "I'm just not a wine drinker."

"Well, what will you have, then? Whisky? Water? What can we get you?" He was straining around in his chair, looking for one of the servants, none of whom were close at hand, while the lawyer shook his head to the offer of whisky and pointed at his full glass of water. Once started, though, Lloyd was hard to stop.

"Anyone else? What are we missing? Hey? Mustard! Anyone want mustard?" As his guests unanimously declined, the great man turned toward his son, still intent on his food. "Maxwell! We need mustard. Go get us some. Four or five jars."

Mac answered calmly, as quietly as he could when speaking to his father, which was loud enough for those of us nearby to hear the peevishness in his voice. "There will be a man here in a moment, father. Talk to the servants."

"But I'm talking to you, Maxwell! I asked you to do it!" Lloyd paused, then added with a grin, "You don't like me calling you Maxwell, do you?"

Again Mac showed a practiced restraint. "The guests might not know who you're talking to."

Lloyd pounced on this. "They will when you get up and get us the damned mustard!" he shouted, and laughed uproariously. His son poured himself another glass of wine, while the rest of us tried to figure the appropriate response to such a public exchange. Someone had evidently been listening at the kitchen door, and one of the burly, slouching servants entered bearing little plates of mustard, just as Lloyd's solitary gales of laughter overcame him and he began to cough. After a bout of coughing into the front of his dinner jacket, he was forced to return to silence for a while, much to the relief of the rest of us.

A few minutes later, having eaten as much as I cared to eat, I pushed myself back from the table and tried my best to loosen my collar. We were seated at the end of the table that was closest to the bigger fireplace, and I was roasting—sweating like a pig into my jacket. The fire had been built up like Nebuchadnezzar's fiery furnace, but Lloyd actually sat with a blanket around his shoulders. He spotted me pulling away and spoke to me—loudly, as always. "Mr. Zachary! You're not trying to get away? Not time to leave yet!"

I was surprised he recognized me and knew my name. "Not at all, Mr. Bingham," and for once I managed to add something diplomatic. "I think you've got the place nicely warmed up for the benefit of the ladies, and I'm a man that melts easily."

He stared at me, thoughtful, and I braced myself for anything from accusation to humiliation, but instead he turned to the rest of the group and asked, "What about everyone else? Anyone hot? Too warm?" He must have perceived some signals of agreement, because he muttered. "This room. Too small. Not big enough for all of these people and . . ." He turned abruptly on Mac. "Maxwell! Act like a host! Get these people out of here and back to the main room for something sweet to put on top of their dinner."

Mac hesitated for a second, since some of them were still working on their meal, but then he stood and called out genially, "Anyone who's finished—let's go back and get a fresh drink and a piece of cake."

I stood to leave with the rest, but Lloyd Bingham stopped me with a raised hand. "Not you, Mr. Zachary. I'd like a word, please." His tone was not that of a dinner party greeting, but I sat down. He had no need to ask for privacy. Even the few who hadn't finished their main course had dropped their utensils and made an exit.

"I owe you thanks, I believe, Mr. Zachary," he said as the stragglers moved past us into the hall, where cakes and confections now dominated the serving table.

"I don't think you do. I offered an empty room in my hotel to Jack Elliston's friends. That's all."

He made a snorting sound into the blanket around his neck that may or may not have been part of the dialogue. "I don't much like Jack Elliston," he grumbled. "But he's been useful. Too goddamn English, but he's helped this thing to happen, no question there. English, but useful."

I didn't much like Lloyd Bingham, but instead of commenting thus, I just said, "Jack is my friend. Perhaps my best friend."

"Well, you're my friend, too, Zachary. Like it or not. Because anyone who helps me win, anyone who helps me make money is who I call my friend."

"Then Jack's a better friend to you than pretty much everyone else here tonight."

The old man sighed. "Sure, sure. Good for me. Good for you. But you did something, too. You brought the Chinese into this." I didn't know whether he meant Uncle Boon specifically or the whole Chinese town. "So I'm guessing you'll make me a good little chunk of money. And your wife's relatives down in San Francisco—you make sure they mention my name down there. Make sure every one of those bastards in California—yellow and white both—make sure they hear who's winning horse races now!"

I wasn't sure what else he had to say, so I tried to remain polite. "I shall ask them to sing your praises as a favour. To my friend." He seemed to think that was funny. I added that I was surprised he even recognized me or knew my name.

"Ha! I know everybody in town, and exactly what they'll do for a nickel. Once I've seen your face, just once, then it's never forgotten. Ten years from now—no problem. People never change. Always done my business by the look on a man's face." He leaned forward and thrust out his chin. "That's my problem. I'm sick. I can't get around, can't see the faces I need to see. Have to trust my son to fix it all, and him—he's the one character I'm unsure about in this world. Is he ready to take over my life? I just don't know." Abruptly he sat up straight and cleared his throat very loudly. "I'm sorry about the heat in here. It's just I can't get warm. Sick."

"I'd heard that. Do the doctors know what . . . ?"

"To hell with them! This thing is killing me. You don't need to give a nice name for something that decides to kill you, and this is going to kill me sooner than later. Forget it! That's not what I wanted to say to you. My God! We're having ourselves a good old chit-chat, aren't we? I wanted to tell you about Roselle."

He paused, looking straight into my eyes, and if it hadn't been so hot, I would have said I felt a chill. "Really?" I said blandly. "What about him?"

Lloyd Bingham snorted again. "You've been seen talking with the man lately. Becoming a pair of right old chums, which seems damned funny, now that I talk to you. You don't appear to be that stupid."

"Maybe I'm not."

"Good. Because that little weasel is a lying, gossiping little thief, and only a total fool would stand with him for a minute longer than it took to get rid of him."

"But you yourself . . ."

"He's never been any friend of mine! Mac brought him home after one of his trips, hired him as *an assistant*." The old man hissed the word. "I think the little snake had some kind of leverage on young Mac. I hate to think my own son could have been stupid enough to think Roselle was trustworthy."

I wasn't growing to like old Lloyd, but I was beginning to feel surprisingly at ease. "You don't flatter your son, do you, Mr. Bingham?" I said.

He shook his head sadly, then he straightened his shoulders. "He still needs work, that's all. I've told this to my boy a thousand times, and he knows it's true—no one ever got to the top of the ladder without somebody stronger kicking his ass up every step! A strong hand for the teacher and a strap on the back for the child! They need it. Deep down they know it, and they quit fighting back soon enough. You've got to bully your people into success! Every child! Every woman! And . . ." He paused, tilted his head thoughtfully. "Maybe three-quarters of grown men."

"And did you teach your son to be a bully, sir?"

He nodded philosophically. "I hope so. Yes, I think so."

I stared at him. I could think of nothing to say. Suddenly he became aware of the silence. "But off you go, Mr. Zachary! I just wanted to warn you about Roselle. You're not getting a piece of the profits from the race, as far as I've heard, so this is your payment—advice that might save your ass. Stay away from Roselle! Now go get yourself a piece of cake and a proper drink." I realized I was still holding my whisky glass. "Wine! Gin!" Old Lloyd grimaced. "Only fit for Frenchies and English pansies!"

I had to laugh as I stood up, agreeing with him to some extent for once. "You speak of our beloved English forefathers, do you?" Before he could object, I added, "You really despise Jack Elliston?"

"No," he objected. "I don't despise the man. I just don't like him. Don't like his talk. Don't like his walk. Born with everything handed to him, and now he's flipping all over the world like a housefly, and his brother on his sleeve to keep him out of trouble. He doesn't tell that story, but you can bet there's a good reason why his own father kicked him out of the country. But he's smart, give him that. He knows horses. I couldn't have done this thing without him. But I paid him well. Gave him the best damn saddle horse I ever saw. What he wanted. Credit to him for recognizing quality. And his brother is a good man."

"Avery? You know Avery? You like him?"

"I certainly do. Maybe he's just doing what he figures is his Christian duty, but he's been here to look in on me several times. More than anybody else. We talk."

I considered it a substantial testimony to Avery's patience. "That's interesting, Mr. Bingham. You don't really look like natural companions."

"Why not? I haven't had much time for religion, myself, but my parents were strong church folk. Father a deacon." He laughed. "And Avery Elliston is the right kind of churchman. Sincere enough, but he knows the way of the world. Been around. Knows what it's like." Cocking his head to one side, he added, "We've even had discussions about me building a church. My father's name beside the door."

"A church?" This did not sound even remotely like Lloyd Bingham.

"Not a big one, but nicely done up. Stained glass. Avery could stay on permanent there." He leaned forward now and assumed a more serious visage. "I'm a dying man, Mr. Zachary. I'm dying. I've got the money. Plenty left over for little boy Maxwell. You think I'm trying to curry favour with God before I croak? Could be. Maybe I just want to leave something behind for folks to remember my father. Oh, yes—and me, too!"

I could think of nothing to say to that but good luck and good night.

As I walked away, he was pulling the frayed blanket tighter over his fine dinner jacket. "Catch one of my boys, Mr. Zachary, send a couple of them this way. I think I've had enough of this party."

Having done this, I lurked about the serving table in the other room, drinking quickly and sampling the various sweets. After a couple of tries, I discovered the one truly good thing about that party—some kind of pastry wrapped around a cherry preserve. As I ate a number of these, one after the other, I looked around for Jack, but I couldn't see him. Eventually it dawned on me that Mac Bingham was not to be seen, either.

So we were each of us conversing with a Bingham.

Suddenly, Jack came striding around the corner of the hallway at the far end of the great room. His hands were behind his back. His face was set. He marched straight toward me. I threw back my whisky, wrapped a couple more pastries in a linen napkin, and was ready when he spoke.

"I think it's time to leave, Zachary. Don't worry—I've already said goodnight to our host."

In the yard, the stable hand trotted off to get our horses. He brought them around quite smartly, and I gave him the pastries in their napkin. He thanked me and I advised him not to get caught with crumbs on his coat-front or table linen in his pocket. During the whole time, Jack did not speak a word, did not even look at me.

Nor did he become any more talkative once we were on our way. It was a mile along before he broke his silence to say simply, "I shouldn't have hit him," and that was that. We had dropped the horses off at the stable and were walking up the hill when I was finally compelled to ask him what had happened. He stopped, and we stood there, facing each other in the middle of the street.

"He won't waive the contract with Miss Green," he told me. "This was all carefully planned. I had no idea. He says he wanted her from the moment he saw her. He informs me that the contract is carefully written, and I believe him. His father's lawyers. He's got the old man to come on side, and they've had it written so that she won't even be allowed to leave the grounds for a full year, more or less. Slavery. She played the fool to sign that thing—I doubt she read any of it—but she was, well, in one of those states."

"I put her in that state, damn it! I'm to blame here, Jack."

"No, Zachary. No. That fear was stuck in her blood after what she'd been through in Washington, and it doesn't just fade away in a day or a week or a month. Her secret was bound to come out and undoubtedly would send her into a panic. She was overcome by it, and she sold herself into slavery because Mac Bingham happened to be there, ready to do it. I should have been there, I should have . . ."

"She can refuse! She just has to refuse, simply refuse."

"They'll bring her up in court—breach of contract or worse—and the whole story will come out before it's done. Somehow they've guessed that she's afraid of the law. The Binghams are stubbornness incarnate, and they are a powerful family. They won't let her go. Mac made very sure I understood that. He knows I care for her. He pushed it in my face.

"He's proving himself to his father, you know. That's what it's all about. He's showing the old man that he can get what he wants. And Jack—I don't believe he just wants her to write his correspondence . . ."

"Of course not," Jack answered evenly. "He told me that straight to my face as well. That's why I hit him."

We stood silent together in the street in the half-light of the gas lamp on the corner. Finally, he said, "I shouldn't have hit him."

I sighed. "Probably not. Did you hurt him?" I asked.

He nodded. "I should think so."

Everyone but the night cleaning boys was asleep by the time I got back to the hotel. I considered that a good thing, as I had no desire to repeat the bad news that I had just received. The strange thing, I thought as I undressed, was that next day we would all be working together to run The Great Race.

Chapter Nine

I COULD NOT SLEEP. CRUEL scenarios plagued me through the night. My head hurt. My bones ached. Then—very suddenly—as dawn arrived, I slept like a corpse. Twice my wife called me to arise, and twice I actually dreamed that I was up and about. Resorting to a merciless strategy, she sent Ross in to rouse me.

The boy growled my name like a bear, twisted the ends of my moustache, and sang songs in my ear. I grabbed him around the waist, hauled him toward me, and tickled him until he howled. Then with a deep sigh I bade him good morning and ran my fingers through his long, dark hair. It was coarse, almost black, and as untameable as the boy himself. He had his mother's hair and eyes, my own pale skin and angular features. For a while, neither of us moved much. I don't hold him often, don't even spend time with him as much as I should—probably more than most men, but not enough to call myself a truly good father. Then I wrapped a blanket around his head and pushed him away.

"I have to wash up, boy. Run downstairs and tell Cook I want a couple of eggs for breakfast this morning."

He ran off down the hall with a long chorus of whooping noises, while I went to the table next to the window. Someone had brought me a basin of hot water some time ago. It was now barely warm, so I soaked my face for quite some time before I commenced the always dangerous job of shaving. I was very tired. I stared into the little mirror for a full minute before deciding that I looked precisely the same as I always do. Then the soap was on my cheeks, the razor was stropped, and Ross was whooping his way back into the bedroom.

"No eggs for you! No eggs for you!" he shouted.

"What? In my own house—my own hotel?"

"Too many guests! Cook fed them all the eggs. The fat American ate five and his wife ate three! Noodle soup for you, like always!"

After shaving for a minute and clearing my thoughts, I asked Ross, who was twirling my bed sheet into a rope, if his Nanny Green was downstairs. This stopped him cold, and he faced me—suddenly downcast.

"She's gone already."

"Gone? With Jack? Did Mr. Elliston come for her?"

"No. With the big, big man. Like an hour ago, and maybe she's not coming back. That's what Jade May says."

"Jade May knows nothing," I told him. "Do you know what time it is?"

"It's morning."

I thanked him for that information, found my watch on the dresser, and discovered that it was past ten. Small wonder that my wife was concerned. She was at the bottom of the stairs as I came clumping down, and she informed me in an irritated voice that it was nearly noon. I did not contradict her.

"Come to the horse race with me, Sue," I asked her instead.

"What? So late you ask me that? The hotel is completely full of guests. You know we had to turn away two different people yesterday? Preparation and cleaning and making up beds does not happen by itself, my husband."

"These people are all here for the race, my dear, and the party time afterwards. Don't fuss over them. When they get home, you could stack them on the roof and they'd fall asleep without a complaint. Let me eat my soup and we'll head for the track."

She walked away shaking her head as if I were suggesting something impossible, but I noticed that she was already dressed to go out, and before we left, she only reminded the staff about arrangements that she had already made. We took the hotel's one good horse and the dogcart, with Ross squeezed between us on the seat. This made things a little uncomfortable, for, being a boy, he had to squirm and stretch every time we passed anything that might be vaguely interesting. That day, there was much more to be seen than usual.

The weather was perfect, so several eateries and saloons were already setting up tables and chairs on the sidewalk, and even into the street. Canvas roofs were being pulled up on poles, and vases of flowers displayed on the tables. Flowers seemed to be the theme of the day, whether for decoration or presentation by the bundle. I would have stopped to buy a bouquet for Sue, but I could see that traffic on Government Street was starting to fill up and slow down. It was still two hours until the first of the two heats, but it appeared as if the whole town was pouring out to make a full day of the festivity. We came to a complete stop at one point, and while we waited a flower seller hurried along past on the boardwalk, off to Beacon Hill where he would empty his cart at an inflated price in no time. I tried to get his attention, but the general commotion was great, and he was far enough away that he didn't hear me when I shouted for him. Sue patted my arm and thanked me anyway. Ross was standing between us on the seat, looking back over the folded canopy at the noise of what I initially thought was a loud argument. Listening more closely, I ascertained that the two gentlemen behind us in the procession were attempting to sing. As if to explain this, a pair of fellows jingled past us with a handcart loaded precariously full of bottles of beer. They could have lightened their load if they had hawked it to those of us waiting, but they were intent on reaching the race grounds—every vendor's dream.

We didn't know what was delaying things some distance ahead at the intersection, but it didn't matter. There was plenty of time, the sun was shining bright, and my family was with me. Smiling. Very briefly I forgot my worries.

Then, in a chilling little epiphany, came a vision of how quickly this would cease to exist if Sue were to discover that she was sitting not with a lucky gold miner come back from the rush, but a wanted criminal, whose gold was the result of robbery and murder. Details such as my professed innocence would be counterbalanced for the worse by my having lied about it all for years. How could she forgive those years of deceit?

I had thought this through enough times now. I would need to kill Roselle, I decided, and hope that some of my fear would die with him.

Mercifully, at such moments of dreadful oppression one can often be rescued by trivialities. Passing the reins to my wife, I jumped down from the carriage and intercepted a fellow selling sugary fruit ices, after which I barely regained my seat before vehicles began to untangle themselves and resume motion. We travelled the rest of the way to Beacon Hill slowly, but without a pause.

Several sections of the fields surrounding the racecourse were being used for the disposal of carriages. At the second turning-off from the road, my wife and son disembarked and went on ahead while I paid a young man to look after the dogcart, untied our basket from the back-board, and followed them. When I caught up, they were moving down the pathway that paralleled the track and connected the various enclosures from behind. Sue was strolling, Ross was matching her pace by frolicking and scrambling in circles. One horse's little yard and the next were separated by a hundred yards or so, each one surrounded by a milling cluster of owners, grooms, stable lads, and the friends of those owners, grooms, and stable lads, as well as numerous intense or jocular spectators—one hand on a lady, the other holding the day's racing card. We paused at the edge of one such company, the group surrounding the second local horse, the grey. It was probably the second largest gathering, after the one at Miss Deception's enclosure, up ahead, where I could already see a crowd of thirty or forty.

Ross, using the prerogative of children, lowered his head and squirmed his way under the forest of elbows, to the front. I placed the wicker basket beside Sue and wove my way forward until I was beside him. The magical atmosphere of the event had by now taken control of the boy, and as he stared up at the racehorse, just now being fitted with a red and blue blanket under an insignificant saddle, his eyes were filled with a great wonder, as if he were witnessing the crowning of a king. The horse's proud owner, propped up on his canes, beard down to his belt, looked enough like an archbishop to complete the picture. After a minute or two, I took Ross's hand and led him away from among the onlookers.

We walked together, still holding hands, with Sue a step behind us. The next enclosure was not so tightly mobbed, and we were able to view it well enough from a bit of a distance. Even if I had not recognized the big chestnut, I would have known her by the clutch of Nanaimo coalmen who stood in a line to one side, as dark and severe as if they had been discussing commodity prices in a boardroom. Their tall black hats seemed to have been purchased in bulk from the same haberdasher.

"Do you think they will make the horse run the race wearing a black hat like theirs?" I asked the boy softly. It was only a decent jest, at best, but Ross laughed to the brink of hysteria, and I had to drag him onward.

I did not have to drag him long. As we approached the next enclosure, where Miss Deception was in the process of being saddled, he suddenly cried out, "Nanna Green!," threw off my hand, and charged into the low levels of the encircling spectators like a lamb burrowing into the middle of the flock.

There was a low wooden platform set up at one side of the enclosure, with chairs set out on it for the elite of Mac Bingham's company. Sarah Green sat front and centre—very straight and stiff, an empty seat on either side. She looked quite beautiful, framed in that pose, but extremely uncomfortable. When she heard the boy's repeated calls, her face lit up in pleasure and relief, and once Ross had wormed his way through the press, she pulled him up to sit beside her and hugged him around the neck.

Any effort on my part to reach the same location was going to be a slow process, so after Sue pointed out the spot where she would be laying out our blanket, I began a circuitous and apologetic journey around the circumference of Miss Deception's crowd of admirers, up to the outside railing of the track itself, and down to the far side of the platform. As I nudged my way through, I was able to see Mac Bingham and Jack standing together in the middle of the course, pointing seriously at this and that. I was satisfied to see that they were not coming to blows for the time being. Then, rounding my way behind the back row of chairs, I met up at the corner with none other than Christy Riordan. We spotted each other simultaneously and embraced like brothers—the excitement of the occasion making this feel quite normal. Then he turned away and I realized that he was stooping forward, engaged in serious conversation. It was Billy Horne. He was lecturing the younger man on race strategy, specifically how to contend with the big black, Ojai.

"He'll bully you right into the fence if you try to pass him on the inside, so you can't allow that to be your only option. Their horse is fast, but our filly can gain a step on him. Just a step, and that's only my feeling. That's what you've got to find out in the first heat. The two of you will leave the rest of these nags back at the start line, but you also want to get some idea if the big black will fade at all in the final stretch. I'm fearing that he will not. And the white-face boy, this Danny, you watch his free hand if you're in close. He never took a swing at me, but you can read in his eyes easy enough that he wouldn't mind taking the chance and hoping the stewards go blind."

Christy stood half-bent over, absorbing every word the other jockey had to say. I stared at Billy Horne in disbelief. The day previous it had seemed to be even odds whether he'd live or die, and now he was back at the track, enthroned with his leg stretched out in front and rested on a wooden crate. I was not the only one gazing in confusion at that leg. It looked like a length of birch tree, swaddled in cloth and painted with plaster.

Christy was called for and strode off to inspect his mount. Billy Horne turned in his seat to look at me and grimaced at the pain that movement caused him.

"Ah, so it's you, Mr. Zachary."

"What in blazes are you doing here?"

"Over the doctor's strict objections, I am here to see this damned race. It may have caused me my livelihood, so I should at least be allowed to watch the finish of it."

"You'll have your leg fall off between heats, I expect, or bleed to death or something! How can you endure sitting here?"

"They make wonderful drugs these days. My only problem might be to not fall into a comfortable sleep and miss the excitement."

"I doubt that, Billy Horne. You're running a risk, though. And what the devil sort of splint have they got you into?"

He tapped the surface with his knuckles. "It's a plaster casting. The latest thing, don't you worry! Proved itself in the Crimea. If you want to worry, you worry about our boy, Christy."

"He'll do fine."

"Yes," Horne agreed philosophically, "I think he will."

Farther up the track, three men wearing red satin armbands around their jacket sleeves were approaching, one of them growling in a low voice.

"Horses, please, gentlemen! Starting line! Horses, please!"

They were ready to start the first heat, which would eliminate all but two horses. It was assumed that this heightened the drama of the occasion and increased the number of wagers, although some felt that it changed the race too much into an endurance event, there being only a short break between the two runnings.

Mac Bingham and Jack finished their conversation and split up—Jack striding toward the other officials, and Mac returning toward the enclosure, where Christy was now nestling himself into the saddle. Miss Deception was looking agitated, which I suppose is a good thing for a horse about to run, and was being held steady by a groom. A few steps to my left, a little boy's voice tried its best to cut through the gathering crowd noise.

"Mister Jack! Hullo! Mister Jack!"

Elliston didn't hear him, of course, but Mac Bingham did, and he reacted immediately, barging his way through the mob, pointing us out to one of the big stable hands guarding the ropes. I figured it was time to get my son away from there and join Sue over on the grass, but I couldn't immediately see a good path to get to him. I was blocked off by Billy Horne's leg. I called out to Ross, but he didn't hear me. It was getting louder around us, and he was still trying to catch Jack's attention, standing on the chair and steadying himself with one hand on Sarah Green's shoulder.

Then, like a gale blowing in, Mac Bingham was upon us, shoving strangers aside and howling. "Get down from there, damn it! Get the hell out of here, boy!"

Frankly, I was startled at this show of emotion. He was acting like a felony was taking place. I squeezed past Billy Horne, apologizing and receiving a great groan in response, and was face to face with Bingham.

"Hold on there, Mac. No harm done. The boy was just saying hello to his teacher."

We were so close together that I could just about name the brand of whisky on his breath as he barked back. "I decide who goes where today, and who gets the hell out of the way. And she's not his teacher anymore. She's my property. Under contract! My property!"

He punctuated this last repetition by giving me a little stab in the chest with his forefinger, which, under normal situations, I would take as an invitation to throw at least one punch. I had a wounded man against my left leg, though, and a small boy trying to climb onto my right shoulder, so I let it pass. Looking past my son, I caught sight of Sarah, who was breathing heavily, one hand up to cover her downcast eyes, as if the sun was suddenly too bright to bear. My stomach began to burn. I may have trodden on Mac's foot as I pushed past with Ross clutched to my waist. In a minute, we were at the spot where Sue had laid out the blanket on the grass beside the pathway. I don't know whether Ross actually noticed much of the confrontation that had just occurred. As for me, it took all of my self-control to keep from running back and doing something rash. If I could have thought of something rash to do, I think I would have done it.

The gun sounded, and a great wave of noise rolled up—a cacophony of shouting and whistling and pounding hooves and hands banging against the wooden rails. We had an excellent vantage point for both start and finish—better than the grandstands, I'm sure—and for a moment, as the dust kicked up by the racers actually settled on our shoulders, I felt a tingle of excitement, but by the time the horses had sped out of sight around the hill, I had almost forgotten their existence. My mind was taken up by the picture of Sarah Green, alone in her designated chair, her expression one that I had seen more than once before, when terror was paralyzing her. By the time the racers came back into view around the other end of the hill, I was paying almost no attention. As predicted, Miss Deception and Ojai were a dozen lengths ahead of the others, pushing only each other, and that somewhat half-heartedly. As the tumult from the spectators crested and fell away, I bent down to tell Sue that I would be back soon, and hurried away to find Avery Elliston.

Perhaps Avery could use his influence with Lloyd Bingham to help Sarah.

IT WAS NO easy thing to move quickly through that congestion of humanity. Once the horses had all crossed the finish line, the whole assembly seemed to rise to their feet and begin ambling along the thoroughfare—looking for friends, looking for debtors, looking for refreshments, heading off to congratulate this fellow or console that other one. It took me ages to cover the few hundred yards to the far turn where the grandstands and the betting podium were set up. Here the crowd was at its thickest. The stands had emptied to half their capacity, the other half having struggled off to find something cool to drink in the hot sun, or to place a second bet after miscalculating on their first. I was glad I was not attempting to work my way through to one of the wagering tables where the men normally employed as bank tellers were now making accounts of who would be winners and losers, shuffling their money off to be held in escrow by the firefighters of Victoria. The tables were arranged in front of the podium itself, which stood six feet high, sixteen feet square, festooned in red, white, and blue bunting. Beside each teller were at least two formidable civil guardians, thrusting banknotes and coin into canvas bags, to be relayed on high for safekeeping until after the final heat. It was here that I would find the Reverend

Avery Elliston, honorary treasurer of the day's wealth. Around the perimeter, a dozen or more firemen, looking very much like archers on a castle wall, grasped the railing firmly. They were in much betters spirits, though, than most castle archers. The beer had evidently already been delivered. Not all the firemen were up on the parapets or transporting money, mind you. As I tried to elbow my way past a food vendor, I was forced to inch through a trio of them, all intent on carrying as many plates of sauerkraut and sausages as they could hold. Slipping into the wake of their leader, I managed to get to the rear of the wooden edifice, where a makeshift flight of six steep steps led upward.

One of the firemen accosted me as soon as I set foot on the bottom step. "Protected area! Off you go."

"I need to speak to the Reverend Elliston. Is he up there?"

"Maybe. Who are you?"

The fellow with his hand on my shirt front seemed to be enjoying his temporary position of authority.

"Zachary! Lincoln Zachary! It's important I speak to him."

We were shouting at each other in order to be heard and, as it happened, loud enough for Avery to recognize my voice from up above. "Zachary, my good man!" he called down, peering over the back railing. Then, "It's all right. Please let him pass. Bring him up. He's my good friend."

The chesty brute confronting me softened immediately and turned his attention elsewhere after tipping his hat in Avery's direction. I ascended.

"Mr. Zachary! How pleasant! How simply wonderful! Wonderful! It's a wonderful day, isn't it?" He was in conspicuous good humour. Before I could answer, we were levered to one side by a bank teller and a guardian of the peace, who carried their canvas bag to a larger one underneath the little table and emptied it within. It was a plain table, with one unoccupied chair beside it. On the table were a glass jar containing a fistful of pansies, and a number of white porcelain mugs. Once the transport of money was complete, Avery pulled me to the table by my coat sleeve. "Wonderful. Marvellous." In one motion, he pulled a partly filled mug to his lips, drained it, shook a few drops out of the empty vessel next to it, and held them both aloft. "Gentlemen!" he shouted. Then, to me, "You will join me in a glass of beer, won't you, Zachary?" I returned half a smile, quite befuddled. "Gentlemen!" he bellowed again, very unclerically. He had to call twice to be heard, but once the surrounding firemen distinguished his voice, they came to his call with amiable attention. He, in turn, beamed upon them with avuncular pride, patting this one and that on a shoulder. The empty mugs were passed hand to hand and returned, full to the brim.

"I didn't know you drank this kind of beverage, Avery," I shouted.

"Normally, I don't." He nodded. "But these boys—good lads every one of them—they more or less insisted, and once in a long while can't be all that bad, can it, Zachary?"

I agreed that it was not and toasted his health. We drank.

"And the health of the fine and fast young filly, Miss Deception," he cried and drank again. I paused, being somewhat taken aback by the fluid I had just imbibed. Avery noticed my wide, watering eyes. "Ah, yes," he laughed. "That. Well, when I told the fellows that I wasn't normally a drinker, they offered to water down the beer for me. From that." He pointed to a large glass jug a couple of steps behind me, full of a clear liquid. "Ha, ha! I let them think they'd put one over on me, as if I'd never tasted purified alcohol! Hmm." He paused. "The beer is a bit green, though," he muttered, placing a steadying hand on the tabletop.

It was, to say the least, a unique atmosphere atop the podium. As we stood there, elbow to elbow with the rest of the security force, drinking our sour fortified beer, it felt almost for a moment as if we were alone, two friends on a sunny day.

"Have you seen Jack?" Avery asked.

"Yes. He's down there somewhere, doing his official stewardly duty."

"Good, good. I hope he's enjoying this. He so looked forward to it, and then all these distractions kept coming up . . ."

"Yes, Avery. That's what I came to speak to you about."

We were forced to pause, as another bag of money arrived to be dumped in the satchel at our feet. Avery pointed me forward, and we shared the fine view from between the forms of firemen, who themselves gawked and cheered at the track, at passing friends, and at any young female of acceptable proportions.

"Avery. Listen, I need to talk to you about Lloyd Bingham."

"Lloyd Bingham?"

"Yes, and Miss Green. Sarah Green."

"Miss Green?"

Again we were interrupted. One of the firemen was pointing down at the money satchel, asking permission from Avery to "nab a bit to buy a few buns for the boys."

"Oh, no! Can't do that!" Reaching into the pocket of his long, black coat, he pulled out a wallet and passed the man the pair of banknotes from it. "We should all put in and get them something, though. They deserve it. Good lads all. Zachary? Have you by any chance got . . . ?"

I passed over the coins in my pocket, and the fellow disappeared to buy bread for the boys. I resumed the conversation.

"Lloyd Bingham, Avery. I understand you know him?"

"Hmm. Well, for all that, I do. I can't say I'm terribly fond of the old whizzler, but I visited him a few times. Sick, you know, very sick. Not long for this world, if he's got it right."

"But he likes you, Avery."

"Likes me? Hmm. Yes, I think you're probably right. Of course I did visit him all the way out there at his farm, but still, I wonder what effect it is I have over these dismal old rich people? I don't much like *them*. This Bingham actually talked about building a church for me, you know."

"Yes, he told me that. He likes you."

"Of course he's dying, you know? Hears the devil's clippity clop footsteps and wants to store up just a few quick treasures in heaven, where moth and rust do not so on and so forth."

I interrupted. "Did you know that his son had hired Sarah Green to be his personal assistant?"

I don't think Avery heard me. "Or a monument for himself," he continued. "If he built a church, he'd probably insist on a little family throne in it, across from the choir, perhaps."

"Avery!" The murmur and laughter of the crowd seemed to be growing even louder.

"He might even want to be buried under the nave, like some medieval knight . . ."

"Avery! About Sarah Green working in that house!" He heard at least part of that.

"Miss Green? Lovely young woman. Ask Jack."

"Jack knows, Avery. He's very concerned about her. We need you to talk to Lloyd Bingham."

"Bingham? I believe the old dog quite likes me, you know, Zachary?"

"Yes. We need you to talk to him about Miss Green."

"Absolutely! My highest recommendations. I shall relay my highest regards . . ."

I realized that for the time being, it was hopeless. It would have to wait for later. At least, I thought, I had introduced the topic. Our best chance at getting the contract quashed was to have Avery intervene, but there was no time now to discuss it. I had some difficulty making my way through the press to the top of the steps at first, then from somewhere between the podium and the track came a distant squeal of female distress, followed immediately by gales of laughter from the firemen, who all rushed forward to the front rail. The rear of the platform emptied enough for me to shake hands with Avery, then descend.

I thought the start of the second heat must be soon approaching, so I was in a hurry when I got down, but before I could take more than a few steps, I halted. It was Roselle, standing like a Shakespearean ghost in the shade of a large maple tree. He called to me.

"Beddoes! Hey there, partner!" I strode over and told him to shut up. "Don't worry, Beddoes," he replied, "or let's just call you Zachary."

"People could hear you, Roselle. Do I need to explain to you again that you can only inform on me once? If someone hears you . . ."

"Relax, partner. No one is paying attention to you."

"Well, get the hell out of here, and leave me alone."

"I needed to tell you about the changes I decided on."

I could feel a bristling at the base of my neck. "Changes? Changes to what? We haven't decided on anything."

"I have. First of all, I'm dissolving our partnership."

"We never had a partnership."

"Good. I'm glad that's settled. Now, money. You give me my gold and I go away. All of it. Tomorrow."

"Go to hell."

"You're right that I can only reveal your identity once, but starting tomorrow night, I'll begin asking questions here and there. A few rumours. The longer you delay, the greater the chance that one of my little hints will come home to roost later on."

He was right, of course. He had me. "I can't do a thing tomorrow. It's Sunday. I need to have access to my bank."

"Ha! You can get that gold whenever you need it—*and* change it into cash! No white man banker involved for you, is there?"

"Who told you that I . . . ?"

"A Chinaman! You're not the only Yankee in this town who has connections with the Chinamen!" He laughed. "But I won't rush you. Monday, then."

I seemed to feel a cold breeze. White Lee had been to his money changers only the day before, trading almost all my remaining gold for currency. I could not imagine them discussing business with Roselle, but I couldn't see any other explanation.

"So you can buy information in Chinatown, can you?"

"Anyone sells information—for the right price," he laughed. "Your yellow friends are not immune." He probably saw me tensing up, and continued quickly. "I'm not greedy. I'm being more than reasonable here. Four pounds. I bet you have forty. After that I'm gone, and you won't have to think of me for years. Maybe never. I've decided to go to the South Pacific. I've been talking to some whalers and traders, and I think I'll buy a little island all my own, where the sun shines every day of the year. Get myself six little kanaka wives—one for each day of the week and they can fight over me on Sunday. You can do that down there, if you've got the gold. Four pounds. Sunday."

"Monday," I growled.

"Monday then, at the Watson Brothers Saloon, just down and across from my hotel," he said brightly.

"After supper Monday night. Eight o'clock. I'll be waiting with the gold in the saloon." At that, I stomped away. I didn't know why I had insisted on that particular time and day, but I felt like I should insist on *something*, just for my own self-respect.

A swell of noise went up from the crowd. The horses were being led back out onto the track.

Glancing back once over my shoulder to ensure that Roselle was out of sight, I wound my way through the swirling throng and took a place in a short lineup leading to the middle betting table. From my inside coat pocket I drew about ninety per cent of my life's savings.

For a moment, I literally could not breathe. My face felt frozen. My mind stopped.

A sour fellow with pock-marked skin demanded my wager. I handed him the money, and as he counted it, I murmured, "On the filly. Miss Deception," in a hoarse voice. Then, with a nondescript scrap of paper in my hand, I blundered back toward my family.

Ross jumped up and down when he saw me, ran forward, and dragged me back to the red wool blanket on the grass. He had painted a moustache on his upper lip with mustard. Sue pointed to the starter standing just down from us in the centre of the track, speaking up to the two riders. The man called Danny said something, and they all laughed. I knelt beside Sue, put my mouth close to her ear, and told her that I loved her very much. She was shocked, and still looked frightened when she gazed back toward the starting line.

Since there were only two horses in the final heat, an unusual sort of technique was used to start them—at least it seemed unique to me, but I am no authority on horse racing. I don't know whether it was done to even up their chances for attaining the inside track, or whether it was used simply for dramatic effect. Both competitors were led about twenty feet behind the starting line, and facing away—opposite to their true direction. It was unnatural to the racing animals, and they fought their riders a bit, delaying matters for a minute.

Against the starter's protests, Christy Riordan let Miss Deception stroll a full turn across the track at her leisure, and when she was beside her home enclosure, Christy shouted out for Mac Bingham. The big man, hearing his name repeated at volume, ran out onto the edge of the track. Without any word of explanation, Christy threw his whip down at Bingham's feet and turned away again. Then both horses settled into their positions. Bingham was furious. He cursed all Irishmen in general and Christy Riordan in particular, then reluctantly picked up the whip and stalked back to his position. The starter, evidently satisfied, walked away, holding his pistol in the air, while the horses stomped restlessly in place, backs to the start line. He walked to a spot a dozen paces off.

Then he fired the pistol.

Danny and Christy were both ready, but it was young Mr. Riordan that gained the initial advantage as the two horses spun in a half-circle, kicking up great sprays of red dust, legs and hooves flailing in all directions. Ojai was undoubtedly the stronger of the two animals, but fleet-footed Miss Deception cut a slightly tighter turn, and by the time they crossed the official start, she was on the inside rail and about a head in front. Once they were past, the perspective from our viewpoint changed immediately. In a couple of seconds, we could see only hooves and haunches. A couple more, and all we saw was a cloud of red dust. Everyone on the hillside was on their feet. The spectators in the grandstands were screaming. From their angle, they could see the horses for a bit longer, around the turn, although no one in all of Beacon Hill kept silent, whether they could see the runners or not. I looked toward the public betting podium and saw the distant figures of the firemen jumping up and down in a long double line. I half-expected to see the railing collapse.

It seemed that the suspense was actually audible, in the form of a slowly rising rumble. The apprehensive crowd held its breath and turned, waiting for the arrival of the horses.

Ross was leaping about, licking at his moustache between screeches of "God save the Queen! God save the Queen!" Sue looked up at me, reached out, and touched my lips. "Why . . . ?" she began to ask.

The horses rounded the corner into view, head and head, neck and neck, as we knew they would be. Coming out of the turn, Christy and Miss Deception made use of their slim advantage in position, pulled tight to the rail, and charged—wide-eyed, bent forward, straining for the extra inch. Suddenly, I realized that she was ahead—less than half a length—of the big black stallion. There was only a hundred yards to go. Danny and Ojai, of course, knew this as well, and the inches of separation between the boots of the two jockeys began to shrink. When they came level with us, they were almost even, almost touching.

I have tried to review my memory of what happened next many times. On the whole, I have confidence in what I saw. Then again, having returned to the exact position beside the racetrack later on and resuming the same sight lines, I cannot be sure. It seemed quite clear at the time, and the result bears out that what I saw was probably true, but there was dust and there was distance. I have not heard other spectators refer to the details that I witnessed, but I remain confident.

Christy and Danny were leaning forward on their toes. Danny flailed at Ojai's haunch with his whip, up and down in an accelerating rhythm. Christy appeared to be shouting in the filly's ear, although his tensed body remained almost frozen. And then I truly believe I saw the big black horse turn his head for an instant toward Miss Deception. This could not have been effected by the jockey—it was the horse himself, plunging his shining head at her, as if to force her into the rail. And Miss Deception snapped back. How she could do this, restrained so by stress and momentum and reins and harness, I cannot properly tell. As I have said, it was not popularly acknowledged afterwards, but I believe I saw the stallion nip at her, and the filly nip back.

Then they both almost went down.

The crowd emitted a gasp of shock as one. Women screamed. But neither animal completely lost its footing. Ojai, though, was suddenly careening at an angle, almost throwing his rider before he pulled the horse up short. Miss Deception, after a momentary stumble, ran straight forward, across the finish mark.

We three howled like dogs and danced on our blanket.

From the edge of my vision, I spotted Jack Elliston running down the dirt track, and I stepped away from my family. Jack was in the company of two other stewards, and they were all on the scene almost instantly, even before the various grooms had reached the horses to calm them and release the riders. Questions were shouted, although of course I could not hear the exact words over the din of the multitude. I called to Sue that I would be back straightaway and jogged toward all this action, followed—predictably—by my son.

The spectators on the raised dais beside the winning team's enclosure were in an uproar—shouting, dancing, back-slapping. At the centre of this, I could see Sarah Green being led by a red-headed heavyweight down to ground level. She alone, of all the company, still looked distraught. I angled toward her, and she looked up in time to notice me. She called to me.

"Mr. Bingham wants me down there! Beside him at the presentation."

I started to answer her, hardly noticing the big redhead, until he shoved at my shoulder. "Back off, mate!" he bellowed.

"She's my friend!" I called back, but she was already disappearing into the crowd.

"Zachary! Zachary!" I turned to hear who was shouting my name and saw Billy Horne, rocking precariously on his chair, his huge white leg threatening to capsize him. I tried to steady him, just as the man assigned to attend to him arrived to take charge. Over the fellow's shoulder, Billy shouted, "Tell Christy that I love him! Tell him he's a perfect genius!"

As he spoke these words, Ross, driven wild by the excitement of it all, screamed to me. "Who is that? What is this?" and for some reason, kicked Billy Horne in the leg. My son is beyond all prediction The poor man howled, but I had no chance to apologize as he was ferried away from the general hubbub. Logically speaking, he had no business being there in the first place.

I don't know precisely what I thought I was doing at that point. I wanted to be where Jack was, and a gap in the melee allowed me to slip under the rope and onto the track. As I arrived there, near the opening to Miss Deception's enclosure, I saw Danny scratching his jaw and shaking his head to the stewards, indicating that he was claiming no foul, then, almost as one, the stewards definitively pointed at Miss Deception and declared her fairly the winner. Once again the crowd went wild.

Jack spotted me then. He pointed in my direction and shouted that I should stay exactly where I was. Briefly, he conferred with the other officials. Ross was now clinging to my leg, gazing up at me in rapture, as if I, personally, had arranged for the race to be so exciting and so poetically perfect. Then, unexpectedly, I found myself looking up at Danny, who had paused the black stallion beside me.

"Good race!" I shouted.

He recognized me and laughed. "Yes," he answered, "it was."

"Your Mr. Smith in Chicago won't think so!"

But he shook his head. "No. No, Smith just likes to run the race!"

And that was as much as I ever knew about that. Then Jack was beside me.

"What a race! Damn it, Zachary! What a race!" I didn't answer because his attention was already focused on the crowd, searching the faces of the spectators. "Sarah," he asked me. "Have you seen Sarah?"

He leaned his ear forward, and I told him that Miss Green was off somewhere with Mac Bingham. "I think Mac wants her on his sleeve when he presents himself with the prize, the trophy, or whatever."

Jack grimaced. Looking farther afield, he pointed in the general direction of the grandstands and asked anew, "Avery? I wonder where my brother is?"

I laughed at that, thinking at this stage that nothing much was awry.

"By now, I doubt that your brother himself knows where he is," I chuckled.

"What? What do you mean? He's with the money and the fire brigade, isn't he?"

"Yes, yes, Jack, but they got him into the festive mood, and he's been drinking with a bit of gusto. Beer and fireman's grain alcohol."

I knew he would be surprised at this, but I expected him to laugh about it or, at the worst, shake his head and suggest that we join the good reverend, but instead he closed his eyes, twisted up his face, and started to curse. One more glance at the place where Sarah Green had been sitting, and he turned on his heel.

"What, Jack? What?" I demanded.

He halted, considered for a second, then grabbed my coat sleeve. "You'd better come with me, Zachary. God only knows what Avery's done by now." Seeing my blank expression, he added, "Liquor in any quantity is pure poison to my brother."

"He looked fine when I saw him. No need to worry. He was getting a little spiritual, a little emotional . . ." I stopped. Jack's eyes were glazed. He was having visions.

"Come on. We'd better hurry." And he was off.

I bent down, took Ross by the shoulders, and spoke in my sternest paternal tone. "You go back and find your mother, boy. Hurry up, before the crowd gets moving. Tell her to get the buggy from the field and head for home. I'll be there directly. Quick now!"

He ran off in one direction, and I chased Jack Elliston in the other. I caught up to him as he was working his way with great difficulty through the masses. Everyone was headed either to the grandstand area to see the prize presented, or to the wagering podium to cash in their betting tickets. I checked to ensure that my own ticket was safe, stuffing it deep down into my pocket. Once through the general flow, we climbed a few feet up the slope and hurried along the hillside as quickly as we could, pushing our way through gorse and broom, scrambling over boulders. As much to catch my breath as anything, I took hold of Jack's arm as we paused, trying to get a view of the back side of the raised platform.

"Why so worried, man? Avery is full grown and stable. A little liquor . . ."

"Damn it, no! I can't allow it—it will all go wrong! It's happened over and over, and the rascal promised me never again. He promised me!"

"But what harm could he do? He's surrounded by the ever-loving fire department."

Jack was not mollified. "A madness comes down on Avery, and he hears the voice of God when the booze gets between his ears. With luck, he's only healing the sick and raising the dead by now, but he has been known to go forth and smite the ungodly."

"So he might try to smite someone. It can't be all that bad for a race day."

"People do not take kindly to being smitten by a clergyman."

We scurried onward, down the slope on our backsides, and on toward the back stairs of the podium, where a tightly bunched group of guards and bank tellers were arguing among themselves. "Get the manager!" one fellow shouted, and another called after, "Get Mr. Bingham!"

We could see no sign of Avery.

Jack grabbed one of the grumbling, dishevelled firemen and questioned him.

"It's that preacher," the man spat. "He's taken off with all the money."

"I never trusted the son of a bitch," his neighbour added in a surly tone.

Without comment, Jack and I bulled our way between the two. We penetrated to the core of the tragedy in time to hear one of the tellers wailing his excuse to his employer, who had just arrived. "It was you who put the preacher in charge, sir!"

"He was *not* in charge!"

"He acted like he was in charge, and he told me he was taking the money down to be sorted and counted, sir."

"Damn it!" The bank manager turned his attention to the nearest of the firemen. "And what the hell were you boys doing?"

The nearest, drunkenly wiping the sweat off his face, groaned, "We was watching the race, Mister. You *said* we could watch the race!"

Then Mac Bingham's very loud, very angry voice bellowed out over the small assembly, demanding to know what was going on. Before he spotted us, Jack and I squirmed our way loose, cut across a field of scrub bush, and circled back toward the clearing where the horses were kept. As we caught sight of The Commissioner tethered to a line with several other mounts, Jack halted. "Avery's horse is gone," he observed. "I was hoping he'd pass out before he got this far. Damn and blazes! Now we've got to chase him."

"But why . . . ? Why . . . ?"

"Don't try to figure. It's the devil's own logic inside Avery's brain. We have to find him before those angry bastards chase him down. Where's your horse, Zachary?"

The words were just forming on my lips to tell him that we had come in the hotel buggy, when I heard the sound of wagon wheels on the roadway, which was only twenty feet away now, past a screen of trees. Overlaid atop this sound was a shrill little voice calling out repeatedly, "God save the Queen!"

Jack ran off to collect his horse, shouting, "Meet me at my boarding house!" and I ran straight through the trees to intercept the little dogcart. I had no time to look for a proper path. The thorny bushes ripped one of my trouser-legs, and a vindictive twig stabbed under my arm and directly up into my nose. When I burst out of the bushes onto the road, I found myself just behind the rattling wheels of the little carriage.

"Hello!" I bellowed. "Stop there!" It was loud enough to frighten both Ross and Sue, as well as our horse. Then, as I scrambled to get on board, I was almost run down by Jack Elliston, galloping through on The Commissioner. Once I was onto the bench with the reins in my hand, I drove the buggy harder than it had ever been driven. It was not intended to pound along like it was escaping hell itself, and I feared at first that we would all be rattled to pieces.

I made no friends that day by my manner of driving. Through Ross and Sue's hasty efficiency, we had managed to place ourselves ahead of most of the returning racegoers, but there were a few carriages already on their way back into the city. I passed at least three of these, taking more than my share of the road and running the risk of everyone winding up in the ditch. Both Ross and the horse seemed to enjoy this exercise. Sue hid her head under a scarf. We were rumbling down Government Street a very short time later.

My son has an ability that continuously amazes me. He can, at times, decelerate from being frantic to being in the deepest of slumbers in less than one minute. Almost immediately once we were off the worst section of the rutted hard-pack and onto the relatively smooth dirt of the city street, his eyes began to flicker open and shut. Sixty seconds later, his eyes were closed, his mouth gaping open, and he was drooling against his mother's breast. This forced a change in my plans. I had thought to drop the two of them off there, on the main street, and turn toward the Elliston apartments down Fort, but I could scarcely expect Sue to carry the sleeping boy all the way to the hotel. And so I drove, trying not to express my impatience to my family. I didn't really know what my role was in helping Jack rescue his brother from the predicament he was in, but I felt a great urgency to arrive before the police, or Mac Bingham's men, or even the firefighters. This, not to mention the fact that Avery was carrying around my life's savings in his bag.

Arriving in front of the Celestial, I saw the boot boy dozing on a porch chair and called for him to come and take charge of the horse, who seemed to enjoy running more than any reliable cart horse should, then I took Ross from Sue's arms and hurried inside. I carried him up to his own room, dropped him softly on his bed, and continued on without a pause. I did, however, detour into my own room, where I threw my suit jacket on a chair, after transferring my wagering ticket to my trouser pocket. Ten seconds later, I was bounding down the stairs and back to the buggy in my long black coat, with my old felt hat atop my head.

The horse pulled me enthusiastically down Government to Fort, and down Fort to the boarding house. I did not see Jack, but I had not expected him to be outside, so I was pulling the poor beast to a halt, ready to jump down, when I spotted a small boy running from the house, coming toward me. When he reached the buggy, he shouted out, "Who are you?" like the captain of the guard. He was about twelve years old—a dangerous and unpredictable age for a child.

"I am Mr. Zachary."

"Good. The other fellow said you was to go down to the mission." (He actually pronounced it like "Domitian," but I didn't figure he was referring to the Roman emperor.) "Do I still got to stay here? I only got given but one penny."

"Then go to hell, lad." I should have been more explicit here, instead of just yielding to my mood and insulting the boy. Later on he would be in the same spot and give the same directions to the angry men chasing the Elliston brothers. I drove back down Fort to Wharf Street.

Avery spent a good deal of his time at the mission. It was his chosen spiritual project, and I didn't disagree much with his choice. Not being a humanitarian myself, though, I hadn't been inside the place more than once. It wasn't far from the brothers' lodgings, and I was rounding the corner watchfully within a couple of minutes. There was no crowd of angry gamblers on the street yet.

The mission was really only a bland dwelling, neither very large nor particularly small. At one time it had been painted white, but erosion by the sea breeze had now altered it to an unpromising grey. Inside, church services were held in an otherwise bare sitting room, where the down and out sat on wooden benches to earn their soup. After the meal, any number of varied, wayfarers slept on the bedroom floors—veterans of various conflicts involving booze and bad luck.

I didn't need to go inside the house this time either. The Ellistons were sitting, side by side, on a moss-patched wooden bench in the front yard. I took the wagon off to one side and tied it to a fence board, then walked slowly over to join them. All urgency was gone. Avery was slumped against his brother's shoulder, and he was weeping. On the ground, close to his feet, was the canvas bag, stuffed so full of money that the buttons threatened to burst. Jack did not actually look at me, although he lifted his off hand in a sort of greeting and continued to stare at the ground five feet in front of him. I bypassed them at first, walking to where Avery's horse, wandering free in the yard, was starting to browse through the lonely flower bed next to the front stairs. I led her to a spot beside the woodshed where she could crop down the high grass if she wished, and secured her there. The Commissioner was tied to the fence on the street.

I stood behind them for a bit, listening to Avery's forlorn ramble. "It's the same thing all over again, and I'm the fool. I'm the fool again! The dog that returns to his vomit."

"You're just stupid when you drink . . ."

"Stupid! Vile! Wretched!"

"Stupid—that's all, and that's enough. But we've got through it before, and we'll get through it this time."

"A fool. A Biblical fool. Proper translation: *one devoid of moral sensitivity*."

"Nonsense. Your moral sense is . . ."

"It's so much like that business at Kent, isn't it, Jack? The one that got us kicked out of England."

"Not as bad. That was three long days before we found you, and damage that couldn't be undone. This time we've still got the money, and look— you're almost sober."

"Those fine young firemen will tie ropes to my arms and legs and tear me apart, and I'm not sober. No! Just look! Everything is still rolling and rolling . . ."

It sounded as if he might be ready to weep again as I stepped forward into his sight. "Well, then. I'm glad we caught up to you," I said, rather lamely.

He jerked himself upright, if only for a moment. "Zachary! Hello there. My goodness, have I dragged you into this?"

"I'm just here for the entertainment, old man. We'll laugh about this over dinner in a couple of days."

He shook his head and stared forward, wide-eyed, like a prisoner in the dock. "No, I don't think so, Zachary. The wages of stupidity and drunkenness do not pass over so easily. You see, I've done this sort of thing before—been kept out of jail only because of the family name. Father sent me abroad, cast me out like a demon out of a pig, before I could ruin us all. Poor Jack had to come along . . ." Once again he slumped against his brother's shoulder as tears flowed from his eyes. "Jack was charged with keeping me out of trouble, but it seems that no man is capable of such a thing. Least of all myself."

"Oh, come now, brother. We haven't done so bad."

"There was Baltimore, straight out of the gate."

"We were just starting out then. We hadn't got the arrangement settled properly. After that . . ."

"After that, I promised. I promised you, didn't I?"

Jack nodded. "You promised."

"As I had promised others before you. Including Father, and a couple of magistrates."

"Ah!"

"I'm not good with promises, and I should be. I'm a minister. I'm an ordained clergyman, a reverend, a man of God—or that's what they say if they don't know better. Not good with promises. I'm sorry, Jack. I'm so sorry."

"You've said that already. Enough."

"Broken promises and vows, like a string of beads around my neck. If only I was Catholic! The Romans are so much better at vows and things, you know. If I was Catholic, I could become a monk and take a bunch of vows—total abstinence among them—and just live in a little room. A vow of silence, even. I could take one of those. I wouldn't mind. All this talking and talking. I wouldn't mind doing without that. Maybe that's it, Jack. I can go to some monastery—maybe in France. I like the French. God wouldn't mind me bowing to the Pope if he knew I didn't mean it, and you could go home at last . . ."

There was a pause. Jack leaned over, picked up the canvas bag, and set it in front of him. He gave it a kick.

"What the devil were you thinking, Avery?"

The poor man leaned his head back and concentrated, as if it was indeed a difficult matter to recall. Then, "Yes, what was I thinking?" He straightened himself up. "Actually, it came to me when you visited me up there on the wooden platform thing, Zachary . . ."

"Avery! I didn't . . ."

"No, of course you didn't. We were just talking—talking about Lloyd Bingham, I think, and the true spirit of giving. What was it you came to see me about back there, my friend?"

"Nothing," I answered. "It doesn't matter."

"Correct. But we talked about giving, and I looked at all that money, and suddenly, it struck me very clearly that it should be given to the poor!"

"But it wasn't yours to give, Avery!"

"Yes, Jack, but here's the thing. I realized something important. Or at least it seemed important at the time. I thought about whose money it actually was, and I realized that between the time that it was wagered on one horse or another and the time that some horse actually wins the race, well, it doesn't belong to *anybody*! It's just sort of in between, and it might as well be given to the poor! But I thought I'd better be quick about it, before the race was run, and I'm afraid I had to make up a story to get past a couple of people—but the firemen were all watching the race—and I got on my horse and rode off to give it to the poor." He spoke the last words softly, and gazed sadly toward the dark windows of the mission. "But when I got here, the poor weren't home."

"And you thought everyone would just let it pass, and the poor would just . . ."

"It seemed logical to me at the time. I could explain it to everyone and they would see. I could defend it on the basis of Holy Scripture."

"And perhaps you thought Zachary and I would hold them away while you explained?"

He shrugged. "I hadn't thought it all through, but it seemed at the time . . ."

"Well," I interrupted, "I think our first bout of explanation is about to arrive."

Three riders on horseback were coming around the corner. They spotted The Commissioner and trotted toward us.

"Do you recognize them?" Jack asked me.

"One of them. The man in the front is one of Bingham's ranch men. Probably all three." They looked very unhappy. "I suppose it's my fault they found us. I should have told the boy you left at your lodgings to keep his mouth shut."

Jack shook his head. "Sooner or later . . ."

Avery rubbed his eyes. "I would have preferred a bit later," he mumbled sadly.

They fairly leaped from their horses and scampered over to stand in a line before us, looking sinister. They didn't know exactly what to do next. I stood beside the bench, at Avery's shoulder. Finally, the man I had recognized pointed and spoke.

"Is that the money?"

Jack reached out one foot and pulled the canvas bag behind his legs. "It is. All of it. We were just about to take it back to the racetrack. My brother got a little confused about his duties. He got sidetracked."

As comment to this, the big man snorted. "We'll take the money back."

Jack shook his head. "No. It's our job. We don't even know who you are."

"We're sent to find the money. We'll take it back."

"No," I said. I think I spoke a little louder than the other two. "We'll take the money back."

He looked at me, drawing in his breath and rocking back his shoulders so as to look formidable. Then he saw that I was standing with my old friend, the long-barrelled Colt .45 Peacemaker, hanging loose at my side. This is another method of looking formidable. He looked at me in silence for a second, probably gauging whether I was likely to actually shoot him. Eventually he spoke in the same tone as previous. "If you think we're going to let you . . ."

Briefly there, in the front yard of the ramshackle mission house, I felt like the defiant and reckless young man I had once been, rather than the domesticated soul who wanders the countryside as his preferred form of pleasure. I raised the barrel of the gun and pointed it at his foot. He couldn't hold himself and stepped back, drawing his foot away. I followed it, aiming at a spot just above the toe of his boot. Frankly, even I didn't know if I would shoot.

The three men stepped back three paces.

"Avery," I said, "I think you should come with me in the buggy. Bring the money bag, and we can put it behind the seat. Jack, you can ride behind us, why don't you? And you three . . ." I tried to put a bit of contempt into my voice. "You can lead us there, out in front, so you look very important."

And that was the order in which we set off.

We rode slowly now, at a pace suitable for a one-horse buggy. At first Avery, sitting next to me, assumed a reasonable appearance of slightly inebriated dignity. A few minutes later, he looked again like he was on the verge of tears. Just as it seemed he was going to nod off to sleep, he pulled himself straight on the seat next to me and asked a question.

"Mr. Zachary. You didn't tell me, and I can't remember—what did you come up to ask me during the races? Was it not something to do with Sarah Green? What were you meaning to ask me?"

"It doesn't matter anymore," I told him.

THERE WAS SOMETHING of an unpleasant scene when we arrived at Beacon Hill, but that was all. A huge cry of derision went up when the banker announced that the money had arrived and was ready to be divided up. A couple of the firefighters made the almost obligatory threatening gestures toward Avery and Jack, but Avery was to remain only an object of general suspicion, rather than prosecution. For their own benefit, rather than ours, Bingham and his associates chose to maintain the story that Avery had simply misunderstood his orders and tried to transport the money to the Bank of British Columbia in town.

Quietly and discreetly, with an expression that I can only describe as bashful, I presented my scrap of paper to an erstwhile bank teller, and in return received an astonishing amount of money.

It was only later, when I returned home, that I realized I had never had any bullets in my gun.

Chapter Ten

AFTERNOON WAS FADING INTO THE cool of evening by the time I asked our poor horse to drag me one more time into the centre of Victoria. By one standard, I should have been euphoric with the huge fistful of banknotes in my pocket, but the debacle with Avery Elliston had drained me. I felt like an irritable outsider as I witnessed the scene in the city centre. The racing public had returned to town, quickly forgetting any post-race irregularities, and local entrepreneurs had now enticed a good number of the winners to spend their sudden wealth on food and drinks for their less fortunate friends. Add to this the number of unlucky characters without friends who simply wanted to drown their sorrows, and an intoxicated, intoxicating mix filled the bars and saloons, spilling out onto the street in an unruly festival. Every self-professed musician who could squeeze a squeeze-box or strum a mandolin was now wandering hopefully between diners and drinkers, occasionally being given a coin, either to play or to go away.

When I reached the hotel, dinner was already in progress. A chair had been reserved—I believe it was for me—but the table was as full as I have ever seen it, and louder than anything that did not involve Chinese people playing games with tiles. There were two different Americans and a group of business people from up the island. Every one of them seemed to be taking a turn at describing the race as if they had been the only person to witness it. I chose to eat my bowl of stew in the kitchen, and was just mopping up the last of the gravy with a corner of bread when the first of the other diners excused themselves from the table. Among these was my father-in-law, who I intercepted at the base of the stairs and diverted into the empty back parlour. I confess, he looked very tired, and I almost changed my mind about consulting him at this late hour. His eyes brightened, however, as soon as he began to speak about the race.

"My wealthy son! You good and rich now?"

I forced a smile. "A little richer."

"Your uncle Boon is so happy. So happy. He pretty rich now too, I think."

"He was rich before he came here."

"Yes. True. Always better to be a little more rich."

"I didn't see him in there. Did he not come back to the hotel?"

Old Lee clapped his hands in delight. "They make special dinner for him. Celebration!" And with that, he rattled off about a half-dozen names of Boon's Chinese hosts—names that I did not recognize but evidently were impressive. Lee finished with a solemn observation: "Lot of Chinese men now a little bit more rich. Thanks to Boon. Thanks to you and me!"

I laughed, my spirits for a second raised by the old man's glee. "What about you? Were you not invited to the celebration?"

He waved dismissively. "Too tired. Out in the sun all day. Very tired." Then he winked, and whispered, "But I too am a little bit rich now!" and added, "Thanks to you, my son!"

"I'm relieved that Miss Deception did not let us all down. But before you go get some rest, I'd like you to think about something. I need to know something, and the sooner I can find out, the better."

"What, what, what?"

"Well, it seems, father of my bride and partner in my finances, that someone you deal with has been telling tales, gossiping about business."

"What is this? Who is this?"

"It would appear that someone who changes our gold for currency has been telling the story to someone who wishes me harm."

I was glad I had taken him into a quiet corner, because his cry of protest and disbelief lacked all decorum. The gist of what he said was that this was unthinkable—that the man with whom he dealt had secrets of his own to guard and he guarded the privacy of his clients very attentively.

I calmed him down a bit and told him, "It isn't a lot of secrets that were shared—only that I traded gold for money from time to time. This ugly man Roselle knew about it, and he claimed to have learned this from his Chinese contacts."

"Chinese contacts! Goddamn bitch!" His English expletives where no less heartfelt for their inappropriate juxtaposition. "Who is this Roselle?"

"I told you—a nasty man who means me harm. The story he got from the money changer doesn't have much to do with it, but it rather bothered me, all the same. Just think about it, and the next time we do that sort of business . . ."

"I will go. Right now."

"No, no. You don't have to . . ."

He paid no attention to me. He was already in the boot room looking for his coat. I felt a little bad at having caused the tired old men to feel such distress, but I knew he was too stubborn to reason with in such a mood, so

I retired to the front porch to smoke a cigar and dwell upon things. Oddly, the prospect of abandoning Sarah Green to a disastrous employment in the Bingham household worried me more than my own predicament with Roselle. It was my foolish curiosity that had precipitated her tragic decision, and now I feared that she faced a year under a contract that would destroy her.

In spite of my gloom, I had to marvel at the beauty of the twilit dusk, which felt like the first summer evening of the year. It wasn't long before Sue joined me, after ensuring that our guests knew where they were going and our staff knew their duties. She sat on the chair next to mine, the two of us hand in hand, silent for a minute, until I was ready to speak. I told her what had happened after the race, about the fiasco involving the money, and the things we hadn't previously known about the Elliston brothers. I recounted some of the threats and insults and lamented the state of Avery's battered mind and soul.

"What about Sarah? How is Miss Green?" she asked as I paused to relight my cigar.

I shook my head sadly. "We have arranged a meeting tomorrow at noon out at the Binghams' farm—just myself and them—so I can give over the rest of Miss Green's belongings that are still here. I guess I intimated that I had one more thing to say at that time, although I don't know what that will be. Avery and Jack will go out there with me, but Mac already made it clear that they wouldn't be allowed onto the property. They won't even let Jack say goodbye to her."

"Not surprising. Dangerous for Mr. Bingham. He knows they are in love."

"In love? It's a bit early to say that, isn't it?"

"Not at all. Yes. They are in love."

I shrugged. A minute later, Sue asked me, "And what else do you think you can say to Mac Bingham?"

Sweeping the cloud of cigar smoke aside, I answered that it was nothing, just a spur-of-the-moment comment to justify a meeting with Miss Green. Through a screen of cigar fog, I saw a man walking down the middle of the street toward us.

"You have no idea of some way we might help this poor woman?"

I grimaced. "I'm going to take a substantial pocketful of gold with me—enough to be double the wages of a *personal assistant*, but I doubt that they'll look at it. This is now a matter of principle to them, on top of everything else. And we pretty much ruined his moment of glory at the racetrack . . ."

The man walking down the street was beginning to take shape. As I watched his approach, it became a familiar shape, and a welcome one.

"So it's you!" I called out.

"Did you doubt me?" he shouted back.

"I didn't realize the letter would get there so fast. You must have run out the door the minute you read it? Did the ferry . . . ?"

"I know a few fellows with boats. Finding this hotel was probably the hardest part. A bit out of the way, don't you think?"

"I gave you good directions. I know you can read."

"Yes, I can. And here I am."

I turned to Sue. "This is my wife, the finest woman in the world. And Sue, this is Mr. James G. Swan, late of Olympia, Territory of Washington. Bring your bag up here, Mr. Swan, and let me shake your hand."

Greetings were exchanged all around, then I picked up his travelling valise. "The hotel is full of people here for the race, but we'll move the two Americans in together and give you one of their rooms," I suggested. My wife overruled me.

"If you don't mind sleeping in a room downstairs near the furnace, Mr. Swan, there's a clean bed already made up."

"You mean Christy's bed?" I asked. "Where's Christy?"

Sue frowned apologetically. "I had not yet told you. He could not find any of you after the race, and all the others were so mad about things. He came and picked up his belongings and went home to Sooke."

"He went home? He'll never get there before dark."

"I said this as well, but he tells me his horse knows the way in the dark and goodbye to you and to Jack and so on."

"Did the fat bastard pay him properly for winning the race?" I growled.

Sue answered in a more ladylike tone. "I believe he was satisfied with his win and with his payment."

I thought to myself that sooner or later I would meet up again with young Mr. Riordan and ensure that this was the case. "Well, then," I said, turning to Swan. "Let's show you to your room."

"I'm sure it'll be just great. Thank you indeed, ma'am. I'd appreciate it if my bag winds up next to the bed, but . . ."

Sue broke in. "You have something else to attend to, Mr. Swan? Do you wish to . . . ?"

"Actually, I'm sort of in the middle of something up there." Swan pointed up the hill and around the corner. "I have a card game going up there with some new guys I met, and I told them I'd only be gone for a round or maybe two. They said this place was just a stone's throw off, rightly enough, and I'm afraid they'll give away my place at the table if I take too long. I just came down to say hello, here I am, and maybe, Zachary, would you care to come up and have a drink? We could talk."

Sue took possession of the valise. "Off you go then, you two. If you arrive late, Mr. Swan, and if my husband has become too drunk to come home, please tap at this door, and Jade May will be on duty to let you in and show you your room."

He thanked her graciously, with an odd bow and a swoop of his hat, after which we scuttled off up the hill. As we rounded the corner, Swan asked me, "Have you told your wife all about me, then?"

"Good Lord, no," I replied. "Why would I do that? She's truly a fine woman, and she's used to being left in the dark."

Driven by an unerring instinct, James G. Swan had managed to find one of the worst saloons among the many in Victoria in which to pass the time until he could find me. I don't even know the name of the place, and I lived two blocks away. To reach it, one had to walk down a long, dark corridor off the street, between a stationer's and a greengrocer's. On this particular day, however, even this backwater dive was almost fully occupied. Swan walked straight across the room to where a battered round table was surrounded by four poker players and an empty chair. Addressing the other players without any sort of greeting, Swan said simply, "Anybody tries to sit down here, you point him over to me, right there. I'm sitting down to talk to my amigo for a while, but this is still my place." This was met by a couple of grunts and nods. Swan and I took a table in the corner and called for beers, which were duly delivered. I paid.

"A bustling little town this is," Swan began. "I had no idea there would be such an energy about some English colonial swamp."

"It's no swamp," I bristled, "but neither is it normally so energetic. The horse race is what it's about. Did I mention in my letter about the horse race?"

"No, you did not, or I would have got here faster and with more money in my pocket."

"You did well to get here as quick as you did, and knowing you, I suspect that whichever horse you bet on would have wandered off into the trees halfway home. Did I tell you about our predicament with the young lady?"

"Yes, you did mention Miss Naomi, and for the record, I resent your comment regarding my knowledge of racehorses. Miss Naomi is the reason I came here on the proverbial eagle's wings."

"Sarah. You had best get used to referring to her as Miss Sarah Green.

And although the situation has changed since I wrote you—several times, I think—she still needs some help."

He sat up straight in his chair and a gleam came to his eye. "How can I help?" he asked, very serious.

"I don't know," I was forced to tell him, after which I explained in detail what was at stake and the obstacles that confronted us. He listened without interruption, then sat pondering all that I had told him. A certain length of time passed and another glass of beer disappeared before he leaned forward and spoke.

"You're lucky you thought of me," he whispered, as though Mac Bingham's agents were leaning over his shoulder. "I had an inkling of what we might be facing. I came prepared. I brought along certain documents. They might prove useful. If we handle this properly, we may be able to extract Miss Naomi—Miss Sarah, that is—without a fight. Although if they want a fight, you can count on me. You know that."

I did indeed know from experience that my new partner was never one to shrink from a scuffle. I listened to his description of the document in question and shook my head. "No. It won't do. We're talking about a woman's long-term prospects. We have to be straightforward and simple about this. Believe me, I have never been one to shrink from a roundabout strategy, but this won't do. Too much deception. When too much depends on illusion, then things go bad in a hurry."

"Nonsense. It will gain us the high ground, and we'll beat the daylights out of the bastards if they try to come back on us."

"We would put Miss Green under even more pressure, more suspense. She is a fragile woman. Her emotions are fragile, at this point."

"Then what the hell did you call me all this way for, Zachary? What do you want me to do?"

Again I needed to calm my friend. "Originally," I said, "I thought your talent as an expert on the law would be of use . . ."

"I am a notary, which is one step above a lawyer!" he crowed. "Have you ever noticed how close those two words are to each other—*lawyer* and *liar*? My personal integrity . . ." He crashed his beer glass down on the table. I tried to divert his choler to the matter at hand.

"You are still very important, friend Swan!" I assured him. "But now it looks as if we may need your fists and your feisty spirit, rather than your legal expertise."

"I brought a gun!" he shouted, to the consternation of all in the small room.

"Good God!"

"Just in case."

"I dearly hope we do not need it, Swan, but your heart is in the right place. As things stand, we may need to storm the bastions of the . . . hmm . . ." I lost the metaphor in mid-speech. "You know what I mean. We might just need to charge in and grab the woman. Hide her for a while. Send her abroad when it's safe!"

I may have neglected to mention that by this time, more than a few beers and a couple of whiskies had passed between our lips. Still, this drunken scheme was about all I had to offer, and Swan took to its mixture of violence and intrigue with enthusiasm.

"They'll be watching the port of Victoria," he observed. "We're on an island, you know . . ."

"I had noticed."

He pondered.

"You're sure we can't make use of that document? It's perfect, I assure you."

"Sorry, Swan. These are educated men. It wouldn't do."

A new fellow—large, English or Scottish—arrived, coming down the dark corridor singing. He stood at the doorway and shouted to all in general, "The perfect day at the races, it was!"

Without missing a beat, Swan shouted back. "Yeah. But the wrong horse won."

The man hollered back that the filly was the best and fastest horse on this half of the continent, which began a loud and hotly contested argument that betrayed not for a minute that Swan knew nothing whatsoever regarding the day's events. Then the Scotsman got too thirsty to continue, and Swan abruptly shifted his attention back to me.

"Right, then. Let's go get the woman. Darkness will be to our advantage."

"No, no, no, Swan! This must be carefully thought out and carefully executed. We don't know anything yet—the layout of the house, where Miss Green's room is, and when she's there. The place is a ranch house—filled with at least a dozen mean sons of bitches."

"I'll look after the guards while you rescue the girl. We can meet up later."

"We don't even know if she's home and awake and ready to be rescued, damn it."

"Well, then, what the hell can we do?"

"Nothing tonight. That's for sure. Tomorrow we are scheduled to meet Mac Bingham at his house around noon. We're going out there with our two allies in this affair, the Elliston brothers."

"Tough guys?"

"As a matter of fact, no. English gentlemen. Jack could hold his own in a bit of action, I suppose, but Avery is a churchman, a minister."

Swan groaned and stared at the ceiling.

"But Jack is brave and he's smart and he has the biggest incentive of all, the most at stake. He loves Miss Green. He wants to marry her."

"Of course he does," Swan retorted. "So do I. So would any normal man. If you weren't already married, I'd say you either loved her or you're a pansy, and I'd knock you down."

"Tomorrow we will survey the premises carefully, inside and out, and learn what we can that might be useful later. I'm taking her a few things she left at the Celestial. They're in a bag, and I'll enclose a note to tell her to be ready."

"But tomorrow," Swan insisted, "if we see an opportunity . . ."

"No, my man! A hundred times, no. Patience is difficult, but we must be patient, for the poor woman's sake."

"She's not such a fragile thing, Zachary. Remember, she did in Hans Chapman Canon with one blow when the chips were down, and escaped up here by raw grit."

"Yes, indeed, and she has all my respect for that. But if you could see her now! She may have used up all of that grit. I think she still sees Canon's ghost sometimes."

At that, I called it enough and suggested we head back to the hotel. It had been an exhausting day for me. Swan demurred, saying that he was running a streak of luck at the card table. He assured me he could find his way later. We both stood up, and just as I was on the threshold of making my exit, we saw the Scotsman approach the players, put one hand on the vacant chair, and ask them if he could join the game for a while. It was like a jolt that straightened my companion's spine.

"You can have my place in the game immediately after one of us has kicked the other out into the alley," he growled, setting his beer glass on a neutral tabletop. The Scotsman, heretofore in a jolly mood, viewed him in amazement.

I intervened.

"James," I said firmly, "you are in Victoria now. We do not fight in saloons in Victoria."

His eyes widened. "Never?"

"Occasionally," I admitted, "but not over something like this."

He stood thoughtfully, wavering a bit, then he looked around the room. "Do you have music?" he asked.

I shrugged. "Not normally."

"Then you just . . . ?" His voice trailed off.

"Pull up another chair," I suggested. "Play cards."

"But *that*'s my chair!" He pointed.

Leaning past him, I passed the Scotsman a twenty-five cent coin. "If you'll just find another empty chair, sir . . ."

I knew it would not be the last time that night that James G. Swan felt his manhood being challenged, but I couldn't watch over him any longer. I walked home in the dark, found the place all quiet, and reminded Jade May to watch for Mr. Swan's arrival and to take him down to the furnace room and show him his bed.

Then I went to my own, and collapsed into a deep sleep.

IT WAS A deep sleep, but short. I was awake by four, out of bed by five. Dawn showed a glum day of light rain, which properly suited my dispirited mood. Ten minutes, and I was at the kitchen table, demanding to know from Cook why it took so long to boil coffee. By six, I was merely sullen, my temper mollified by the first mouth-scorching cup. I had several sheets of paper from the front parlour bookcase, and I was idly scribbling and sketching with a stub of pencil. I drew a rectangle to represent Bingham's house, and scratched in the few details about its interior that I could remember from the party. Three-quarters of the area was therefore empty. On the back of the same page, I tried to rough out a map of the surrounding land—the road, the drive, the yard, with its multiple shacks and stables. It had been dark when I was there. I wasn't sure whether the geography round about was hilly or flat, forested or open. Turning the page sideways, I began to print out names: me, Jack, Avery, Swan. Beside this list, I marked out another: Bingham Sr., Bingham Jr., 4 to 8 men??? (More??) Below these lists, I wrote the name of Sarah Green. After this I scowled, drew circles around some names, pointed arrows at others.

Horses? I scrawled. Fire?

Attempting to pour myself another cup of coffee, I managed to spill a large pool on top of my paper, and although I cursed as if I had ruined something important, there was really nothing lost.

There was a gradually increasing clamour at the top of the stairs, the sound of guests packing bags down the hall, talking among themselves, getting ready to leave. I paid little attention until I realized that the party concerned was Uncle Boon, with his sundry servants and associates.

"My dear Boon," I addressed him once he had reached the ground floor. "I had no idea you were leaving so soon. No one informed me . . ."

"Busy man." He smiled. "And me too. I got to be busy back in San Francisco before I get forgotten. Ways of business! Such sad ways!"

"I agree, sir. I wish we could have spent more time together, discussed things at length."

"But I have my vessel prepared. Docked up. Ready to go. Yes, I would enjoy to stay in this fine place. This fine city. Talk about business. Talk about pleasure. Too bad!" I nodded agreement. "So I thank you, husband of the daughter of my nephew. Such fun. Make a little money always is fun, too. Thank you, thank you. Always doing good for me!"

Sue was mostly business, as always, ensuring that Boon's perfectly competent staff did not need any assistance from the rag-tag bunch of fumblers that we ourselves employ. Old Lee stood at a respectful distance, grinning, wringing his hands, already wearing his coat and hat in preparation for the walk down to the dock. Sue would not be accompanying the group, so she accepted thanks from Uncle Boon and gave him her respects. Lee found a moment to slip over to my side. He grasped my forearm and as he whispered, I realized he was quite agitated. "News! I have news. Later. Soon."

Boon assured us that he had a good bowl of breakfast waiting on his boat and led the party outside, where they quickly assumed exactly the same order of procession that I had seen on their arrival. White Lee and I were momentarily unsure of where we should place ourselves in this parade, but Boon motioned us to join him at the fore, and we walked there, three abreast, down the hill toward the port. After a brief interval of silence, the Chinese gentleman turned his head to me and began to speak in a low tone.

"Mr. Zachary, please excuse this unpoliteness. My quickness to speak. Also, please excuse impertinence. Not wishing to meddle in your affairs. Total respect for all your ability. Time is so short. We have not found time to talk. Very unfortunate. Busy men, busy times."

"Another time, Uncle. Another visit."

"No! But it is right now that you have difficulty with a bad man. Hard not to see, not to notice."

I looked across to my father-in-law, who had dropped back a half-pace, and was now staring at the buildings on his side of the street as if he had never noticed them before. "Well," I admitted slowly, reluctantly, "there is an issue with a certain man that I must soon resolve . . ."

"Mr. Roselle. Not a tasteful man."

I was a bit shocked that he knew this much, but I carried on. "I'm sure that it will soon be come and gone and myself none the worse. These things happen, and they generally work themselves out so that . . ."

"Look! There is the dock. And my little ship! You must come aboard just for a moment and see. Admire. Make me feel proud. Oh, and back at your hotel, I have left a man for you. His name is Fu."

"What?" I could not resist spinning around to see that bringing up the rear of the procession was only one bodyguard, not two.

"Fu is a good man. Very, very strong. He is obedient and he has orders that there is no limit to what he will do to solve this problem. This Roselle problem."

"Uncle! I'm sure I can handle this myself."

He nodded vigorously. "I am sure also. My total respect. Only with Fu, these things maybe are done quicker. Far away from you, if you think is best."

"Really, sir, you don't need to do this for me."

He stopped, facing me, and the whole line stopped behind him. "Yes," he said solemnly. "I must do this. I have not forgotten how my son was rescued by you from the sea. And then hospitality all the time! Maybe for me never another chance to repay." We resumed our previous pace. "If you do not find a use for Fu, then he return to me in San Francisco. But in a meantime, he might follow you a bit." He held up one finger. "Oh, and regrettable, but one more thing. Fu speaks very little bit of English. Six word. Maybe ten. If you need, nephew Lee can be used to speak to him."

I REMEMBER LITTLE else of the loading, the short tour of the boat, and the final farewell. The next memorable thing occurred on the way back home, when White Lee excitedly told me what he had learned from the Oriental money changer the night before.

What he had learned gave me the beginnings of a plan, and a faint whisp of hope.

Reaching the hotel, I wandered past a roomful of breakfasting guests in the dining room. I hardly registered their presence. I returned to my place at the kitchen table, and, after a minute, pulled a fresh sheet of paper forward, along with the pencil. Then, in block letters each two inches high, I wrote: HE HAS A SECRET!

WHEN JACK AND Avery arrived about an hour later, they found me outside sitting in the doorway of the old shed, staring at the timbers and planks still stacked to one side in the rain. I had not seen the carpenters in several days, and I was already beginning to tire of the project. The

Ellistons were both wearing rainproof capes, and Avery had exchanged his normal hat for a wide-brimmed affair I hadn't seen before. They tied their horses to the rail at the front of the building and, as they approached, both of them opened the fronts of their dark green vests—Jack to reach his pipe and tobacco pouch, and Avery to draw out his pocket watch from the vest pocket of a light brown suit—again unfamiliar to me—that looked to have been tailored to his form several pounds in the past. It occurred to me that although he wasn't exactly disguising himself, he was about halfway there. It was he and Jack, though, who registered surprise, looking past me into the shed, for standing there, at a respectful distance, was my new companion, Mr. Fu.

"Good day, sir," Avery called to him, to which he nodded thoughtfully.

"I don't remember *him*," Jack stated in a low voice. Indeed, Fu was a pretty memorable figure, dressed as he was in the uniform of a Chinese cowboy-soldier.

"On loan from Uncle Boon," I told Jack. "Helping me with a different affair. I'm afraid he doesn't have much English. Would you fellows like tea or anything before we head out?"

"There's not a lot of time, is there?" Avery noted, and we others agreed.

"I'll just go inside and get my coat. Is the rain letting up, do you think?" We all gazed upward speculatively, but no one had a very strong opinion on this. "Well, it's not so bad, anyway. I'm sorry this had to take place on a Sunday, Avery. You'll miss services, I guess."

"I'm certainly not needed at the church," he replied regretfully.

That was enough spoken about that situation. "Do I presume that neither of you came up with fresh ideas overnight as to how we should address our erstwhile friend, Mac?" Avery shook his head sadly, while Jack just stared at the mud by his feet, the picture of dejection. I tried to assume a positive, decisive tone. "Well, then. Mr. Fu, why don't you come inside with me."

We went in by the kitchen door, and found White Lee keeping warm by the cookstove. I got him to translate to Fu my desire that he should stay at the hotel, that my "other business" would not get under way until the morrow. He accepted the instructions with reluctance, but slipped off without objection. As he left, I noticed Jade May wiping down the dining room table and I asked her about James Swan.

"Did he make it home safely last night?"

She nodded.

"What time did he get in?" I asked, for there was still no sign of him having emerged from his basement lair. Jade May's command of English numbers was not good, so again my father-in-law translated.

"Almost dawn," he told me. "The girl says she called down breakfast time twice already, but he just sleeps."

"Very good, Jade May. Now you go get some sleep yourself. You have worked a long night." As she departed, Sue bustled into the kitchen on her morning rounds, and I explained to her about Swan. As I did so, I scribbled a rough map on a paper at the table. "If he really insists," I said, "he can come out and take a look around at the Bingham place, but tell him we don't really need him today. He had a plan figured out before he came, you see—a crazy plan, and it didn't fit the situation at all. Still, he might feel left out, so here's the map, and he can use Old Peter if he wants—he can get him from the stable. Keep an eye out for him, would you, my dear? And tell him that I'm glad he's here, and I think I will need him very much for something tomorrow."

"Tomorrow?" Sue inquired, never being one to miss an implication. "What will you need Mr. Swan's help with tomorrow?"

"Nothing, nothing. I just don't want Swan to feel he's made a useless trip."

One quick run up to my room, then I gathered my coat and hat from the boot room and went out to join the Ellistons. The hotel's carriage was already waiting, the canvas top in place. In one hand I carried a dry woollen blanket, rolled up and tied with string. In the other I had Sarah Green's second embroidered travelling bag, which contained the clothing and small belongings that she had left behind when she departed with Mac Bingham the previous day. In my left pocket, I had a small leather pouch filled with gold. In my right pocket was my revolver. Gold on one side, gun on the other—an apt metaphor for the twin options of negotiation.

We rumbled away, travelling in silence.

The road going north and east toward Saanich was level and straight on the whole, low forest and farms spreading out on either side, now hung with a low mist. The rain had almost stopped, but it was cool and damp, as if yesterday's summer sun had been a malicious jest and now we were back in the frigid wet of winter. The way was wide enough for Jack to bring The Commissioner alongside the buggy, and we talked.

"You know they won't let Avery and me past the gate," he said. "What are you thinking to do? What *can* we do?" It was almost a rhetorical question.

"Well, Jack, let's remember that it's better to use a bit of patience and eventually succeed than to rush into things and lose completely." A very few years previous to this, I would have laughed in the face of anyone saying such a thing—maybe worse. "I'll try things one at a time. Maybe Mac will surprise us and show some common sense and decency."

"Yes, that would be a surprise, all right."

"First, I'll offer again to purchase Sarah's contract. I brought enough gold with me to make an offer that is double or triple a fair amount."

"Of course you understand, Zachary, that I will certainly . . ."

"Never mind, man. If he accepts, then everyone will be happy, but I doubt it. He has lots of money, and he's already refused me once."

"You know what he really wants, of course? He wants . . ."

"Never mind, I say. The second thing I'll do is utter vague threats, dire implications. Thunder and lightning, floods and hellfire. I'll think of something, but it won't carry a lot of weight. He believes he can whip me with one arm behind his back."

"Whatever you threaten, I can figure a way to make it happen!"

"Eventually we could fix him, I'm sure, but I don't want to leave that woman in his house a minute longer than necessary, so I will advance as quickly as necessary to my third course of action, which, unfortunately, relies to a large extent on bravado, illusion, fast talk. And luck, of course. A lot of luck."

And with that, I called for Avery to ride up alongside and, side by side, we trotted along while I told them what Old Lee had learned from the money changer—who also sold opium—that Roselle, while waiting to buy some, must have seen Lee trading some of my gold for cash. Since Roselle had already broken the code of confidentiality, the man had no qualms about telling Lee that Roselle purchased the drug quite regularly for his employer, Mr. Bingham.

"Well, that is certainly believable," Jack interjected. "It explains certain things, in a way." Then, to me, "So we threaten to expose him as a drug fiend unless he releases Sarah from her contract?" He spat into a puddle of water. "This is flimsy stuff, Zachary."

"I know it is. It all depends on the relationship between father and son—I believe that it would be a hard thing for Mac to be exposed as an opium user in front of his father. It's a sign of weakness. Maybe if we're lucky, he'll panic as soon as the word *opium* is used. He might just relent and let me buy her out of her contract. Flimsy stuff. We're down to flimsy chances."

We had reached a narrower spot in the road, so Avery had to step up ahead of us and speak back over his shoulder. "All this intrigue is very worrisome to me, Mr. Zachary. Do you suppose instead that Miss Green might be persuaded to just take your hand and walk away as quickly as you can? Surely Mac wouldn't assault a woman! Surely the fellow must have some fear of God and the Queen in his bones!"

It was my turn to shake my head. "I've considered that sort of thing over and over, Avery, and I cannot believe she could do it. And neither does Mac Bingham. He's a bully, and he has a bully's logic. He learned it from his father, who bullied *him*. It's not even logic really, but once a bully has seen you back down, he knows you'll back down again. He knows you won't fight back. He has already faced Sarah down once, and now he can prove that he's won the day completely. And he's right, in a way. Sarah Green is terrified of public exposure, and Bingham knows that. I don't think he knows anything specific, but he's seen the fact that she positively will not risk having to appear in a court of law. She believes it would surely cause her past to be exposed and her to be hanged as a murderess."

IF WE HAD ever been under the delusion that we were welcome at the Bingham estate, it would have been quickly erased by the extremely large man standing in the centre of the drive, where it joined the road.

"You can all stop right there," he shouted as we approached. "No one goes any farther. Only one. Who's the hotel man?"

"That would be me," I answered.

He took a step forward and peered into the carriage. "I thought you was supposed to be a Chinaman. You a Chinaman?"

"I don't believe I am, sir, but I am the hotelkeeper, and I am going in to talk to Mr. Bingham, so stand aside."

He stood his ground, like a human cedar tree. "No horses. No buggy. Just you."

It was just as well. I pulled the carriage a little bit ahead and off to the side, one wheel on the grass. Jack and Avery dismounted and tied their mounts to the backboard. "You might as well sit in here under the cover while you wait," I suggested. "That breeze has a chill in it." Jack waved the idea aside, still glowering at the guard in the driveway, but Avery climbed up and sat on the buggy bench. "There's a blanket under the seat there, if you want. Why don't you warm it up in case we're lucky enough to have a passenger on the way back."

While he tugged at the string around the blanket, I took down Miss Green's travelling bag and paused, mentally reviewing my various options. The three of us were tight together, a dozen paces from the big guard.

"You feel confident about this?" Jack whispered. "I don't see anybody else around. Mac's not worried about us. If you want, we could just try a charge at the front door and . . ."

"Not today, Jack. Who knows? Maybe another day when we're better prepared, but not today." After a moment's thought, I took the .45 revolver from my pocket and set it discreetly under the seat of the buggy. "I think today we just try our best to get results by talking."

Jack maintained a low voice as he asked, "Do you really think Mac is so ashamed of being an opium user? I mean, Mac wasn't dragged away from a den of prostitutes, or anything, was he?"

"Opium is disgusting to Lloyd's kind of people. It's a drug. Worse yet, it's Chinese. Remember, he sent someone else in secret to buy the stuff."

"Still . . ."

"I'm pretty sure his father knows nothing about it." I scratched my chin and grimaced. "I hope that's true. I hope he won't just call our bluff. Revealing a secret is like setting off a bomb—you can only make it explode once. After that, you're finished."

I took a couple of steps down the road, then turned back to the brothers. "One more thing, just in case. There is a fellow who may yet show up here. A friend. An eccentric friend, and he'll be riding my horse, Old Peter. Catch him up on what's happening if he arrives while I'm inside, and tell him to wait."

"If he's riding Old Peter," Jack opined, "he won't be here before this evening at the earliest." I ignored the slight on my horse's behalf.

With my back as stiff as I could make it, my posture as threatening as a person can manage while carrying a ladies' travelling bag, I strode past the guard down the hundred feet of muddy clay, banged once on the front door, and entered the Bingham house.

I was certainly not expecting to be faced with the person who stood up from his chair in the entry hall to confront me. I had never seen him before—I would certainly have remembered. He was built with the proportions of a street-side rain barrel, bald on the top of his head, with a long spray of bright red hair coming down on the sides and behind. His expression was blank. He said nothing. I was afraid for a second that he would attack me like a guard dog, but a voice called out from behind him. It was the voice of not Mac, but Lloyd Bingham.

"Mr. Lincoln Zachary, I expect. Let him past. You're a bit early for a Sunday morning, Zachary."

I thought of knocking the mud off my boots, then decided against it, and strode forward. I found him seated in the pale light coming through the front windows, behind a large desk that had been pushed into the great room sometime since the dinner party. He was in a wheelchair—a fancy one with rubber tires like a bicycle, and strong enough wheels to carry the bulk of Lloyd Bingham. He wore a robe over his regular clothes, and he had a blanket spread over his legs.

"Maybe a few minutes early. I was fairly sure you wouldn't be off at church."

"Ha! As if I had any truck with churches! You can pass that along to your friend the whisky priest, too. There was a moment of weakness when I thought he might be honest—might even be a friend. Just a moment of weakness. But let me tell you, I'm sick to the point of dying, but I'm not weak. Pain and death mean nothing to me. Neither does public opinion.

I won't be building any churches—or anything that doesn't bring back a profit."

A very strange new possibility came to my mind as Lloyd spat out his speech.

"I don't think he ever wanted anything to do with your idea of a church, Lloyd." I hoped he was one of those men who dislike being addressed on a first-name basis by their juniors. "You're looking pretty frail, pretty pale today, all right." This was true, although I said it mostly in an attempt to be offensive. "Maybe you should start building churches and hospitals right away. Get yourself something to mention to the devil when you arrive down there."

He laughed. Unfortunately, he seemed to enjoy this kind of talk. "My son will·be doing the building in the future," he said proudly. "The boy has plans to spend every penny of my money, just building and building. He'll be running this colony in ten years." As he said this, he inclined his head to the far end of the room, where Mac was now getting to his feet after prodding the logs of the fire in one of the two large fireplaces.

"I'll be running a pretty damned big part of the business around here, at any rate, Zachary. Yes, and I think I have a place for you."

"A place for me?"

"Yes. Hong Kong!"

Father and son burst into gales of laughter. Silently, I had to admit that it was a pretty good joke, but I retained an exterior showing only boredom.

"I'm here to see Miss Green," I spoke flatly.

It was Mac who replied. "She's in her room. We don't need to disturb her. I've given her the day off to acquaint herself with the surroundings and rest up after the excitement of yesterday."

"I'm surprised you're not off somewhere counting your pot load of money."

"I pay other people to do that for me," he replied with a grin.

"Money's not the important part," his father threw in. "We proved we could organize a race bigger than there's ever been in this little city, and then we won it, fair and square. I wanted to prove that to all the hypocritical bastards in this town who laughed at me a few years ago when I got hoodwinked on the other race. I hope every one of those sheep-grinning bumpkins bet their bundle on the American horse. I got some respect back."

"But winning a pot load of money feels good, too, doesn't it, Father?"

I interrupted their self-indulgence. "I would like you to call Miss Green down here, please. I have her belongings."

"She's up in her room. She may still be sleeping." Mac smirked.

"I don't think so."

Sarah had just arrived, and was standing in the entranceway between the great room and the stairs. I couldn't guess what her emotional state was exactly, but she had the look of a schoolchild awaiting some sort of permission.

"Ah, Miss Green!" Bingham chortled. "We don't need you down here, girl. Off you go."

"Yes we do," I growled.

"You can give me her bag. I'll take it up later."

"I know you don't care much for propriety, Mac, but I do sometimes. I would like her to come and inspect her belongings in my presence, so I am assured there's nothing missing." Very deliberately, I carried the travelling bag over and placed it on one of the wooden chairs sitting against the wall by the entranceway hall. Then I took a step back.

Mac had no rationale for denying me in this, but he was a suspicious type, and he hesitated for a long moment before he sighed. "All right. Tiresome, very tiresome. You may come and get your bag, Miss Green. Do take a look inside, for Mr. Zachary's delicate peace of mind."

Her steps were measured and tentative. Her shoes echoed like steel boots on the polished wood floor. She flicked her attention back and forth between Mac and myself, managing to appear relatively calm, or at least she did not seem prepared to cry and fly. She breathed deeply and focused her eyes on the bag on the chair. When she reached it, she bent over, undid the four big buttons and looked inside. She saw the message on the piece of paper: HE HAS A SECRET.

She hesitated then—frozen in concentration, but did not show her feelings, for which I was grateful. I stepped forward quickly and whispered to her.

"You must pay close attention. It's our one chance to take advantage."

Then, just as Mac was beginning to protest my speaking to her, I turned and addressed the Binghams in an ostentatious, businesslike manner. "Before the lady leaves, gentlemen, I want to renew my offer of financial compensation to have her released from the contract that you foolishly offered and she foolishly accepted." Sarah slumped into the chair next to the one with the bag.

"I like the contractual arrangement just as it is, thank you, Mr. Zachary." Mac spoke with an air of suspicion.

"Really, Mac? Even smart men get into bad situations from time to time, but it's only a fool who misses the way out of it when he gets the chance."

Again, he laughed as if he had heard a tremendous joke. "You're just bitter because she belongs to me and not to you."

"She doesn't belong to you, Mac. She just works for you. And you don't have a use for her. She's a governess, for God's sake!"

"She's a clever girl. I'll teach her. I know exactly how to get exactly what I want from a woman!"

"She doesn't want anything to do with you, Mac."

He shrugged. "Not important. Women change opinions like a man changes hats. I can teach her what she wants and what she doesn't want."

I reached into my pocket as I stepped toward them, and the burly red-headed doorman made a move to charge at me, but I pulled out only the gold pouch. "Two and a quarter pounds of gold, Mac." I held it out. "It's got to be triple what you'd pay her for a year if you were a generous man, and I know you're not. Take it and hire yourself a pair of secretaries who are already educated."

I was not surprised that Mac shook his head with mock regret, but I found it interesting that Lloyd Bingham sat forward, serious, thoughtful.

"Maxwell. Listen, my boy . . ."

"Father!" The younger man's voice held mostly a tone of anger, but in addition, a pleading tone. "We have discussed this, Father. I want this woman. We don't need this peasant's money."

Lloyd's interest in my proposition was only fleeting. He relaxed suddenly back into his chair and chuckled. "I'm surprised at you, Zacahary. Trying to buy and sell people on the Lord's Day!"

As they shared their private moment, I turned back toward Sarah. Once again she looked like a child, small and withdrawn in her chair, in her secret world. I tried to smile at her, to hold her eyes with mine, to send a message of cheer and challenge. I couldn't be sure she even saw me.

Then the main door burst open.

"Step aside, you burly son of a bitch! I am a United States deputy marshal, and I have business with your betters, you overfed lump. Don't make me knock you down!"

I had not expected this at all, but as soon as I heard James G. Swan's voice, I realized that something along this line was bound to happen. I should never have written to him in Olympia. Mac was standing beside his father now, behind the desk, and he looked quizzically in my direction. I turned away. One couldn't see much more than the back of the redhead, who blocked the opening of the entry hall, but an exchange of grunts and a bit of shoving was evident before Lloyd shouted, "What the hell is going on?"

Once again the raspy cry. "I am a US deputy marshal on important business, and I demand . . ."

"Step aside, Leroy. I need to take a look at this character."

The guard complied, and Swan took a few steps forward, blinking, pushing his hat back on his head. His bravado was admirable, I suppose, but he didn't look like much. He hadn't shaved or brushed his hair, and he was still wearing the same trousers, striped suspenders, and dirty white shirt in which he had played cards and then slept. He clutched a folded paper in his hand, and cleared his throat. "I am a . . ."

"I don't care if you're the president of the United States, boy! We are not in the United States! And as far as that goes, you look about as much like a lawman as the Pope's mother." He turned to me. "Is this weasel one of your lot, Zachary?"

I held my hands up. "I have no idea what's going on here," I answered, which was true.

"Thank you for seeing me, Mr. . . . ." Swan now began in a conciliatory voice.

"Bingham," I threw in. "Mr. Lloyd Bingham and Mr. Mac Bingham." It was about as much help as I was going to be able to give my almost accomplice.

"Mr. Bingham. And Mr. Bingham. I forgot. I'm not good with names. Here." He unfolded the paper in his hand, stepped up to the desk, and thrust it forward. "This document serves as my identification and outlines the basis of my case."

Lloyd took it and glanced at it briefly, Mac peering over his shoulder. Neither man looked impressed, but before they could respond, Swan set into his speech like a lawyer—or a notary, I suppose. "I have been on the trail of this woman," he began, stabbing a finger in Sarah's direction, "halfway across the country, through the Washington Territory, and up here to the Colony of Vancouver Island . . ."

"It's British Columbia now."

"Whatever you wish. This woman, Naomi Phillips, also known as Sarah Green, among other names, is a known confidence trickster and swindler of honest money, who has been the ruin of more than one good man and is now, I believe, out to insinuate herself into this place and steal you blind, as well as ruin your honest family name."

As he spoke, Swan waved a Socratic fist and gradually raised the timbre of his speech to end on a climactic high note. In a different time and place, he could have been a decent preacher, or a politician.

"Who the hell do you think you are?" Mac burst out.

"Do you expect us to believe this tripe?" Lloyd added. "Do you think we're children? Idiots? Leroy! Get this half-wit out of here!"

Within an instant, the stocky redhead had Swan by the collar and his trouser bottom, spinning him around in a half-circle. Swan squawked and struggled, but the doorkeeper was as solid as a stump. Holding his victim at arm's length he proceeded deliberately toward the door. Swan's feet were mostly off the floor, his face gasping red as his own collar choked him. I couldn't stand back from it, much as I wished I could.

"Hey!" I shouted, shoving one leg into their path. "There's no need to . . ."

As usually happens when too many people push in too many directions, somebody tripped over somebody else and we three collapsed into a heap. Swan was quickest to regain some of his balance, and he brought a knee up into Leroy's nose. There was blood. I was on my knees. Swan was on his feet. The redhead was still prone, covering his face with his hands. Swan was angry now, and as he coiled his leg back to direct his boots properly into the other fellow's midsection, I crawled forward and grabbed his ankle.

"Stop it!" I shouted. Trying to keep from kicking me, Swan's momentum upended him. He landed on my back, with his elbow on the side of Leroy's neck. Leroy emitted a cry of anguish.

"Grab him, Leroy!" Mac shouted, keeping his position beside his father's wheelchair.

"Get some help! Hit somebody, Maxwell!" Lloyd bellowed.

And above all this echoed the piercing cry of Miss Sarah Green.

"Stop it! Shut up, all of you! Be silent! Sit still!" This last, pointing her finger at James Swan. And once we had all paused in amazement, she turned her attention to the father and son behind the desk. "And now, it is time for you two to listen."

"Father," Mac smiled, "I think I heard a mouse . . ."

"Please be silent, Mr. Bingham!" And he was silent. He was taken aback by the unfamiliar stance and the expression on Miss Green's face, as were we other three men when she turned to us. "Mr. Zachary, Mr. Swan, please stand up. You look foolish."

"And who the hell is . . . ?" Lloyd pointed a gnarled finger.

"Mr. James Swan is a lawyer and private detective from the Territory of Washington, City of Olympia. He has been acting for some time on my behalf. I was unable to contact him yesterday or today to inform him that I have not been harmed, and that we no longer required his services. Mr. Zachary has also been making enquiries, and he has just two minutes ago informed me that our suspicions have been confirmed regarding the secret that you have been maintaining for some time."

"Secret?" Mac mumbled, totally mystified.

"We wanted to be absolutely sure before we began formal dealings with you. Now our research appears to be complete, and we will not be at any risk for a charge of libel or slander. We know your secret."

Mac repeated the word. "Secret?" His eyes fluttered as he was searching desperately for some idea of what she might know that he wished to keep secret. Standing by the entryway door, Swan looked sideways at me with the same mystified expression. Miss Green was remarkable. She looked like a Greek statue—some goddess dealing out vengeance on a bunch of mortals. If I had not recognized the need for gravity, I would have laughed and clapped my hands.

"Don't worry, gentlemen," she continued. "We will not ruin your good name in public, not even besmirch it with rumours. We will keep the matter completely in silence for a very small price. I wish to leave immediately. My contract must be cancelled."

Mac had thought long enough. "I have no secrets! Anything I've done, I'm proud to say that . . ."

But his father spoke out.

"Be quiet, Maxwell! Why do you always have to be so hot-headed in business? You don't even understand it half the time!"

My belated suspicions were being confirmed with every word.

Sarah began speaking again, like a high magistrate giving her summation. "You realize, I hope, that we are doing you a great service by keeping this matter confidential. Part of me feels that after the discourtesy with which I have been treated, I should go directly to *The Colonist* and have you exposed to ridicule, and who knows what else? I admit that they might not wish to print it, because you wield a certain amount of power here in Victoria, but even then, there are always other ways to make things public. For myself, I have been appalled to learn what I have learned. Disgusted. I can only guess what your business associates will say . . ."

She gained confidence and volume with each new bit of rhetoric she invented. I literally held my breath, hoping that she would not utter some specific word or detail that would betray the fact that she was bluffing. She carefully did not. My respect for her intelligence, which had always been estimable, grew still greater.

We were fortunate, I saw, in two things. Firstly, I had written, in my note to her, that "*He* has a secret," not that "*Mac* has a secret," which is what I had believed at the time. We had arrived at the Bingham estate armed with the wrong secret, directed at the wrong man. The Chinese moneylender had only told Lee that Roselle had been purchasing opium for "his employer," and I had jumped to the wrong conclusion. The second bit of good fortune was that Sarah, in order to keep her concentration and her nerve, was looking everywhere about her as she spoke, but not directly into the face of either man, father or son.

"That's enough! Garbage and nonsense!" Mac exploded. "We have no secrets. We have nothing to hide. It's time I had you . . ."

"Don't be such an ass, Maxwell." Lloyd spoke very calmly, albeit disrespectfully, to his son. "Everybody has secrets, you blithering monkey mouth. How do I know what you've been up to, once I sent you off to some college back east? Hey? I've got a feeling that you started running up a long list of stupidity as soon as you were away from my guidance. I'm beginning to think Zachary was right. We're better off without this viper of a woman in our house."

"Father! These are lies and nonsense. They're bluffing, and making us look like fools!" He turned to us. "All right, I'm calling your bluff. What the hell kind of secret do you have that you think you can peddle to the newspaper?"

Sarah spoke calmly to me. "Shall we tell them, then?" Turning back to the Binghams, she pointed at Leroy and added, "I remind you that we are speaking in front of the servants . . ."

I took one step forward. "I will mention two things: Roselle. And the Chinese town."

Now it was the senior Bingham's turn to erupt. "Roselle! My God! You see what happens when you bring your nasty little friends home, Maxwell! Roselle! I should have known. All right! Miss Green, you can get out of my house. Right now, you ungrateful strumpet! Get out."

Mac was now reduced to pleading. "Father, Roselle was just a clown I met at a card game in San Francisco. He worked off his gambling debt doing odd jobs for me, and I sent him packing. I have big plans, and I need this woman to . . ."

"You need a nursemaid. That's what you need, you idiot child. Woman! Get out! Get out!" Lloyd had managed to clamber to his feet from the wheelchair, and the blanket fell on the floor. "All of you get out of here! I refuse to listen to any more of these accusations!"

I allowed myself a smile. Lloyd Bingham was happy enough to let anyone in general know that he was sick—dying, perhaps—but to admit that he was taking Chinese opium to ease the pain would strike at his pride. He was sick, but he refused to be weak. Killing the pain with something you bought from a Chinaman was weak. Then a new thought: What if his only sickness was the opium itself? Leaning forward onto his desk, all he could do was stretch one long bony finger out, pointing toward the door.

But Sarah did not flinch. If anything, her chin rose a little higher and there was suddenly confidence in her stride as she stepped directly toward that finger. "I am most happy to leave, sir. But first . . ." She reached across the desk, pushed aside a couple of other sheets of paper, and lifted up the employment contract. For what seemed like a very long moment, she held it in the air, looking from one of the men to the other and back. It was one of the bravest, fiercest moments I have ever witnessed. Then she ripped the document into four pieces, which she threw in their faces. Lloyd Bingham actually ducked.

"Goodbye, Mr. Bingham. Goodbye, Mac. You may send my belongings to Mr. Zachary's hotel, and they will be forwarded to me."

Then she spun around, snatched up the travelling bag, and led the way to the door at a brisk pace. Then she stopped and turned.

"Leave me alone. You should know that I once killed a man much like you. With a brick."

She continued walking.

For a moment, Mac only stared with an open mouth. In the end, he couldn't quite stand it. "Wait!" he screamed. "Wait, you bunch of lying . . . !"

"Shut up, Maxwell! Sit down somewhere."

Sarah turned as I held the door open for her. Red-headed Leroy stood motionless in the corner, like a gargoyle. Mac had followed us as far as the entryway hall. "You needn't worry," she said, still in a businesslike tone of voice. "The Ellistons and I will be leaving Victoria as soon as we can arrange things. Mr. Swan is returning to Washington. And Mr. Zachary is in business, and would not want your stupid scandal to be associated with him."

We left the door open behind us. I realized that Sarah did not even have her coat, but no one wanted to turn back, even for that. Probably all of us still felt that something might go wrong—that Mac would need to make one more gesture.

And he did.

He began by shouting to the huge gate guardian, who stood now between us and the Ellistons, beside the carriage, which they had brought around to the end of the driveway.

"Stop them! Stop them and hold them there!" Then he hurried over to the side of the house and called around for help from that direction. Two lanky blond fellows and a heavy-set Negro came running.

If there was any one man capable of holding all five of us at bay, it was the guard at the gate. He must have been six and a half feet tall and was broad across the chest. He had a limited array of teeth. He faced us, leaning forward on the balls of his feet, and clenched his fists, holding them in front of his belly. Then he stepped methodically in our direction. Perhaps I was gradually developing into a gentleman, because my reaction was to place myself in front of Miss Green, where I held my ground. There was a blur of motion to my right.

The honourable James G. Swan, notary public, began his charge running head up, like a sprinter, but at a distance of about eight feet, he lowered it like a bull. The bigger man stood ready to accept the impact, but unknown to him, he was also being attacked at speed from behind by Jack Elliston, who pounded a shoulder into his back, bowling him forward. Thus, his head was at the same level as Swan's when the two collided, quite squarely and with full force of momentum. The sound was short, simple, and horrible—like two unripe melons smacking together.

The two men fell side by side like dead fish tossed onto the ground. For a second, neither moved, and I thought the worst. The bigger man remained in that supine position, but by the time Jack and I had reached their side, Swan had regained consciousness, lurched to his feet, and was standing in a bewildered boxer's pose. He was pointed sideways, mind you, defiantly facing the gatepost. There was still a lot of shouting, mostly that of Mac Bingham, coming from the direction of the house, and when we turned that way, the three ranch hands, with Bingham striding along not far behind, came toward us. I don't think James Swan could see them or recognize what was going on, as forceful as his posture may have seemed.

Sarah Green ran directly to Jack and grabbed hold of him. It was a very strange embrace for reunited lovers. She had hold of his shirt front with two clenched fists, her face pressed against his chest. She was shaking—not crying, but shaking—shaking head to foot. He wrapped his arms around her shoulders and stared forward, unable to move.

So it appeared to be up to me. I stepped to the centre of the muddy drive and tried quickly to decide on the best strategy for fighting three men, all of them at least as big as me and in better physical condition, but immediately the three skidded to a halt, visibly frightened. I had little time to marvel at how I had achieved such a ferocious reputation before

I realized that Avery Elliston was now standing at my shoulder with my big Colt .45 pointed forward at shoulder level. The barrel hardly wavered as he cocked the hammer with his thumb. I felt exceedingly glad that the English gentry were well schooled in the use of firearms.

"That's enough for you fellows," Avery said loudly. "This business is nothing to you, and it's over. Off you go." The only movement of the gun barrel was a calculated aiming, first at one man, then the next. None of them said a word. Together they began to ease away from us.

Mac Bingham had stopped halfway between the confrontation and the front door to the house. "Go get them! Stop them!" he continued to shout, and as he did so, one could hear another angry voice bellowing from inside, demanding that Mac come back immediately. For a moment, he managed to ignore his father. "Charge them! He won't shoot! He's a preacher, just a preacher!"

It was the black man who replied to this assertion.

"He don't look like no preacher."

It should be noted that a man pointing a large revolver at your face almost never looks like a minister of the gospel. The three men turned and walked away. As they passed Mac Bingham, he too turned and trudged toward the house, totally dispirited.

I drove the little dogcart slowly home, with Miss Green squeezed into the seat between me and Avery, the blanket wrapped around her. James Swan had evidently galloped Old Peter most of the way from town in his haste to make a fool of himself, and now the poor beast was barely capable of stumbling along behind the cart with an empty saddle. In a comparable form was Swan himself, whose skull may have been cracked in his recent collision. He was still groggy and very unsteady, but we managed to prop him up on Avery's mare and Jack rode The Commissioner along tight against him, close enough to catch him if he started to fall. It took us all ten minutes, maybe twenty, before we were composed enough to speak.

In part, I think it took us that long to believe we would not be pursued. I leaned past Sarah, who had stopped shaking and now seemed merely exhausted, and spoke to Avery.

"Thank you, my friend, for stepping up back there. They wouldn't have stopped and let us go if it wasn't for you."

He considered this, brow furrowed, for a moment, then replied. "You know, Mr. Zachary, if you insist on carrying that big brute of a pistol around with you, you should consider putting some bullets in it."

"Ah! Well, I was bound to forget *something* the way I was running around in circles. I remembered the gun was empty when I was halfway here from town. I didn't think *you* noticed it."

"Of course I noticed it. Good heavens, man! I am an ordained minister. I wouldn't go pointing a gun at people if I knew it was loaded."

He murmured something to Miss Green and she murmured something in return. Our progress was leisurely. The poor cart horse had rather enjoyed his breakneck run the day before, I think, and now he was returned to the tiresome business of dragging three grown adults along on a muddy road. I held the reins and watched the clouds.

Living near the seacoast and being accustomed to long, rambling walks, I have developed an appreciation for the varieties of cloud. Someday, perhaps, I will publish a study or a long lyric poem. There were filmy flights of low mist, come up from between the trees and off the little ponds that dot the fields, and these, gaining some height, scurried around and inland like migratory birds calling each other on. Behind these, the larger, more sedate bulk of white shifted its weight a bit, and a few shafts of brighter daylight broke out, then disappeared again, as if the sun were peering down at us. We passed three teams of horses pulling three ploughs for three men, shoulder to shoulder, breaking up a field. There is little Sabbath rest for a farmer in the spring. Halfway home was marked by Kendrick's place—dairy cows in the pasture behind a market garden in front of a little general goods store that fronted on the road. He was a man who would make something of himself.

At last I felt enough time had passed for me to speak to Sarah Green.

"You were very brave back at the house," I told her. "I was proud and impressed. Very brave."

She must have been considering things along the same line, because she answered immediately. "Brave? No, I was not brave. Brave is when you have a choice, and you do the hard thing. I had no choice. I had run out of options." I thought she was finished speaking, but she only paused. "When I was brave—that was back in Olympia, at the farm. There was blood, a dead man. There were the children to be cared for all through the night and helped onto a stagecoach next day, and there was hiding and running and then starting all over again. That was brave, I think. Just for those few days, I was a brave girl."

"Yes, you were," I agreed, "and you are still amazingly brave and clever. My God, that was clever the way you bullied the Binghams about with nothing but a secret that you didn't know. My only fear was that old Lloyd would go into an apoplectic fit."

"I was so afraid that I would say the wrong thing. Or that I would still sound weak." She turned to me. "What *was* Mac Bingham's secret, Mr. Zachary?"

I shrugged. "Nothing, as far as I know. I thought when we started out that he had an opium habit, and only when I was talking to the two of them did I realize that it was Lloyd Bingham for whom Roselle was buying the stuff. And there's nothing wrong with that, but I believe he was afraid of his son thinking of him as a weakling—forced to get help from the Chinese, of all people. A master doesn't do business with slaves. He's a bully, is old Lloyd, and appearance is everything to a bully." I shook my head. "Mac's only problem in this world is that his father is a bigger bully than he is."

"They are both of them more evil at close range than they are at a distance."

I didn't want her to elaborate on that. "Never mind. You have beaten them, because you are brave and clever and quite marvellous."

She showed just a hint of a smile. "I think perhaps I might try a new career as an actress . . ."

"You shall not!" Avery erupted. "God protect us! That is too unworthy an idea even to be spoken aloud. Even in jest."

"Dear Avery! It was only a joke. But I shall have to think of something. I really can't stay in Victoria, much as I love dear young Ross."

"Well, just say the word to Mr. Zachary, and we'll stop the carriage and I'll go back to hold onto Mr. Swan while Jack comes up and proposes to marry you! He's only waiting for things to calm down for a few minutes so he can ask you. You'd have him, wouldn't you? Good heavens, girl. An actress!"

She actually managed a smile.

We passed a place called Twin Eagles—a log building that now served as an ale house—and Swan called up to us that he needed a drink and this was just the spot. Jack shouted him down with the bad news that today was Sunday and the place was dark. The poor man lapsed back into his dizzy silence.

For most of a mile we were slowed to a crawl behind a big wagon loaded high with hay. The road was low here, close bordered by boulders and brush, so there was no place for him to let us by. Eventually, he turned off into a field to deliver his load, and we increased our pace. We were by then passing between high stands of birch and maple, but getting close to the first real town buildings.

"All right, then," Sarah said abruptly. "I suppose we should stop."

I pulled the carriage as far as I could off to the side of the narrow road, while Avery imperturbably asked, "I should go and fetch my brother?"

"If you really think it's a good idea," she answered, her voice faint and full of air.

Avery only needed to speak a few words to Jack, to whom this was evidently a straightforward course of action, albeit in an unusual location. As he strode forward to the carriage, I jumped down and walked off a ways into the maple forest, where I relieved myself against a tree. Thus far, I thought, the day had been a great success.

Chapter Eleven

WE TRAVELLED ALL TOGETHER AS far as the Baxter residence at the south end of town, near James Bay. Baxter was an older man, a mining engineer and some sort of high-hat in Avery's church. He and his wife lived in a house that was large by Victoria's standards, and while they weren't exactly expecting us, they had on a contingency basis already approved the idea of having Sarah stay with them for a while. For a number of reasons it was preferable to having her return to the Celestial Hotel.

Jack and Avery stayed behind there, to introduce the newly affianced Sarah Green to the Baxters, while James Swan, transferred from the mare to the carriage, accompanied me back to the aforementioned hotel, where both of us intended to have a midday sleep after a difficult morning. Swan was, as usual, inclined to have a drink or two to level his spirits and dull the pain in his head before taking to his bed in the basement, but I managed to propel him first thing into the kitchen, where Old Lee prepared for him a large cup of his headache tea. This is a remarkably effective remedy.

My father-in-law has some sort of Chinese potion to deal with everything from constipation to consumption, and I am skeptical about the majority of them, but his medicinal concoctions for headache and for insomnia—they may, in fact, be the same beverage—are both first rate.

As for me, I was merely exhausted, but I intended to keep the man company at the kitchen table until he was ready for his nap. Then my wife appeared in the doorway and silently gestured from behind Swan's back that she wished to speak to me in private. I could see from her expression that it was a matter of some concern.

We moved to the front parlour and sat facing each other by the far window. It was a measure of her distress that she questioned me only briefly about the events at the Bingham estate. Did all go well? Was there violence? Where was Miss Green now? I answered her likewise, in short sentences. At last she broached the subject on her mind.

"That man, Roselle?" She spoke this as a question. I replied only by repeating the name with distaste.

"Roselle. Yes?"

"He was here while you were out today."

The mixture of foreboding and sudden anger made me feel almost nauseated. "What did he want, Sue? What did he say?"

She drew in a long, deep breath. "He was looking for you, and when I told him you were not available, he said he hoped you were making good plans for tomorrow night. I said I did not understand, and he told me there was a lot of things about my husband that I do not understand, a lot that I do not know. I told him this was surely not his business, and he insisted that it was, in fact. Then he was going to say more. I became rather frightened. He was going to say something to me, and then he did not."

A rush of anger normally supplies me with a concomitant burst of energy, but this time it did not. I felt drained and light-headed. It wasn't right for a scoundrel like that to speak to my wife while I was away.

Things had suddenly, subtly changed.

"You can't listen to anything he says, my dear," I offered lamely.

Her response was quick. "I am afraid that he knows about you. Does he know enough to be very dangerous?"

I was confused. "Does he know *what* about me? What do you mean?"

"I think he knows about your troubles of the past, about the bad business from the gold mining days in Barkerville. Does he know your real name?"

"What? My real name is Lincoln Zachary!"

She took my hand in hers and brushed it across her cheek, then held to it firmly. "Your name is always Lincoln Zachary to me," she said softly. "Or something different. Whatever you wish. Your heart is true. Names are nothing."

Lies come fairly easily to me in moments of need. I have never professed otherwise. Now, though, I could find nothing false to say. "What do you know?" I asked.

She shrugged lightly and lowered her eyes. "I am your wife. I know that you are a good and honest man. Or mostly honest. You have done something before you came here, something up there, far away and now long ago. You stay away from police and the law and you live more quietly and carefully than any other man with such white skin. Part of you has always been hidden. I am your wife, and I have no right to see into every corner of you. You hide whatever you want to hide. I do not know it—no need to know it—but I know that it is there, and I know that if someone says you are bad, then they are wrong. If someone says you have done something very bad and you must be punished, then . . ." For a second, she was also at a loss for words. Then she spat out, "Then they should be plucked up by the devil and away they go to burn in hell."

She spoke this last phrase quite loudly. Across the room, at the front desk, Jade May stood up from her stool and, without looking in our direction, slipped down the hall and away. As she left by one door, James Swan showed himself at the other.

"I'm very tired," he rasped.

"Is your head feeling better?" I asked.

"Some better. I'm going down to bed."

"Be careful on the stairs."

Sue and I sat there for a while in silence before I resurrected the desultory conversation.

"I didn't realize you suspected anything."

Her gaze widened in surprise. "You thought I believed when you arrived that the east wind just blows in young strangers full of gold to solve all our problems? Oh! And this stranger does not show his face in daylight for a whole month, but nothing to worry about that!"

"I wish you had informed me that you knew."

"That I knew what, my husband?"

I sighed. "That you knew the things I always wanted to tell you, but I was too afraid."

She spoke to me briefly in Chinese, something none too complimentary, I believe. I do not recall her doing that before or since, so I forgive her.

"I did not do the things I am accused of doing, Sue. Not the really bad things."

"Of course not. I knew that!"

I thought for a minute.

"What about your father? Does he know all this stuff?"

"It is not the place of a wife to discuss her husband with another man." Then she added, "But he is not stupid, either."

A couple of the last hotel guests of the weekend came down the stairs, and she left to attend to their departure. I walked slowly up to my room, removed my shirt and stockings, and lay on the bed. I did not sleep, however. I considered.

Things *had* suddenly, subtly changed.

THAT NIGHT AFTER supper, once things were cleared away, I went for a stroll in the gathering dark, but I did not go alone. Old Lee accompanied me, as did Boon's man, Fu. We ambled in silence, thoughtfully. Out of habit, I suppose, Fu walked two steps behind. It was fully dark by the time we found ourselves across from the Watson Brothers Saloon, which was now lit only by a pair of lanterns as someone swabbed the floors with a mop. Since it was Sunday, all drinking and carousing had to be done in private premises, and the caterwauling sound of celebrating came to us from more than one direction as we took up places in the mouth of an alleyway across from the saloon. Gambling winnings should be spent continuously, as soon as they are collected and, after such a big race, it would take some people several days to squander it all.

I sat on an empty wooden barrel, with Lee standing on my right and Fu on my left. I pointed out a few things to Lee, and he translated for Fu's benefit. Roselle's hotel was on the near side of the street, two doors to our left. The saloon was across the way and to our right. Both gas lamps on that street were on the other side. We were equidistant between them, in the deep dark. There wasn't much else to see. I tried to visualize the possibilities. If the street was empty when Roselle started across to the saloon, and if he chose to walk down the boardwalk on this side, he would pass right in front of our alley and we could take him. I knew that we had to take him. My mind would not let me picture what must happen next. If, however, Roselle crossed the street when he came out from his hotel—which seemed likely for a nervous man—he would be walking under the gaslight all the way, possibly with passersby in view, and never closer than thirty feet from our alleyway.

If we mishandled our assault, bystanders would become involved and I would be a walking dead man.

As I contemplated this situation, I became aware of the approach of several people walking in a bunch—walking down the middle of the street. It wasn't a terribly noisy group, but I could hear conversation and noticed that it was in neither English nor Chinese. The group of six men were speaking idly among themselves in Spanish. While they were still too far away for me to distinguish their features, I saw that among the various dark, shuffling figures walked one man whose bright white skin and hair reflected unmistakably in the artificial light. It was the redoubtable equestrian known as Danny.

I hopped down, on an impulse, and strolled out to intercept the troop. He recognized me immediately and hailed me with a broad smile.

"Hullo! I know you—Bingham's pal. Sorry, but I don't remember if I know your name."

"I'm no longer Bingham's pal," I corrected him, "but you've got the right idea. I'm Zachary—Lincoln Zachary. And you'd be Mr. Smith, I think."

He laughed. "Sometimes Mr. Smith. Maybe. But mostly I prefer to be Danny."

"You and the boys are just out for a stroll? I'm sorry that our little city doesn't offer much entertainment on a Sunday night. Did you find a place to eat?"

"Yes, we did, and not too bad for plain food. I liked it. Hard to please Mexicans, though. And they'd rather be in a place with strong drink and somebody to fight."

"Again, I'm sorry. No one selling liquor on the Sabbath, and no one looking for a fight tonight. Maybe tomorrow."

"You schedule these things in this town, do you?"

I cannot claim that I knew *why* I was saying it, but it came to me with the feeling of a minor epiphany that I should tell him, "Why yes. As a matter of fact, there's a bit of a brawl scheduled for tomorrow night, this time, right about the spot where we're standing."

Again he laughed, a pleasant, easy laugh. "Are you issuing us a challenge, Mr. Zachary?"

"No, no! Not at all!" I assured him. "I'm not a man for fighting, and I won't be taking part myself. I just happen to know that it's on for about eight-thirty tomorrow, once the officers of the peace have done their rounds and passed this place by. You're welcome to pick a side and join in, if you have the time."

"Really? What a gracious invitation, sir! Our boat leaves Tuesday, but it might be nice to meet some of the locals on less formal terms than at the race."

"The race—sorry about that race, Danny."

"Not at all. I enjoyed myself."

And with that, Danny and the Mexicans headed off in one direction while I collected my friends and went in the other, trying desperately to figure a way to make this chance meeting work to my advantage.

THE FULL MEASURE of inspiration did not strike me until a long time after midnight, by which time it was too late to discuss matters with my accomplices. I arose, though, at the same time as my wife—well before dawn—lit the fire in the cookstove, which our cook has sternly forbidden me to do, and began the process of making coffee. In the middle of my reprimand from Cook, just as the brew was ready to be poured into cups, my friend Swan arrived up from his basement lair, professing that he hadn't slept so long in years without the aid of liquid sedation. Mr. Fu came out to the kitchen soon after and took tea silently at a chair in the corner. The last member of our company was my father-in-law, and I sent my son to fetch him about an hour later. When we had all breakfasted, we retired outside to the shed, where we sat in a rough circle on lumber and firewood blocks. Fu smoked a cigarette, I drank coffee, Swan did both.

I began to explain.

"There is a man named Roselle. You know him, Lee, and Fu has seen him talking to me one day at Beacon Hill." Lee translated this to Fu, and the bodyguard seemed to know immediately to whom I was referring. (This translation process punctuated the whole of our conversation, and slowed things down considerably.) "This Roselle has threatened me with slander and blackmail—very dangerous things to me, which I can't ignore, nor can I trust him to keep his word if I pay him the money he wants."

"What's this slander?" Swan asked. "What's he threatening to say?"

"That doesn't matter, James."

He nodded. "So it's the truth—the stuff he says he'll spill."

I grimaced. "Part of it. The important thing is that it would indeed ruin me. I can't allow him to talk—not a word of it. I can't let it happen."

"So we are going to . . . ?" Swan let this hang there as a question. I answered it with my head down.

"You will help me to waylay the bastard, then you leave me alone to do what I must do."

There was a fairly long silence as I let this sink in. Oddly, it was Fu who eventually spoke, addressing me, then awaiting a translation, an answer, and another translation. "Mr. Fu wishes to know whether you are sure the man is working alone, or whether he might have associates."

It was a good point. "I strongly think he's by himself in this," I said. "No one likes the fellow. He's suspicious and greedy. We have to proceed on the assumption that he's working on his own. He's taken the sorts of precautions that intimate that much, as well." Setting aside my coffee cup, I leaned forward and drew a sketch in the dirt, showing the street with Roselle's hotel, the saloon, and the alley. "This is the place he has set out to meet me—the place we three visited last night."

"What? Where was I?" Swan demanded.

"Asleep. No matter. You and I can go back there and take a look later this morning. I need to be very sure of the layout." I pointed at my lines in the dirt, to the spot indicating the entrance to the alley. "We will be here, Fu. Well before eight o'clock." The translation of this was delayed by the fact that Old Lee objected to being absent from the actual operation. I convinced him that he was too old to fight and would be too conspicuous in that neighbourhood at that hour. He grudgingly related my words to Fu, who nodded in assent.

"What about me?" Swan asked.

"You will be here, lingering outside Roselle's hotel. You'll see him come out, and no doubt he'll be nervous, careful, watchful. The first problem is that there might be someone else passing by or hanging about at that moment on the street. If that happens, you need to delay Roselle, make some kind of advance and talk to him until things are clear of witnesses. The other thing is that he'll probably prefer to cross the street to where the streetlights are. Somehow, you need to convince him to walk on our side so that he passes by close to the front of the alley. Then we dash out, grab him, and get him back into the dark. I haven't figured out the best way to do that yet. It has to be done, though. We can't run all the way across the street, knock him out, and drag him away. It would be in full view of the saloon. It's dicey enough as it is, just snatching him from a few steps away. We'll need to figure out a way to keep him on the right side of the street."

Swan was rolling himself a second cigarette. "Why don't we just catch him right when he comes outside, walk right up and shoot him— kill him?"

I was taken aback. "What? No! What? Swan, have you ever killed a man?"

He nipped the loose ends of tobacco away. "No. Of course not."

"Well, it's something you don't want to do! It's a terrible thing, a horrible thing that changes everything in the world, and you don't forget it. You don't get used to that memory."

He looked at me for a minute, then lit his cigarette and answered softly, solemnly. "I'll take your word for that, Zachary."

"Thank you, James."

"But I bet the Chinaman would do it." He nodded toward Fu.

"No! Lee, don't tell Fu any of that stuff we were just talking about. Listen! We are not going to be nice to Roselle, but if somebody has to kill him, it will be me." I grimaced. "But I may not need to kill him. You two will be gone. I will decide."

"Kill him . . . You'd just leave him there for the police to find?"

"He's a nasty little bastard that nobody in this town ever liked. The police won't waste a lot of time on it."

AN HOUR LATER, James G. Swan and I stood on the street outside Roselle's hotel. I described his appearance and then pointed out the proposed start and finish of his brief journey, and the alleyway where Fu and I would be lying in wait. I also brought to his attention the two gas lamps, both on the saloon side of the street.

"He'll want to cross over straight from the hotel," I said. "You need to greet him like a friendly stranger, strike up a conversation, even though he'll be suspicious of you. You can do that, James."

"I can do that. It's a bit of a specialty of mine." I did not ask him to elaborate on that.

We stood together in silence. We considered. Swan drew a short breath, held up one finger. "Yes. I believe I remember something that's been done before."

"What's that?"

He turned me around so that I was facing the direction Roselle would be going as he tried to cross the street, then faced me with an earnest look on his face. "Excuse me, sir," he said—a bit too histrionically for my taste. "I'm a stranger in the city of Victoria, just here for the horse race, and I was looking—discreetly, you understand—for a place where a gentleman might be entertained by a pretty lady. Can you confirm that there is such a place just above that saloon?"

"What?" I happened to know that the younger of the Watson brothers lived above the saloon, with his wife.

Swan beamed at my response. "Well, it seemed that way to me, sir. Just now I looked up at the windows above the saloon and saw a young woman dressed in nothing but her own skin."

"What?"

"Yes, sir. Come over here. You can get a clear view from right here, in front of the alley."

I slapped him on the back and pronounced him a veritable prince of thieves. Before we departed, we walked farther down the alley and found a cooperage there, with a stack of barrels and crates, behind which I could have my final confrontation with Mr. Roselle in complete privacy. As we walked back to the hotel, I reviewed the situation, and as I did so, my anger gradually and steadily rose and cemented my resolve.

"Do you know," I said to Swan, "that the bastard came to my hotel yesterday and threatened my wife?"

"Threatened your wife? I know your wife. Did she strike him?"

"No," I replied. "She's too good. She left it up to me."

THE THREE OF us—Swan, Fu, and myself—left the Celestial Hotel at about ten minutes past seven that night, seen off at the front porch by Old Lee, still out of sorts because I would not let him come along. We were halfway to the potential scene of our crime when a ridiculously obvious fact came to our attention.

"It's still too light," I observed. "We can't show up there yet. Three strange men hanging about between the buildings . . . ?"

"I thought it would be darker by now," Swan said. I agreed and, turning to Fu, tried to point out our predicament to the Chinese speaking member of our expedition. By a certain rolling of the eyes and gestures at the horizon, he indicated that he had already realized the error in timing.

We were forced to turn aside and sit down next to a wagon shed, watching the sky for almost a half-hour before we proceeded any farther. It still seemed disturbingly bright at a quarter to the hour, but we now had little choice. By the time we got to our destination, though, the shadows were satisfactory.

We walked the length of the street, past the saloon and past the Seaview Hotel, to the corner, where there were empty lots both to east and west. Once more we spoke briefly, commenting on this and that, then we returned, Swan dropping away casually across from the Seaview, while Fu and I continued on to slip into the alley after assuring ourselves that no one else was on the street. It was a dreary little avenue, already feeling like midnight, apart from the Watson Brothers Saloon, which, from the sound of things, was capturing the last dregs of horse-racing money still needing to be squandered on a Monday night. My companion and I allowed our eyes to adjust to the comforting darkness, then found places to sit on opposite sides of the narrow passageway. I stood against the wall. Fu seated himself at the end of a stack of firewood.

Roselle was late. This should not have surprised us; it was a logical bit of strategy, but it was nonetheless irritating. I found myself becoming more nervous by the minute. Almost five minutes past the hour, one pair of pedestrians—a man and woman—walked down the street and passed us, then a few minutes later, a short, fat fellow went the length of the far boardwalk and into the saloon. Swan was soon afflicted by the same disquiet as myself and chose to wander down for a visit at ten or twelve minutes past eight. I didn't think he should be abandoning his post, and I told him so, but he protested in an agitated voice.

"I can't stand there forever pretending there's a stone in my boot."

I directed him back, suggesting he place himself behind a corner of high fencing until he spotted movement at the Seaview. "I'll look even more suspicious if someone notices me there."

"No one will notice you, Swan. It can't be more than a few minutes. He won't risk the chance that I'll give up and go home, or even come after him up in his room." He grumbled a bit, but turned to leave, then I stopped him. "I've had one more thought, since you're already here. I mean, what if he decided to go over there early, and he's already inside the saloon? Why don't you stroll past the windows on your way back, and see if someone of his description is sitting in there, waiting? Anyone who looks like it might be Roselle. I can't go over in case I get caught out there in the street when he walks out of his hotel."

This agreed, Swan made his way leisurely across, up the three steps to the boardwalk, then slowly past the bar windows, peering inside. Once past, he jumped down to the ground, came casually back across the street, and without stopping, spoke out loud as he passed the alleyway.

"Nothing. Just one big gang of low-downs all together at a circle of tables."

I felt better for knowing this much.

Swan disappeared behind his bit of fencing. I stood. Fu sat, sullen but stolid. I began to wish that I had brought Old Lee along or could converse directly with this unknown subject of my uncle Boon. The minutes dragged by like a slug. I wished I could voice my thoughts and my emotions to the mysterious Mr. Fu. I wanted to speak out loud the anger and frustration I felt. I was angry that Roselle was blackmailing me, but I was equally angry that I could find no alternative way of dealing with the problem than killing him. Was I even capable of killing him like that? Maybe if I was able to say these things out loud, Fu would be able to slap me on the back, look me in the eye, and convince me that God was on my side.

He looked like a decent sort of man, so far as I could see in the semi-darkness of the space between derelict buildings.

Then I heard Swan's voice. He spoke in an unnaturally loud voice, I thought, although I could not hear his words distinctly. I stuck my head out from between the buildings to see him striding across to the Seaview. I glanced both directions quickly enough to ascertain that no other passersby were coming our way. Fu was on his feet. We stood together.

The distant conversation lasted no more than half a minute, after which an exchange of chuckles and murmured comments approached our position. They were in front of the very building to which we held our backs, and Swan let out a long, protracted laugh. The other man responded in kind as they stepped in front of us.

I reached out and grabbed his shoulder, sending him spinning into the shadows. Fu met him there with a vicious blow to the spot where stomach meets ribcage, and he bent double with a fearful gasping exhalation. Swan followed the flow of things by bringing his knee up into the man's face. He collapsed onto the ground, writhing, semi-conscious. It all happened in such an efficient flurry that I was unable to call out for them to stop. It was the wrong man.

He was, even spread out on the ground, squirming, most unlike the reprobate Roselle. He was taller than Roselle by several inches, heavier by ten pounds at least. We rolled him over onto his back.

"He has a moustache!" I hissed.

"Yes?" Swan retorted.

"I didn't tell you Roselle had a moustache!"

"You didn't tell me he didn't!"

The moustache in question was now soaking up a considerable flow of blood. The stranger's eyes were rolled back in his head.

"What are we going to do with him?"

"How the hell would I know?"

"This is not my fault!"

"He's starting to come around." As Swan said this, he delivered a short, swift kick to the right side of the man's head, thereby delaying his revival by a few minutes. The air went out of the poor man with the slow susurration of a dying snake.

And then Roselle arrived.

"You bunch of stupid bastards," he said. He was standing with his back to the street. He held a pistol in his right hand, stretched out in the manner of a person not accustomed to using such a device. "Stupid bastards!" he repeated.

My shoulders sagged like a caught-out schoolboy. I opened my mouth, preparing to speak, although I do not know what I meant to say, when Fu stepped in front of me moving confidently, moving very fast. He reached our foe in two long strides, grasped his wrist in one hand, the pistol with the other, and twisted it loose. All in the same motion, he crashed his forehead into Roselle's face. The gun rattled past me into the alley. Roselle went limp. Fu dragged him into the deeper darkness.

Even the loquacious James G. Swan found nothing to say. I gaped. Fu snatched up the revolver, flipped open the magazine, and emptied the bullets from their chambers into his coat pocket. The gun itself he pushed under his belt at the small of his back, adjusting his coat over top. He had lost his broad-brimmed hat in the scuffle, and he now retrieved it and set it square on his head. Then he turned to me and spoke. His accent was fairly heavy, but his English was rather good for someone who supposedly did not speak the language at all.

"I will see to this. You go. Go home to your home."

With that, he picked up Roselle by one arm and one leg and threw the man almost effortlessly over his shoulders. Then he hurried away down the lane, past the cooperage and out of sight. It was the last I ever saw of Mr. Fu. It was also the last I saw or heard of Roselle.

"Bloody hell!" Swan whispered.

"Bloody hell!" I agreed.

I might have stood there in silent contemplation for a considerable length of time, but my partner spoke again.

"This one's coming around," Swan said sharply.

My first impulse was to jump forward and protect the poor bystander from further assault, but Swan was making no such move. Instead, he was bending over the man, speaking softly, raising his head with one hand. "Are you all right?" he cooed.

The big fellow shook his head, then grimaced, thinking better of it. He wiped the worst of the blood off the lower part of his face with the back of his hand.

"What in God's name happened to me?" From that single sentence, I couldn't be sure whether his accent was Scottish or Irish.

Swan helped him to a sitting position. "Good," he said. "You're still alive and kicking."

"What . . . ?"

"I'm afraid it was those miserable swine over there," Swan informed him. "Those Mexicans, damn their eyes!"

I hadn't seen them appear, didn't know they were even there, but five or six of Ojai's handlers were loitering in the street, almost directly across from us. They must have come along while Swan was directing the stranger toward his ambush.

With great effort and growling all the while, our unwitting victim managed to struggle to his feet. Without hesitation, he stepped forward, bellowing at a most impressive volume. "You wicked, godforsaken sons of bitches!" he shouted out, and began to march across the street. The Mexicans looked amazed as they watched the man's methodical, incomprehensible approach—bloodied but unbowed—howling out every imaginable profane insult toward them, individually and grouped together as the sons of their native land. He was Irish, I think now. One of them took a few steps forward to meet him, saying something I didn't catch, and was promptly levelled by a single blow.

Then all manner of shouting and commotion broke loose. Swan dashed past me, running to the aid of the person he had so recently kicked into unconsciousness. Someone from inside the saloon spotted what was happening, and the place emptied into the street in an instant. I stepped forward just far enough to see the confrontation erupt into a full blown riot.

I was still trying to digest the vision of Fu galloping away with Roselle on his back. I felt sick to my stomach.

It looked to be a reasonably well-matched rumble, considering that Mexicans typically fight harder and meaner than any member of the varied citizens of Victoria. Swan was in his element and needed no assistance from me. I hoped he would eventually make it back to our hotel. If not, I would retrieve him from the local jail. Staring out over the top of the fray, I caught sight of Danny's pale frame, leaning against the distant gaslight standard. He was smoking a cigar, smiling broadly. When he saw me, he waved.

I waved back, turned, and started for home.

Chapter Twelve

THERE WAS THE BUSINESS OF the banns to be dealt with—they had to be read or posted, or whatever—so I suppose it was two weeks, perhaps three, before Jack Geoffrey Cecil Elliston was duly wed to Miss Lucinda Thorpe, also known as Naomi Phillips and Sarah Green, the Reverend Jervis Quick presiding. The couple decided that only friends of them both should be invited to attend, so it was a small ceremony indeed. My wife and I were there, of course, Sue standing in as the bride's woman of honour, while Avery stood up for Jack. Ross carried the rings. The Baxters were there, and James Swan, who arrived late, looking very sombre, and left the church before the benediction was spoken. Apart from that, there were only a pair of spinsters, stalwarts in the church, who had never missed a wedding held in that place and refused to be put off now.

The next day, James Swan reported to me that, using his remarkable skills as forger, actor, and liar, he had searched out the terrible letter that Roselle had left for his friend Hec Simmonds—the letter exposing me as

Zachary Beddoes. It had been left in the hands of someone at the Bank of British Columbia who readily handed it over when Swan produced his hastily prepared false identification. I could guess from the condition of the envelope that James's curiosity had got the better of him and he had read the letter, but I was neither angry nor worried at the thought

Two days later they were gone—Jack, Sarah, Avery—all my friends. Jack has since written to say that his father considers Sarah (as I will always know her) to be the Queen of Creation, particularly since she will soon make him a grandfather. Avery has taken a position as chaplain to a hospital in Nova Scotia, hoping, he says, to "find a few more disciples among the fishermen." The chances of him staying out of trouble are probably about even. Nova Scotia is a province of Canada, and it appears that Nova Scotians and British Columbians shall soon be countrymen, living thousands of miles apart. What a strange new world.

I was devastated when they left. For three days, I sat in my room at the hotel, drinking whisky and writing passages in this journal of events. On the fourth day, my wife forcibly evicted me, insisting that I go for a walk at the very least. I strolled the length of the town, stopping on the way back at a saloon, where I fell in with three interesting fellows. One is a watchmaker, the second is an undertaker, and the third insists on describing himself as a spy.

They are more practised drinkers than I—although I thought I could hold my own at first—and it was two days before I returned home. The aftermath of that lapse into misconduct is another story completely.

ABOUT A WEEK after that, James G. Swan and I were seated on chairs behind the Celestial Hotel, mugs of chilled tea in our hands, as the carpenters resumed work on our new carriage shed. At last, he cleared his throat and made a pronouncement.

"I've decided not to go back, Zachary," he informed me. "I'm going to stay here in Victoria."

"Really? Good to hear it! I haven't many friends—we can spend time together."

He grimaced and looked up at the sky. "I'd like that," he said. "I'd like it very much, but I'm afraid my work might turn out to be a problem with that."

"Your work? You'll be too busy? What do you plan to do? Notary?"

He shook his head. "No. No, you can't just go from one country to another and be a notary in both places. Can't be done."

"Then what will you do?"

He leaned forward in his chair, and his eyes brightened. "I've already rented a location, down at the far end of Fort Street. I'll live there starting tomorrow, and work out of there as well."

"What will you do?"

"I'll provide a variety of services—many of them pretty philanthropic. I'll help immigrants from all over getting settled here in the colony. I'll smooth out business problems that importers and exporters have with their paperwork. People who have lost their documentation and can't prove their citizenship will come to me, and I'll see it straight."

"So you're going to make a living doing forgery?"

"I sincerely hope so. I think it might not be good for you though, to be associated with me too much. Sooner or later I'll start to attract attention from the law, and you . . ."

I knew what he meant, and I couldn't help but agree.

We get together now a couple of times a month. I look forward to these times—his stories, his company—but we generally meet outside of the public eye. We go riding together on the country roads. He rides Old Peter, who he appreciated from their first ride together and purchased from me for the sum of one dollar. I used that dollar to buy The Commissioner from Jack Elliston when he left Victoria.

The Commissioner is definitely too much horse for me, but I am improving. My horsemanship is improving.

Acknowledgments

THIS BOOK HAS BEEN WRITTEN over a long period of time, and I have been assisted by too many people to accurately recall. I should, however, mention the kind assistance of people at Washington State University as well as Ruth Stubbs and the Quesnel Museum.

As well, I don't believe most readers recognize the huge contribution given any author by good editors, and I would like to mention in particular the patient, exhaustive advice given me over the years by Ruth Linka, Edna Sheedy, and Sarah Weber, as well as by Jay Connelly of Oolichan Books.

One segment of the novel is historically true, names unchanged (and as accurate as the reporting of the old *Washington Standard* can make it). The story in Chapter Five of Charles Mitchell, the young slave who escaped to Victoria and almost caused an international incident, sounds fantastic but is quite true, although no one seems to know what became of him once he reached British Columbia.

STAN KRUMM was raised about fifty miles from the historic town of Barkerville. He has always been fascinated by its landscape and history—drawn into flights of fantasy by the fields and forests of the Quesnel River valley. When his novel *Zachary's Gold*, about the gold rush of the 1860s, was published, *BC Bookworld* called it the summer fiction "book to read." Stan lives in Quesnel, where he has a business, a wonderful family, and a cat named Max.